Veiled Betrayals: Cracking the Cultural Code of Middle Eastern Espionage

© 2025 by Mike Hajjar

For permission requests, please contact:

Stealth Press

An imprint of Stealth Investigation Services PLLC

10222 W Warren Ave

Dearborn, Michigan 48126

Email: stealthpi23@gmail.com

ISBN (Paperback): 979-8-9937984-0-0

ISBN (eBook): 979-8-9937984-1-7

Library of Congress Control Number: 2025923407

Printed in the United States of America

Cover design by Stealth Investigation Services PLLC

Author photograph courtesy of the author

10 9 8 7 6 5 4 3 2 1

First Edition

Veiled Betrayals

Cracking the Cultural Code
of Middle Eastern Espionage

Mike Hajjar

PREFACE

When I first laid hands on the dusty stacks of Iraqi Intelligence Service (IIS) files in 2004, I had no idea they would become the blueprint for this book or reshape how I saw the world of espionage. As a young man born and raised in Iraq's tribal heartland, I learned early on that understanding people wasn't just useful; it was survival. In those close-knit communities, where every word carried the weight of honor or betrayal, I absorbed lessons from elders about reading motives in a glance, resolving conflicts with patience and wisdom, and knowing when bravery meant holding back rather than charging ahead. Those insights stayed with me through my service in the Iraqi Army during the Iran-Iraq War, where quick judgment in chaos could mean life or death, and through the upheaval of the 1991 Gulf War, which forced my family into four years of exile at Saudi Arabia's Rafha Refugee Camp, a harsh forge that sharpened my sense for human resilience amid shared hardship.

Little did I know those foundations would prepare me for the seven years I spent as an intelligence analyst with the United States Government, immersed in tens of thousands of IIS documents spanning the 1970s to 2003. Those files weren't cold records; they were a masterclass in the raw mechanics of intelligence: recruitment ploys that twisted loyalties, surveillance operations that turned shadows into spies, interrogation tactics that broke minds through cultural precision, and fronts that hid betrayal in plain sight. Day after day, often in shifts stretching eight to twelve hours, I dissected how IIS officers thought, executed daring missions, and navigated the minefield of human behavior. I could anticipate an operation's twist before turning the page, recognizing each officer's unique rhythm: the meticulous planner layering deception, the bold executor striking with precision timing. It felt like unlocking a hidden code, one shaped by Eastern tradition yet timeless in its psychology. My philosophy emerged from those years: intelligence isn't about gadgets or brute force; it's about decoding the cultural and psychological patterns that govern us all.

That journey continued as I earned my Master of Science in Criminal Justice and Security in the United States, refining those insights, and through my work with the U.S. Department of State on the P2 program, investigating thousands of cases for Iraqis who collaborated with American forces and learning to find truth amid tangled narratives. Today, leading Stealth Investigation Services in Dearborn, Michigan, and serving Middle Eastern and Arab communities, I apply those lessons daily: resolving disputes where honor collides with reality, dissecting stories for hidden motives, and navigating mindsets shaped by the same cultural forces I grew up with. Hundreds of cases have only deepened my conviction that espionage, at its core, is a human endeavor, one where understanding betrayal's whisper can avert catastrophe.

This book is the culmination of that lifetime, distilled not from borrowed theories but from the raw grit of real operations and personal reflection. In many instances, the concepts presented here arose from firsthand analysis and original thinking, blending the IIS's shadowy lessons with practical strategies for recruitment, asset management, surveillance, and counterintelligence. The ten case studies, drawn directly from never-before-published files, bring these lessons to life, revealing triumphs like a precision strike in Qum and failures born of cultural blindness. Whether you're an officer sharpening your craft, an analyst decoding reports, or a reader intrigued by the human side of spycraft, these pages will challenge how you see the shadows.

Writing this was not easy; it meant revisiting the moral gray zones of a craft that can save lives yet shatter them too. But if it helps one more reader navigate the Middle East's complexities with wisdom, empathy, and restraint, then it has achieved its purpose.

Welcome to the code, may it serve you well.

Mike Hajjar Dearborn, Michigan, November 2025

ACKNOWLEDGMENTS

No book emerges from isolation; it is the product of countless influences, conversations, and shared experiences that shape its pages. I am deeply grateful to those who have walked this path with me, knowingly or unknowingly, whose contributions made Veiled Betrayals possible.

First and foremost, to my family: my roots in Iraq's tribal community taught me the enduring lessons of honor, loyalty, and human insight that form the foundation of this work. Your stories and wisdom, passed down through generations, have been my greatest teachers. To my wife and children, thank you for your unwavering support during the long hours of writing and reflection; your patience and encouragement turned ideas into reality.

I extend my profound thanks to the United States Government for the opportunity to analyze tens of thousands of Iraqi Intelligence Service (IIS) files between 2004 and 2011. This immersion not only honed my analytical skills but revealed the intricate world of Middle Eastern espionage that inspired this book. To my colleagues at the U.S. Department of State's P2 program, your collaboration in investigating cases tied to U.S. operations in Iraq deepened my understanding of human narratives under pressure, lessons that echo throughout these chapters.

To the mentors and professionals who guided me from my early military service in Iraq during the Iran-Iraq War, where I learned the realities of high-stakes decision-making, to my academic pursuits earning a Master of Science in Criminal Justice and Security, your insights have been invaluable. In my current role leading Stealth Investigation Services in Dearborn, Michigan, serving Middle Eastern and Arab communities, continues to refine these ideas through real-world cases. I am deeply thankful to my clients and team for the trust that fuels this ongoing journey.

A special note of appreciation goes to the unsung figures whose stories, drawn from the IIS archives, bring this book to life. Though anonymized, your experiences, successes and failures alike, offer timeless lessons for all who venture into the shadows.

Finally, to the readers who pick up this book: thank you for joining this exploration. May these pages not only inform but inspire a deeper understanding of the human side of intelligence. Any errors or oversights are mine alone; the wisdom belongs to the collective experiences that shaped me.

Mike Hajjar Dearborn, Michigan, November 2025

CONTENTS

INTRODUCTION

Entering the Shadows: Culture and Psychology as Weapons in Middle Eastern Espionage

Step into the shadowy world of Middle Eastern intelligence, where cultural mastery and psychological insight are not just tools; they are weapons. In this region, the art of espionage is not a game of gadgets and disguises but a delicate dance of understanding human behavior, tribal loyalties, and communal values. Success demands more than technical skill; it requires fluency in the unspoken codes that govern life in the Middle East and Arab world. This book is your guide to that world, drawing on real-world operations, cultural nuances, and the hard-won lessons of those who navigated its complexities.

Written for intelligence officers, analysts, and curious minds alike, this book offers a rare glimpse into the cultural and psychological forces that shape intelligence work in one of the most complex regions on Earth. Whether you are navigating the streets of Baghdad, managing a source in Tehran, or analyzing behavior in diaspora communities across the West, the lessons here are universal. They reveal not only how people in these societies think and act but also how to turn that understanding into operational success. My purpose is clear: to illuminate the cultural and psychological norms that define the Middle East and Arab world, and to show how these factors, along with others, mold behaviors, influence thinking, and present unique challenges to intelligence professionals. This exploration goes beyond theory, delving into practical strategies for recruitment, asset management, surveillance, counter-surveillance, and the use of fronts and covers, all while grappling with the ethical dilemmas that define the craft.

At the heart of this book lies a simple truth: culture is the key to intelligence. The Middle East and Arab world are defined by deep-rooted traditions, such as family honor, tribal allegiance, and communal identity, that influence every decision, from the mundane to the monumental.

These norms are not mere background noise; they are the lens through which people view loyalty, trust, and betrayal. For case officers, grasping these dynamics is essential. A misstep in cultural etiquette can shatter trust in seconds, while a well-placed gesture of respect can open doors that no amount of coercion ever could. Consider the weight of tribal bonds in Iraq or the intricate balance of honor and shame in Iran: these are not abstract concepts but operational realities that can make or break a mission.

But culture is only half the equation. This book also delves into the psychological landscape of the region. Arab and Muslim communities, whether in the Middle East or abroad, often exhibit distinct mentalities, such as a tendency toward exaggeration in reporting or a heightened sensitivity to honor and shame. These traits are not stereotypes; they are patterns shaped by history, religion, and social structure. Understanding them is critical for interpreting intelligence, managing assets, and predicting behavior under pressure. I've focused particularly on teaching case officers how to navigate these personalities, how to decode the embellished narratives, build trust with individuals who prioritize honor over self-interest, and operate effectively within these communities. The book extends this insight into modern tools like surveillance and counter-surveillance, where psychological awareness can mean the difference between detection and evasion, and explores the strategic deployment of fronts and covers, which turn everyday roles and businesses into invisible platforms for influence.

Drawing from my own philosophy and eight years of work analyzing tens of thousands of documents from Saddam Hussein's Iraqi Intelligence Service (IIS) files for the United States Government (2004 to 2011), this book bridges theory and practice. Those files, spanning the 1970s to 2003, covered the full spectrum of intelligence tradecraft, from recruitment and execution of operations to surveillance, counter-surveillance, covers, assassination tactics, and the nuanced ways of dealing with diverse human minds. They revealed how the IIS used timing, reverse psychology, emotions, and religion as a cover, twisting personalities, culture, religion, criminals, and everything related to the intelligence world. Each department had its own specialties, and the collections we analyzed made those of us working on them feel like graduates from the Eastern school, akin to the Soviet tradition. It was 8 to 12 hours of daily shifts, reading and analyzing the IIS tactics, how each intelligence officer thought, executed operations, and what they were looking for. Over time, we reached a level where we could anticipate outcomes before even finishing a file, understanding each officer's style of conducting espionage. This immersion, combined with my subsequent work with the U.S. Department of State on the P2 program, investigating cases for individuals who worked for the U.S. Government in Iraq during the American presence, and my current role as a private investigator within Middle Eastern and Arab communities, has shaped the insights here. It is not a dry academic treatise, but a hands-on manual forged in the fires of real operations. The insights in these pages stem either from my personal perspective or from the raw, unfiltered realities documented in the IIS files.

The book is structured into 21 chapters and 10 case studies, each designed to build your understanding step by step:

• The chapters serve as a comprehensive guide to the people of the Middle East and Arab countries, how they think, act, and behave, and how their worldviews are shaped by cultural and psychological forces. From recruitment techniques tailored to collectivist societies to strategies for managing sources bound by tribal codes, these chapters equip you with the tools to decode and influence behavior. They cover operational challenges, cultural nuances, practical lessons for intelligence work in the region and its diaspora communities in Western countries, the critical roles of fronts and covers in espionage, and the evolving arts of surveillance and counter-surveillance.

• The case studies bring these concepts to life with ten real stories from the IIS files, tales of espionage that have never been published until now. These are not polished Hollywood scripts but gritty, real-world accounts from the shadowy corners of intelligence. You'll read about successes, like the surgical elimination of a dissident imam in Qum, and failures, such as a botched recruitment in Tehran undone by cultural ignorance. Each case study is followed by a detailed analysis, breaking down what drove the triumphs and what triggered the disasters. Case officers can extract practical lessons from these stories, while readers fascinated by the intelligence world will enjoy a front-row seat to the minds of IIS operatives, how they thought, what they got right, and where they went wrong.

This book is not just for the intelligence community. It is for anyone captivated by the human side of espionage, the calculations, the risks, and the moral dilemmas that define the craft. Whether you are a professional seeking to sharpen your skills or a member of the public eager to learn about intelligence work in Middle Eastern and Arab communities, both in the region and abroad, these pages will pull you in. The stories and lessons transcend borders, offering insights into how cultural and psychological factors shape not just espionage but human interaction itself. They also extend into the practical realms of surveillance, where the art of unseen observation meets the challenge of evasion, and the strategic deployment of fronts and covers, which turn everyday roles and businesses into invisible platforms for influence.

As you dive into the chapters and case studies, you will discover:

• How to read the unspoken signals of loyalty and betrayal in Arab and Muslim communities.

• Why understanding exaggeration and narrative style is crucial for interpreting intelligence from the region.

• How to recruit and manage assets in societies where family and honor outweigh personal gain.

• What the IIS achieved, and catastrophically lost, in their most daring operations.

• The intricate techniques of surveillance and counter-surveillance that can make or break a mission in high-stakes environments.

• The power of fronts and covers as tools for penetration, manipulation, and long-term operational success.

In the end, intelligence work is about people. It is about seeing through their eyes, speaking their language, and anticipating their next move. This book is your key to mastering that art in one of the world's most enigmatic regions. Welcome to the game.

PART I:

THE CULTURAL
BATTLEFIELD

CHAPTER 1:
CULTURAL FOUNDATIONS AND THE INVISIBLE BATTLEFIELD

THE TERRAIN BENEATH EVERY OPERATION

Culture is the invisible battlefield beneath every act of intelligence. In the Middle East, Arab, and Muslim worlds, it does not merely influence the mission; it defines it. Every conversation, every hesitation, every look across a tea table carries meanings born of centuries of collective memory. To navigate this region is to walk through a field of invisible boundaries, each charged with loyalty, pride, and survival.

An officer who cannot read these codes enters blind. For here, culture is not a backdrop; it is the air the operation breathes. A single misplaced gesture, an unguarded question, can ignite suspicions that take months to extinguish. But to the officer who listens deeply, culture becomes a weapon sharper than technology. The quiet knowledge of how a family thinks, how a tribe forgives, how faith binds, these are the true tools of influence.

THE COLLECTIVE HEART

In this world, individuality is a foreign rhythm. The Middle East lives by a collective pulse where belonging outweighs ambition and honor is inherited, not earned. From birth, each person learns that their name is more than their own, it carries the weight of generations. A misstep stains the bloodline; a triumph lifts an entire clan.

This collective order gives life meaning but denies solitude. Decisions are not made in private; they echo across family councils and neighborhood whispers. A man's pride belongs to his brothers. A woman's honor belongs to her household. To act alone is to risk exile.

For the intelligence officer, this truth overturns every Western instinct. Appeals to personal advancement or ideological conviction often fail here because identity is plural. To reach one person, you must speak to the circle around them, to their elders, their faith, their unspoken obligations. Every recruit is the visible end of an invisible chain.

THE WEIGHT OF LOYALTY

Loyalty is the region's unbreakable currency. It is born not from contract but from survival, a living inheritance that stretches across generations. To belong is safety; to stand apart is peril.

Within these loyalties live unspoken rules: who one may speak to, who one may question, and whose hand one must kiss before speaking freely. Disloyalty is not a moral flaw; it is a crime against blood. And yet, this same loyalty, when understood, can be redirected. It can be turned from obstacle to conduit.

An officer must see that every decision, every hesitation, every truth withheld is shaped by this invisible code. A source who seems open may still carry the weight of cousins, uncles, or patrons whose invisible presence governs their words. Persuasion that ignores these ghosts is not persuasion; it is offense.

THE PAST THAT NEVER DIED

The roots of these loyalties lie deep in history. In the deserts and mountains where central governments were weak and danger constant, survival depended on kin. The tribe was the law, the court, and the shield. A man's lineage was his insurance against death. Centuries of empire and occupation have changed flags and names, but not instincts.

Today, that same architecture of belonging operates in boardrooms, ministries, and militia camps alike. A general may wear a modern uniform, but the mind beneath it still hears the voices of ancestry. To understand this is to understand why states may fall, yet tribes remain. In every negotiation, the officer faces not only a person but the ghosts of their forefathers watching silently over their choices.

THE PSYCHOLOGY OF THE COLLECTIVE

Psychologically, collectivism is both armor and restraint. It provides emotional security, the comfort of identity defined by group acceptance, yet it also suffocates independence. A Middle Eastern recruit is rarely torn by ideology alone; his conflict is emotional. Cooperation with an outsider feels like betrayal not of belief, but of belonging.

This is the battlefield of the mind where intelligence work must fight its quiet wars. The officer's task is not to dismantle loyalty but to reinterpret it, to show that cooperation is not treason but protection, that silence endangers the family more than disclosure ever could. It is persuasion through reframing, not force.

THE OPERATIONAL IMPLICATIONS

These cultural bonds create obstacles that cannot be bypassed, only understood.

- Clash of loyalties: Family duty outranks all other obligations. Promises made to a service or an officer are fragile beside promises made before kin.
- Amplified risk: Exposure threatens not just the individual but their entire household. Fear of collective punishment is a powerful deterrent to openness.
- Emotional strain: Guilt corrodes trust. The psychological cost of betrayal can turn a cooperative source into a silent ghost overnight.

To operate effectively, an officer must blend the patience of a diplomat with the discernment of a psychologist. Relationships, not results, become the first objective. The report is the consequence, not the goal.

ANTICIPATING THE STRAIN

Conflicted loyalties twist truth into fragments. Half-truths replace confession, and silence masquerades as prudence. An officer must learn to hear what is not said, the slight pause before an answer, the careful avoidance of certain names, the change in rhythm when family or faith enters the discussion.

A source under cultural strain will rarely defect suddenly; they will fade. Their tone grows ceremonial, their words safe, their meetings perfunctory. The untrained officer sees compliance. The experienced one sees withdrawal.

THE ART OF ENDURANCE

In this region, recruitment is not an act; it is a process measured in months and memories. Each small gesture, remembering an elder's illness, attending a local celebration, or sitting quietly through an hour of silence, becomes currency in the emotional economy of trust.

Respect is not a tactic here; it is survival. An officer who displays arrogance or impatience invites exile. The one who listens, who drinks the tea even when it is the third round and the day is long, will find that doors begin to open without being knocked upon.

THE LONG GAME OF TRUST

In the Middle East, time itself is a language. A rushed man is distrusted, a patient one respected. Recruitment here does not move through urgency; it moves through rhythm, through repeated gestures that prove sincerity long before intent is spoken.

Trust is not built in words but in presence. A foreign officer who keeps returning, same hour, same street, same quiet tone, begins to absorb legitimacy by endurance. Over time, he stops being the outsider and becomes the familiar stranger, tolerated first, then trusted. In the eyes of the community, persistence is proof of integrity.

The first contact must be more listening than asking. A calm tone, an interested silence, a shared story told at the right moment all speak louder than promises. In this environment, emotional patience is tactical intelligence.

READING THE INVISIBLE WEB

Beyond family lies a living network of alliances, tribes, business interests, clerical hierarchies, militia affiliations. Each connection functions as both pathway and trap. The officer's first mission is not to persuade but to map.

Who controls social access? Which voice is feared in the market? Whose name, when spoken, lowers others into silence? Such observations reveal power in its purest form, unrecorded, unspoken, but absolute.

Inside every neighborhood lies an unseen chain of authority that the untrained eye misses. The real decision-maker may be the imam's brother, the shopkeeper who extends credit, or the mother whose kitchen hosts unending conversations. Information flows through these domestic corridors faster than through ministries. The officer who learns to listen in kitchens rather than offices begins to see the real structure of control.

INTERMEDIARIES AND CULTURAL ANCHORS

No foreign presence succeeds alone. Entry must come through intermediaries who possess moral weight, respected traders, local elders, or men of faith whose handshake validates your existence.

The wrong intermediary can destroy a mission. A man from a rival sect or tribe brings contamination. His introduction labels you long before your words are heard. But when the right intermediary steps forward, suspicion transforms into respect. The asset no longer meets a stranger; he meets someone vouched for.

In the Arab world, a single sentence, "He is with me," carries more protection than any official badge.

MANAGING THE EMOTIONAL ECONOMY

Every man carries three kinds of needs: security, dignity, and belonging. In the Middle Eastern context, these are magnified by communal scrutiny. A man may endure hunger, but not humiliation. He may live in poverty, but not disgrace.

The officer must design incentives that speak to these inner equations.

- Security: Offer discreet protection, not through threats but through practical measures, ensuring his family's safety, arranging travel, providing quiet assurance that he will not stand alone.
- Dignity: Frame cooperation as moral courage, not betrayal. Show him that what he risks is balanced by the honor of protecting others.
- Belonging: Never isolate him. Keep his cooperation connected to his social circle's survival, so his conscience sees participation as defense, not desertion.

Each meeting must reduce shame and replace fear with control. When the officer achieves this balance, loyalty becomes self-sustaining.

THE LANGUAGE OF GESTURE

Words are rarely enough. Meaning is conveyed through tone, pauses, and ritual actions that outsiders overlook. The way one accepts tea, the sequence of greeting, or the moment one touches the heart after shaking hands, these gestures carry volumes.

In a recruitment meeting, silence is never empty. It can be a test. The experienced officer learns to let quiet moments breathe. The man across from him may be searching his face for contradiction, weighing respect against suspicion. A single uncontrolled glance, a hint of haste, can end months of progress.

True fluency is not linguistic; it is behavioral. The one who mirrors cultural tempo without mimicry becomes invisible, and in intelligence, invisibility is mastery.

HANDLING CONFLICTED LOYALTIES

Every recruit will reach a breaking point where fear and loyalty clash. It may come after a sermon that denounces betrayal, after a rumor that outsiders are watching, or after a family elder warns him to stay silent. The officer must anticipate this moment as if it were inevitable.

Do not fight the guilt. Allow it space. A short withdrawal is not failure; it is breathing. Pressing too soon fractures trust. Instead, reaffirm the source's moral identity, remind him that cooperation protects his people, that the information he provides may prevent suffering. Turn his inner storm into a defense of what he values.

Cultural operations fail not from lack of courage but from impatience with conscience.

OPERATIONAL TECHNIQUES FOR CULTURAL TERRAIN

- Context mapping: Identify not only the target but his environment, relatives, patrons, rivalries, and faith-based affiliations. Influence flows through them.
- Symbolic engagement: Use culturally grounded rituals, visit during Ramadan evenings, attend weddings, send condolences. These gestures build memory that lasts longer than arguments.
- Incremental disclosure: Never ask for more than what feels safe. Let each truth shared normalize the next.
- Emotional calibration: Adjust tone based on social setting. In public, humility is protection. In private, quiet confidence earns trust.
- Adaptive pacing: Let the group's rhythm dictate progress. Time, not pressure, creates allegiance.

FIELD AWARENESS: THE MORAL MAP

A seasoned officer learns that cultural operations require more than observation; they demand self-discipline. The field does not forgive arrogance or insensitivity. A misjudged joke, a careless question about faith, a failure to greet properly can unravel months of work.

The Middle East remembers. Offense lingers, but respect multiplies. Every gesture of restraint reinforces credibility. Every moment of genuine curiosity earns a place in memory. An officer who moves through the field with ethical clarity gains more protection than one armed with deception alone.

Ethics here are not academic; they are operational. To humiliate a man before his peers is to mark yourself permanently. But to honor him, even subtly, can open doors that would otherwise remain bolted.

THE INTELLIGENCE MINDSET

Cultural mastery is less about knowledge than rhythm, knowing when to act, when to wait, when to fade into the background. It is about learning to think in the cadence of the society around you.

This mindset requires emotional endurance. A good officer must endure boredom without restlessness, insult without retaliation, and uncertainty without panic. It is not enough to speak Arabic or recite customs; one must feel the tempo of a region where relationships move at the speed of trust.

In the end, intelligence in the Middle East is less about gathering secrets than about understanding silence, the unspoken loyalties and quiet moral calculations that dictate every move.

Conclusion: The Living Core of the Mission

Culture is not the setting of intelligence work; it is the mission itself. The officer who understands loyalty commands it; the one who misreads it is devoured by it. Every family tie, every faith ritual, every communal habit can serve as either shield or weapon. The difference lies in perception.

To master this environment, the officer must live within it, not above it, not against it. He must treat respect as tradecraft, patience as armor, and humility as strategy.

The lessons of this chapter are not philosophy; they are survival. Here begins the real work, turning this cultural fluency into recruitment power, where knowledge becomes influence and observation becomes control. Chapter 2 continues this evolution, revealing how these cultural codes transform from understanding into deliberate operational design, the point where empathy becomes leverage and culture itself turns into a weapon.

CHAPTER 2:
TURNING CULTURAL KNOWLEDGE INTO OPERATIONAL POWER

THE SHIFT FROM UNDERSTANDING TO ACTION

Cultural understanding is the first weapon of intelligence, but mastery begins only when knowledge leaves the page and enters the field. The Middle East does not reward theory; it rewards presence. The officer who studies from a distance sees the map but not the terrain. To survive here, one must feel the rhythm of life that moves through narrow alleys, quiet courtyards, and crowded mosques where loyalty speaks in whispers and betrayal in silence.

Building on the foundation of cultural fluency from Chapter 1, this chapter transforms comprehension into controlled influence. It teaches how to move from observation to participation, from knowing people to shaping their decisions. In this landscape, recruitment is not an act of persuasion but an act of alignment, of bringing a man's moral compass into orbit with your mission without him realizing he has shifted.

THE ART OF PRESENCE

Building on the endurance principles outlined in Chapter 1, presence in Arab and Muslim societies evolves from mere consistency to strategic integration. Every movement is a message: the way you cross a threshold, remove your shoes, or accept coffee signals education, humility, and belonging.

An officer must learn to move without friction, to exist inside the environment until the air no longer reacts to his presence. This goes beyond listening; it's about applying quiet observation to operational ends, altering the psychological field so the community not only tolerates you but begins to reveal its inner dynamics. Authenticity cannot be performed; it must be earned through gestures that open doors to influence.

FINDING THE GATEKEEPERS

Extending the cultural anchors from Chapter 1, gatekeepers become operational pivots in the Middle East. Access is governed by networks of trust anchored in legitimacy: the imam who interprets morality, the merchant who extends credit, the family elder who speaks with history behind him. These figures are the arteries through which influence flows.

Choosing the wrong gatekeeper is operational suicide. A man of low status or questionable lineage carries no moral weight and can taint an entire mission. But when the right gatekeeper introduces you, you inherit his credibility. Suspicion softens; even hostility becomes courtesy.

A single introduction from the right mouth can replace months of surveillance. The key is discernment, knowing who truly leads, not who claims to. In the Arab world, authority often speaks softly. It sits in the corner of the room, silent until it decides to bless or dismiss you. Use these introductions to pivot into deeper recruitment, turning vouching into a pathway for secure meetings.

READING FAULT LINES

Every society carries its quiet fractures: jealousies between clerics, rivalries between tribes, resentments within political factions. To an outsider, these look like background noise; to an officer, they are the map of opportunity.

The art lies in listening for tension without appearing to. A smile that doesn't reach the eyes when a name is mentioned, a proverb chosen too carefully, a silence that lasts one breath longer than it should: these are signals that power is not as united as it seems.

The officer must treat these tensions not as weapons but as keys. Exploiting them crudely breeds enemies; using them gently creates allies. Influence grows when you help a man recover dignity that someone else denied him. In this region, respect is the rarest currency. Offer it, and even resentment turns to cooperation. Operationally, map these fault lines to identify vulnerable targets for initial approaches, turning internal discord into recruitment leverage.

THE ARCHITECTURE OF MOTIVATION

Western intelligence often mistakes greed or ideology for the primary levers of persuasion. In the Middle East, neither stands alone. Beneath every choice lies a moral equation that weighs honor, belonging, and divine accountability. To ask a man to betray his world without redefining what loyalty means is to ask him to destroy himself.

The officer's task is to translate cooperation into virtue. You do not tempt him with gain; you convince him that action preserves what he loves. You present truth as protection, not betrayal. You show him that silence serves the corrupt while his courage safeguards the faithful. When belief becomes the bridge, loyalty follows naturally.

Every offer must fit the man's moral rhythm. The devout require sanctity; the ambitious require recognition; the fearful require safety. The key is not manipulation, but resonance. When your purpose echoes their private values, recruitment feels inevitable, almost moral. Apply this by tailoring pitches to specific profiles, such as framing financial incentives as family security for the subsistence-driven or ideological realignment for the zealous.

THE BALANCE OF FEAR AND DIGNITY

Fear moves people only when wrapped in dignity. Threats alone harden resistance, but fear that is given meaning transforms into self-preservation. The officer must never humiliate, even in control. In collectivist societies, humiliation stains deeper than injury. A humiliated man cannot be trusted; he will wait for the day to restore his pride, and when that day comes, it will cost you everything.

Instead, the officer should offer a controlled escape from fear, a path that allows the source to preserve self-respect while cooperating. Dignity is oxygen; take it away and the human mind suffocates. Offer it back, and the heart opens. In practice, this means de-escalating high-stakes moments with empathetic debriefs, ensuring the source feels empowered rather than coerced.

Building Early Trust

Trust grows through rhythm, not revelation. Small acts, performed repeatedly with consistency, create emotional gravity. Remembering a child's name, inquiring about a relative's illness, offering help without being asked, these acts forge bonds that no bribe can buy.

In a world where loyalty defines identity, a foreigner who honors another's family earns something far greater than affection: protection. When a man begins to defend your reputation in your absence, you have crossed the line from tolerated to trusted.

At that point, recruitment is no longer a negotiation; it is an evolution. Operationally, use these early bonds to test low-risk tasks, gradually escalating to information exchange while monitoring for cultural alignment.

Mastering the Psychology of Influence

The Human Equation

Recruitment in the Middle East is less about manipulation than emotional geometry. Every person holds a pattern of fear, pride, faith, and desire. The officer's role is to read that pattern and apply just enough pressure to make the lines converge. There is no formula, only the discipline of observation and the courage to wait until the right line moves.

The first step is to understand that every recruit is fighting two wars: one against external risk and another within his conscience. The first is easy to manage with security; the second can destroy the mission if ignored. When a man betrays his world, he must rebuild a new one inside himself to survive. The officer becomes both architect and confessor in that reconstruction.

Emotional Synchronization

A skilled officer mirrors the emotional tone of his environment. If a man is grieving, you grieve with him. If he jokes, you smile softly. This is not mimicry but psychological synchronization, a shared wavelength that communicates sincerity without speech.

Emotion is the true language of recruitment. It travels faster than logic and cuts through suspicion. The more a source feels understood, the less he fears exposure. In a society where shame is the sharpest weapon, empathy is disarmament.

A single sentence, spoken at the right moment with true emotional resonance, can succeed where months of planning fail. It may be as simple as You did what you had to do, or I know you only wanted to protect them. These words reframe guilt as virtue and turn hesitation into resolve.

Aligning Moral Logic

The Middle East is not a moral void; it is a moral labyrinth. Every act must be justified within the logic of faith, honor, or duty. An officer who ignores this will always be seen as an outsider, clever perhaps, but soulless.

To win trust, you must operate within the subject's moral code, not against it. When a man believes that your purpose protects his people, he no longer serves you; he joins you. The goal is not to erase his convictions but to reorient them.

Faith is a bridge, not an obstacle. A devout man can be guided more easily through theology than through argument. Show him that truth, not silence, is divine justice. The Qur'anic call to honesty, the duty to protect innocents, the obligation to confront corruption, these are not tools of deception but instruments of moral logic that transform cooperation into righteousness.

SUBTLE SECURITY

Operational communication must move like conversation, not command. Instructions hidden in normal dialogue are far safer than coded transmissions. A proverb, a gesture, or even the placement of a cup can deliver meaning undetectable to outsiders.

For instance, a changed seating position may signal danger; a repeated phrase may confirm contact. In the Middle East, culture already encodes meaning; the officer's task is to use it, not to overwrite it. These become invisible forms of security, impossible to decode without cultural context. The most successful officers blend tradecraft into daily life so completely that even the source forgets it is tradecraft.

When tradecraft speaks the language of culture, it becomes invisible. A prayer meeting becomes a rendezvous; a marketplace becomes an exchange point; a wedding becomes a cover for coordination. In such operations, the safest plan is the one that looks most ordinary.

Operational safety in this environment cannot appear foreign. Disguise must look like custom, and communication must sound like ritual.

SUSTAINING COOPERATION

Every successful recruitment must evolve into endurance. Trust decays when left unattended. An officer must cultivate a rhythm of reassurance: small acknowledgments, consistent tone, steady presence.

The source must feel that cooperation strengthens his identity, not weakens it. Each interaction should restore a sense of purpose. By keeping the moral alignment alive, protecting his sense of doing good, the officer ensures that loyalty becomes habit.

When the mission depends on information flow, the smallest emotional fracture can cause silence. Therefore, vigilance is constant. Watch his words, but also his silences. When he grows formal, when his eyes drift, when humor disappears, danger is near. Reconnect before withdrawal becomes betrayal.

THE ETHICS OF CONTROL

Every officer faces a private test: how far to push, how much to manipulate, how deeply to lie. The best officers operate under moral discipline as sharp as any operational rule. Deception without respect corrupts judgment. Respect without control loses the mission. Balance must be absolute.

Never humiliate a source, even in private. Never mock his faith or his fear. These are not weaknesses; they are the architecture of his world. To tear them down is to destroy the ground you stand on.

There will be times when you must deceive him for his safety, when truth would shatter his courage. This is not cruelty; it is stewardship. The true professional knows that power without restraint breeds collapse. The strongest officer is the one who can lie without arrogance and command without contempt.

THE PRICE OF IMMERSION

Working in the Middle East demands emotional immersion. To gain access, you must live inside their world, eat their food, share their silences, and bear witness to their pain. Over time, the lines between role and self blur. You begin to think in their metaphors, to feel their loyalties. You become both observer and participant.

This is where danger turns inward. Too much empathy clouds judgment; too little turns you into a ghost. The professional must walk that razor's edge, close enough to understand, distant enough to decide.

Many officers fail not from exposure but from exhaustion. They absorb too much of what they see. The suffering, the contradictions, the human warmth mixed with brutality; it seeps into the conscience. The antidote is ritual: a routine of detachment, reflection, and renewal. The mission must never replace the self.

THE SCIENCE OF PATIENCE

Patience is not waiting; it is controlled motion at the speed of trust. In this region, events unfold according to social tempo, not operational schedules. One must learn to recognize the cultural pace, the pauses between decisions, the ceremonies that precede approval, the delays that are tests of respect.

The officer who tries to accelerate the process often destroys it. A premature request feels like disrespect. The right question asked too soon can sound like insult. But a delayed approach, seasoned by familiarity, can turn skepticism into loyalty. Patience is not the absence of strategy; it is the perfection of timing.

THE CULTURAL MIRROR

Every operation reflects the culture that hosts it. When done with sensitivity, intelligence work becomes a mirror of society's values rather than an intrusion. Each conversation reveals how identity is built, how people reconcile fear with faith, and how belonging shapes truth.

The best officers come to see that culture is not an obstacle but an ally. Its rules, once understood, offer protection. Its rituals create cover. Its hierarchies define predictable patterns. To master this mirror is to transform complexity into clarity.

Conclusion: Culture as the Engine of Control

Recruitment in the Middle East is not a transaction of secrets; it is a negotiation of meaning. The officer who understands this moves unseen through a landscape of loyalty and silence. He persuades without pressure, influences without exposure, and turns culture itself into the architecture of control.

The art of recruitment lies not in dominating minds but in synchronizing with them, aligning emotion, faith, and reason until cooperation becomes an act of identity. This is the evolution from cultural fluency to operational power.

As this chapter closes, the officer steps beyond understanding and into influence. The next phase, explored in Chapter 3, delves into the human mind itself, revealing the psychological mechanisms that drive loyalty,

fear, and deception. There, the tools of persuasion sharpen into the instruments of control, and the boundary between culture and cognition
begins to vanish.

CHAPTER 3:
DECODING HUMAN BEHAVIOR AND COMMUNICATION IN MIDDLE EASTERN INTELLIGENCE WORK

NAVIGATING THE HUMAN LANDSCAPE

Every intelligence officer eventually discovers that the hardest map to read is not geographic, it is human. In the Middle East and the Arab world, that map is layered with centuries of power, faith, and survival. Every handshake carries calculation, every silence carries meaning, and every act of loyalty is tied to something larger than the self.

Extending the cultural structures from Chapter 1 and the recruitment frameworks in Chapter 2, this chapter dives into the emotional, psychological, and behavioral heart of intelligence work. It explores the forces that make people in this region unpredictable yet profoundly patterned, the shifting pulse of politics and religion, the personality traits forged by history, and the deeply traditional forms of communication that reveal more than words ever could.

Here, intelligence officers learn that behavior is never random. It is coded in honor, guided by faith, and shaped by the delicate balance between pride and fear. Understanding these patterns is not about manipulating people: it is about predicting them, turning volatility into actionable foresight.

The question that drives this chapter is one that haunts every operative who has ever worked in the Middle East: When a single event can rewrite loyalties overnight, how do you tell the difference between fear, faith, and betrayal?

THE SHIFTING POWER OF POLITICAL AND RELIGIOUS CURRENTS

In the Middle East, the environment itself is alive with movement. Political upheavals, clerical decrees, or even rumors of reform can shift loyalties faster than any negotiation. Building on the adaptive loyalties discussed in earlier chapters, this volatility demands officers treat loyalty as fluid, a response to external pressures rather than a fixed trait.

The officer who mistakes adaptation for betrayal risks losing not only his asset but also the rhythm of the mission. To succeed, one must understand that political and religious shifts act as emotional earthquakes. The ground does not just shake once, it continues to tremble, reshaping the landscape long after the first shock.

HOW EVENTS RESHAPE MINDS

Political or spiritual events do not merely alter opinion; they redefine identity. When power changes hands or when a new clerical edict is announced, people do not just reconsider their loyalties, they reconsider who they are within the moral order.

A new leader can trigger fear, opportunism, or inspiration. Each emotion changes how information is shared or withheld. A religious decree can sanctify old loyalties or turn them into sins overnight. An outbreak of unrest transforms ordinary citizens into participants, observers, or informants depending on how they perceive danger and belonging.

This constant fluidity makes operational discipline both difficult and essential. It demands that officers read emotion as closely as they read intelligence reports, using tools like real-time sentiment tracking to anticipate shifts.

Common Triggers and Their Hidden Mechanisms

1. Power Vacuums: Leadership changes, from coups to resignations, create ripples of fear and calculation. People rush to

re-align with whoever appears strongest. A once-loyal source may suddenly hesitate to meet, not because of deceit but because of uncertainty about who truly holds power. Officers must learn to track small behavioral clues: a shift in tone, sudden silence, or a repeated phrase that echoes new rhetoric. Operationally, use these moments to insert protective narratives that position cooperation as a hedge against instability.

2. Faith Mobilization: Religion, more than politics, moves emotion at scale. A single sermon, broadcast from a pulpit or shared online, can reframe a moral universe. The devout who once saw cooperation as patriotic may wake up seeing it as betrayal. Faith can transform logic into fervor and fervor into flight. The key is not to fight belief, but to anticipate its direction and realign the mission before conviction becomes withdrawal. In practice, monitor social media echoes of sermons to gauge asset vulnerability.

3. Social and Economic Pressure: When economies collapse or protests fill the streets, personal survival becomes political. People huddle closer to their kin, tribes, or sects. Fear drives unity, and unity excludes outsiders, including officers who once felt like family. Yet within this tightening circle lies opportunity: those marginalized by the new order often seek quiet alliances for protection. Leverage this by offering discreet economic relief tied to ongoing collaboration.

OPERATIONAL CHALLENGES DURING UPHEAVAL

Distorted Intelligence: Under stress, assets begin to repeat rumors as fact, projecting their own fears into reports. Verification must become a daily habit, not a procedural step. Cross-check through multiple channels before acting, incorporating digital signals like app usage patterns.

Emotional Displacement: Anger or guilt can manifest as hesitation, silence, or erratic communication. The officer must become part handler, part counselor, steady, unreactive, and quietly available, using debriefs to recalibrate without pressure.

Opportunism: Some will exploit uncertainty to renegotiate their value. When loyalty becomes a bargaining chip, reaffirm shared goals subtly before trust erodes into transaction, perhaps by escalating rewards incrementally.

STRATEGIC ADAPTATION: TOOLS FOR OFFICERS

1. Emotional Temperature Checks: Ask simple, open questions about how people feel about current events, not to collect information, but to assess inner balance. Answers to "What do you hear in the mosque?" often reveal more about fear and faith than the sermon itself. Log these for pattern analysis.

2. Scenario Forecasting: Before major events, imagine how they might alter your asset's emotional or moral alignment. Build contingency plans in advance, alternate contacts, emergency language cues, or delayed operations until stability returns.

3. Timing as a Weapon: In unstable climates, time heals suspicion. Wait for calm before resuming persuasion. Every delay, when strategic, can preserve an entire network, using tools like encrypted check-ins to maintain low-profile contact.

Better View: Events do not just shake loyalties; they rewire perception. An officer who rushes after tremors only stirs more dust. The skilled handler observes until clarity re-emerges, not because he is passive, but because he knows that human equilibrium always returns, and when it does, trust can be rebuilt on the foundation of his patience.

CULTURALLY FORMED PERSONALITY TRAITS: MAPPING THE INNER LANDSCAPE

If Chapter 1 described culture as the skeleton of society, and Chapter 2 taught the muscle of recruitment, then personality is the pulse, the beating rhythm that gives movement and unpredictability to human behavior.

In Middle Eastern contexts, personality is rarely individualistic. It is shaped by history, hierarchy, and collective struggle. To understand a person's mind, one must first understand their world, a world where honor replaces ego, patience replaces impulse, and silence often carries more power than speech. This section advances prior discussions by focusing on decoding these traits for predictive analysis.

KEY TRAITS THAT DEFINE BEHAVIOR

1. Calculated Caution: Decades of instability have made caution a survival art. People watch before acting, listen before answering, and test before trusting. An officer must interpret delay not as resistance but as evaluation. The moment a source begins asking questions of their own, it means progress. Curiosity is the first step toward cooperation. Operationally, use this by embedding low-stakes probes to accelerate evaluation without alarm.

2. Communal Identity: The self is inseparable from the group. An individual does not act alone; they carry their family, tribe, and faith into every decision. Convincing one man may require convincing his invisible circle, the elders, the cleric, the spouse who interprets his morality. Recruitment here is never one-on-one; it is one-to-many, even if the others are never in the room. Differentiate from prior frameworks by mapping extended networks via digital footprints for targeted influence.

3. Resilient Endurance: A lifetime of sanctions, conflict, and

scarcity creates stoicism. Emotional restraint is not indifference; it is dignity. Officers who misread calm as detachment miss the subtle cues of fatigue or quiet defiance. Watch for micro-signals: the slowed breath, the eyes that do not return a gaze, the hand that stops gesturing mid-sentence. These are emotional leaks in otherwise guarded minds. Employ wearable tech or video analysis for real-time cue detection in high-risk meets.

4. Honor as Moral Currency: Honor is not vanity; it is spiritual capital. It dictates behavior in every social setting, from politics to the family home. Losing it is worse than death because it stains generations. A wise officer never bargains directly with honor; he works through it, presenting cooperation as a way to defend or restore it. Build on earlier dignity discussions by integrating honor into risk assessments, quantifying it through social media sentiment.

OPERATIONAL IMPLICATIONS

Testing the Surface: Assign symbolic tasks before operational ones. Loyalty revealed through small risks is stronger than loyalty declared through words.

Building Around Communal Duty: Always link cooperation to protection of family, of reputation, of faith. Frame every exchange within this cultural code, and it ceases to feel like betrayal.

Balancing Toughness with Empathy: Never mirror aggression with aggression. In this culture, composure under tension earns respect. A single display of temper can undo months of quiet investment.

Guarding Dignity: Humiliation, even accidental, poisons trust beyond repair. If offense occurs, restitution must be immediate and public enough to restore balance. A gesture, a visit, or a phrase of respect can mend what pride once broke.

Field Reflection: In Iraq, a veteran Iraqi intelligence officer once said: "The hardest men to read are the ones who smile with their eyes down. They are not hiding hate; they are hiding pride." He was right. The emotional landscape here is not defined by openness but by restraint. A Middle Eastern man who speaks softly may carry the weight of unspoken fury or deep trust. Only patience reveals which one.

Better View: Each personality is a network of contradictions, loyal yet pragmatic, proud yet cautious, devout yet flexible. The officer's art lies not in simplifying these contradictions but in navigating them, using the right note at the right time. A word too sharp cuts; a pause too long cools. The best operatives learn to read the emotional pulse beneath still waters, where loyalty and fear coexist in delicate balance.

THE CULTURE OF ARGUMENT: THE ART OF VERBAL COMBAT

In Middle Eastern and Arab societies, conversation is never neutral; it is a form of contest. Argument here is not an act of hostility but a language of respect and intelligence. To argue is to engage; to stay silent is to withdraw. In this region, silence ends relationships faster than anger.

An officer working in this environment must unlearn the Western instinct to avoid confrontation. In the Arab world, confrontation is not necessarily conflict; it is connection. It is how trust, intellect, and courage are tested in real time. This builds on prior communication insights by emphasizing debate as a diagnostic tool.

THE ANATOMY OF DEBATE

1. Verbal Sparring as Social Theater: Long before microphones and politics, Arabs refined debate in markets, coffeehouses, and mosques. These were arenas where words replaced swords. Eloquence proved wisdom; quick wit commanded admiration. For an intelligence officer, understanding this tradition means

recognizing that intensity is not aggression; it is an expression of authenticity.

2. Emotion as Logic: Western reasoning separates emotion from argument. Middle Eastern reasoning blends them. Passion is not loss of control but proof of sincerity. When a man's voice rises, it is not necessarily anger; it is emphasis. When his eyes flash, he is not attacking; he is testing if you are real. The officer who responds with calm detachment risks appearing cold or arrogant. Instead, mirroring tone and tempo builds parity, the foundation of mutual respect.

3. Honor and Endurance in Dialogue: In argument, withdrawal signals weakness. To stand your ground, politely but firmly, earns respect. Yet, true mastery lies not in winning the argument but in ending it with dignity. When both parties can leave the discussion believing they have prevailed, the relationship strengthens.

OPERATIONAL STRATEGIES FOR VERBAL COMBAT

Read the rhythm, not the volume: A raised voice may mark trust, not danger. Watch for tone more than sound. When the rhythm softens after heat, it signals emotional release, an opening for connection. Record sessions for post-analysis to spot recurring patterns.

Mirror energy without mimicry: Engage emotionally, but never theatrically. Match intensity through empathy, not imitation. A small nod, a reflective pause, or a phrase like "I understand your point, my brother" can reset tension without submission.

Yield strategically: Allow the source to "win." In many cultures, compromise equals concession; in the Arab world, it equals wisdom. When you let someone have the final word, you preserve their dignity, and with it, your access.

Use disagreement as diagnosis: The way a person argues reveals personality more clearly than how they agree. Do they appeal to faith, history, or emotion? Each method exposes their core motivator. For the observant officer, every debate becomes a psychological map, informing future handling tactics.

Field Example: During an operation in Basra, a handler spent two hours debating the meaning of loyalty with his source, a local merchant. The discussion grew heated, attracting attention. Yet afterward, the merchant laughed and said, "Now I know you're not like the others; you don't fear truth." That night, he shared information he had hidden for months. Argument, when respected, becomes a form of vetting: use it to calibrate trust levels mid-operation.

Lessons from the Art of Argument:

- Patience wins power: Allow emotion to flow; do not interrupt its rhythm.
- Respect translates through resistance: Gentle disagreement can strengthen credibility.
- Clarity emerges after passion: Truth often surfaces once the emotional layer burns away.

In this context, the officer is not simply collecting intelligence; he is participating in a cultural ritual of testing and affirmation. It is not the debate that matters, but what remains unsaid after it ends.

Better View: In the West, logic convinces; in the Middle East, presence does. The officer who listens, argues, and laughs as a local does not simply gain information; he earns identity within the culture itself.

INTEGRATING OBSERVATION, PSYCHOLOGY, AND COMMUNICATION

By now, the intelligence officer has seen that no single factor, culture, faith, or personality, works alone. They weave together like threads in a complex fabric. Success lies in seeing the pattern rather than the parts.

An officer must learn to think in systems of influence: External pressures (political or religious shifts), internal psychology (fear, pride, loyalty), and interpersonal expression (debate, silence, tone). Together, they shape every reaction, every choice, every betrayal or confession. This integration advances prior chapters by synthesizing into predictive models.

THE THREE-LAYERED FRAMEWORK

1. Environmental Awareness: Track how social events and religious climates shift a person's sense of security. A Friday sermon or televised speech may undo weeks of trust. Use AI-assisted monitoring for trend prediction.

2. Psychological Profiling: Identify the person's primary drivers. Are they ruled by guilt, pride, or fear of dishonor? Each demands a different handling tone. Develop custom profiles with behavioral baselines.

3. Communication Mastery: Adapt speech patterns, pacing, and metaphor to align with local norms. A single misplaced idiom can expose foreignness; a well-chosen proverb can create kinship. Train in dialect variations for authenticity.

PRACTICAL INTEGRATION TOOLS

- Dynamic profiling: Update emotional assessments constantly. An asset is not a fixed file; he evolves daily: use encrypted apps for real-time updates.
- Cultural anchoring: Use shared symbols, family, nation, religion, as emotional stabilizers, embedding them in comms protocols.
- Narrative immersion: Embed mission goals inside personal stories. When cooperation feels like destiny, loyalty becomes emotional, not transactional. Craft narratives based on local folklore for resonance.
- Emotional timing: Choose the right moment for persuasion, after relief, not during fear. Schedule around cultural calendars like religious holidays.

- Cross-loyalty awareness: Understand that each source serves multiple masters: faith, family, and self. The goal is not to replace these loyalties, but to nest within them, creating layered commitments.
- Field Reflection: A Lebanese journalist once said, "We don't follow one leader; we follow whoever speaks to our conscience today." For the intelligence officer, this means loyalty must be renewed continually, not demanded, but inspired through adaptive engagement.

THE OFFICER'S MINDSET

Middle Eastern operations demand emotional agility. The officer must be at once patient and assertive, compassionate yet guarded. Those who rely only on logic miss the human temperature that drives decisions. Those who drown in empathy risk losing objectivity. The art lies in standing inside the culture emotionally, yet outside it operationally: feeling without absorbing, seeing without judging. Differentiate from prior mindsets by emphasizing predictive intuition honed through simulation training.

Advanced Field Insights

- Behavioral mapping: Document every emotional fluctuation, when they hesitate, joke, deflect, or contradict themselves. Patterns reveal more than confessions; analyze via data logs for anomaly detection.
- Emotional recalibration: Use reassurance as maintenance. When fear spikes, remind them of earlier moments of courage. Link the present mission to their past pride. Memory, in this region, is a weapon of stability: deploy it via personalized callbacks.
- Strategic storytelling: Craft mission narratives that echo collective legends, stories of loyalty, sacrifice, and redemption. In the Arab psyche, stories carry moral weight that logic cannot reach; use them in debriefs to reinforce bonds.
- Controlled vulnerability: Share small truths about yourself. Admitting minor weaknesses, a sleepless night, a difficult mission, humanizes you. It invites reciprocity and breaks the barrier of mistrust without compromising authority. Limit to vetted scenarios for security.

- Better View: In intelligence work, data builds strategy; emotion builds access. The officer who masters both, controls not only the mission but also the meaning behind it.

Conclusion: Turning Volatility into Vision

The human landscape of the Middle East is not chaos; it is choreography. Each political tremor, each surge of faith, each burst of emotion follows hidden rhythm. The successful officer listens for that rhythm until it becomes second nature.

Politics and religion may set the tempo, but psychology defines the melody. Argument adds harmony, and trust becomes the refrain that repeats across operations.

When an officer learns to hear this symphony, the tremor of fear, the pause of honor, the rise of conviction, he moves from collecting intelligence to conducting it.

To operate in this environment is to live inside a living equation: Culture shapes thought. Thought shapes emotion. Emotion shapes action.

Understanding that chain is what separates the ordinary investigator from the master of human terrain.

As the book moves into Chapter 4, the focus expands from individuals to collectives, from decoding the human pulse to orchestrating networks of loyalty, influence, and survival. Here, the lone operative's insight evolves into strategic vision, where culture and psychology merge into the larger art of controlling environments rather than merely navigating them.

CHAPTER 4:
ENTERING THE CIRCLE: INFILTRATING GROUPS AND BUILDING TRUST

READING THE LIVING NETWORK

Groups are not buildings you enter; they are climates you learn to breathe. Militias, political factions, religious circles, and community networks are social ecosystems with their own seasons and storms. They grant safety, status, and identity, and they punish betrayal with consequences that are social, economic, and sometimes lethal. What looks like a single organization is more often a shifting constellation: a leader's fall, a funding cut, or an ideological fissure can redraw loyalties overnight. Chapters 1 through 3 laid the groundwork: cultural maps, how minds tilt under pressure, and the basic art of recruitment. This chapter moves from the individual to the collective. It shows how to locate the seams in a living system, how to slip a thread through without tearing the fabric, and how to convert access into sustained, actionable intelligence.

THE ANATOMY OF A GROUP

Every group has a structure, and every structure has a brittle point. Understanding that architecture is the first operational task.

- Leadership concentrates power. Decisions are often made by a handful of people who embody authority through charisma, lineage, or ideology. That concentration makes a group fast and coherent, but it also produces leverage. When authority rests on persona rather than on formal institutions, influence moves with personality. A leader can be the group's greatest strength and its most fragile hinge.

- Secrecy is a currency. Decision-making and sensitive knowledge are compartmentalized. Information is a string of fragments distributed across many hands. Direct access to core facts is rare; what you can gather most often comes from periphery conversations, ritual behaviors, and the mundane logistics that reveal priorities: who supplies food, who signs the rent, who pays the phone bills.

- Adaptability is the rule. Groups survive by shifting. Rivalries, money flows, and external shocks force rapid reconfiguration. That volatility creates windows. A faith decree, an arrest, an influx of cash, or a disputed promotion can open cracks that were invisible a week earlier.

THE DEFENSIVE PERIMETER: HOW GROUPS KEEP OUTSIDERS OUT

The walls around groups are rarely just walls. They are overlapping systems of surveillance, obligation, and reward.

Mutual monitoring turns members into guards. Social norms, honor codes, and reciprocal obligations create a dense web in which members police each other. Every conversation is tested against expectations; every newcomer is scanned not only for behavior but for lineage and patronage.

Material and social incentives tie people in. Homes, jobs, protection, and access to patronage are real anchors. Emotional rewards, such as status, ritual recognition, and the sense of belonging, bind more tightly than cash. Leaving the group often costs far more than the short-term gain of betrayal.

Rules are moralized. Written orders are rare; the group's rules live in stories, symbols, and ritual practice. Religious language, militia vows, and public oaths transform compliance into a moral duty.

FINDING THIN PLACES: WHERE THE WALLS PAUSE

Operational advantages lie where watchfulness slips or incentives loosen. These thin places are the aim of every insertion strategy.

Fissures appear in ordinary ways. Disputes over money, tensions between old-guard and newcomers, or a leader's perceived failure create moments of doubt. New recruits and peripheral supporters are often less enculturated and therefore more malleable. External stressors, such as arrests, sanctions, or supply shortages, accelerate reassessment. Your task is to map these frictions and be present when they widen.

BECOMING ONE OF THEM: FITTING WITHOUT LOSING YOUR COVER

Infiltration is not a costume change. It is a slow, social recalibration. You do not mimic; you grow into a role.

To integrate effectively:

- Match rhythms before you match rhetoric. Small signals matter: prayer times, the cadence of speech, the way tea is poured, the placement of shoes at the door. These details do two things. They lower suspicion and they buy you time to observe.

- Enter along the edges. Low-profile roles are safer and more useful than dramatic positions. Someone who repairs radios, delivers goods, or manages paperwork can learn more than a charismatic newcomer who demands attention. Peripheral roles also attract less scrutiny.

- Use social friction to learn hierarchies. Engage in benign arguments, raise small practical questions, and listen to how authority is asserted and negotiated. The tone of a dispute reveals orders of influence more reliably than public statements.

RECRUITMENT WITHIN THE CIRCLE: TAILORED MOTIVES THAT HOLD

Keeping people inside a group willing to share requires reasons that feel authentic, not transactional. Motivation must be calibrated to culture, status, and fear.

- Offer protection that looks like solidarity. Safety framed as communal care, such as a discreet relocation, a believable explanation for absence, or a mediated reconciliation, fits cultural norms and reduces the appearance of betrayal.

- Create paths to influence. Showing a recruit that cooperation can enhance their status within the group is more durable than cash. Small public gains, such as a favorable word, a steady supply, or a minor promotion, strengthen ties and cloak the relationship in plausible benefit.

- Solve everyday problems in culturally intelligible ways. Aid that respects values, such as finding work for a sibling, helping with a dowry, or arranging a medical visit, shifts priorities without breaking honor. These are not bribes. They are interventions that decrease the cost of cooperation in the recruit's frame of reference.

DETECTING DRIFT: PREVENTING THE SOURCE FROM SNAPPING BACK

People change. Pressure, guilt, new alliances, or renewed faith can pull a source back toward the group. Mitigation is constant rather than episodic.

- Monitor behavior continuously. Small lapses in availability, inconsistent details, or sudden shifts in tone can be early warning signs. Compare what a source says with what you can observe through logistics: travel, financial flows, communication patterns.

- Validate through redundancy. Cross-check facts using multiple, independently verifiable methods. Relying on a single source is a structural weakness; corroboration turns brittle intelligence into resilient understanding.

- Use graduated tests. Give low-risk tasks designed to demonstrate reliability. These tasks should simulate real pressure in miniature so you can see how a source reacts without exposing them to catastrophic failure.

STRENGTHENING THE SOURCE: PSYCHOLOGICAL AND CULTURAL PREPARATION

Effective handling is not only procedural; it is psychological. A source that can withstand communal pressure will deliver more and cost less.

- Chunk tasks into achievable steps. Small assignments reduce anxiety and build confidence. Each successful small act becomes a building block for larger cooperation.
- Anchor actions to values. Recast tasks in the recruit's language of honor, responsibility, and community benefit. If cooperation can be framed as protecting family or preserving community dignity, it becomes ethically resonant rather than purely self-serving.
- Train for stress. Role-play expected interrogations, rehearsed confrontations, and community testing. Visualization and practice of responses make reactions more predictable and therefore more manageable.

OPERATIONAL PLAYBOOK: PRACTICAL ROUTINES THAT SUSTAIN ACCESS

Field discipline turns insight into durable operations. These are the routines that keep work secure when groups shift.

1. Real-time Monitoring Maps Movement in Power. Track changes in leadership, supply lines, and interpersonal disputes. Timelines and overlays reveal patterns that a single snapshot misses.
2. Adapt your Insertion to Mood. If the group grows anxious, become quieter and more dependable. If it relaxes, increase your visibility through service roles that solidify trust.
3. Refresh Motives Regularly. Offers that worked yesterday may fail tomorrow. Keep benefit structures aligned with the group's evolving needs.
4. Institutionalize Warning Signs. Create scripted debriefs and checklists that probe emotional and practical commitments.

Make these part of the standard cadence so potential drift is spotted before it becomes derailment.

5. Sustain Cultural Fit. Reinforcement is not flattery. Remind recruits of rituals, phrases, and small acts that keep their public identity coherent with private cooperation.

ETHICS IN THE FIELD: DECISIONS THAT OUTLAST OPERATIONS

Every practical gain involves moral cost. In places where affiliations are family and faith, the choices you make echo for years.

- Minimize destabilization. Short-term disruption can cascade into long-term harm. Plan for consequences beyond the immediate operation.
- Protect the uninvolved. Collateral communities deserve consideration. Preserve livelihoods and social fabric wherever possible.
- Balance immediate advantage with future access. Ethical restraint is not weakness. It protects long-term capability and keeps doors open for future work.

CASE VIGNETTES: SMALL LESSONS IN ACTION

A mid-level logistician once handed me the name of a supplier during the chaos of a winter food shortage. He did it because the small club of men he trusted now had children to feed. The information was operationally modest but strategically rich. The lesson was simple: when a group is stressed, practicality can outweigh ideology. Another time, a young recruit faded after a leader returned from a pilgrimage with renewed fervor. We had failed to anchor his cooperation to a public value. Our support had been private and personal; it should have been framed as communal stewardship.

These vignettes repeat a theme. Moments of tension reveal what a group cares for. They are the places where an officer who pays attention can trade quiet assistance for enduring access.

Conclusion: The Slow Work of Steady Access

Groups are never static. They are living systems that respond to stress, reward, and narrative. The officer who knows how to read those responses and how to make offers that look like care rather than betrayal will find more than information; they will build relationships that survive leadership changes and ideological storms.

This chapter provided the map and the tools: how to locate seams, how to enter through the edges, how to construct motives that fit local logic, how to test and strengthen sources, and how to balance the tactical with the ethical. The work is never glamorous. It is patient, methodical, and humane. It prepares us for the sharper instruments ahead.

What follows in Chapter 5 is a closer look at harder skills and operational tradecraft: handling direct confrontation, hard evidence collection, and managing disclosure under pressure. The foundations laid here, such as cultural leverage, psychological preparation, and procedural discipline, will determine how well those harder tools are wielded, and at what cost.

CHAPTER 5:
THE DISCIPLINE OF PRESSURE: COERCION AND DISCLOSURE

COERCION AS CRAFT, NOT CRUELTY

Coercion, in its true form, is not a hammer. It is a scalpel. In the Middle East, where identity is built on layers of faith, tribe, family, and honor, the use of pressure must be as subtle as the fabric of loyalty itself. Force alone cannot bend what pride holds together. The region's history has shown that men will endure pain before betraying belief, but they will trade silence for understanding.

To coerce without destroying is to master balance: the delicate art of control through comprehension. Where earlier chapters taught the anatomy of culture, recruitment, and psychological profiling, this chapter walks the tightrope between persuasion and pressure. Here, coercion becomes less about power and more about perception: understanding how to make a man see cooperation as salvation rather than surrender.

THE ARCHITECTURE OF RESISTANCE: HOW PEOPLE HOLD THEIR GROUND

Resistance in the Arab and Islamic world is not random. It is structured like a fortress with four concentric walls, each made of moral stone.

1. The Wall of Honor: The first wall rises from the individual's sense of dignity. It is the conviction that one's silence protects family, faith, or cause. This is where many interrogations fail: by attacking the very identity the subject is sworn to defend.

2. The Wall of Belonging: Behind honor stands loyalty. A man in the Middle East often sees himself as part of a living chain: tribe, party, sect, neighborhood. To betray one link is to break

the whole chain. Only when he sees cooperation as preserving that chain, not severing it, does the wall weaken.

3. The Wall of Fear: Once physical or psychological pressure begins, fear takes over, not of pain, but of shame: the fear of being seen as weak. This is where cultural understanding matters most. In Arab societies, humiliation is worse than defeat. A skilled officer applies discomfort without disgrace.

4. The Wall of Survival: At the final stage, survival eclipses ideology. Hunger, fatigue, or the loss of perceived control breaks the fortress from within. But even then, the officer must move carefully, for victory gained by humiliation breeds revenge.

Operational mastery lies in timing: knowing when resistance turns from conviction to exhaustion, when words become bargaining chips, and when silence hides the need to be understood.

THE REGIONAL PSYCHOLOGY OF PRESSURE

Throughout Middle Eastern history, power and persuasion have danced together. Ottoman intelligence relied on persuasion through status and promise; the British in Mandatory Iraq used moral arguments dressed as diplomacy; Ba'ath-era Iraq blended ideological loyalty with pragmatic survival. Across all these systems, the most effective interrogators understood one universal rule: belief bends faster than fear.

When an officer frames disclosure as an act of defense, of faith, family, or national honor, the subject's mind begins to rewire. Cooperation becomes righteous. The act of speaking turns into an act of protection.

Historical vignette: In 1986, an Iraqi officer interrogating a captured Iranian engineer never raised his voice. He began by discussing prayer, then the engineer's family, then how both sides were "sons of the same God led astray by politics." By the third night, the engineer was volunteering information about power lines feeding Iranian radar stations. He did not feel broken. He felt understood.

THE PHYSICS OF PRESSURE: HOW TO APPLY FORCE WITHOUT VIOLENCE

Physical coercion is crude; psychological pressure is precise. The art lies in measured escalation, where silence, time, and moral framing become instruments more powerful than force.

- Phase One: The Human Mirror. Start with presence. Sit across, say little. Allow silence to fill the room until discomfort becomes reflection. In many cultures, silence signals authority. The subject begins to talk to fill the void.
- Phase Two: Controlled Discomfort. Remove routine. Disrupt sleep cycles slightly, not as torture, but to disorient rhythm. In the Middle East, routine is security. Breaking it shifts mental patterns. Offer tea, then take it away. Offer cigarettes, then wait. Every small disruption is a message: control is fluid, and you control less of it than you think.
- Phase Three: Moral Reframing. Introduce the concept of redemption. Ask what their children would think if their actions caused more death. Use communal logic: not guilt, but legacy. In collectivist cultures, the future of one's bloodline often outweighs personal endurance.
- Phase Four: Release Valve When resistance reaches its breaking point, ease tension with empathy. Offer a cigarette. Speak softly. The body follows tone; adrenaline recedes. The moment of calm is when truth leaks most naturally. The officer who listens rather than shouts, wins the real battle.

READING THE BODY: SIGNALS OF COLLAPSE

Words lie, bodies don't. In coercion, physiology is a language of its own.

- Breathing: Shallow at first, then deep and erratic when internal struggle peaks.
- Eyes: Shifts from defiance to distance. The gaze avoids, not out of fear, but calculation.
- Hands: Tremor fades when surrender begins: the body accepts its new reality.

- Voice: When pitch drops and sentences shorten, resistance has become fatigue.

The experienced officer reads these signs like field coordinates. They show when to hold, when to pause, and when to release pressure to harvest truth rather than break spirit.

THE TURNING POINT: WHEN SILENCE BREAKS

The moment of surrender is rarely dramatic. It's not tears or confessions: it's a sigh, a look, a question like, "If I tell you this, will you protect my family?" That is the instant of transition. Coercion has become trust.

From that moment forward, interrogation becomes negotiation. The officer must stabilize the subject, offer believable protection, and frame the act of disclosure as moral duty. The best handlers never celebrate that moment. They treat it like surgery: precise, sterile, and solemn.

STABILIZATION AND CONVERSION: TURNING FEAR INTO COOPERATION

Information alone is temporary. The goal is transformation: turning the source from coerced informant into voluntary collaborator.

1. Reassure: Explain the purpose behind the act. Frame cooperation as preserving life or justice, not betrayal.
2. Protect: Ensure safety or at least the illusion of it. Offer relocation, cover stories, or controlled anonymity.
3. Reframe: Help the subject see himself as a protector: of innocents, of his people, of truth.
4. Reintegrate: Prepare psychological exit routes. A man who believes he can still live with himself becomes sustainable.

Vignette: In Basra, a militia driver gave away the location of an arms convoy after an officer showed him a photo of a bombed school, saying quietly, "The man who planted those weapons took your son's classroom."

The driver whispered the coordinates an hour later. He didn't see it as betrayal. He saw it as vengeance turned to redemption.

ETHICAL BOUNDARIES: THE INTELLIGENCE OFFICER'S LINE

Ethics in coercion are not a luxury; they are a weapon of legitimacy. The difference between control and cruelty is accountability.

- Minimum force: No act that dehumanizes can produce reliable truth.
- Cultural respect: Never mock faith or lineage: the insult lasts longer than the operation.
- Documentation: Record every interaction. Transparency protects both the agency and the officer.
- Chain of command: No coercive action should be unilateral. Authority without oversight is corruption in uniform.

An officer's strength is not in what he can do, but in what he chooses not to do.

THE PSYCHOLOGY OF THE OFFICER:HOLDING POWER WITHOUT LOSING HUMANITY

Coercion tests not only the subject but the handler. Long exposure to fear and guilt corrodes empathy. The officer who learns to compartmentalize without hardening survives longer: both operationally and morally.

To stay human, professionals learn quiet rituals: writing reports with reflection, sharing tea after a session, walking at dawn to empty the mind. These are small acts of preservation: reminders that restraint is strength. Without them, coercion devours its practitioner.

Conclusion: Control, Compassion, and Consequence

Coercion in Middle Eastern intelligence work is not about domination. It is about choreography: moving pressure and empathy in rhythm until resistance folds into reason. The finest officers never crush; they convert. They understand that to break silence, one must first understand the silence itself.

The art of coercion is therefore not violence but calibration. It is patience shaped by insight, control softened by compassion, and authority tempered by ethics. It is the moment when fear becomes dialogue: when truth, coaxed rather than beaten, changes the course of events.

The next chapter will build upon this foundation, moving from human pressure to structural manipulation: exploring how disinformation, controlled leaks, and engineered perception shape the battlefield of intelligence without a single shot fired.

CHAPTER 6:
MASTERING MOTIVATIONS AND TRUST IN SOURCE MANAGEMENT

THE HUMAN ELEMENT IN INTELLIGENCE

In every operation, there is a moment when all the maps, surveillance footage, and intercepted calls amount to nothing more than silence: until a human being decides to speak. That decision, more than any technology or tactic, determines the success or failure of an intelligence officer's work. In the Middle East, where loyalty and reputation often outweigh contracts or ideology, the mastery of human motivation is not just a skill; it is survival.

This chapter explores the delicate art of source management: understanding what drives cooperation, sustaining trust under pressure, and transforming fragile alliances into enduring partnerships. It builds upon the foundation of cultural literacy from Chapter 1, recruitment strategy from Chapter 2, psychological insight from Chapter 3, group dynamics from Chapter 4, and the discipline of pressure from Chapter 5. Together, they form the living architecture of intelligence relationships.

In volatile environments, such as Iraq after invasion, Syria during civil fracture, or Lebanon's sectarian labyrinth, the officer's greatest weapon is not coercion or money. It is empathy guided by discipline. When applied with precision, empathy does not soften the mission; it strengthens it. It becomes the invisible bridge between necessity and trust, turning fear into dialogue and uncertainty into continuity.

DECODING MOTIVATION: THE ENGINE BEHIND COOPERATION

Every source has a reason to talk. The difference between fleeting compliance and lasting loyalty lies in how well that reason is understood. Motivation in intelligence is rarely simple; it is layered: a negotiation between need, pride, fear, and belonging.

- Power and financial security. Money opens doors, but it rarely keeps them open. In unstable societies, where economic opportunity is scarce, financial incentives can secure initial cooperation. Yet without meaning attached, those incentives dissolve as quickly as they are paid. The officer's task is to translate money into identity: to make the source see each payment not as a transaction but as a measure of trust and worth. In post-conflict Iraq, for example, payments to informants were tied to community reconstruction projects: rebuilding schools, restoring wells, repairing mosques. The money bought more than information: it purchased dignity. A man who once spied for cash began to see himself as a protector of his neighborhood. The intelligence officer, by aligning reward with purpose, created a bond stronger than any contract.

- Desperation and survival. Desperation often opens the first door to co-operation. A man seeking safety for his family will take risks he would never take for ideology. But the officer must not mistake desperation for loyalty. Fear fades when the danger does. The art lies in converting fear into partnership: offering tangible support that turns short-term survival into long-term engagement. After a coercive encounter, as discussed in Chapter 5, stabilization is essential. Promises of relocation, contact protection, or legal assistance transform the relationship from control to care. The subject begins to see the officer not as a captor but as a lifeline. Survival, reframed as collaboration, becomes a shared mission.

- Revenge and ideological conviction. Anger can be an engine, but it burns quickly. Many sources enter cooperation driven by revenge: against rivals, commanders, or entire factions. Others are propelled by ideology: the belief that they serve a higher truth. Both are volatile. The officer's challenge is to channel emotion without becoming hostage to it. In one Lebanese case, a young man agreed to provide information on a militia that killed his brother. His rage made him reckless, pushing him to overpromise and take risks beyond his capacity. The handler reframed his motive: revenge as justice, anger as guardianship. By connecting his grief to the protection of other families, the officer stabilized his purpose and preserved his usefulness.

- Legacy and recognition. For many in Middle Eastern societies, the deepest motive is legacy: the desire to be remembered with honor. Recognition, especially when framed through family pride, can inspire remarkable loyalty. Officers who learn to speak to this cultural truth often find that one sincere compliment achieves what months of persuasion cannot. An asset in Basra once whispered, "My father died unknown. At least they will remember my name." That single sentiment explained years of cooperation. In a culture where honor is communal and memory sacred, the officer who ensures that a man's contribution will not vanish has secured more than a source: he has gained allegiance.

- Operational method. Create a motivation profile for each source. Record not just their needs but their symbols of pride: family names, mentors, personal losses, local heroes. Update the profile quarterly, using Chapter 3's behavioral observations. Motivation, like loyalty, is alive; it must be studied, nurtured, and adapted.

ETHICAL SOURCE MANAGEMENT: THE INTELLIGENCE OFFICER'S COMPASS

Ethics in intelligence is not idealism; it is structure. In regions governed by reputation and fear, the way an officer treats his sources becomes his signature: one that spreads silently across markets, mosques, and tribal councils. A single act of betrayal can close a dozen future doors.

- Safeguarding well-being. Every source is under pressure. Their families may be unaware, their communities unforgiving. The officer's role is not to remove risk: that is impossible, but to manage it responsibly. Provide escape routes, secure meeting locations, and emotional support disguised as operational briefings. Teach them how to think under suspicion, how to behave during community questioning. Role-playing and rehearsal, introduced in Chapter 4, are invaluable: simulate confrontation so they are not destroyed by it when it arrives.

- Preventing exploitation. Exploitation is operationally tempting but strategically suicidal. A source coerced into compliance will always search for exit. Consent, even when subtle, produces better intelligence. Conduct "trust renewals": deliberate conversations confirming that cooperation remains voluntary. This reinforces dignity and prevents ethical corrosion.

- Preserving objectivity. Affection and pity are silent poisons. When emotional closeness clouds assessment, officers begin to see what they wish rather than what is. The cure is triangulation: cross-check all reports through independent channels and behavioral indicators. Use Chapter 3's micro-analysis techniques to compare emotional tone and factual consistency. If contradictions appear, verify before confronting.

- Reducing collateral impact. In honor-driven cultures, a single rumor of betrayal can destroy families. Before acting on intelligence, assess the social blast radius. Ask: Who suffers if this leaks? Consider the sons, brothers, and employers of your source. Collateral harm breeds cycles of silence. Protecting those outside the operation is as critical as protecting those within. Operational lesson: In Mosul, an informant's exposure led to the burning of his cousin's shop. The officer's next recruit came only after he personally delivered compensation to the family and asked forgiveness in the name of "justice, not shame." Ethics became repair, and repair restored access.

THE POWER OF REINFORCEMENT: MAKING LOYALTY A LIVING HABIT

Trust is a living organism. It breathes through attention, recognition, and respect. Neglect it, and it decays. Recognition does not require extravagance; it requires sincerity.

- Enhancing confidence. In regions where self-worth is often tied to social perception, affirmation is fuel. A private thank-you, a shared coffee after a successful task, or even a respectful handshake can raise morale. Compliments should tie action to meaning: "You did not just help us: you protected families."

- Deepening trust. Gratitude creates equality. It humanizes the relationship, transforming command into partnership. When emotional closeness invites manipulation; too much control breeds rebellion. The key is emotional intelligence without emotional dependence.

- Sustaining commitment. Over time, fatigue and paranoia can erode loyalty. Regular reinforcement acts as maintenance: small acknowledgments that prevent emotional drift. The best officers never assume loyalty is permanent; they renew it through steady, genuine contact.

- Cultural sensitivity. Praise must match the culture. Public honor may empower a tribal elder but endanger a discreet informant. Learn which form of appreciation fits which environment. In conservative circles, an indirect compliment: "Your words have saved lives," carries more power than overt acknowledgment.

- Technique. Maintain a reinforcement log for each source. Record gestures, affirmations, and observed reactions. Over time, these notes become a diagnostic tool for emotional stability and emerging risks.

COMMUNICATION AS TRUST IN MOTION

In intelligence, communication is not just dialogue; it is choreography: tone, timing, and silence performing in sync. Each culture has its rhythm, and the officer must learn to speak it fluently.

- Tone and delivery. A Calm, measured tone invites honesty. A raised voice, even when unintentional, signals dominance and shuts down conversation. Use modulation as a tool: lower your voice when demanding truth, pause before acknowledgment. The silence after a question often reveals more than the answer itself.

- Body language. Respect begins with posture. In Arab and Persian cultures, leaning slightly forward signals engagement; maintaining open hands shows peace. Eye contact varies: direct for urban elites, moderated for traditional or religious interlocutors. Mastering these small codes can mean the difference between suspicion and trust.

- Adaptability. Each source brings their own emotional language. Some crave formality; others relax in humor. Flexibility is the hallmark of mastery. Authenticity is not imitation, it is resonance. Mirror tone, not character.

- Active listening. Listening is an operational act. Repeating key phrases or summarizing points signals comprehension and respect. This not only clarifies information but also reinforces the illusion of shared purpose. In Syrian operations, questions like, "What do you think happens next?" often reveal deeper motives than any interrogation. Technique: Use active listening as psychological reconnaissance. It identifies what matters most to the speaker and where vulnerability lies.

STATUS AND SYMBOL: AUTHORITY AS ASSURANCE

Authority, when used wisely, comforts. In chaotic environments, people trust stability. In the Middle East, where social perception shapes legitimacy, the smallest details, such as a pressed shirt, a punctual arrival, or a composed demeanor, communicate power without arrogance.

Use subtle affiliation. Mentioning mutual acquaintances, religious respect, or shared origins builds belonging. A simple phrase like, "My uncle prayed with your imam" can erase miles of suspicion. These are not deceptions; they are bridges built on cultural grammar.

Symbolic gestures amplify this effect. Sharing a meal after a debrief, attending an Eid visit, or offering condolences after a loss communicates kinship. Yet overdoing it creates unease. The officer must walk the thin line between approachable and enigmatic: visible enough to be trusted, distant enough to remain respected.

REPAIRING FRACTURES: REBUILDING TRUST AFTER DAMAGE

Even the strongest relationships fracture. A late payment, an exposed operation, or a perceived slight can undo months of progress. The officer's response determines whether that fracture becomes permanent.

- Acknowledge and own. Never let silence fill the gap. In Arab cultures, delayed apology often reads as arrogance. Admit error directly. Say less, mean more.
- Rebuild with action. Words heal little without consistency. Assign smaller, safer tasks to restore momentum. Let the source experience your reliability again, not just hear about it.
- Cultural repair. Reconciliation must fit cultural grammar. For a tribal informant, an apology may involve a meal or shared tea. For an urban operative, a quiet meeting in private is enough. In some cases, involving an elder or intermediary restores face for both sides. Vignette: In Yemen, an informant withdrew after a perceived betrayal during a sting operation. The officer did not argue. He appeared at the man's home with gifts for his children, sat in silence, and drank tea. Two weeks later, the man called back with information. In that silence, trust had been rewritten.

THE OFFICER'S PSYCHOLOGY: MANAGING ATTACHMENT AND AUTHORITY

Every handler walks a psychological edge. Too much empathy invites manipulation; too much control breeds rebellion. The key is emotional intelligence without emotional dependence.

After years in the field, many officers develop micro-rituals to keep their humanity intact: writing after debriefs, reflecting before assignments, avoiding alcohol during operations to keep clarity of conscience. These are not weaknesses but safeguards. Without them, trust corrodes into cynicism, and cynicism kills more sources than any rival agency.

Conclusion: Turning Contacts into Allies

In the theater of Middle Eastern intelligence, loyalty is not bought; it is cultivated. Every interaction, from the first handshake to the last coded message, carries a moral weight. The true mastery of motivation lies not in manipulation but in understanding.

To manage a source is to manage a human life caught between duty and danger. It demands patience, integrity, and awareness of the invisible lines that connect one heart to another across languages, tribes, and wars.

This chapter, standing on the pillars of culture, psychology, and ethics, closes the first arc of your professional foundation. It prepares you for the next stage: the advanced recruitment and counter-intelligence strategies ahead, where the principles of trust you have learned here are tested against deception, double agents, and the shifting sands of loyalty itself.

When technology fails and silence stretches across the wires, only one thing remains: the fragile, unspoken contract between the handler and the human soul who risks everything to speak.

CHAPTER 7:
ADVANCED ASSET RECRUITMENT: TAILORING APPROACHES FOR SUCCESS

REFINING THE ART OF INFLUENCE

Recruiting an asset is not a transaction; it is a choreography between risk and persuasion. In the Middle Eastern theater, where loyalty and reputation interlace like a woven carpet, recruitment requires finesse that borders on artistry. Every pitch, every pause, every shared cup of tea carries strategic weight.

This chapter builds on the foundations laid in Chapter 2's recruitment frameworks, Chapter 3's psychological profiling, Chapter 4's penetration of groups, Chapter 5's coercion ethics, and Chapter 6's trust and motivation management. Together, they converge into a single discipline: refined recruitment, the process of turning potential into allegiance through precision, patience, and psychological clarity.

Elite case officers distinguish themselves not by aggression but by calibration. They know when to reveal intent, when to conceal motive, and when to let silence do the work. In environments shaped by tribal hierarchies, ideological pressure, and state surveillance, recruitment is not a singular event; it is a living campaign that unfolds in layers.

THE MULTIFACETED SPECTRUM OF RECRUITMENT: UNDERSTANDING THE PATHWAYS

Recruitment in its advanced form is not linear. It moves along multiple tracks shaped by context, awareness, and psychology. A skilled officer understands these distinctions intuitively, shifting between them like a chess player adjusting strategy mid-game.

- Direct recruitment: precision with the cognizant. Some assets know their value. They understand their access, their leverage, and their potential price. Direct recruitment is therefore an act of negotiation between two professionals: one offering purpose, the other bargaining over risk. Success depends on presence. The officer must project authority without arrogance, clarity without exposure. Each word must carry consequence. The case must be personal: connect mission objectives to what the target values most: legacy, status, or family honor. In a Gulf-state energy ministry, a senior engineer once hesitated when approached. The officer noticed a framed photo of his late father, a tribal elder once dismissed by the regime. The pitch shifted instantly: cooperation was framed as restitution, a way to restore the family name. The man accepted the next meeting. Direct recruitment often begins not with power, but with precision empathy. Use Chapter 3's emotional temperature checks during these engagements. Breathing pace, eye shifts, or finger taps signal stress or openness. The officer who reads them well controls tempo without appearing to.

- Indirect recruitment: The subtle architecture of influence. When visibility is danger, influence must be invisible. Indirect recruitment works through accumulation: small gestures, repeated contacts, layered trust. It begins without pitch, without even naming intent. The goal is to let cooperation appear self-discovered. In Damascus, a translator for a political office was never asked to spy. She was instead asked to "help clarify" regional documents for a journalist friend. Months later, she was offering internal meeting summaries voluntarily. Influence had become participation. Indirect recruitment borrows from Chapter 4's group dynamics. By embedding oneself plausibly, as a colleague, confidant, or cultural insider, one creates a moral bridge instead of a moral threat. It is slow, meticulous work, but it yields assets whose cooperation feels natural rather than coerced.

- Voluntary assets: Harnessing the proactive. The eager volunteer is both a gift and a trap. Self-initiated collaborators often bring urgency, idealism, or desperation. Self-motivated partners come with self-selecting risks. The officer must dissect that motive quickly. Is it ideological? Financial? Emotional? Using Chapter 6's motivational profiling, separate the stable from the transient. A volunteer driven by belief is a torch that burns bright but short; one driven by belonging can become a lifelong ally.

Field vignette: In Cairo, a university professor offered information "for the good of Egypt." His first reports were genuine, but his later demands for public credit exposed vanity. By reframing his role as "silent guardian of national stability," the handler realigned his need for recognition into quiet pride. Recruitment succeeded not by accepting enthusiasm, but by refining it. Tactical rule: Boldness suits the aware, subtlety suits the unaware, and discernment governs the eager. Recruitment is not uniform persuasion; it is psychological tailoring.

ADVANCED RECRUITMENT: THE ELEVATION OF STRATEGY

Where Chapter 2 introduced the mechanics of approach, advanced recruitment elevates the art into orchestration. The officer no longer targets individuals; he targets systems: networks, rivalries, ambitions, and loyalties that bind people together.

The goal is not merely access, but influence through placement. An officer might begin with a minor intermediary: a driver, a fixer, a secretary, then use that contact to reach the elite. Each tier is approached differently: incentives at the bottom are material; in the middle, relational; at the top, ideological or moral.

For example, in Baghdad, an officer seeking access to a militia's financial wing befriended a local contractor who supplied uniforms. Through that relationship, he was introduced to a quartermaster, then to a logistics officer. Within months, financial records flowed discreetly. The path upward was invisible but deliberate: each link recruited through motives aligned to their level of influence.

Fault lines identified in Chapter 4 become strategic entry points. Rivalries within a group can be converted into ladders for recruitment. The key is subtle exploitation: never breaking trust, only redirecting ambition.

PSYCHOLOGICAL PROFILING: READING THE MIND BENEATH THE MASK

Every human carries contradictions. Advanced recruitment depends on seeing them before the subject does.

- Trait dissection: Predicting behavioral limits. Traits reveal how a person handles pressure. Adaptable individuals require constant challenge; rigid ones crave security. By testing reactions: through controlled uncertainty, silence, or unexpected questions, an officer can map tolerance thresholds. The "graduated model" from Chapter 5 applies here: pressure, pause, and reward build an accurate psychological blueprint without overt interrogation.

- Emotional currents: The power below the surface. Emotion is the undercurrent of every decision. Pride, resentment, nostalgia: these currents define loyalty far more than ideology. A handler who detects an emotional gap can fill it with meaning. When a former army captain in Mosul spoke of betrayal by his commanders, the officer didn't counter his anger; he redirected it. Cooperation became restoration, not treason. Use Chapter 6's reinforcement tools to keep such emotions alive. Recognition and gratitude are levers that deepen identity alignment.

- Cognitive lenses: Breaking the filters of perception. People see the world through inherited biases: tribal, religious, ideological. Understanding these lenses lets an officer reframe reality without confrontation. A skeptic trusts data; a loyalist trusts story; a believer trusts scripture. Recruitment dialogues must match those languages. In Tehran, an engineer suspicious of Western motives was convinced through technical discussion, not ideology. The officer appealed to precision, not politics. Adjusting to perception keeps communication frictionless and influence invisible.

OPERATIONAL FLEXIBILITY: MASTERY AMID UNCERTAINTY

The operational field never stays still. A power shift, a new surveillance regime, or the death of a contact can dismantle months of effort. Adaptability is not optional; it is the core survival trait of elite recruiters.

- Environmental fluidity: Reading the shifts. Learn to sense change before it becomes visible. A quieter marketplace, a delay in calls, altered body language from intermediaries: each may signal surveillance or suspicion. Scenario forecasting, from Chapter 3, trains the mind to anticipate these tides. A flexible officer adjusts the playbook mid-mission without losing tempo.

- Motivational refinement: Keeping the flame alive Motives decay if left unattended. A once-committed asset may fade into apathy or fear. Ethical debriefs, modeled in Chapter 5, offer a method of renewal: regular check-ins that reassess safety, reaffirm values, and reignite purpose. Adjust incentives as circumstances evolve: what began as financial might need to become protective, ideological, or familial.

- Proactive foresight: Anticipating the invisible. Advanced operations often fail because officers react too late. Anticipate betrayal, interference, or burnout before signs appear. Maintain contingency assets: couriers, dead drops, or cultural mediators, ready to absorb sudden disruptions. Use Chapter 4's real-time monitoring techniques to detect tension early. Field vignette: In northern Syria, a sudden leadership purge threatened an ongoing recruitment. Instead of retreating, the officer pivoted: shifting communication to the target's sister through coded family messages. The connection survived because the handler had pre-planned alternate routes of influence.

THE RECRUITMENT ECOSYSTEM: MAPPING THE WEB OF INFLUENCE

No asset exists alone. Each operates within a web of alliances, debts, and rivalries. Understanding that ecosystem turns recruitment from persuasion into engineering.

- Affiliation mapping: The social cartography. Every contact has satellites: relatives, co-workers, patrons. Chart them. The weakest link is often the strongest doorway. Before a pitch, map who owes whom, who envies whom, and who fears exposure. Chapter 4's network modeling offers a framework for visualizing these interdependencies.
- Influence spheres: Calculating reach. An asset's real value lies not just in what they know, but in whom they can sway. Some control decisions quietly, through family or faith circles. Others amplify influence through social credibility. Assess which sphere offers more long-term advantage and adapt accordingly. Sometimes, the quieter ally carries the louder echo.
- Systemic impact: Predicting the ripple. Recruiting one node can destabilize the entire web. Before final commitment, run simulations: How will others react? Will the group suspect, fracture, or rally? Chapter 5's ripple analysis becomes crucial here. Stability after recruitment matters as much as acquisition. A successful operation that collapses its network leaves intelligence without continuity. Field vignette: In Jordan, recruiting a tribal security liaison threatened internal hierarchy. Instead of direct approach, the officer first recruited the man's son, framing cooperation as generational progress. The elder later joined voluntarily. Controlled ripple replaced shockwave.

THE HANDLER'S DISCIPLINE: MASTERY OF PRESENCE

Advanced recruitment demands emotional stamina. Each interaction carries moral gravity; each promise becomes a thread in a web of consequences. The best handlers maintain equilibrium: neither seduced by success nor paralyzed by guilt. They operate with quiet humility, understanding that influence without integrity is corruption disguised as craft.

Between meetings, elite officers review their own motives. Are they pursuing the mission or their own ego? Reflection is as operational as surveillance. The ability to remain centered amid deception distinguishes the professional from the exploiter.

Conclusion: The Pinnacle of Recruitment Craftsmanship

At its height, recruitment becomes a mirror of the human condition: a study of trust, ambition, fear, and faith interwoven under pressure. The officer's role is not to manipulate but to orchestrate: to align human drives with operational purpose without breaking their essence.

Advanced recruitment fuses everything that came before: the cultural fluency of Chapter 1, the strategic empathy of Chapter 2, the psychological decoding of Chapter 3, the network insight of Chapter 4, the ethical restraint of Chapter 5, and the motivational mastery of Chapter 6. Together, they form the blueprint of professional excellence.

What begins as persuasion matures into partnership. The recruited asset, once a target, becomes a co-architect of intelligence. The handler, once a stranger, becomes a custodian of faith and fear alike. This delicate equilibrium, where influence meets respect, defines the true elite.

As we turn to Chapter 8, we enter the domain of cultural memory and historical imprinting: understanding how collective narratives shape perception, resistance, and loyalty. The lessons of recruitment will now evolve into influence at scale: how to recruit not just individuals, but entire beliefs.

CHAPTER 8:
CULTURAL MEMORY AND RECOGNITION: TURNING STRANGERS INTO ALLIES IN SECONDS

MEMORY AS LEVERAGE, NOT COURTESY

In Western training programs, remembering someone's name is taught as a basic courtesy. In the Middle East and the Arab world, it can be a weapon. A recalled name can peel suspicion off a tense exchange, open a guarded door, or turn a cautious contact into a cooperative source. It can also expose you if you get it wrong.

To operate in Arab, Iraqi, Levantine, or Gulf environments, an officer must understand one truth: memory here does not serve the individual first. It serves the group. This is where many Western officers fail. They assume that being forgotten means being dismissed. They interpret a missed name as disrespect. They press for personal recognition when the culture is not built on the personal.

That misreading is dangerous.

In collectivist societies, as we explored in Chapter 1, identity is inherited, layered, and relational. You are not simply "Ali." You are "Ali, son of Hatem, from the Abu Mohammed line, the ones from the southern farms who stood with the party in '91." The unit of identity is not the self, but the network. Loyalty is defined by belonging. Memory obeys that law.

This chapter examines how that cultural logic shapes recall, trust, and rapport. It explains how to work inside that logic without insulting it. It offers a memory technique taught within the former Iraqi Intelligence Service that officers used in face-to-face human intelligence work. It shows how a single remembered name, delivered in the right way, can collapse social distance in seconds.

It also makes something else clear. Knowing how to remember is not just about respect. It is about survival.

THE CULTURAL CONTEXT: WHY NAMES DISSOLVE AND FAMILIES DO NOT

In many Western settings, forgetting a name risks being seen as rude. In many Arab and Middle Eastern settings, forgetting a name is normal. The difference is not intelligence. It is priority.

In Western individualist societies, the person is the core unit. A name is therefore a primary tag of status. You remember me, therefore you value me.

In tribal, clan, sectarian, and patronage-based systems, the group is the core unit. Names matter, but lineage matters more. Titles matter more. Affiliation matters more.

When two men meet in Basra, they may not immediately ask "What is your name?" Instead, they will ask "Who are your people?" The question is not rude. It is a map request. It is an attempt to place you inside the living web of tribe, neighborhood, militia, religious current, political patron, and economic sponsor. This is how security is calculated. This is how risk is read.

That has consequences for memory. The mind is trained to store affiliation, not bare identity. A person becomes "the cousin of the man who supplies diesel to the checkpoint," or "the widow's nephew who handles the phones at the office," or "the one from the mosque who sits in the second row behind the Imam." The tag attaches to role and belonging.

In Chapter 4, we learned that groups regulate trust through internal surveillance, shared protection, and ritualized loyalty. In that environment, personal identifiers are less useful than positional ones. People get remembered not as individuals but as nodes within the structure. The habit persists across daily life.

For an outsider, this can feel like indifference. It is not. It is structural loyalty.

This is why, in an operational meeting, a source might fail to recall your first name but will remember with perfect clarity that "you are the one who drinks tea without sugar and who said he knew my uncle's people near Hillah." That is not forgetfulness. That is cultural accuracy.

HISTORICAL CONTINUITY: MEMORY AS LINEAGE, NOT POLITENESS

This pattern is not new. It is an inheritance.

For centuries, tribal and clan networks across Iraq, the Levant, and the Arabian Peninsula survived through oral record. Genealogy was not casual knowledge. It was strategy. It determined alliances, revenge obligations, marriage disputes, grazing rights, blood money, and protection claims.

A Bedouin elder could recite eight generations of a neighboring family by heart. Not because he loved them, but because that knowledge determined whether his sons would ride with them or bleed because of them. Memory, in this frame, is a defensive perimeter.

The Ottoman-era administrative system in the provinces of Mesopotamia and Greater Syria recognized and exploited this. Authority often moved through notables, tribal sheikhs, and clerical patrons who anchored communities. What mattered to Istanbul, and later to Baghdad and Damascus, was not the identity of one man. It was the loyalty chain that followed him.

Modern intelligence work in the region still swims in those waters. Militia commanders are remembered as "Abu so-and-so," not for intimacy, but because the kunya ties them to a paternal image of authority. Religious figures are remembered by title. Business intermediaries are remembered by function. What persists is role.

Understanding that order prevents costly misjudgments. If a source forgets your name, it does not always mean you have lost standing. It may mean you have not yet been assigned a place in their social map. Your objective is to claim that place, and then protect it.

PSYCHOLOGICAL PERSPECTIVE: MEMORY FOLLOWS EMOTIONAL WEIGHT

Human memory is not neutral. It prioritizes whatever feels important. In individualist cultures, individual recognition carries emotional gravity. In collectivist systems, the emotional gravity sits inside belonging, duty, obligation, and shared narrative.

This is the same logic we studied in Chapter 3 when we looked at psychological profiling. People recall and repeat what protects their internal balance. In the Middle East, that balance is deeply social. A man will forget the name of someone he just met, but he will never forget who insulted his cousin three years ago at a funeral. That memory is not petty. It is political.

Officers must internalize this: When interaction lacks emotional or social stake, it is not coded as important. It passes without imprint. That is why cold contact, especially from an outsider, is fragile. You do not yet carry social meaning. You are not "inside" the person's moral field.

Your job is to enter it.

The fastest way to enter it is to speak to the values that anchor memory: dignity, family continuity, protection, spiritual framing, local loyalty, and shared grievance. When you attach yourself to one of these anchors, you stop being a stranger. You become context. You become relevant.

At that moment, they start remembering you.

MODERN TENSION: TECHNOLOGY AND THE SPLIT GENERATION

Globalization and digital platforms are changing memory behavior unevenly across the region. Younger urban contacts in Beirut, Amman, Doha, Najaf, and Istanbul now live in social media environments where personal branding matters. They are more likely to remember individual handles and names. They are more likely to expect you to remember theirs.

Older tribal, religious, or militia-linked contacts often remain in relationship-based memory systems. They notice whether you greeted their cousin by title, whether you remembered the grandfather's health, whether you said "your people" instead of "your family" because "family" sounds biological but "your people" sounds communal.

Officers cannot assume uniformity. This is where Chapter 9's status mapping becomes critical. A clean shirt, a respectful greeting, and a correct title can establish rank in one room while doing the same in another room makes you look artificial.

To operate across that divide, match your recall style to the dominant value system in front of you. In a high-rise café with graduate students, self-identifiers matter. In a village council, lineage does.

THE IRAQI INTELLIGENCE SERVICE RECALL TECHNIQUE: A FIELD TOOL FOR SURVIVAL

Intelligence services in Iraq developed a pragmatic memory method for human source handlers operating under surveillance and time pressure. It is striking not because it is complicated, but because it accepts the cultural reality of selective recall and compensates for it.

The method is simple.

1. Mindful Isolation. After meeting someone, even briefly, take two seconds of mental withdrawal. Look down. Close your eyes. Tilt your head as if thinking. This physical pause creates an intentional imprint point. It tells your brain: mark this.
2. Internal Naming. In that small pause, repeat their name silently, linked to their face. Say it in your mind as a complete phrase.

"This is Khalaf. This is Khalaf's face." Do not say only the name. Say the connection. The mind remembers pairings better than isolated data.

3. Anchor Association. Attach that person to a detail that mattered in the meeting. A broken thumbnail. A missing molar. A slow blink. The smell of diesel on his clothes. The way he said "ya akhi" before disagreeing. The association does not have to be flattering. It only has to be personal.

4. Quiet Daily Reinforcement. At the end of the day, revisit the faces you met aloud in your mind. Not in a report. In memory. Re-walk the conversation. Re-say the name. Re-see the face. The repetition moves it from short-term engagement memory into usable recall under stress.

The IIS system emphasized that this was not just for courtesy. It was for deconfliction. In high-threat environments, misidentifying a man at a checkpoint could get you killed. Remembering a cousin's name could get you waved through.

This technique fits naturally with tradecraft from Chapter 5. It creates reliability without pulling out a notebook in public, and without asking "remind me again what your name is," which can broadcast that you are an outsider.

PRACTICAL APPLICATION: TEACHING RECALL AS A TRUST WEAPON

Teaching this recall discipline to an asset is both tactically useful and psychologically powerful. It turns you from user to mentor. That shift is everything.

Frame the method as a professional skill. Tell the source that remembering names is how serious people operate. Present it not as your need, but as their advancement. Pride is one of the cleanest motivators, as we covered in Chapter 6. When a source begins to view themselves as a professional, their reliability improves and their anxiety decreases.

Guide the practice in neutral settings. Do not rehearse in a sensitive place. Use a market stall. Use a tea vendor. "Who sold you that bread? Say his name in your mind. Now close your eyes. See him. Say it again." Calm repetition builds confidence. Confidence builds initiative.

Lead by example. Use the source's name correctly, and do it often. Use their preferred form. Some men prefer kunya, some prefer formal first name, some prefer title. Listening to how others refer to them tells you which one preserves their dignity. Matching that choice signals deep respect.

Highlight the payoff. Tell them plainly: "When you remember, you gain status. When you gain status, people talk more easily. When people talk, you control the room." In cultures where status is currency, this logic resonates immediately.

In Baghdad, teaching this technique to a low-level intermediary changed his usefulness overnight. He stopped referring to "the guy with the green shirt" and started giving first names, family ties, and affiliations. That shift allowed full network mapping, connecting directly to the recruitment ecosystems described in Chapter 7. A basic cognitive adjustment turned him from a messenger into an access broker.

BEYOND NAMES: USING NARRATIVE, STATUS, AND RHYTHM AS MEMORY SCAFFOLDS

Names alone are not the main memory carriers in the region. Story is. Rhythm is. Rank is.

- Narrative recall. People in oral cultures remember through sequence. If you ask, "Who was there," you may get fog. If you ask, "Tell me what happened first, then what happened next," details emerge. Time structure triggers recall. This method should be used in debriefs. It produces cleaner timelines and fewer invented fillers.

- Status recall. Tie details to recognized figures or known hierarchies? "Was anyone connected to the sheikh from the west road?" "Was anyone from the mechanic's cousin's crew." Associating unknowns with known anchors improves precision. It also respects the cultural reality that influence transmits through position.
- Mnemonic repetition. Religious life in the region is built on repeated recitation. People absorb and retain phrases through rhythm and repetition. You can borrow that same structure. Quietly repeat a key name in a measured cadence while the source recalls contextual details. You are building neural grooves the same way a sermon does.

These techniques align with Chapter 3's principle that memory is emotional, not mechanical. You are not extracting data. You are helping the mind relive the moment with structure.

RAPPORT AND RECRUITMENT: WHY THIS MATTERS IN FIRST CONTACT

Recruitment, especially indirect recruitment as explored in Chapter 7, depends on one fragile exchange: the first serious conversation. That conversation is not always about money, ideology, or revenge. Sometimes it is about recognition.

In a world where most people feel used by someone, the simple act of greeting a man by name on the second meeting sends a powerful signal. You were worth remembering. Your existence registered. You are not furniture.

That feeling, as discussed in Chapter 6, is addictive.

This is why skilled officers sometimes introduce small memory displays early. "Your brother is still working nights, yes." "You were sitting at the back of the shop last time." "Your cousin brought us tea." These are signals of attention and respect, and they flip the relationship from interrogation to alliance.

It is also why getting it wrong can be fatal. Mixing names, confusing lineage, or misattributing tribal origin can trigger immediate distrust. You are then marked as careless, and careless in this environment can mean dangerous.

OPERATIONAL IMPLICATIONS: MEMORY AS CONTAINMENT AND PROTECTION

Accurate recall is not only for rapport. It protects operations.

In Chapter 5 we discussed the ripple effects of disclosure. A single slip in a name during a hostile confrontation can expose a source, ignite suspicion inside their group, and destroy months of access. A single misidentification can place the wrong person under pressure, collapsing a neutral clan into an enemy.

Strong recall shields against these spirals. When you know who is who, you do not accidentally feed one faction the name of someone tied to another. You do not falsely accuse the cousin of a man you are trying to recruit. You do not fracture a network you intend to harvest.

In other words, disciplined memory is operational containment. It keeps the blast radius small.

It is also a layer of officer security. Recognizing a surveillance tail by face and name lets you track patterns, predict escalation, and prepare preemptive countermeasures without obvious signaling. This is life or death in high-pressure follow environments.

BRIDGING GENERATIONS: MOVING BETWEEN OLD MEMORY AND NEW MEMORY

As the region continues to hybridize, officers must be bilingual in memory culture. You will move, sometimes in the same day, between a young contact who expects you to remember his first name, Instagram handle, and preferred nickname, and an older sheikh who cares less if you remember his name than if you remember his family's standing.

Mastery lies in adapting instantly without looking artificial.

With the young contact, individual recognition is the bond. Use his name easily. Refer to details he shared about his ambitions. Speak to personal identity. With the elder, respect his collective identity. Refer to "your people," "your fathers," "your standing." Do not overuse his first name if the room is watching. He may interpret that as shrinking him down to a level below his title.

This flexibility is part of status navigation, which will become central in Chapter 9. Status in the region is not self-declared. It is socially observed. Your behavior either elevates someone's status or undermines it. Choose elevation.

Conclusion: Memory as Relationship Architecture

In Middle Eastern intelligence work, remembering a name is not a trick of manners. It is entry. It is tribute. It is allegiance offered in miniature.

Understanding why names are sometimes forgotten prevents you from misreading allies as enemies. Teaching recall methods gives your assets sharper tools and deeper pride. Using names correctly at the right time becomes a lever that moves trust, cooperation, and silence.

Most importantly, disciplined cultural memory protects lives. It prevents accidental exposure. It strengthens cover stories. It contains fallout. It preserves networks that took months to build and seconds to lose.

Every remembered name is a statement: I see you, I place you, I respect the structure that made you. That statement is often the first stone in a bridge that will carry intelligence back across danger.

In the next chapter, we will examine status itself. Chapter 9 moves from memory to hierarchy. We will study how power is displayed, negotiated, and enforced across tribal councils, militia rooms, religious circles, and elite business networks. We will learn how status can be borrowed, traded, undermined, and weaponized, without ever raising a voice.

CHAPTER 9 :
THE ART OF ASSET SELECTION: CRAFTING INTELLIGENCE EXCELLENCE

STRATEGIC CHOICE AS THE CORE OF MASTERY

Every successful operation begins long before recruitment, surveillance, or disclosure. It begins with the quiet calculation of who is worth trusting. Asset selection is not a clerical process; it is judgment refined into art. The wrong choice collapses a mission. The right one changes history.

This chapter moves beyond recruitment into refinement. It merges the cultural literacy of Chapter 1, the psychological decoding of Chapter 3, the motivational management of Chapter 6, the adaptive strategy of Chapter 7, and the cultural memory of Chapter 8 into a single framework: how to recognize, sculpt, and sustain assets who can think, adapt, and endure.

Selecting an asset is not only about competence. It is about potential under pressure: the unseen strength that reveals itself when fear enters the room. The skilled officer reads not the résumé but the rhythm of the person. Every twitch, every pause, every hesitation during conversation is data. Every remembered name becomes leverage.

In the Middle Eastern field, where hierarchy, pride, and honor shape behavior, asset selection demands both logic and empathy. The officer must read culture as fluently as he reads faces.

ASSESSING CAPABILITIES: READING READINESS BEFORE IT IS TESTED

Reliability under pressure defines an asset's true worth. Selection must therefore measure three pillars: mental agility, emotional steadiness, and physical endurance.

- Mental sharpness. A valuable asset processes complexity quickly. They can adapt to shifting narratives, understand partial information, and draw conclusions without panic. The officer observes how they interpret confusion: do they freeze, or do they improvise?

- Emotional fortitude. Pressure reveals integrity. In the field, calm is currency. An asset who can maintain composure in interrogation, delay, or confrontation will outlast one who performs brilliantly but unravels emotionally.

- Physical Endurance Surveillance, border crossings, or long observation missions demand stamina. Yet physical capacity is more than strength; it is the ability to function while hungry, afraid, or sleep-deprived.

Advanced Assessment Building on Chapter 3's psychological profiling, officers must test, not assume. Conduct conversational stress simulations: change plans mid-discussion, alter timelines, introduce hypothetical danger. Watch for micro-signals of adaptability. Test recall, as introduced in Chapter 8, by asking the individual to recount details from earlier meetings. Under stress, the mind reverts to habit; sharp recall signals discipline.

In high-threat environments, this multidimensional evaluation reveals more truth than any dossier. It distinguishes potential from pretense.

SCALING MISSIONS: GROWTH AS A LOYALTY MECHANISM

Assets mature through experience, not promises. Throwing them into deep operations prematurely ensures collapse. Gradual exposure, on the other hand, binds them to the mission through shared endurance.

1. Stage One: Controlled Simplicity. Begin with low-risk tasks: observation, note-taking, or routine delivery. These build comfort with tradecraft while giving the officer data on discipline and communication reliability.

2. Stage Two: Structured Challenge. Once confidence forms, introduce complexity: coordinating multiple contacts, handling

funds, or reporting indirectly. These intermediate tests reveal initiative and composure under divided attention.

3. Stage Three: Mission-Critical Role. Only proven assets, those who demonstrate discretion, judgment, and internal motivation, should advance to high-stakes operations. These roles demand precision, not speed.

4. This progressive model mirrors the graduated pressure approach of Chapter 5: strain, observe, recalibrate. As capability rises, so does trust. Each success becomes an emotional anchor: a memory of triumph that strengthens future loyalty.

RESPECTING STATUS AND PRESERVING STRENGTH

The Middle East is a landscape of pride and hierarchy. Every individual occupies a rank, within family, sect, profession, and age group. Pushing beyond those limits without recognition invites rebellion.

- Recognize boundaries. Do not force an asset into roles that threaten their dignity or social standing. An engineer might accept covert data gathering but refuse physical surveillance. Respect that distinction.
- Detect strain early. Fatigue appears in speech before it appears in body language. Forgetfulness, irritability, or sudden silence may signal overload. Recall Chapter 8: memory lapses are not always disrespect; sometimes they are signs of exhaustion or fear.
- Adapt plans, not people. Modify the mission timeline or task load. Tactical patience preserves long-term capability. In the intelligence profession, endurance outweighs urgency.

Sustaining an asset requires humanity masked as professionalism. Behind every operative is a human being who wants to be respected, not consumed.

STRENGTHENING WEAKNESSES: TURNING FLAWS INTO FUEL

Every person has cracks; good officers see through them, great ones reinforce them. Vulnerability is not a liability: it is an entry point for growth and loyalty.

Mental tools. Use guided self-reflection to encourage the asset to anticipate stress and visualize successful outcomes. Psychological rehearsal, taught discreetly, builds control under tension.

Emotional anchors. Connect duty to purpose. Align assignments with values: family protection, social stability, or justice. In collectivist cultures, duty that's bound to meaning produces steadfastness.

Physical preparation. Subtle conditioning matters. Teach posture discipline, breath control, and energy pacing for long tasks. Simple techniques become survival mechanisms in extended operations.

Field Example: Afghanistan. A field agent plagued by anxiety during stakeouts was retrained using Chapter 6's reinforcement strategy. His nervous scanning became structured vigilance: counting vehicles, noting intervals, assigning meaning to noise. Anxiety converted into situational awareness. Weakness became method.

CULTURAL NUANCE: THE MAP BENEATH THE MISSION

Culture defines who can be trusted and how far. Tribal links, sectarian loyalty, and family pride dictate where risk begins and ends. Ignoring these structures means recruiting a body without understanding the blood that flows inside it.

- Affiliation mapping. Identify an asset's kinship, religious, and political alignments. These networks are both armor and chain. A cousin in a rival militia can destroy an entire operation if overlooked.
- Conflict avoidance. Never assign tasks that force moral contradiction.

A man will risk his life for his tribe but will not betray it for you. Frame cooperation as service to his people, not betrayal of them.

- Leveraging ties. Position the mission as honor work. "Your information protects others." "Your eyes keep the peace." When contribution is framed as communal service, loyalty deepens.

Chapter 8's lesson on memory applies here: remember the affiliations your assets hold. Forgetting a family tie is more insulting than forgetting a name.

TECHNOLOGY'S EDGE: THE MODERN FILTER OF SELECTION

In today's field, the right candidate must blend traditional loyalty with digital literacy. The battlefield is both physical and virtual.

- Skill priority. Seek assets comfortable with secure apps, encrypted communication, and discreet data transfer. Tech literacy multiplies operational reach.
- Risk defense. Train early against digital traceability: metadata, GPS tagging, image recognition. A single careless photo can undo months of stealth.
- Adaptive mindset. Favor curiosity over perfection. The best asset is a fast learner who embraces new methods without arrogance.

Example: UAE Operation During surveillance of a financial hub, a tech-savvy source used encrypted channels to transmit data through an innocuous business chat, bypassing state monitoring. His comfort with hybrid space, half social, half operational, extended the network's reach.

Technology will never replace human intuition, but it can amplify it. In Chapter 4, we saw that every group polices itself; technology, properly applied, polices those who would otherwise betray themselves.

CROSS-CULTURAL AGILITY: THE NEW INTELLIGENCE CURRENCY

In a region of overlapping identities, the best assets are cultural translators. They can move between dialects, codes, and expectations without suspicion.

- Local insight. Prioritize those who speak not only the language but the rhythm of place. An accent or phrase can betray outsider status faster than any surveillance slip.
- Behavioral flexibility. Observe how the candidate shifts tone, eye contact, and gesture in mixed company. True agility lies in subtle transition: how easily they become local among locals.
- Training for nuance. Use immersive drills. Role-play scenarios where cultural missteps cost credibility. Teach when to shake hands, when to avoid, when to defer, when to lead.

As shown in Chapter 8's globalization discussion, the hybrid generation, fluent in both digital and traditional systems, is the most potent resource. They bridge old loyalties with new communication codes.

ETHICAL BALANCE: INTEGRITY AS STRATEGY

Selection carries moral gravity. The handler's power must be measured against conscience. Exploitation creates short-term compliance but long-term rot.

- Transparency and consent. Define the mission risks clearly. Informed cooperation creates responsibility and pride.
- Safety Over ambition. No target or report is worth a destroyed life. Protecting the source protects the mission.
- Mutual benefit. Assets who feel respected will protect their handler as fiercely as themselves. Mutual dignity breeds resilience.

Chapter 5 warned of coercion's limits; Chapter 6 showed how ethical care anchors loyalty. Here, ethics become operational armor. A respected source rarely betrays the hand that preserved their honor.

OPERATIONAL SECURITY: GUARDING THE CORE

A brilliant source without discipline is a liability. Instill protection habits from the start.

- Need-to-know boundaries. Information spreads fastest through ego. Starve ego with compartmentalization. Share only what sustains function.
- Secure communication. Standardize code names, schedules, and verification routines. Teach discretion not as paranoia, but as professionalism.
- Threat awareness. Drill situational sensitivity: when to sense a tail, when to pause a meeting, when to walk away. In high-risk zones, instinct saves lives faster than orders.

Linking to Chapter 7's lesson on adaptive operations, assets must be selected for self-awareness as much as courage. The one who notices is worth more than ten who obey.

BUILDING TRUST: THE QUIET CURRENCY OF COOPERATION

Every method, from recruitment to selection, ultimately depends on trust. Without it, even the best tradecraft collapses.

- Consistency. Keep promises. Honor schedules. Pay on time. Reliability is the simplest and most persuasive proof of integrity.
- Inclusion. Treat assets as partners, not tools. Ask opinions. Let them shape part of the strategy. Ownership strengthens commitment.
- Respect. Use names, recall personal details, observe dignity, applying Chapter 8's memory principles. Remembering a son's graduation or a mother's illness is worth more than an extra payment.

When an asset senses authentic regard, loyalty transcends transaction. They stop working for money and start working for you.

Conclusion: Crafting Excellence

Asset selection is the intelligence officer's most consequential art. It merges science with instinct, ethics with precision, and psychology with empathy. Every candidate represents both risk and opportunity: a potential ally or a future adversary.

Through the lenses of capability, culture, technology, and morality, officers sculpt individuals who can think, act, and endure within the fog of intelligence work. A well-chosen asset embodies conviction, not just competence.

This chapter brings together the lessons of all that came before: the cultural fluency of Chapter 1, the psychological architecture of Chapter 3, the ethical clarity of Chapter 5, the trust discipline of Chapter 6, the strategic flexibility of Chapter 7, and the cultural memory of Chapter 8. Together, they converge into operational craftsmanship: the ability to choose not merely who will serve the mission, but who will survive it.

In the next chapter, we will move from selection to evaluation: exploring how to measure, refine, and recalibrate performance in real time. For now, remember: the difference between success and disaster in intelligence rarely begins in the field. It begins with the choice of who stands beside you when the world turns against you.

CHAPTER 10:
REASSESSING TRANSFERRED ASSETS: SAFEGUARDING THE OPERATION

THE FRAGILE MOMENT OF TRANSFER

In intelligence work, there are few events more delicate than the transfer of an asset from one handler to another. On paper, it looks administrative. In reality, it is surgery.

You are not just inheriting a source. You are inheriting trust, dependence, fear, vanity, pride, guilt, survival instinct, and the story the asset tells themselves to live with what they are doing. You are stepping into a relationship that may have taken years to build in whispers and glances, under pressure that never stops.

Handled well, reassessment during transfer stabilizes the network, sharpens the flow of information, and reinforces operational security. Handled poorly, it can detonate everything. A careless tone, a premature demand, a single question that sounds accusatory rather than respectful, can cause an asset to withhold, fabricate, or disappear.

This chapter is about control through clarity. It explains how to reassess a transferred asset without destabilizing them, without insulting the previous handler, and without leaving blind spots that expose the mission. It blends psychological profiling from Chapter 3, trust and reinforcement principles from Chapter 6, selection criteria from Chapter 9, and adaptive flexibility from Chapter 7.

The core rule is this. Loyalty is never static. It moves. It erodes. It re-anchors. You must measure it in real time, not assume it from history. Reassessment is how you measure.

THE REASSESSMENT PROCESS: A DISCIPLINED SEQUENCE

Reassessment is not about interrogating the asset. It is about learning who they have become. You proceed in stages, not to intimidate, but to observe.

1. Analyze historical performance. Study the entire record. Read every report, debrief, behavioral note, missed meeting, tension moment, apology, flare of ego, and moment of silence. Do not skim. You are looking for patterns. Did their reports remain consistent in tone, or did they shift from simple and direct to defensive and overly detailed? Did their initiative rise or fall? Did they start offering information without prompting, then later retreat into short answers? Were there unexplained gaps in availability? Did they begin referring to "they said" instead of "I saw?" These are not just stylistic changes. They are indicators of stress, divided loyalty, or fading access. This is where Chapter 8's memory discipline becomes operational. You must internalize these historical signals so you can recognize them later without having to visibly search through notes. A transferred asset will test whether you know their history. If you visibly do not, they may conclude you are temporary, unworthy, or unsafe.

2. Probe current access and method. Do not assume the asset can do what they used to do. Power shifts, leadership rotations, arrests, relocations, religious pivots, and simple politics can close doors overnight. Your task is to confirm whether they can still have meaningful reach. Ask them, calmly, to walk you through how they obtain their information. Not just what they hear, but where they stand when they hear it. Who was present.

How often they see those people now, compared to before. You are not only validating access. You are also listening for whether they now rely on rumor, post-event gossip, or old relationships that are no longer alive. An asset who keeps reporting after losing access is not always a traitor. Sometimes they are afraid to lose relevance. Sometimes they think your approval, your attention, and the rhythm of reporting are the only things keeping them safe. That fear produces invention. You must identify it without humiliation.

3. Spot behavioral red flags. Behavior changes faster than access. Watch for new nervousness, artificial formality, unusual coldness, blaming language, sudden politeness, or rehearsed phrases. Note whether they deflect with compliments instead of answering directly. Note whether they start using excessive honorifics with you that they did not use before. These signals are not random. Sudden stiffness can indicate they have been warned. Overly warm familiarity can indicate manipulation. Distancing can signal resentment toward the transfer itself. As we studied in Chapter 6, tone tells you what words conceal.

4. Cross-check intelligence in real time. You must test content with subtlety. Take a detail from their previous report and reintroduce it incorrectly in conversation. If they correct you quickly and easily, recall is intact and likely authentic. If they agree with the false version just to please you, they may be performing, not reporting. Do this gently. The point is not to catch them in a lie. The point is to study how they handle contradiction. That behavior under contradiction tells you how they will perform under external pressure.

5. Reevaluate drivers and risks. People change. Motives shift. A man who once cooperated for money may now want status. A

woman who once cooperated out of fear may now feel morally justified and become more daring than you want her to be. Likewise, new threats may exist that did not exist before: debt, illness in the family, blackmail, political exposure, new surveillance, or quiet pressure from rivals. You must re-map these drivers. They are your new leverage points and your new danger points. Treat reassessment as a living process. Repeat it periodically. Document emotional shifts. Compare what they say about themselves today to what they believed about themselves last year. Expect movement. Movement is the truth.

THE CRITICAL EYE OF THE NEW CASE OFFICER: SEEING WITHOUT PROJECTION

When you inherit an asset, you also inherit the old handler's bias. That bias may be loyalty, complacency, distrust, affection, guilt, or pride. You cannot allow it to blind you.

You approach with fresh eyes.

Start by listening more than speaking. Let the asset talk in their natural rhythm. Are they open, guarded, transactional, performative, wounded, proud? Do they narrate their service to the previous handler like a badge of honor? Do they test you to see whether you show respect for that history?

Your goal in the first engagements is not to dominate, but to read.

Do not assume that long-term cooperation equals long-term loyalty. Long tenure can create entitlement. Entitlement can produce sloppiness. Sloppiness becomes exposure. An asset who has been "in the system" for years may believe they are untouchable. That arrogance is a map of how the previous officer fed their self-image.

This is where the vulnerability matrices from Chapter 9 guide you. Identify their weaknesses and triggers early. Note insecurity, pride, fear of abandonment, hunger for praise. These are not psychological curiosities.

They are the hinges on which control rests.

Your role is to restore equilibrium. You respect what they were, but you redefine what they are. You make clear, without insult, that the relationship has entered a new phase. You signal that stability continues, but standards have changed.

DIFFERENTIATING RELIABLE AND UNRELIABLE SOURCES: READING THE SLOPE, NOT THE SNAPSHOT

An unreliable asset is not always a liar. Sometimes they are desperate. Sometimes they are exhausted. Sometimes they are compromised and afraid to admit it. Your task is to distinguish declining reliability from temporary strain.

You evaluate three dimensions.

- Technique. How are they gathering information now? Do they still physically observe, listen in person, and engage direct contacts? Or do they increasingly report what "people are saying?" The more remote the method, the higher the contamination risk. Secondhand channels multiply distortion.
- Access. Ask for the names, roles, and affiliations of the people they claim to speak with. Cross-check those names against what you already know from network mapping in Chapter 7 and cultural affiliation mapping in Chapter 1. If the claimed network has shrunk, do not shame them. Quietly reduce their tasking or reposition them. An asset who feels cornered will invent.
- Behavioral stability. Reliability is not only what they give you. It is how they show up. Are they punctual? Do they appear at agreed locations without repeated rescheduling? Do they respond at expected cadence or start going silent, then flood you with too much detail to compensate for guilt? Is their tone agitated, or unnaturally calm? These are early warnings. You address them through disciplined, respectful con-

frontation. Never humiliate. When you humiliate, you force an asset to defend ego rather than correct behavior. Corrective pressure must be clean. As covered in Chapter 5, confrontation without humiliation stabilizes the relationship and preserves usefulness.

ADVANCED TECHNIQUES FOR EVALUATING RELIABILITY: STUDYING THE MIND IN MOTION

To protect a network, you must see the fracture before it shows.

- Behavioral mapping. Track posture, breathing pace, gaze contact, fidget patterns, word choice, and honor language across meetings. Build a behavioral baseline, then watch for deviation. A sudden lean back when answering. A new habit of avoiding eye contact on certain topics. An unusual stiffness during greetings. These are not theatrics. They are data.

- Psychological sketching. Maintain a living mental portrait of the asset. What they fear. Who they respect. Whom they envy. What they need in order to feel whole. Update this portrait after every meeting. Do not lock them to who they used to be. A person's narrative about themselves is a survival instrument. When that narrative changes, so does their loyalty profile.

- Intelligence validation. Embed micro-tests in natural conversation. Repeat a detail from last week's report, but phrase it slightly wrong. Ask them to retell a routine event in chronological order, as discussed in Chapter 8. People who lie, often struggle with ordered time because they invent from effect backward. People telling the truth often narrate forward with sensory detail. Professional practice: maintain a Reliability Ledger. This is not just a log of accuracy. It is a chronological record of tone, confidence, stress level, pride, fear, anger, and compliance. Over time, that ledger becomes predictive. You will see downturns before they appear in the content.

MANAGING TRANSFERRED ASSETS IN HIGH-RISK ENVIRONMENTS: REASSESSMENT UNDER FIRE

In volatile regions, reassessment is constant. Everything moves at once: political loyalties, militia leadership, clerical influence, tribal alliances, policing pressure, money flow. Your asset feels that movement in their bones. You have to read it before it breaks them.

- Affiliation mapping. Rebuild the social map around the asset. Who protects them now? Who resents them now? Who suspects them now? Who has risen in their environment and who has fallen? This is not optional. In Chapter 4, we saw how group structures watch and punish their own. A shift in one faction can turn your asset from insider to liability without warning.

- Tightening security After transfer, increase security discipline. Shorten exposure windows. Vary meeting locations. Reduce predictable patterns. Limit what you share until you are certain their channels are not compromised by surveillance, debt pressure, or coercion.

- Countering threats Look for stress indicators: sudden spending, improved clothes without explanation, unexplained new fearfulness, visible fatigue, late communication at unusual hours, changes in personal hygiene, or emotional withdrawal. These can indicate blackmail, religious pressure, debt leverage, or rival recruitment attempts. Here you apply Chapter 7's foresight discipline. You do not wait for a crisis. You model it in advance. You ask: if they are pressured, who pressures them first? Who would approach them if someone discovered their cooperation? How would that approach likely be worded? You prepare counter-language before it is needed. You give them defensive storylines before they are needed.

THE ROLE OF POLYGRAPH TESTING: TOOL, NOT THEOLOGY

The polygraph is often misused by insecure officers who want certainty and cannot live without it. Truth does not live in a machine. It lives in relationship, consistency, and verification.

- Friend sources. Long-term assets who have risked their lives repeatedly should not be casually tested. A surprise demand for a polygraph can destroy years of goodwill and turn loyalty into quiet resentment. With them, rely first on corroboration, ledger analysis, and subtle behavioral tests.
- Volunteer sources. Self-initiated informants are often driven by ideology or ego. With them, the polygraph adds little. Better to test them through task performance and narrative control. If they claim moral conviction, watch whether their behavior matches their declared cause over time.
- Covert recruits in hostile structures. Assets embedded in militias, clerical networks, security offices, or tribal councils face lethal exposure if the testing process itself becomes visible. Bringing them to formal testing locations can be more dangerous than useful. In such cases, indirect verification, cross-source triangulation, controlled misinformation placement, and pressure-free recall tests protect both asset and mission.

The polygraph should never replace judgment. It should only confirm what judgment and observation have already suggested. Its value is psychological, not mystical.

NAVIGATING EMOTIONAL AND CULTURAL DYNAMICS: THE INVISIBLE LAYER OF TRANSFER

Transfers are emotional events. You cannot treat them like paperwork.

In Arab and Muslim societies, loyalty is often personal before it is institutional. An asset might have trusted their old handler as a brother, a protector, or even a confessor. Losing that handler can feel like abandonment, punishment, or demotion. If you do not acknowledge that emotional wound, you create quiet hostility.

You manage this in stages.

- Fresh relationship. Do not pretend to be the same as the previous officer. You are not. Do not imitate their speech, their posture, their warmth. You will seem false. Instead, build your own channel. Let the asset adjust to you as a new center of stability.
- Bridge meeting. When possible, arrange at least one overlapping meeting with the previous handler. This is a ceremonial transfer of legitimacy. The old handler's presence says: you can trust this person. That reassurance is critical in collectivist cultures where mentorship and sponsorship define safety.
- Cultural sensitivity. Withdrawal, caution, and testing behaviors are not disrespect. They are recalibration. The asset is figuring out how to survive under new authority. This is the same dynamic described in Chapter 6 when we discussed emotional repair after operational strain. Your task is to let them stabilize without forcing immediate intimacy. Use Chapter 8's techniques here. Remember their family names. Recall their affiliations. Refer to previous details naturally. When you do this, you prove continuity. You signal: your story did not die with the last officer. You are still seen.

Conclusion: The Quiet Art of Continuity

Reassessment is not suspicion. It is stewardship.

When you inherit an asset, you inherit risk, and you inherit responsibility. Your duty is to verify that their loyalty still aligns with mission reality. Your duty is also to preserve their dignity while doing it.

The reassessment process protects more than just the operation. It protects the human bond that makes intelligence possible. Behind every operative is a human being who wants to be respected, not consumed.

Every element in this chapter—historical analysis, behavioral mapping, affiliation revalidation, controlled testing, emotional bridge work—serves one purpose. To turn uncertainty into structure.

This is where the entire arc of the book converges. Culture from Chapter 1. Human psychology from Chapter 3. Coercion control from Chapter 5. Trust and care from Chapter 6. Recruitment craft from Chapter 7. Memory and status fluency from Chapters 8 and 9. All of it lives here, in the ability to receive something fragile and keep it alive.

The officer who masters reassessment does not simply inherit assets. He inherits networks, preserves continuity, and extends influence without rupture. He prevents collapse before it begins.

In intelligence work, that is how quiet power is built.

PART II:

ADVANCED APPLICATIONS AND PSYCHOLOGICAL MASTERY

CHAPTER 11:
DECEPTION AND MASKS IN MIDDLE EASTERN AND ARAB INTELLIGENCE OPERATIONS

THE MASK IS NOT ALWAYS A LIE

In the Middle East and the Arab world, deception is not only tolerated, it is expected. It is woven into negotiation, hospitality, protection, prayer, commerce, and survival. In a region shaped by instability, foreign pressure, and internal rivalry, concealment is a form of self-defense. The mask is not always a lie. Sometimes it is a shield. Sometimes it is a courtesy.

For the intelligence officer, this matters.

Western services often view deception in binary terms: honest or dishonest, cooperative or obstructive, loyal or treacherous. That frame does not hold here. In Arab societies, deception is frequently an act of loyalty, not betrayal. It is a way to preserve dignity. It is a way to avoid humiliating someone publicly while quietly refusing them in private. It is a way to show caution without provoking confrontation.

This dynamic connects directly to the collective loyalties described in Chapter 1, the behavioral decoding of Chapter 3, the emotional management and trust work in Chapter 6, and the ethical restraint themes in Chapters 5 and 9. Deception in this environment is not just operational behavior. It is cultural grammar.

The officer who misreads it as hostility damages the asset. The officer who understands it can recruit through it, negotiate inside it, and build trust without demanding an honesty that the culture itself considers reckless.

Deception here is not always an obstacle. Often, it is the map.

HISTORICAL AND CULTURAL CONTEXT: WHY MASKS BECAME NECESSARY

To understand deception in Arab and Middle Eastern environments, you must understand the political and social memory that formed it.

For centuries, power in this region has often been unpredictable, personal, and punitive. Shifts in regime, militia control, tribal authority, religious authority, and foreign presence created an environment where what you said publicly could get you killed privately. Survival demanded calibration.

Three forces carved this habit into the culture.

- Legacy of instability. Borders moved. Armies changed flags. Leaders who were praised one week were condemned the next. Open defiance in such an environment was suicide. People learned to say one thing in the square and believe another at home. This was not cowardice. It was rational adaptation.
- Social hierarchy and obligation. As we saw in Chapter 1, loyalty is collective before it is individual. A person stands not alone, but as the extension of family, sect, and tribe. Direct statements that would expose a cousin, shame an elder, or implicate a patron become morally impossible. Evasion, redirection, and polite misstatements protect more than the self. They protect the circle.
- Adaptive resilience. Generations of navigating danger without direct confrontation produced a functional respect for indirection. The ability to avoid answering directly, without offense, without escalation, became a sign of intelligence. It remains so. A man who can speak without committing is considered wise, not slippery.

This is why, in many Middle Eastern settings, deliberate vagueness does not always signal resistance to you. It signals loyalty to people you cannot see. It is often a quiet message: I am managing multiple loyalties at once. Do not force me to break one in your presence.

An officer who understands that tension can work with it. An officer who ignores it will break the source.

PSYCHOLOGICAL DYNAMICS: DECEPTION AS EMOTIONAL STRUCTURE

Deception in this context is not usually about greed. It is about psychological balance. It protects identity.

- Guarded perception. As explored in Chapter 3, most people in the region assume hidden motives as a default. Not because they are paranoid, but because experience taught them that every offer has a cost, and every question carries a purpose that is rarely said aloud. To survive, you must assume motive. Therefore, you must also conceal yours.

- Honor and shame. Honor is not a performance in this region. It is memory. It is inheritance. It is your father's name carried into tomorrow. Openly admitting weakness, fear, regret, or desperation can be socially lethal. So people present strength even when they are afraid. They edit their story to protect how they will be remembered. That is concealment, not to deceive you, but to preserve dignity in a culture where dignity is oxygen.

- Fluid identity. In many Arab environments, a single person can legitimately occupy different personas based on audience. The humble servant in front of an elder can become the negotiator in front of a rival and the protector in front of a younger cousin. These are not lies. They are roles. They serve order.

To an outsider, this looks like duplicity. To an insider, it is maturity.

For the officer, this is critical. Your source does not have one face. He has multiple faces that are all real. If you insist on one consistent face across every setting, you are not asking for honesty. You are asking him to violate his own survival logic just to make you comfortable.

That is not good tradecraft. That is cultural arrogance.

OPERATIONAL NAVIGATION: WORKING INSIDE THE MASK

In this environment, demanding blunt clarity too early is not just ineffective, it is provocative. It forces the source into either open defiance or false compliance. Both are destabilizing. The professional approach is to let the mask breathe, study it, and slowly narrow it.

- Read what is not said. When a source hesitates before a name, changes subject, or offers a beautifully phrased answer that reveals nothing concrete, that moment is not failure. It is a signal. It tells you where the fear sits. It tells you which topics carry collective danger. Instead of pushing, mark it. Return to that space later under a different light, through family framing, moral framing, or shared-risk framing.
- Give time room to work. In Chapter 6, we stated that trust accumulates through rhythm. The same applies here. Culturally, direct exposure of truth is rare at first contact. It is earned through consistent presence. A calm handler who returns, maintains tone, and does not humiliate becomes safe to tell the truth to. The truth is not given to the clever. It is given to the safe.
- Use indirect prompts. When you ask, "What did you do?" you corner pride. When you ask, "How does someone in your position usually handle that situation?" you allow the asset to speak truth without self-indictment. This reduces shame cost. Reduced shame means more honesty later. This is not softness. This is controlled intake.
- Match communication style. Silence, lowered voice, a respectful pause before answering, invoking God's name before giving an opinion, all of these behaviors signal emotional weight. Mirror the pacing without theatrics. Matching local rhythm builds credibility without imitation. It shows that you understand how conversation carries status.

Field application: One of the cleanest tests of deceptive tension is repetition over time. Ask the same question in three different meetings, spaced apart, with slightly different framing. If the core story remains the same, and the emotional tone remains consistent, then what you are hearing is stable. Stability in this region is more important than elegance.

TRUST INSIDE A CULTURE OF MISTRUST: TURNING MASKS INTO CHANNELS

Trust in Arab and Middle Eastern operational settings is not built by demanding honesty. It is built by reducing the perceived cost of telling you the truth.

You do this in three controlled ways.

- Validate their caution. Say it out loud. "I understand why people here are careful with what they say. It protects families." When you acknowledge that secrecy is rational, you remove the accusation. You are no longer the foreigner demanding disclosure. You are the listener who understands the risk.
- Consistency as proof. In Chapter 6, we established that reliability is the purest form of respect. Show up when you said you would. Deliver on what you promised. Protect what they gave you. In environments of layered deception, consistency is interpreted as moral quality. That consistency is often the reason an asset eventually tells you the unvarnished version.
- Reciprocal vulnerability. Controlled self-disclosure is a tactical instrument. You do not dump personal biography. You strategically allow a small truth, fatigue, stress, danger that you have also had to navigate. In collectivist cultures, shared burden creates legitimacy. When you reveal that you, too, carry risk, you lower the status gap. Lowering the gap invites confession.

The goal is not to erase deception. The goal is to make deception unnecessary between the two of you.

ETHICAL DISCIPLINE: DECEPTION WITHOUT COLLAPSE

All officers operating in this space eventually face the same temptation: to manipulate the cultural acceptance of deception for fast gains.

That is a path to failure.

- Respect autonomy. Never exploit the fact that an asset fears exposure. Never weaponize their instinct to conceal against them. If you force them to betray their protective instinct, you have not recruited them. You have broken them. Broken assets do not last. They also do not forgive.
- Honor as boundary. As explained in Chapters 5 and 9, the concept of honor is not aesthetic. It is structural. You cannot demand a confession that would destroy a man's standing in front of his people and expect him to remain loyal to you afterward. Your operational need does not outrank his social survival.
- Carry consequences forward. Short-term deception by the officer can produce immediate intelligence. It can also poison the ground for future operations in that family, that district, that religious circle. The region remembers. Your reputation moves faster than you do. If you are known as someone who humiliates or discards sources, access will quietly be closed at the tribal and clerical levels.

Ethics is not branding. It is access preservation.

The officer must therefore wield deception as a controlled tool, never as a default. You conceal when it protects the mission, protects the asset, and prevents unnecessary harm. You do not conceal to satisfy ego or speed.

Deception, in other words, is part of your discipline, not your identity.

READING THE MASK: PRACTICAL FIELD CUES

In practice, deception in this region often follows recognizable patterns. You can learn to read them without confrontation.

- Over-formal politeness. When a source shifts from relaxed speech to ceremonious phrasing, you are no longer in rapport. You have entered protected ground. They are distancing. Something is wrong behind the surface.
- Excessive detail. Overly ornate description can signal fabrication, but it can also signal fear. Some sources drown you in detail to convince

you of their continued value because they feel you doubt them. This is as much psychological reassurance as it is potential distortion. Apply the reliability ledger discipline from Chapter 10: track not only content accuracy but also emotional state when they deliver it.

- Deflection through honor. If a source repeatedly invokes someone else's virtue instead of answering directly, "He is an honorable man," "That family is respected," this is often a request to stop pushing in that direction. You are close to a line that, if crossed, will feel like an attack on collective dignity.

In these moments, step back. Not out of fear. Out of tactical patience. Pushing through honor barriers is how you turn a controlled asset into a silent one.

Conclusion: Deception as Cultural Signal, Not Just Operational Obstacle

In the Middle Eastern and Arab operational space, deception is not always treachery, and truth is not always loyalty. Masks are social instruments. They protect families. They prevent humiliation. They maintain order in rooms where power is dangerous and unstable.

For the intelligence officer, the task is not to rip the mask off. The task is to understand why it is there, read what it is hiding, and gradually make yourself the one person in the room who does not require it.

This chapter extends the logic built across this work: Chapter 1 taught that identity here is collective, not individual. Chapter 3 taught that behavior here is emotional, not random. Chapter 5 taught that pressure without respect destroys more than it collects. Chapter 6 taught that trust is sustained, not granted. Chapter 9 taught that you must choose the right human before you can shape them. Chapter 10 taught that loyalty changes over time and must be reassessed, not presumed.

Chapter 11 adds one more layer. It teaches you that deception in this environment is not the end of communication. It is often the beginning.

If you can operate inside that reality without arrogance, if you can see concealment as cultural logic rather than a personal insult, you stop fighting the environment and start navigating it.

That is the difference between extraction and influence. That is the difference between getting information and building a network that survives.

CHAPTER 12:
RECRUITMENT AND CONNECTION THROUGH A TRANSLATOR: HOLDING TRUST ACROSS A DIVIDED LINE

THE HUMAN BRIDGE

In Western training, translation is treated like a technical function: convert words from one language into another and proceed. In Middle Eastern and Arab operations, that assumption will get you killed.

In this environment, language is not just informational. It is moral. It is social. It is performative. It carries honor, intention, and allegiance. It communicates status before it communicates content. A raised eyebrow can outweigh a sentence. A pause can carry more meaning than a paragraph. A poorly timed smile can collapse the credibility you spent three months building.

When you recruit or handle an asset through a translator, you are operating inside a triangular structure: officer, translator, asset. That triangle is not neutral. It is alive, charged, and unstable.

The translator is not a cable. The translator is an actor in the room: a living filter with their own loyalties, fears, instincts, pride, and understanding of what "respect" sounds like. Every word you speak will be reshaped by that filter. Every answer you receive will come to you already interpreted. And the asset is watching both of you at once, judging which of you holds authority, which of you holds empathy, and which of you can actually protect them.

This chapter accepts that reality instead of fighting it. It builds directly on Chapter 1's cultural foundations, Chapter 2's recruitment logic, Chapter 6's trust discipline, and Chapter 8's focus on recognition and presence. Its purpose is to show you how to run a recruitment or sustain one, when your voice is not the voice being heard.

Because here is the truth: the presence of a translator is not a weakness in your approach. It is a stress test. If you can build loyalty through a third party, you have built something that can survive distance, disruption, or handover. You have created loyalty to the mission, not just to your accent.

Field Note: Keep your eyes on the asset when the translator speaks. Your voice may pause, but your presence must not. Eye contact is control in this environment. It says: I am with you, even when someone else's mouth is moving.

THE TRIAD: RECRUITMENT UNDER TRANSLATION PRESSURE

Direct recruitment is intimate. You read the rhythm of the other person's breathing. You match tone. You shift tempo when you feel fear rise. You use silence like a scalpel. You let respect sit in the air until the other person reaches for it.

Insert a translator and that intimacy fractures. You now work inside triadic tension. Three bodies. Three agendas. Three interpretations of loyalty.

Three predictable stresses emerge.

- Filtered perception. The asset does not hear your voice. They hear an approximation of you. Your urgency, your restraint, your sincerity, your respect, all of it is rerouted through someone else's delivery. If that delivery is too soft, you will seem weak. If it is too harsh, you will seem arrogant. If it is too casual, you will seem unserious. This matters because, as established in Chapter 6, trust here is not built only on what you say. It is built on how you seem to carry yourself under moral weight.
- Divided focus. In Arab and Muslim societies, people read character before they read content. They are not only listening. They are watching. And in a translated meeting, they are watching two people at once. You become the figure of authority. The translator becomes the figure of familiarity. The asset evaluates the alignment between the two. Any misalignment triggers suspicion.

- The translator's imprint. Translators are never neutral. They bring their own dialect, their own status posture, their own internal moral logic. They may unconsciously protect the asset by softening you. They may unconsciously protect you by softening the asset. They may insert their own spin to "fix tone." This is not sabotage by default. Sometimes it is loyalty. Sometimes it is ego. Sometimes it's just a survival instinct.

The danger is simple: the bond you think you are building may actually be between the asset and the translator, with you sitting outside the emotional channel. When that happens, you are funding a relationship that does not belong to you.

Operational Tip: Before the first meet, give the translator explicit instruction: "Mirror my tone." "Do not summarize. Translate." "Flag emotional shifts, not just verbal content." Then lock down one more rule: Key pledges, promises, assurances, red lines, must be delivered as close to verbatim as possible. Those lines form identity in the mind of the asset. You cannot afford "creative interpretation" there.

CLOSING THE DIVIDE: HOLDING PRESENCE WHEN YOUR VOICE IS BORROWED

Your main task in a translated recruitment is to keep the core bond between you and the asset, not between the asset and the intermediary. You accomplish that with controlled technique.

- Unify the frame. Before the asset speaks freely, establish the structure aloud. Look at the asset, not the translator, and say (through the translator): "I am here to work with you directly. [Translator's name] is our bridge. What you say comes to me. What I say comes to you." This is important. In collectivist cultures, roles define legitimacy. You must define roles clearly. You are signaling that the translator is part of you, not the other way around.
- Align posture and rhythm. You and the translator must read as a single instrument. If you sit forward and speak softly, and the translator leans

back and delivers with theatrical bravado, the asset will receive mixed signals and doubt honesty. Before the meeting, rehearse posture, cadence, and level of emotional intensity. You are not choreographing a performance. You are eliminating discord.

- Maintain visual tether. When you speak, speak to the asset, not to the translator. When the translator delivers your words, keep your eyes on the asset, not on the translator. When the asset responds, watch the asset's eyes and shoulders while the translator speaks in your ear. This does two things. First, it preserves direct rapport, which preserves authority. Second, it lets you read micro-reactions in real time: tightening of the jaw, a flick of contempt at a name, a protective glance at the door. You cannot afford to lose those details. Chapter 3 taught us that emotion often leaks through the body before it leaks through the mouth. That is even more true when language is buffered.

- Use culturally resonant nonverbals. Some meaning travels without needing translation. In this region, placing a hand briefly over the heart can signal sincerity or respect. A slow nod while the translator speaks can signal acknowledgment. A softened expression when family, illness, or risk is mentioned signals care without weakness. These gestures are not decoration. They are operational cues. They bypass linguistic interference and tell the asset: I am not hiding behind process. I am here.

- Interject name and recognition. As we established in Chapter 8, recognition is currency. Use the asset's name at key points. Not constantly. Precisely. Use family references or status markers that they value. "Your judgment matters here." "You're calm under pressure, I respect that." These lines cut straight through translation because the asset sees that they are being specifically seen. That lowers suspicion and locks you, not the translator, as the point of validation.

Field expansion: Agree on discreet micro-signals with the translator, a tap of the pen for "slow down," a slight lift of the chin for "press harder," a palm-down gesture for "soften your delivery." Spoken corrections in front of an asset can fracture authority. Silent steering preserves it.

SELECTING THE TRANSLATOR: YOU ARE CASTING, NOT HIRING

A translator in this setting is not logistical support. They are a live operational variable. Treating them as interchangeable is amateur work.

Criteria you cannot ignore:

- Cultural precision. Dialect is not cosmetic. A Najdi Saudi does not speak like a Damascene Syrian. A Lebanese Shia from the southern villages does not frame respect the way a Gulf Sunni businessman does. If the dialect alignment is wrong, you trigger distance. Worse, you can trigger unwanted affiliation. Your presence can be interpreted as backed by a rival group. This is not linguistic snobbery. It is survival. In this region, dialect maps to identity, and identity maps to safety.
- Emotional attunement. The translator must be able to read tension. They must feel when the asset's formality is fear, when their humor is defense, when their silence is anger, and quietly flag that for you after the meet. You want someone who can tell you, "When you mentioned his cousin, he withdrew. Don't push there yet," not someone who says, "It went fine."
- Temperamental fit. Your translator's energy must complement the asset's psychology, not yours. A proud, high-status tribal elder will not tolerate an overeager, informal translator who interrupts or embellishes. A nervous younger asset, on the other hand, may respond better to warmth and reassurance than to clipped professionalism. You are matching currents, not resumes.
- Operational instinct. A good translator understands when literal accuracy will escalate danger and when fidelity is essential. They know when to soften and when not to soften, and they know to tell you when they did it, so you are not operating on a false read of the room.

Guiding Tenet: You are not just recruiting the asset. You are, in a sense, recruiting the translator as co-architect of the relationship. If they do not believe in the moral frame you are selling, protection, dignity, purpose, they will never sell it well. And make no mistake: they are selling it alongside you.

Field Note: Create and maintain a shared micro-glossary with the translator. Lock down how you want key terms rendered: protection, loyalty, risk, honor, urgency, promise. In Arab and Muslim societies, the wrong word, even if technically accurate, can suggest insult, weakness, or manipulation. Do not leave those pivots to improvisation.

THROUGH THE ASSET'S EYES: WHAT THEY ARE READING THAT YOU MAY NOT

Remember how Chapter 9 stressed that selection hinges on how a person reads you, not just what they give you. That applies here with twice the force. The asset is evaluating not just what is said, but who is really in control.

They are asking themselves:

- Whose face carries authority? Does the officer look decisive, composed, anchored, or does the translator seem to be running the exchange while the foreigner sits like a client? If they conclude the translator is the real center of gravity, they will bond with the translator, not you. That creates a fracture you may never fully repair.

- Do these two operate like one unit, or like strangers in the same room? If your posture and tone do not match the translator's delivery, you look false. False is dangerous in this region. As we established in Chapter 11, deception here is accepted, but only when it feels culturally coherent. Incoherence is interpreted as threat.

- Does the officer respect me? Respect is read visually: did you greet properly, did you sit in the right place relative to perceived status, did you acknowledge hardship without pitying them, did you offer tea or accept it. And crucially: did you look at them, or did you spend the entire interaction looking at your own interpreter like a superior talking through staff.

Operational **Insight:** When possible, initiate ritual yourself. Shake hands or place a hand on your chest before the translator says anything. Accept tea from the asset's hand, not passed through the translator. These small moves establish direct human contact. You are telling the asset: I recognize you as a man, not as a file.

MANAGING STRAIN IN THE MIDDLE: KEEPING THE LINE CLEAN

The translator stands in a pressure channel. They feel loyalty to you, an obligation to the mission, and often cultural kinship with the asset. If you ignore that pressure, it will express itself in places you cannot see. If you manage it, it will work for you.

- Unify purpose. Before the meeting, and again after, make the mission explicit with the translator: "We are not here to collect lines of text. We are here to build a secure working relationship. Your job is not just to translate. Your job is to help me prove that I am reliable." When a translator internalizes that frame, they stop freelancing tone for ego and start managing tone for effect.

- Debrief after every contact. You cannot assume you "got the same meeting" the asset got. You must ask. After each session, pull the translator privately and ask direct, tactical questions: "Did any phrase I used land badly?" "When did they pull back?" "When did they lean forward?" "What did they respect?" This is not politeness. It is calibration. It is how you avoid repeating the wrong approach in the next meet.

- Protect the translator's dignity. If you correct them, do it privately. Shaming them in front of the asset will poison the triangle. The translator will retaliate, consciously or not, by cooling your warmth in delivery or over-softening your strength. You cannot afford that. As Chapter 5 made clear, humiliation in this region never dies quietly.

THE REWARD: WHEN IT WORKS

When recruitment through a translator is executed correctly, something rare happens.

The asset stops seeing three people in a room. They start seeing one structure.

Your authority. The translator's cultural fluency. The mission's moral frame.

That structure, if built patiently, produces more than compliance. It produces initiative. Once the asset feels recognized, protected, and respected, even across language, they begin to act. They stop waiting to be asked and start volunteering. They start offering texture, not just fact. They start warning you when danger is forming.

That is when you know the bond has crossed the language barrier and turned into allegiance.

Foundation of faith In Arab societies, loyalty is rarely born from logic alone. It is born from felt certainty. Certainty that you see them. Certainty that you respect their standing. Certainty that you will not expose them and then disappear.

If you can generate that feeling through an intermediary, you are operating at a professional level. You have turned a structural liability into a force multiplier.

Conclusion: The Translator Is Not Your Mouthpiece. They Are Your Instrument

Recruiting and managing an asset through a translator is not a workaround. It is advanced tradecraft.

It requires: Cultural discipline from Chapter 1; Recruitment timing and moral framing from Chapter 2; Behavioral reading from Chapter 3; Emotional steadiness from Chapter 6; Respect calibration from Chapter 8; Status control from Chapter 9; Non-humiliating pressure discipline from Chapter 11.

The translator sits at the center of it all. They can carry your respect forward or bleed it out. They can reinforce your authority or quietly replace it with their own. They can make you unforgettable or make you irrelevant.

Treat them accordingly.

Build alignment before the first word. Hold presence with your eyes, not just your voice. Capture after-action notes. Maintain a living translator brief, tone choices, preferred metaphors, sensitive terms, nonverbal cues that landed well, and update it after every session. That continuity becomes its own form of trust.

In the end, you are not just translating language. You are translating intent, protection, and dignity. When you do that correctly, the asset does not feel managed through a stranger. The asset feels chosen.

That feeling is what turns a conversation into cooperation, and cooperation into loyalty that survives distance, politics, fear, and time.

CHAPTER 13:
BRIBERY IN INTELLIGENCE OPERATIONS: CONTROLLED CORRUPTION, MANAGED LOYALTY

THE OLDEST LEVER IN THE ROOM

Bribery is older than borders.

Before treaties, before alliances, before formal recruitment, someone quietly offered someone else what they did not have: money, access, safety, forgiveness, in exchange for what they could not afford to give. That moment is bribery. And in intelligence work, it is still one of the most effective, most dangerous tools an officer will ever touch.

In Iraq, particularly during the sanctions era, the Iraqi Intelligence Service understood this with clinical clarity. Sanctions starved institutions, starved families, starved loyalties. The IIS weaponized that starvation. Bribery there was not sloppy, desperate cash-for-secrets. It was engineered dependence. It turned hunger into obedience and necessity into leverage.

Western services use the same dynamic, but they dress it differently. They call it "quiet support," "facilitated opportunity," "family assistance," "outplacement." The label is theater. The function is the same. You are altering a person's decision-making by controlling their material reality.

To treat bribery as crude corruption is to miss what it actually is: behavioral modification through controlled relief.

This chapter studies bribery as it actually operates in Middle Eastern and Arab intelligence environments. It connects directly to: – Cultural honor and belonging from Chapter 1 – Motivational and psychological architecture from Chapter 3 – Trust and stewardship from Chapter 6 – Status and selection from Chapter 9 – Ethical restraint from Chapter 11

The point is not to glorify the act. The point is to understand its power, its risks, and what it does to everyone in the room.

BRIBERY'S LINEAGE: HOW IT BECAME DOCTRINE, NOT IMPROVISATION

Bribery is not an accident of desperation. It is a designed instrument.

In unstable environments, loyalty is often unreliable because identity can be bought, threatened, shamed, reclaimed. Bribery steps into that chaos and imposes a new gravitational center: whoever feeds you becomes, in time, whoever owns you.

The Iraqi Intelligence Service refined this into policy during the sanctions era. When salaries collapsed and state support eroded, the IIS quietly stepped in where the government could not. A cash gift framed as "assistance," a favor for a brother at a checkpoint, a medicine supply routed around embargo: each one created obligation. And obligation, repeated, hardened into loyalty.

This is the critical point: the money was only the first layer. The second layer was pride. "We take care of our people. You are now under our wing." That language turned the bribe into belonging.

Western services built parallel structures under softer branding. Reconstruction funds. Business favors. Placement within a foreign NGO. Tuition for a nephew. Medical evacuation. These are bribes wearing suits and signatures. They are justified as "partnership support," but they run on the same current: controlled dependency.

Across cultures, bribery flourishes where institutions are weak and fear is high. In much of the Middle East, where blood ties outrank written law, bribery is rarely seen as moral decay. It is seen as realistic negotiation with power.

The danger for the officer is arrogance. Bribery works so quickly that it tempts you to believe you have loyalty where you actually have appetite.

HIGH-RISK, HIGH-YIELD: WHY BRIBERY IS BOTH IRRESISTIBLE AND LETHAL

Chapter 2 established that incentives are essential to recruitment. Bribery is the incentive stripped down to its rawest form. It ignores ideology. It does not bother with moral reframing. It speaks to the pressure point directly and says: you don't have to suffer if you choose me.

It is fast. That is why it is used.

It is also fragile. That is why it destroys officers who lean on it too early.

If the first bond between you and a potential asset is money, you have not recruited a human being. You have hired a service provider. The moment a competitor pays better, or fear spikes higher than what you're offering, you lose them. Or worse: they keep taking your money and feed you dressed reports that flatter your assumptions.

Used recklessly, bribery creates false confidence. Used correctly, it seals a bond that was already forming.

The professional rule is simple: Bribery is not an opener. Bribery is a stabilizer.

You do not start with it. You use it when the person is already leaning in, already thinking in your direction, already quietly justifying cooperation to themselves. At that point, the bribe is not "payment for betrayal." It becomes "support for a choice I was already on the edge of making." That difference is psychological armor. It keeps the conscience from revolting.

This timing discipline is the line between control and collapse.

THE PSYCHOLOGY: WHAT MONEY ACTUALLY BUYS

Money does not buy loyalty. Money buys permission.

It buys permission for a person to cross a line internally without falling apart. It gives them a story they can live with.

To use bribery with precision, you must understand the emotional mechanics that sit under it. Those mechanics appear again and again in Middle Eastern and Arab environments.

- Dependency. When someone cannot feed their family, money stops being "currency." It becomes oxygen. Refusing oxygen is irrational. Accepting it starts to feel inevitable, not shameful. In this frame, taking your offer is not corruption. It is survival. Survival is morally clean.
- Pride. Many men in this region, especially those from tribal or traditional structures, cannot tolerate pity. Handing someone cash like you're throwing scraps creates insult, not loyalty. You must frame payment as recognition, not charity. "I am supporting someone valuable," not "I am rescuing someone weak." The first builds status. The second kills it.
- Fear. When a target believes they are already at risk, money can feel like shelter. It says: "You are not alone anymore. There is now a force invested in your safety." You are no longer offering income. You are offering coverage. In Chapter 6 terms, this is not payment. It is reassurance.
- Fatigue. People break quietly. Years of pressure, humiliation, or double-life stress will grind down even the proud. At that stage, bribery is not greed. It is relief. It says: "You can stop struggling alone." That relief is addictive. Once you give it, you own the rhythm of their calm.

This is why bribery works. It is not just financial leverage. It is emotional sedation. You are not buying their mind. You are buying quiet inside their chest.

RECRUITMENT TIPPING POINT: WHEN THE OFFER BECOMES UNAVOIDABLE

There is always a moment in recruitment when the subject hovers. They are in psychological free fall. They are leaning toward you, but a part of them is still clinging to the old loyalty, the old story.

That is the moment bribery becomes decisive.

- Immediate relief. Food. Rent. Debt forgiveness. Medical care. School fees. Legal trouble "resolved." In Middle Eastern settings, helping with a family obligation is often more effective than giving direct cash. It lowers the shame cost. It also ties you to their people, not just to them. That widens the dependency network.

- Long-term stability. Not a one-time envelope, but a recurring line. Quiet, predictable support. A path to eventual relocation. A job for a brother. This creates interdependence. "If I stop, they lose." That becomes its own form of psychological trap. You are not paying for information. You are constructing a future that cannot exist without you.

- Exit promise. In collapsing environments, a regime about to fall, a militia about to fracture, an arrest wave coming, bribery can also mean extraction. Safe passage. Paperwork. A path out. At that point, you are not just buying cooperation. You are offering survival beyond the end of the world.

This stage is dangerous. It turns you from a handler into a lifeline. Assets saved this way tend to become loyal, but they also tend to become entitled. You must be ready to manage that entitlement, or it will metastasize into control they try to exert over you.

FORMS OF BRIBERY: IT IS NOT ALWAYS A STACK OF CASH

Cash on the table is the image. Reality is more disciplined.

- Digital transfer. Accounts, crypto, prepaid channels. These provide distance. They also erode the emotional bond of the hand-to-hand moment. The cleaner the transfer trail, the colder the relationship. Use only if you're deliberately keeping distance.

- Facilitated opportunity. Visas. Pilgrimage access. University placement for a son. A job inside a foreign contractor's supply chain. These are not experienced as "bribes." They are experienced as "respect." They create a story that the asset can tell his family without shame.

- Indirect support. You don't hand the money to him. You pay his brother's medical bill. You get his cousin out of a checkpoint jam. You keep his father's name clean in a municipal dispute. That is power in its purest form. That is you inserting yourself into his honor network. He cannot easily walk away from that.

- Payment for restraint. Sometimes you are not buying action. You are buying inaction. "Do not warn them." "Do not pass this on yet." "Delay this message two hours." That is bribery too. But it feels cleaner to the recipient, because they can still tell themselves: "I did nothing."

Understand this: the most effective bribes are the ones that do not feel like bribes. They feel like dignity being restored.

PLANNED BRIBERY: THE SLOW OPERATION

When you have the luxury of time, you do not improvise. You engineer.

1. Map Pressures. Before you offer anything, you need a full pressure assessment. Who does he owe? Who is sick? Who is angry with him? Who humiliates him? Who protects him? Bribery without target mapping is a waste.

2. Test Receptivity. Float small gestures early: paid transport, covered meal, discreet problem-solving. Watch the reaction. Look for guilt or insult. Look for relief. Look for entitlement. That response tells you which lever to pull.

3. Lock Delivery Cover. Never hand something you cannot explain. Money through a "cultural gift." Approval routed through a local intermediary. Assistance framed as "a favor called in." You are not only paying. You are manufacturing deniability in case this ever surfaces.

4. Present the Offer as a Partnership. Never frame it as "I give,

you obey." Frame it as "We are now aligned. I take care of mine." You are inviting them into a circle. You are not hiring them like labor.

5. Deliver at the Emotional Peak. Hit at need, but before humiliation. If you wait until they are fully broken, they will accept, but they will hate you for seeing them that way. Hatred rots loyalty.

6. Monitor the Aftermath. After payment, watch for a behavioral shift. Do they show initiative? Do they stall? Do they get careless? Do they begin to leak your existence? Your first bribe is not a conclusion. It is diagnostic.

SUDDEN BRIBERY: WHEN THE WINDOW OPENS AND YOU HAVE SECONDS

The field rarely grants you perfect staging. Sometimes the moment just drops.

A father talks about a child's illness. A man mentions a debt with eyes lowered. A woman who's never asked for anything finally asks for something indirect.

These are live fractures. They close quickly if you mishandle them.

- Detect the fracture. You need to hear not just the words, but the tone. Shame plus urgency is the signal. As covered in Chapter 3, desperation in this region rarely speaks loudly. It leaks.
- Offer relief with respect. Your first words matter. "Let me help" is too direct and risks making them feel exposed. "We can solve this" is better. It implies shared burden, not rescue.
- Move immediately. In sudden-need situations, the window is short. Deliver before they can reconsider and push you away. Delay breeds pride. Pride kills access.
- Then step back. After you deliver, do not linger in triumph. Do not gloat in subtle ways. Do not "check in" five times in the next two

days. Give them space to rewrite the story in their head. They must be allowed to believe they acted with agency, not desperation. That narrative is what will let them keep working for you.

CULTURAL NUANCE: BRIBERY IN ARAB AND MIDDLE EASTERN SETTINGS

This is where outsiders get reckless.

In much of the region, what you think of as bribery may be read instead as hospitality, respect, obligation, or negotiated reciprocity. And what you think is a generous offer can be read as humiliation.

- Hospitality cover. Gifts, favors, quiet assistance routed through socially acceptable rituals, these allow both sides to pretend this is "relationship," not "purchase." That pretense is not weakness. It is protection. It keeps the asset's honor intact.
- Status transfer. If you are seen as a figure of power, foreign, connected, resourced, your aid elevates the recipient in their circle. They can say, "They came to me. They trusted me." That is status. Status is addictive. This is how bribery binds without ever being named.
- Face protection. In this region, exposure equals humiliation, and humiliation outlives money. A bribe that becomes known can permanently destroy the target's standing and get you killed for causing it. You are not simply paying. You are accepting stewardship of their face.

Honor is the line. Violate that, and you are not just cut off. You are marked.

ETHICAL TENSION: WHAT BRIBERY DOES TO THE OFFICER

There is an additional cost most manuals ignore: what repeated bribery does to you.

Each time you solve someone's desperation with money, you reinforce the idea, in them and in yourself, that their pain is a tool. If you are reckless, you begin to see people as levers instead of human beings. That moral erosion is operationally dangerous. It makes you sloppy. It makes you cruel in small ways. And in this region, cruelty is remembered.

Four specific risks demand constant discipline:

- Escalation. Once you start paying, expectations grow. The "favor" becomes "support." The "support" becomes "salary." The "salary" becomes "you owe me." If you don't control escalation, you will lose authority and end up paying to be disrespected.
- Dependency. If their entire security now depends on your pipeline, you own them. That sounds like control. It is also a liability. If your pipeline is cut—rotation, bureaucracy, budget, exposure—they may panic and expose you in retaliation.
- Reverse leverage. Assets who get comfortable may threaten to reveal the arrangement unless you increase payment or protect them from consequences. Bribery without exit architecture turns into blackmail.
- Institutional rot. Inside services, habitual bribery can attract officers who prefer the shortcut. They stop cultivating loyalty. They stop doing the hard psychological work from Chapters 2, 6, and 11. They become bankers, not handlers. At that point, you're not running assets. You're running payroll.

MITIGATION: STAYING IN CONTROL

To use bribery without letting it own you, you enforce limits.

- Buffer yourself. Do not be the one physically handing cash if you can avoid it. Use controlled intermediaries, approved channels, or cover mechanisms. This protects you if the payment ever surfaces.
- Set boundaries early. "Here is what I can do. Here is what I cannot." Say it clearly. Ambiguity invites escalation. Clarity preserves respect.
- Start small. Do not start high. Start with limited relief. Watch output. If their reporting improves in clarity, initiative, and relevance, you have a viable channel. If it does not, you are being harvested.
- Plan the exit before the first payment. You must know how you will ta-

per or disengage. This includes giving them a story they can live with afterward: relocation, new cover employment, "transfer of responsibility," anything that lets them keep dignity when the money stops.

PROFESSIONAL GUIDANCE: BRUTAL TRUTHS YOU CANNOT IGNORE

Bribery cannot replace rapport. It can only accelerate it.

You must understand what the person wants to protect, not just what they want to gain. Protection is often more powerful than profit.

Never humiliate. If the payment feels like pity, you did damage, not work.

Track behavior, not gratitude. "Thank you" is worthless. Initiative under risk is priceless.

Keep records secure and need-to-know. History has a long memory and a violent bite.

Conclusion: Money Is Not the Point

Bribery is not about currency. It is about narrative.

You are giving someone a new way to explain their choices to themselves. You are building them a justification they can live with when they look in the mirror, when they stand in prayer, when they face their brothers.

When you do it with precision, the bribe is not "I sold out." It becomes "I protected my family," "I preserved my dignity," "I survived." In that frame, the asset will keep working. They will not see themselves as bought. They will see themselves as chosen.

When you do it without precision, you buy reports, not loyalty. And you pay for them again and again until the entire structure rots.

Bribery is a blade. Used with discipline, it opens doors no ideology ever could. Used without restraint, it cuts the hand that wields it.

In the next chapter, we move from the transactional to the personal: field practice under live pressure, where improvisation, ethics, survival instinct, and human need collide without warning, and where a single offer, gesture, or sentence recalibrates the entire operation in seconds.

CHAPTER 14:
IIS RECRUITMENT METHODS: ARCHITECTURE OF CONTROL

INFLUENCE AS DOCTRINE

The Iraqi Intelligence Service did not recruit. It harvested.

Under Saddam Hussein, the IIS built an intelligence machine that treated every Iraqi body, every Iraqi relationship, every Iraqi living abroad, as exploitable terrain. There were no civilians in their worldview. There were only assets not yet activated.

What made the IIS formidable was not simply brutality. Brutality alone burns fast and dies loud. What made the IIS dangerous was systematized influence. They fused cultural fluency, psychological leverage, compartmented structure, and operational patience into a model that turned loyalty into an engineered product.

They did not ask, "Can we turn this person?" They assumed the answer was yes, and then worked backward to find how.

This chapter is not nostalgia for a regime. It is an analysis of method. It draws directly on cultural dynamics from Chapter 1, behavioral analysis from Chapter 3, motivation control from Chapter 6, bribery architecture from Chapter 13, and status/selection logic from Chapter 9. It examines how IIS recruitment worked at scale: how they identified targets, applied pressure, disguised offers as loyalty, and then locked the result into a machine that would outlive any individual officer.

The IIS model is not admirable. But it is instructive. It shows how influence becomes infrastructure.

THE IIS PHILOSOPHY: NO ONE IS OFF THE BOARD

The first principle of IIS recruitment was simple: everyone can be used.

There were no "civilians" in the Western sense. The student in a foreign university, the merchant on the Jordanian border, the imam in a provincial mosque, the cousin of a diplomat's wife, the man who poured tea in the ministry hallway—every layer of Iraqi life was viewed as an access point.

This mindset was not random predation. It was doctrine. It rested on four pillars that, together, formed a repeatable system of control.

1. Ambition without Ceiling. The IIS did not recruit only elite figures. They built dense networks across all social classes.

2. Students. University students were prime targets. They were young, hungry for status, and mobile. A student sent abroad for "study" was quietly tasked with monitoring exiles, dissidents, and opposition narratives. That student believed he was serving Iraq, not serving an intelligence service. The IIS understood, as we outlined in Chapter 7, that ideological framing works best early, before self-interest hardens.

3. Businessmen. Businessmen moved money, goods, and information across borders even when Iraq itself was politically isolated. They were used as couriers, brokers, funders, buyers, smugglers, and soft diplomats. If sanctions closed a door, a businessman opened a window. Many were not approached as spies. They were approached as patriots who could "help the homeland maintain dignity under Western pressure." The appeal to national pride disguised commercial leverage as duty.

4. Religious figures. Mosque leaders, clerics, and preachers carried moral authority. The IIS understood that moral authority, in the Arab world, is louder than political messaging. So, they penetrated religious spheres not only to collect information but to

shape narrative. As covered in Chapter 3, sermons can redirect loyalty overnight. The IIS invested heavily in controlling the sermon.

5. Spouses, relatives, domestic circles. Power does not live in offices alone. It lives in kitchens. The spouse of a military officer, the brother-in-law of a diplomat, the cousin of a provincial chief often carried gossip, frustration, private compromise. The IIS quietly turned these domestic nodes into informants. Not through ideology. Through leverage. Through need. Through fear of exposure.

6. Drivers, clerks, translators. The IIS understood something Western services often overlook: access is not always at the top of the tree. The driver hears the unscripted conversation. The clerk handles the document before it is shredded. The translator knows who is lying in the meeting because he listens for tone, not just words. These "minor" assets became control points. Disposable to leadership. Priceless to the service.

7. This wide targeting lattice meant Iraq lived under layered surveillance. People did not just fear the state. They feared each other.

8. Opportunism as Method. IIS officers were trained to treat every human encounter as exploitable. There was no such thing as casual contact. A conversation in a market could become an opening. A family funeral could become a soft assessment environment. A visa request could become a point of leverage.

9. Opportunity was not luck. It was doctrine.

10. Officers were taught to recognize stress signatures:

11. A businessman whose contract failed and whose pride is wounded.

12. A mid-ranking officer passed over for promotion and quietly bitter.

13. A student abroad drinking heavily and complaining of isolation.

14. A relative of a regime insider suddenly "on the outside" after an internal fall.

15. Those signatures were not noted and filed. They were acted upon. The IIS did not wait for recruits to come forward. It caused the moment of vulnerability, then arrived with the solution.

16. The rule was: exploit the wound immediately, then become the one who stops the bleeding.

17. Cultural Alchemy. The IIS learned to turn Iraqi and Arab social codes into operational leverage.

18. Honor. Honor here is not vanity. It's lineage, reputation, and moral credit. The IIS would frame cooperation as honorable, and dissent as shameful. You are not "spying." You are preserving Iraq against traitors, agents, heretics, thieves. They turned state obedience into moral defense.

19. Shame. Shame is nuclear in collectivist societies. Affairs, addictions, quiet desperate acts under sanctions, all became leverage. But the IIS did not always weaponize them through open blackmail. More often, they hinted at exposure, then offered protection instead. You do not threaten a man's reputation and then demand. You threaten it and then rescue him. That rescue becomes permanent control.

20. Loyalty reframed. In Chapter 5, we described moral reframing under coercion. IIS officers were masters of that technique. They could make compliance feel like duty to family, not duty to regime. "Work with us and your children will be safe. Refuse, and your children will live in a country run by enemies." That framing swallowed objection and recast obedience as paternal responsibility.

21. Social ritual. Tea, condolence visits, weddings, religious holidays—these were operational environments. An IIS officer understood that in Iraqi culture, once you enter someone's grief or someone's celebration, you move from stranger to familiar. Familiarity grants access. Access grants leverage. Cultural ritual was not courtesy. It was access engineering.

22. Tactical Precision. The IIS did not rely on one method. It ran a menu and selected what matched the individual. Their core levers included:

23. Financial inducement. We explored bribery in Chapter 13. The IIS executed it with discipline. For businessmen, it looked like "investment." For students, it looked like "support." For clerics, it arrived as "donation to the cause." Money did not appear as payment. It appeared as confirmation of value.

24. Sexual entrapment. Compromise through intimacy was standard, especially for targets who projected moral conservatism. A liaison was staged, photographed, then quietly archived. The threat was rarely shouted. It was allowed to sit in the subject's mind. The psychological effect was: "You belong to us now, and no one else has to know."

25. Ideological grooming. The IIS understood how to wrap self-interest in patriotic language. "Western powers want to break Iraq." "The Zionists want to humiliate you." "Only loyalty prevents national humiliation." This script was especially effective on students and junior officers who wanted to believe they were serving something larger than their own survival.

26. Staged access. Conferences, trade delegations, cultural exchanges, religious visits abroad—all were used as controlled environments to spot, assess, prime, and harvest. What looked like diplomacy was also fishing.

The sophistication here matters. The IIS did not reduce people to fear alone. Fear alone is unstable. They preferred a blend: a soft bribe, a moral story, a social bond, a quiet threat. Fear was the lock, not always the first key.

THE SYSTEM BEHIND THE METHOD: HOW THE IIS SUSTAINED CONTROL

The IIS's recruitment success was not only due to aggressive field officers. It was due to structure. Saddam understood something most authoritarian leaders do not: paranoia without organization wastes itself. So he built an intelligence architecture that channeled paranoia into process.

THE EVOLUTION: FROM INTERNAL ENFORCER TO GLOBAL ARM

Initially, the IIS existed largely to police Iraq from within. Dissent, whispers, clerics getting too bold, Ba'ath Party rivals—this was the early focus. But as Iraq's isolation deepened, global reach became survival. Exiles became threats. Smugglers became lifelines. Foreign sanctions became battlefields.

Directorates specializing in assassination, external operations, and foreign cultivation emerged. The service shifted from "watch the street" to "reach the world."

This matters because it shows how recruitment doctrine followed geopolitical pressure. When Iraq could not rely on formal diplomacy, it relied on informal control networks. Students in Europe, merchants in Amman, expatriates in London and Damascus became unofficial embassies of regime influence. Some knowingly. Most not.

COMPARTMENTED LAYERING: HOW THEY AVOIDED COLLAPSE

The IIS rarely allowed a single recruited source to see the full chain.

A trader in Jordan might move funds "to help a friend in trouble" and believe he was doing business. Those funds might support a student in Paris who believed he was defending Iraq's reputation at debates and gatherings. That student's reporting might then be routed back through an officer in Directorate 18, who would launder it as "cultural sentiment analysis," which would feed internal security narratives in Baghdad.

No one in that chain saw the whole organism.

This produced two operational advantages:

Betrayal became difficult. You cannot expose what you do not fully understand.

Loyalty became elastic. If one node failed or fled, the others could continue without clarity on what was lost.

For modern officers, this is the lesson: redundancy and compartmentalization are not just security practices. They are psychological practices. They deny any one human the sense that they are indispensable. Control increases when the asset believes they are replaceable.

THE DIRECTORATES: MACHINERY OF MANIPULATION

The IIS did not operate as a single monolithic "spy agency." It was an ecosystem. Different directorates specialized, overlapped, and watched each other.

- Directorate 4 (Secret Service). This was the HUMINT core. Handlers. Recruiters. The officers who walked into lives and sat in living rooms. They cultivated businessmen, clerics, community influencers, and foreign contacts. They were the face of the net.

- Directorate 5 (Counterintelligence). They watched everyone, including other IIS officers. Their job was to detect penetration, test loyalty, and pressure-test sources. If Directorate 4 brought you in, Directorate 5 tried to break you to see if you held. This internal stress test echoed what we explored in Chapter 10: reassessment is not optional. It is survival.

- Directorate 8 (Technical Operations). Surveillance, communications intercept, covert listening, photography. They enabled leverage. You cannot blackmail a man with what you never captured. Directorate 8 made sure you captured it.

- Directorate 9 (Special Operations). Assassinations, abductions, deniable violence. They were the fist. Their existence mattered in recruitment because their shadow sat in the room. When a handler hinted, "You know how these things go if someone chooses badly," everyone knew what that meant without it needing to be said.

- Directorate 14 (Internal Counterintelligence / Security). The shield. They existed to keep foreign services from penetrating the IIS. They also quietly monitored domestic loyalty within Iraq's institutions. They were the reason fear felt omnipresent. If you thought of flipping, you assumed Directorate 14 already knew.

- Directorate 18 (Foreign Operations / Expat Networks). The outreach arm. They cultivated Iraqis abroad, sympathetic foreigners, businessmen, sympathetic journalists, buyers, smugglers, sympathizers cloaked as cultural liaisons. They handled exile communities the way a botanist tends a greenhouse: pruning, feeding, replanting when necessary.

OPERATIONAL SYNERGY: HOW RECRUITMENT BECAME PIPELINE, NOT PERFORMANCE

The real sophistication of the IIS was that these directorates did not work in isolation. They chained.

- Identification. Directorate 18 spots a vulnerable Iraqi medical student in Europe. Intelligent, isolated, patriotic, financially strained.

- Cultivation. Directorate 4 steps in. Friendly contact. Small favors. Moral frames. "You represent Iraq's dignity abroad."
- Validation. Directorate 5 runs quietly in the background. Family connections checked. Past loyalties mapped. Weak points cataloged.
- Control. Directorate 8 captures leverage material. A photo. A recording. A moment of vulnerability that can be weaponized later if needed.
- Protection/Threat. Directorate 9 provides the silent backdrop: "Do not become a traitor. You know what happens to traitors."
- Continuity. Directorate 14 monitors for signs of drift. If drift appears, pressure is applied early. The asset is either corrected or cut.

What looks like a single recruitment conversation is, in truth, an organ system. Intelligence is not just the handler in the room with the target. It is the entire organism wrapped around that moment, tightening or relaxing as needed.

LESSONS FOR THE MODERN OFFICER: WHAT THE IIS MODEL STILL TEACHES

The IIS legacy is stained with brutality. But brutality is not what made it function. Its strength came from something colder: discipline.

Several enduring lessons emerge:

- Everyone is assessable. The IIS assumed that every individual was recruitable given the right mix of pressure, pride, belonging, and fear. You do not have to agree with that morally, but you must understand it operationally. Limiting your pool out of comfort is laziness disguised as ethics.
- Access lives in the ordinary. A president's driver can be more valuable than a president's aide. A wife at a diplomatic dinner can be more dangerous than any envoy. Do not chase titles. Chase access.
- Culture is an operational surface. Honor, shame, duty, family, faith— these are not atmospherics. They are leverage. The IIS proved that cultural codes, when read with precision, can be sharpened into tools

more effective than cash or threats.

- Redundancy is control. No single source should become critical. The IIS layered assets so their network could survive arrests, defections, embassy raids, assassinations. A network that only functions as long as one fragile human keeps committing treason is not a network. It is a liability.

- Fear without dignity fails. The IIS often used coercion. But they also understood that pure terror burns out. They preferred a controlled blend: fear to lock, belonging to hold. Chapter 5 calls this calibrated pressure. The IIS practiced it as policy.

- Internal surveillance sustains external reach. Their counterintelligence units did not just protect secrets. They enforced discipline inside the service. Paranoia was institutionalized to prevent officer complacency. That discipline is why their recruitment machine remained effective even under sanctions and isolation.

Conclusion: Influence Is Not Improvisation

The IIS did not improvise its way into dominance. It built systems.

It built a worldview that saw every human as a usable vector. It built officers who could read pride, debt, loneliness, and fear with predatory clarity. It built directorates that could identify, test, bind, threaten, insulate, and replace assets in a continuous cycle. It built cultural fluency into weaponry. It built paranoia into structure.

For a modern case officer, the value of studying this system is not admiration. It is recognition.

It proves that recruitment at scale is not a conversation. It is an ecosystem.

It proves that loyalty can be trained, fear can be ritualized, and belonging can be weaponized.

And it proves something else: power in intelligence is never just what you collect. It is what you can keep.

As we move into the coming case studies, we step out of doctrine and into practice. We watch what this looks like in contact with real people, prideful, frightened, calculating, devout, and how influence either binds them or breaks them under pressure.

CHAPTER 15:
SOCIAL MEDIA AND DIGITAL PLATFORMS IN MODERN INTELLIGENCE RECRUITMENT

INTRODUCTION

The street is no longer the street.

In today's Middle East, the real marketplace of influence is not the café, the mosque courtyard, or the souk. It is the feed.

Instagram stories replace whispered rumors. Telegram channels replace backroom meetings. WhatsApp voice notes carry more conviction than printed pamphlets ever did. A teenager in Basra can speak to five thousand strangers before breakfast. A minor cleric in Tripoli can ignite outrage across three borders without leaving his chair. A widow in Gaza can become a strategic amplifier in 48 hours, not because of rank or pedigree, but because she is grieving in public, and the world is watching.

For intelligence services, this is not noise. It is a signal.

Social platforms in the Arab and Middle Eastern space are not just tools of self-expression. They are emotional engines, loyalty factories, and early warning systems. They reveal who is angry, who is scared, who is isolated, who is searching for meaning. And that is recruitment space.

This chapter examines how modern officers identify, assess, approach, and shape potential assets through digital platforms in Middle Eastern environments. It connects to the cultural foundation of Chapter 1, the behavioral decoding in Chapter 3, the motivation and trust models in Chapter 6, and the selection discipline in Chapter 9. It also intersects with the coercion logic of Chapter 5 and the bribery dynamics of Chapter 13, because in this digital arena, influence, fear, validation, money, ideology, and loneliness all exist at once, under one light.

This is the new contact ground. It is immediate, intoxicating, and lethal if misread.

THE DIGITAL ECOSYSTEM: WHAT SOCIAL MEDIA ACTUALLY IS IN THIS REGION

Western officers often make a critical mistake: they assume social media in the Middle East is just a copy of social media in the West, scaled with different dialects. It is not.

Here, social media is not just entertainment. It is identity support, political theater, confessional space, rumor mill, safety valve, recruitment pool, and pressure release.

VOICE FOR THE VOICELESS

In many Arab states, traditional media is censored, captured, or distrusted. The average citizen does not expect television or newspapers to tell the truth. He expects them to tell power's version of the truth. Social media becomes the alternative channel: not necessarily for facts, but for emotion.

That difference matters. A person may not post "This is verifiably true." They post "This is how I feel, and you will witness it." That emotional clarity is gold for an officer. You can see pressure building before it explodes.

UNFILTERED GRIEVANCE

Platforms have become confessionals for humiliation and rage. A man who would never criticize a minister in a public square will curse that same minister on a semi-private Telegram channel at 2 a.m. A young woman who would never challenge her community's gender rules in her father's living room will mock those rules on TikTok with a joking filter. These expressions are not trivial. They are declarations of fracture between the person and their environment.

And a fracture is an entry point.

MOBILIZATION ENGINES

In this region, a single viral clip can do more than spread. It can summon. It can pull people into the street. It can harden a narrative overnight. We have seen clerics lose credibility in hours because of leaked voice notes. We have seen militias recruit openly through Telegram rooms disguised as "community defense committees." We have seen false martyr stories gain so much traction in a single night that real men volunteered the next morning to become the proof.

This is not just audience development. This is force generation.

MANIPULATION AT INDUSTRIAL SCALE

This same environment is flooded with disinformation: state-produced, militia-produced, foreign-produced, often layered with religious framing. Manufactured outrage is pushed the same way real outrage is pushed. Conspiracy is fed as comfort. Lies are wrapped in language that feels familiar, sacred, dignified.

For an officer, this means you cannot take any digital performance at face value. You are observing a theater where some actors are paid, some are desperate, and some don't even know they are on stage.

OPERATIONAL REALITY

Social media in the Middle East is not "online chatter." It is a living intelligence surface. It reveals emerging loyalties, new resentments, fresh desperation, and exploitable isolation in real time.

But it reveals it through distortion.

Your task is to separate signal from theater without insulting the culture that produces the theater. If you misread performance as sincerity, you recruit the wrong person. If you dismiss sincerity as performance, you miss the right one.

DIGITAL RECRUITMENT: TURNING NOISE INTO HUMAN ACCESS

Digital recruitment is not blasting offers into inboxes. It is a patient, silent pattern work.

It is behavioral profiling at scale without the subject realizing they have already begun the interview.

The modern case officer can prospect an entire city's worth of temperaments, insecurities, egos, and motives before ever walking into that city. That level of pre-contact access did not exist twenty years ago. It exists now.

Four pillars define the process.

1. Ideological Resonance Mapping. Before you ever speak to someone, you read their stance. Not the slogan they reposted once, but the rhythm of their beliefs over time.

2. You look at who they call "corrupt." Who they call "honorable." What institutions they mock. What sacrifices they glorify. Who they think deserves pity. Who they think deserves revenge. Someone who repeatedly criticizes government betrayal but praises "protection of the innocent" is signaling moral alignment: they are angry, but they still see themselves as defenders, not destroyers. That is a recruitable profile under the "protector" frame from Chapter 2 and Chapter 6. Someone who posts humiliation narratives ("They insulted our people," "They sold us," "No one respects us anymore") is often primed for status restoration, not money. That is a Chapter 9 status-repair profile. Someone who mixes religious justification with calls to immediate action is dangerous, valuable, and volatile. That is a Chapter 5 coercion-risk profile. You can approach them, but only with ideological fluency and containment plans. Tools: pattern-of-life logging, keyword clustering by emotional tone, and sustained

sentiment over weeks, not hours. You are mapping identity, not just content.

3. Psychological Extraction through Open Content. Every consistent poster reveals a need.

4. Frequency reveals hunger. Tone reveals mood discipline. Humor style reveals insecurity. Self-presentation reveals aspiration. Engagement reveals loneliness. The man who posts constantly and receives almost no response is starving for recognition. He is not dangerous. He is vulnerable. He is susceptible to validation. He is susceptible to being told "You matter. You are sharp. You see what others don't." This is not flattery. This is access. The woman who posts infrequently but whose followers hang on every word is something else entirely. She is an influencer. She will not be bribed easily. She will not be steered with cheap reassurance. Her self-worth is already fed. With her, recruitment is framed in legacy, purpose, moral impact (Chapter 6 territory). You do not "buy" her. You invite her into a story large enough for her ego to survive inside it. Tools: tone profiling, trigger analysis (what makes them angry, what makes them go quiet), escalation markers (what topics make them reckless), shame tolerance (what they will mock publicly versus what they defend).

5. Contact through Proximity, Not Intrusion. One of the worst mistakes inexperienced officers make is contacting too directly, too early. "We've been watching you, and we think you're important." That message feels like surveillance, not respect. It triggers flight.

6. Instead, you build digital familiarity. You move into their periphery. You follow. You occasionally react. You enter shared comment threads in a way that feels organic. You signal ideo-

logical or emotional sympathy without promising anything. You do not say, "I agree with you." You say, "That's exactly what no one is willing to say out loud." You're not mirroring belief. You're mirroring courage. That is different. From there, you let them initiate intimacy without knowing they did so. They respond to you. They start addressing you directly. They start tagging you. They ask your opinion. That shift is consent. That is the pivot point where you can move the conversation into more controlled channels. Then, and only then, do you open a private line on an encrypted platform. By that stage, in their mind, you are not a stranger. You are the only one who "understood."

7. Community Mining inside Closed Groups. The region runs on private groups. Neighborhood defense channels. Militia-adjacent "services" chats. Pilgrimage coordination groups. Mourning circles. Women-only social rooms. Diaspora support clusters. Trade and smuggling logistics forums disguised as "import/export opportunities." All of these are live intelligence surfaces.

8. You enter these not as a hunter, but as a listener. Inside, you do not target the loudest voice. The loudest voice is often either leadership bait or theater. You target the second-layer voice: the one who corrects misinformation quietly, who calms arguments without claiming authority, who expresses frustration without losing face. That person has influence and restraint. Influence plus restraint is recruitable. When they challenge leadership inside the group, and nobody expels them for it, you have found credibility. That is value. That is Chapter 7-level material.

DIGITAL RISK: WHY ONLINE RECRUITMENT CAN GET YOU KILLED

Everything you gain in access, you risk in exposure.

There are three core hazards.

1. False Identity and Manipulated Bait. You may think you are grooming a disillusioned militia sympathizer. You may actually be talking to a militia counterintelligence officer running a fishing line for foreign handlers. You may think you are reading a real student in exile. You may be engaging a state-run persona designed to pull you into a traceable communication pattern.

2. Do not assume authenticity from emotional intensity. Rage can be fabricated. So can fear. Corollary: Anyone who moves too fast is a problem. If they volunteer sensitive access unprompted, if they escalate to operational talk without hesitation, assume you are being profiled.

3. Contamination through Metadata. Even when the content of messages is encrypted, metadata still exposes timing, frequency, routing patterns, device signatures. A sloppy recruitment attempt can link your operation to theirs in a way that can later be reconstructed.

4. This is not hypothetical. It is routine counterintelligence practice in the region. If you build dependence digitally without providing tradecraft discipline, you are not recruiting an asset. You are growing a future liability with your fingerprint on them.

5. Misinformation Bleed. Online, lies spread faster than corrections and last longer than clarifications. An asset who lives primarily in digital echo chambers may feed you conviction, rather than truth.

6. That conviction will sound operational. It will feel urgent. It
   will tempt you to act. This is how operations walk into ambush-
   es. Digital reporting must never stand alone. As stated in
   Chapter 5 and Chapter 10, everything under pressure is cross-
   checked. Digital intel is pressure by default. You validate with
   human verification, physical observation, signals confirmation,
   or trusted parallel sources before you move.

PRACTICAL TRADECRAFT: HOW A DISCIPLINED OFFICER WORKS THIS DOMAIN

To recruit in the digital environment without losing control, you apply
structure.

Build the target profile before you speak

Map ideological consistency over time, not just flare-ups. Someone who has
held the same grievance narrative for six months is emotionally predictable.
Predictability under stress is a strong selection factor (Chapter 9).

Map influence

High follower count means reach, not reliability. What matters more is
engagement density and who listens. Who comments. Who defends them.
Who quotes them elsewhere. Influence tells you not only what they can
give you, but what kind of blowback will occur if they disappear.

Map network

Tag patterns, recurring co-commenters, repeated inside jokes. This gives you
the relational graph. You are not just recruiting an individual. You are walking into a web. You must know who will notice if you pull on that strand.

Build rapport with cultural precision

Language in this region is layered. A single phrase signals insider status
or exposes you as an outsider.

Do not attempt slang you do not fully control. Getting dialect wrong kills credibility instantly. Getting honorifics wrong can insult without you realizing it. Your tone must match their register: pious if they present devout, irreverent if they survive through gallows humor, formal if they lead. You are not trying to sound like them. You are trying to sound like someone who understands them. That distinction preserves respect.

Escalate gradually

Do not lunge. You move from open comment to limited private exchange to deeper private exchange to structured backchannel. Each step is its own test. Each step is a chance for them to show fear, arrogance, volatility, greed, instability, duplicity.

If they demand money on step one, they are not an asset. They are a liability hunting for a wallet. See Chapter 13. If they romanticize martyrdom, they are not ready for controlled work. They are a live explosive. You do not recruit explosives; you observe them. If they ask who you work for, you slow down, or you cut.

Train them early

If a digital contact begins to convert into a real recruit, you immediately train protection.

You coach them on what not to post. You coach them on what not to forward. You coach them to reduce political volume publicly so that their eventual value to you doesn't get them killed by their own timeline six weeks later. This is not charity. This is asset preservation. As stated in Chapter 6 and Chapter 10, protection is part of stewardship.

Verify everything

Digital self-presentation is theater. You confirm claims through:

- Secondary digital traces (different accounts linked by pattern).
- Geolocation hints in images or background audio.
- Offline confirmation through separate human sources.

- Tasking them with verifiable, low-risk micro-assignments.

If they lie about something small, they will lie about something lethal. Track that.

ETHICS: THE LINE YOU DO NOT CROSS

Digital recruitment tempts officers into exploiting loneliness, poverty, anger, grief. The platform delivers vulnerability directly to your screen. You will see people bleeding in public. You will know you could move them with a single message.

Here is where Chapter 11's ethical thread applies in full. You are not a predator. You are a professional. That means: You do not fabricate identities solely to emotionally destabilize a target and then capitalize on the collapse. Breaking someone on purpose to "claim" them may look effective short term. Long term, it gives you an unstable, resentful, guilt-ridden source who will eventually either implode or expose you. You do not harvest trauma as leverage if you cannot also manage the aftermath. If you pull someone into your orbit using grief, you now own that grief. You are responsible for stabilizing them. If you cannot, do not pull them. You do not recruit a person into mortal risk just because they are loud online. Volume is not readiness. This is not softness. This is discipline. Assets recruited through cruelty tend to self-destruct under pressure and take you with them.

THE OFFICER'S MINDSET: ADAPT OR BECOME OBSOLETE

The modern Middle Eastern battlespace is digital first, physical second.

That does not mean physical presence is obsolete. It means physical presence now often follows digital shaping. By the time you sit across from a potential source in a car, a café, a clinic waiting room, you should already know:

- Their resentments
- Their loyalties
- Their fears
- Their ego needs
- Their risk tolerance
- Their capacity for discipline
- Their preferred story about themselves

If you walk into that first in-person contact blind, you are operating in the wrong decade. The platforms have given you a gift that previous generations never had: pre-contact psychological mapping at scale. But that gift came with new fragility. You are now visible too, even when you think you are not. The work, then, is a balance:

- Precision without haste
- Access without exposure
- Influence without humiliation
- Recruitment without corrosion

CONCLUSION: THE FEED IS THE FIRST LAYER OF THE GROUND

Social media in the Middle East is not a side channel. It is the terrain. It is where grievance forms, where identity performs, where loyalty declares itself in miniature before it declares itself in public.

For the intelligent, disciplined officer, it is the most powerful early-access environment ever created. You can listen before appearing. You can select before approaching. You can shape before revealing presence. But it is also a mirror. It reflects you back to yourself. If you recruit through arrogance, you will get assets who betray you. If you recruit through respect, you will get assets who endure. The future of recruitment in this region belongs to those who can merge classical tradecraft with digital literacy: reading tone as closely as you once read posture, mapping networks you have never physically walked, and applying cultural fluency to a space where a single careless word can expose you to thousands at once. Master the feed, and you enter conversations before they are spoken aloud. Misread it, and you're already compromised before you ever knock on the door.

CHAPTER 16:
THE ART OF INTERROGATION: MASTERING THE IRAQI INTELLIGENCE SERVICE'S TECHNIQUES IN A CULTURAL CRUCIBLE

INTRODUCTION

An interrogation room is not four walls and a table. It is a battlefield.

Not of fists, but of memory. Not of muscle, but of identity.

The Iraqi Intelligence Service under Saddam Hussein understood this with cold clarity. For them, interrogation was not casual questioning. It was controlled psychological warfare. It was theater. It was ritual. It was an exercise in domination, in which the outcome was rarely in doubt. The question was never simply "Will he talk?" It was "How will we make him believe that talking is his only path to survival, dignity, or redemption?"

Inside that room, everything carried weight. The chair. The silence. The interrogator's posture. The mention of a mother's name. The way a verse from the Qur'an was quoted. Every word and every pause was deliberate.

This chapter studies that craft.

We examine how the IIS built interrogators who could read a man's breathing pattern and tell whether he was lying. We study how they weaponized culture (honor, shame, religion, family), turning them into tools sharper than any baton. We show how they cycled between fear and mercy to break resistance without leaving marks. And we confront the ethical reality: this system produced results, but often at a cost that could never be washed off.

We anchor this discussion in Case Study 4: the interrogation of an Irani-an operative detained inside Iraq. His resistance did not collapse under physical suffering. It collapsed under psychological exposure: the weaponization of his own sense of responsibility to his family and his name.

As you move through this chapter, remember the line that separates mastery from brutality. The IIS crossed that line often. A modern officer cannot afford to.

THE INTERROGATOR'S CRAFT

The IIS interrogator was not trained to "ask questions." He was trained to control the room.

He entered as judge, confessor, historian, brother, and executioner: sometimes in sequence, sometimes all at once. His presence alone was meant to set the tone: "You already belong to me. We are only negotiating how hard I make this for you."

Key elements of the craft:

Command presence

In Iraqi and wider Arab social structures, hierarchy is absorbed from childhood. Authority is recognized, not debated. IIS officers used this to front-load psychological pressure. They did not storm into the room shouting. They entered calm, composed, almost bored.

That calm was the threat.

When a suspect meets a man who is not excited, not angry, not nervous, the message is simple: You are not the first. You will not be the last. We already know.

Submission often begins before the first question.

Cultural and psychological acumen

Interrogators were expected to know who they were facing before the first contact. Tribal background. Sect. Place of origin. Local feuds. Religious leanings. Economic stresses. Family reputation. This is not trivia in

Arab societies; this is leverage.

They were taught how shame operates in a Sunni tribal village versus in a Shi'a urban family network, how a man from a conservative rural area responds to an insult to his honor compared to a cosmopolitan student who cares more about ideological purity than ancestral pride.

They did not apply generic pressure. They applied tailored humiliation or tailored absolution.

Patience as a weapon

The Western stereotype is loud interrogation. The IIS mastered the opposite.

They would sit in silence and let the suspect sweat under his own imagination. They would let him over-talk. They would let him contradict himself. They understood what we covered in Chapter 5: fear grows in the absence of certainty. Silence becomes a mirror. The suspect starts negotiating with himself.

Patience breaks people who believe they are strong.

Reverse psychology

One of their favored moves: accept the lie.

When a suspect finally gives a rehearsed story, the interrogator does not immediately attack it. He nods. He starts treating that lie as if it were already official. He acts as though it convicted the suspect of something far worse.

"You helped them move supplies? So you admit you were aware of their operations. That makes you part of the plan, not just a witness. But I understand. Some men are followers, not actors."

Now the suspect, desperate to prove he is "not as guilty" as the interrogator is implying, begins offering the truth out of self-defense. He corrects the record to save face. He exposes details to protect his ego.

That is not an accident. That is design.

Training the interrogator

The IIS did not assume anyone could walk in and perform this work. They built interrogators.

They forged them.

Training was immersive, brutal, and total. It produced officers who were capable of reading micro-signals in the suspect, and equally capable of suppressing their own.

Cultural immersion

Interrogators were drilled in regional dialects, tribal structures, religious framing, and customs of respect and insult. They were taught exactly how "shame" sounds in Najaf and how "shame" sounds in Mosul: because they are not the same word, even when they are.

They memorized formulas of address: uncle, sheikh, ustadh, hajji. They knew when to flatter and when to withhold basic courtesy.

The goal was to speak like someone inside the suspect's world, not outside it. A man is more easily broken by someone who sounds like his cousin than someone who sounds like a bureaucrat.

Behavioral analysis

They practiced watching.

Blink rate. Pupil dilation. Throat swallowing. A tapping foot under the chair. Shoulders that rise and stay raised. Eyes that jump left when describing details of a timeline.

They ran repeated drills: one trainee played a suspect, another interrogated, a third watched silently and logged micro-behaviors. Afterwards, the observer (not the interrogator) was graded. The IIS believed, correctly, that sometimes the person asking the question misses the signal. The silent witness does not.

Field simulations

They rehearsed interrogations under different emotional tones. One day, they'd interrogate an indignant nationalist. Next day, a grieving father. Next, a zealot convinced God justifies his actions. Next, a quiet, frightened courier who insists he "knows nothing."

They learned to adapt cadence, volume, and moral framing to each profile, not force every suspect into the same mold.

Emotional conditioning

They were trained to take insults without reacting, to listen to lies without showing contempt, to hear prayers for their death without blinking. Their composure was part of the weapon.

If the interrogator remains unshaken, the suspect has no emotional foothold.

SCENARIO: THE FIRST TEST

A junior IIS officer sits across from a respected tribal elder accused of quietly passing information to rival elements.

The elder swears on his family's honor that he has done nothing.

The officer does not slam the table. He does not accuse him of treason. He leans in and says, almost gently:

"If you lie here, your grandchildren carry that shame. Not you. Them."

He doesn't threaten prison. He threatens legacy.

The elder's eyes shift. His hands tighten. The first crack appears.

That is interrogation in this region. Not "Do you admit this?" but "Can you live with what your silence will do to your bloodline?"

Cultural leverage

To interrogate in the Arab world without cultural fluency is to walk in blindfolded.

Family. Tribe. Religion. Honor. Reputation. These are not "themes." They are structural supports of the self. They are pressure points. Push correctly, and a man will fold. Push incorrectly, and he will die before giving you anything.

The IIS understood this difference.

The oath

Many suspects tried to protect themselves with an oath: "By God," "By the Qur'an," "By the honor of my father," "By my children's lives."

To the untrained interrogator, this sounds like proof of truth.

To the IIS officer, it's diagnostic.

If a suspect is innocent, his oath comes calmly. His breathing does not spike. His eyes hold.

If he is lying, the oath arrives too fast. Too dramatic. Too rehearsed. It is performance, not conviction.

The interrogator does not call him a liar. That would give him battle lines to defend. Instead, he says:

"I respect that you said that before God. So if you are lying, the punishment is not mine. It's His. And He punishes through disgrace. Through children."

That reframes the oath. The suspect has trapped himself.

Family as leverage

In collectivist societies, a man's individual fate hurts less than his family's humiliation. Decades in prison? He can imagine surviving that. His daughters whispered about in the neighborhood? Unbearable.

The IIS used this mercilessly.

They would not always threaten harm. They would threaten exposure.

"We will not touch your son. We will simply tell the truth about you in the mosque. Let them decide what kind of father you were."

Most men cracked before that line was crossed.

Religious framing

Scripture was not quoted as comfort. It was quoted as an indictment.

A skilled interrogator could say, "The Prophet said that concealing corruption is sharing in it," and make a man feel that silence itself was a sin. That turns confession from betrayal into repentance.

That is powerful. That is also morally dangerous. Because now truth is extracted through guilt that has been engineered for effect.

SCENARIO: REFRAMING THE DEFENSE

A suspect swears on his children's lives that he is innocent.

The interrogator replies: "Then their reputation is on the table with yours. We will see if it was worth it."

The suspect wasn't protecting himself. He was protecting his self-image. The interrogator turned that image into a liability.

This is cultural pressure with surgical precision.

Psychological warfare

The IIS treated interrogation like atmospheric manipulation. Everything in the room was part of the operation.

They understood what we established back in Chapter 3 and Chapter 5: human beings are not rational under stress. They are narrative-driven. Their mind will race to fill the silence. Your job is to feed the mind the story you want it to believe.

Control of rhythm

They would ask fast, then slow. Gentle, then sharp. They would let a suspect speak for twenty minutes uninterrupted, then interrupt at the one sentence that mattered. That interruption feels like exposure. Panic follows.

Control of time

No clock. No stated schedule. No sense of how long this will last. The interrogator controls duration. Time itself becomes a coercive instrument.

Control of contrast

They would deny comfort for an hour, then offer a glass of tea. That tea becomes more than tea. It becomes mercy. The interrogator becomes not just the threat but the savior.

Once that dynamic is established ("Only I can hurt you, and only I can protect you") dependency begins. Dependency opens mouths.

Control of identity

"You are not a criminal," the interrogator says. "You were used. You were misled. You are better than them. Help me make this right."

That is not kindness. That is recoding. The suspect is being given a way to talk without self-destruction.

This is how the IIS broke seasoned operatives without screaming.

SCENARIO: COLLAPSE WITHOUT FORCE

A captured Iranian asset holds firm at first. His story is clean. His tone is disciplined. He is trained.

The IIS officer does not try to out-argue him on operational detail.

Instead, he says: "Your family will not be touched. But when your village learns what you did, they will spit on your father's grave."

Everything changes.

The suspect's resistance was never about his life. It was about his narrative. Attack the narrative, and the center falls.

THE INTIMIDATION-ENTICEMENT CYCLE

The IIS formalized this approach into a repeatable system. They called it different things internally, but its structure is the same across cases. It is the pendulum.

1. Establish Dominance. The suspect arrives disoriented. Blindfold. Moved at night. Seated in an unfamiliar space. When the blindfold is removed: light too bright, temperature too cold or too hot, room slightly too large or too empty. He feels small. The interrogator is already seated. He is already in control. He does not introduce himself as an equal. He enters as inevitability.

2. Apply Pressure. Not always physical. Often emotional. "This is already bad. Do not make it worse. We already have statements from others. We know who you met." Even if that is not fully true, it is believable. That belief triggers fear.

3. Offer Relief. Then the tone softens. "Listen. You are not the first. I can protect you if you cooperate. I can protect your people. I can write this in a way that does not destroy you." A glass of water appears. A cigarette. A blanket. The suspect feels seen. He attaches to the source of relief. That attachment is leverage.

4. Reapply Pressure. The relief is taken away. Calmly. "Do not insult me. Do not insult yourself. Do not make me change my mind about you." Now the suspect fears losing the only lifeline he believes exists.

Repeat.

The cycle creates emotional exhaustion faster than physical abuse does.

The mind burns through hope and terror, hope and terror, until the subject starts reaching for escape. That escape is confession.

This is how you get statements that seem voluntary.

This is also how you build dependency so strong that the suspect starts cooperating not for self-preservation, but for approval.

PHYSICAL COERCION

We cannot discuss IIS interrogation without acknowledging brutality. When patience failed, they escalated.

Sleep deprivation. Temperature manipulation. Stress positions designed to exhaust, not necessarily cripple. Denial of rest. Psychological isolation. Rhythms intended to produce exhaustion, paranoia, then collapse.

This is the hard edge. It produced results. It also produced false confessions, broken men, and long-term operational blowback.

Here is the operational truth: pain forces words. Pain does not guarantee truth.

The IIS knew this. That is why their first line was always psychological and cultural manipulation, not immediate physical force. Force was escalation, not baseline.

From a modern standpoint, this is the red line. Contemporary services operating under legal and human rights oversight cannot and must not replicate that escalation. The existence of a method does not justify its use.

READING THE SUSPECT: THE OBSERVATION DISCIPLINE

Observation was considered a weapon on its own.

The interrogator watched for micro-signals that exposed stress points and deception patterns. These signals guided when to press, when to pause, and when to pivot to enticement.

Core indicators:

Eye activity

Rapid blinking, sudden aversion of gaze when a specific name is mentioned, darting eyes when constructing a timeline. Each is a tell.

Facial heat and strain

Flushed cheeks, sweat at the brow, jaw clenching during certain topics. These are emotional peaks. Those topics are where truth lives.

Body posture

Leaning back and away when asked about logistics, but leaning forward when asked about ideology? That means logistics are dangerous. Ideology is safe. You now know where to dig.

Hands

Hands tell what the mouth won't. Fingers tapping at certain questions. Hands pulling at sleeves. Wrists tightening. Hands covering the mouth subconsciously when lying. The IIS trained officers to track hands almost more than faces.

Voice

Hesitation. Forced humor. Sudden dryness in the throat. A voice that drops when naming an associate. A voice that lifts (falsely casual) when denying something important.

All of these were logged.

PRACTICAL FIELD TOOL: BEHAVIORAL LEDGER

Professional interrogators kept mental or written ledgers that tracked the suspect's reactions to specific topics in real time. This wasn't "he lied." It was:

- Blinks increased when asked about X
- Jaw tightened when asked about Y
- Calm when discussing Z
- Voice drop on mention of [name]
- No reaction to threat of prison, strong reaction to threat of public shame

That ledger guided the next pass.

TARGETING SPIES

The IIS reserved its most intense methods for foreign intelligence penetrations, especially Iranian assets. They viewed them not as criminals but as existential threats.

In Case Study 4, an Iranian operative is detained after behavioral anomalies expose him. He had visited a controlled site under weak pretexts. He showed the wrong kind of confidence. He carried himself like someone on a mission, not like someone with a normal reason to be there.

Once in custody, he tries discipline. He tries silence. He tries ideological superiority.

The interrogator does not argue politics with him.

He attacks identity.

"You think they will honor you when they learn how you talked? Do you think they will call you a martyr? They will call you a traitor who broke early."

That reframing lands harder than any physical strike. The operative did not fear death. He feared legacy.

He begins to talk.

This is a critical lesson: different targets fear different losses. The IIS understood that. They did not say, "We will hurt you." They said, "We will rewrite what you are."

MODERN EVOLUTION: WHERE INTERROGATION STANDS NOW

The IIS operated in an era and under an authority that allowed them to push past ethical limits. Modern services cannot and must not claim that freedom. The world has changed. Oversight exists. International scrutiny exists. Internal accountability exists.

But the psychological lessons (the controlled pacing, the observation of micro-reactions, the cultural framing, the calibrated respect) remain relevant. They can be used inside ethical boundaries.

Modern interrogation trends emphasize:

Rapport-based extraction

Instead of declaring dominance, the interrogator anchors in empathy. The suspect is not treated as "broken," but as "valuable." This lowers defensiveness and encourages voluntary disclosure.

This approach mirrors what we laid out in Chapter 6: you stabilize their identity instead of tearing it apart. You show them their story can survive cooperation.

Cognitive interviewing

Rather than confront and accuse, you ask the subject to walk you through events in their own order, in their own descriptive language. You watch for inconsistencies between early and later versions. You listen to what they forget and what they repeat.

This is far harder to fake than a single scripted denial.

Digital validation

Modern interrogators do not need to take every claim on faith. They can confirm movements, contacts, communications patterns, digital presence, social media behavior. They can confront a lie gently with proof and then offer a dignified way out.

This reduces the perceived need for hard coercion. Truth can be compelled through quiet exposure rather than terror.

Ethical reinforcement

Ethics are no longer an afterthought. They are operational armor.

Torture produces short-term answers and long-term poison. Abusive methods fracture communities, stain institutions, and discredit collected intelligence in the eyes of allies, courts, and the public. It weakens the service that uses it.

Modern interrogation doctrine, at its best, understands what Chapter 11 and Chapter 13 made clear: power without restraint rots from the inside.

Comparative frame

We can summarize the philosophical split:

IIS model:

Leverage shame, fear, honor.

Break identity, then offer conditional restoration.

Cycle intimidation and enticement.

Use coercion if needed.

Accept moral cost if the result protects the regime.

Modern ethical model:

- Leverage rapport, self-preservation, practical outcomes.
- Preserve identity; offer cooperation as continuity, not collapse.
- Use memory reconstruction and behavioral observation instead of threats.
- Avoid coercion.
- Protect institutional legitimacy alongside operational gain.

This is not softness. It is strategic durability.

ADVANCED TECHNIQUES: WHAT TRULY SKILLED INTERROGATORS DO

Beyond structure and doctrine, the real masters (then and now) operate in subtle space.

Behavioral mapping

They map what triggers stress, what triggers calm, and what triggers pride. Pride is often the key. A suspect will talk not to save himself, but to prove he is smarter than his enemy.

Cultural anchoring

They embed questions in shared values. "You're a man of faith. A man like you protects the innocent. Help me stop this, so no more blood spills." This reframes disclosure as moral responsibility, not betrayal.

Dynamic questioning

They avoid predictable patterns. They let the suspect think the session is drifting, then quietly reinsert the critical line of inquiry when the guard is down.

Stress threshold reading

They do not escalate blindly. They escalate when the suspect shows visible strain but not collapse. Push too little and nothing moves. Push too hard and the subject shuts down or starts fabricating wildly.

Narrative weaving

They do not demand: "Tell me what happened." They offer: "Here's what I think happened. Tell me where I'm wrong." This allows the suspect to "correct" rather than "confess." Correction feels safer. It still produces usable truth.

All of this appeared in Case Study 4. The interrogator did not win because he yelled. He won because he made the asset's continued silence feel like a betrayal of the very people the asset claimed to protect.

ETHICS AND THE COST OF MASTERY

Interrogation leaves marks on everyone in the room.

On the subject. On the interrogator.

The IIS model achieved results, but often at a permanent cost. Men left those rooms cracked, humiliated, hollowed. Some never psychologically returned. Some broke in ways that produced elaborate false narratives just to end the pressure. False narratives contaminate operations. They send officers down blind alleys. They get innocent people killed.

Even inside the IIS, this was understood. The most disciplined interrogators were not the ones who shouted loudest. They were the ones who could get the truth without splintering the subject so badly that nothing that came out could be trusted.

For modern services, the lesson is sharper.

You cannot afford to generate intelligence you cannot defend. You cannot afford to build cases on statements a court will reject. You cannot afford to poison your own networks by earning a reputation for cruelty in cultures where honor and revenge live for generations.

Interrogation is not a license to destroy. It is a test of control.

THE LEGACY

The Iraqi Intelligence Service perfected psychological pressure in an environment where fear was law. They weaponized culture, honor, shame, religion, and family obligation with surgical accuracy. They engineered emotional collapse without always needing to spill blood.

That legacy is both a blueprint and a warning.

The blueprint: Know the mind you are facing. Know the world that built that mind. Shape pressure to that world. Control tempo. Read silence. Break resistance by offering a story the subject can live with.

The warning: Power without restraint corrodes the operator, corrupts the institution, and contaminates the intelligence.

CONCLUSION

Interrogation is not about pain. It is about ownership of narrative.

In Saddam's Iraq, the IIS learned to seize that narrative and bend it around the suspect's throat. They turned confession into obligation. They turned silence into guilt. They turned loyalty into leverage.

Case Study 4, the Iranian operative who shattered not under blows but under the threat of disgrace, is proof of how powerful that method can be, and how dangerous.

For the modern intelligence professional, the lesson is to evolve. Take the discipline, the patience, the observation, the cultural fluency. Leave the cruelty. Replace humiliation with controlled rapport. Replace terror with psychological clarity. Replace domination with guided self-preservation.

Because in the end, the objective is not to break a human being.

The objective is to get to the truth, and to walk out of the room still able to live with how you got it.

CHAPTER 17:
UNVEILING VULNERABILITIES: GENDER DYNAMICS IN MIDDLE EASTERN INTELLIGENCE

THE CULTURAL LENS OF GENDER IN THE ARAB WORLD

In the intricate web of Middle Eastern intelligence, where every cultural cue can be exploited as a tactical advantage, gender remains one of the most potent yet often overlooked tools. Across the Arab world, societal norms grounded in centuries of tradition, religion, and patriarchal authority define strict expectations for male and female behavior. These expectations not only shape daily life but also serve as blueprints for manipulation, turning gender psychology into a calculated weapon of influence.

CULTURAL AND RELIGIOUS FOUNDATIONS

Gender roles in the Arab world are deeply rooted in a social and spiritual framework that elevates male authority and enforces female modesty. These foundations are not simply traditional customs, they are doctrines reinforced by religion, family honor, and social hierarchy. Intelligence agencies such as the Iraqi Intelligence Service (IIS) have long understood that where belief and identity intersect, opportunity for manipulation exists.

- Islamic teachings: The Quran's permission for men to marry up to four wives under defined conditions (Surah An-Nisa 4:3) institutionalizes male privilege and responsibility. The concept of Hur al-Ayn celestial women promised to martyrs links male virtue with sexual reward, blending faith, power, and desire into a singular motivator. This creates a predictable psychological dynamic: men equate control with divine approval.

- Tribal honor: A man's reputation within his tribe depends on the perceived purity and obedience of his female relatives. Protecting this honor becomes both a duty and a public performance. Losing control over a woman's behavior is equated with losing one's identity and status, creating a constant pressure to dominate the domestic sphere.

This patriarchal structure produces both power and vulnerability. Men who must constantly project dominance are often unaware that this performance breeds insecurity. Skilled intelligence officers recognize that contradiction as the precise point where psychological pressure can be applied.

THE PUBLIC-PRIVATE DICHOTOMY

In Arab societies, masculinity operates at two levels: the public arena and the private realm. Publicly, men must appear resolute, moral, and untouchable—the embodiment of honor (sharaf) and dignity (karama). Privately, they frequently seek emotional release or validation through behaviors that contradict those ideals. Intelligence agencies identified this cultural split as an exploitable fault line between image and instinct.

- Public strength: In public spaces, such as mosques, cafés, or tribal councils, men assert control and enforce social codes that emphasize modesty, propriety, and male authority. This rigid performance earns community respect but limits emotional expression.
- Private fragility: Behind closed doors, these same men reveal insecurities and desires repressed by societal judgment. They crave admiration, affection, or forbidden intimacy, which becomes their emotional undoing.

This contrast between pride and vulnerability defines the psychological terrain of many Arab men. As one IIS operative observed, "A man's honor is his shield before the crowd, but his desires are the crack through which truth escapes."

EXPLOITATION BY INTELLIGENCE AGENCIES

The Iraqi Intelligence Service mastered the manipulation of these dynamics through calculated gender-based operations. Female operatives trained in cultural awareness, psychology, and emotional influence became both instruments and strategists. They embodied societal ideals in public while subverting them in private encounters. Their mission was not seduction for pleasure, but for control.

- Seduction as strategy: Female operatives used subtle charm and empathy to attract male targets, understanding that men often confused emotional connection with trust. They drew information gradually, framing disclosure as proof of intimacy or strength.
- Psychological manipulation: By feeding a man's ego or sympathy, operatives created dependency. Targets were encouraged to believe they were in control even as they revealed secrets. Emotional entanglement became the leash that replaced physical coercion.
- Cultural navigation: In public, operatives maintained modest attire and speech to remain above suspicion. In private, they wielded confidence and curiosity to dominate interactions, turning cultural expectations into camouflage.

A prominent example emerged in Dubai in the late 1990s when an Iranian intelligence officer, disciplined yet vain, was methodically compromised by a female IIS operative. Meeting him at a local café, she initiated friendly debates about politics and faith. Over time, the relationship deepened until he felt compelled to impress her. During one visit to her apartment, outfitted with covert recording devices, he disclosed sensitive details about Iran's Gulf network. The operation, executed through patience and precision, became a benchmark for cultural exploitation in intelligence circles.

PSYCHOLOGICAL UNDERPINNINGS

Why do these methods succeed so consistently? The answer lies in the psychology of repression and the illusion of control. Arab men, conditioned to equate dominance with self-worth, experience tension when their public confidence clashes with private vulnerability. Female operatives exploit that friction with precision, offering comfort, admiration, or temptation at carefully chosen moments.

- Cognitive dissonance: The struggle between external pride and internal weakness creates a mental imbalance. Confession during intimacy can serve as emotional release, reducing guilt through perceived trust.
- Disinhibition: Pleasure, admiration, or emotional comfort lowers psychological defenses, making secrets easier to share. The more personal the setting, the weaker the resistance.
- Power projection: Many men view revealing privileged information as proof of control or sophistication. This misperception fuels voluntary disclosure and deepens emotional reliance on the operative.

As one retired Iraqi officer reflected, "A man convinced he's leading the game never realizes he's already been played." These operations demonstrate how emotional intelligence can accomplish what interrogation cannot: truth offered freely, disguised as intimacy.

PRACTICAL INSIGHTS FOR INTELLIGENCE OFFICERS

Understanding gender psychology is essential for modern intelligence professionals operating in the Middle East. Exploiting vulnerabilities is not about moral judgment but about identifying consistent behavioral patterns shaped by culture and pride.

- Target profiling: Focus on men whose reputations depend heavily on moral authority or dominance. The tighter the control they project publicly, the greater the likelihood of private contradictions.
- Operative training: Female operatives must balance grace with strategic intellect: embodying cultural modesty in appearance while maintaining the psychological agility to manipulate or redirect conversations as needed.

- Strategic patience: Such operations cannot be rushed. Emotional rapport builds slowly but produces deeper and more credible intelligence once trust is secured.

Through the calculated use of patience, empathy, and cultural awareness, intelligence officers can transform the most rigid social structures into avenues of infiltration. Gender dynamics, when understood and ethically managed, offer unparalleled access to the private world where power truly resides.

Gender dynamics in Middle Eastern intelligence are far more than background context: they are the blueprint of human behavior in societies defined by honor and repression. The Iraqi Intelligence Service demonstrated that understanding masculinity's dual nature could unlock the secrets of men who appeared untouchable. For contemporary officers, mastering this dynamic requires both respect for culture and control over one's own influence. True intelligence lies not in exploiting weakness for its own sake, but in understanding how identity shapes vulnerability. In the Middle East, where image governs reality, those who read the hidden language of gender hold the key to persuasion, access, and power.

CONTRASTING DYNAMICS: WOMEN'S INFLUENCE IN IRAN

While Arab gender dynamics often expose men's private weaknesses behind public bravado, Iran presents a contrasting landscape. There, strict public codes coexist with robust private authority for women inside the household. This duality creates intelligence opportunities of a different kind: access through trusted domestic channels rather than fleeting moments of personal indiscretion.

The Iranian Gender Paradox

Iran's cultural identity and political system shape gender relations in ways that differ markedly from many Arab states. Under the Islamic Republic, public life for women is tightly regulated: dress codes, gender segregation, and limitations on pubPons behind the scenes. Intelligence practitioners recognized this paradox early on as a source of reliable access.

- Domestic authority: Iranian women commonly make or heavily influence household decisions, financial choices, children's education, social contacts, and sometimes even career moves for their husbands. This domestic sway makes them natural reservoirs of insight into family members' work and social ties.
- Trusted confidantes: Because public roles for men emphasize stoicism, many turn to wives or sisters for emotional support. That trust places women in private conversations where operational details, stresses, and even classified topics are sometimes shared informally.

This paradox—visible public subordination masking private agency—creates a distinctive intelligence landscape. As one IIS analyst put it, 'In Iran, the home is a vault, and women are its keepers.' Understanding that dynamic enables operations tailored to a context where influence is exerted quietly, persistently, and often with great effect.

Exploiting domestic access

The IIS and similar services developed tactics that positioned female operatives within trusted everyday social venues to collect information in passively and ethically ambiguous ways. These operations prioritized long-term rapport and subtle elicitation over direct confrontation, converting ordinary social interaction into intelligence collection.

A prototype of this approach was a discreet beauty salon in Tehran frequented by the wives and daughters of military and government officials. Staffed by female operatives posing as stylists, the salon offered high-quality services while creating a relaxed environment for conversation. Clients spoke freely about family matters, social events, and personal concerns, comments that, when aggregated, painted a revealing picture of local networks and activities.

- Elicitation in action: A general's wife might casually mention late-night meetings; an officer's sister could complain about sudden travel or stress; each remark, recorded and analyzed, can indicate shifts in deployments or internal tensions.
- Mosaic intelligence: Individual snippets, seemingly insignificant on their own, can be cross-referenced over time to form comprehensive intelligence mosaics revealing troop movements, political fractures, or logistical changes.

The salon operation, which ran successfully for several years until regional upheaval disrupted it, demonstrated the power of embedding sources in trusted social spaces. The approach's strength lay in its camouflage: it fit existing cultural patterns and therefore drew little suspicion while producing steady, high-value intelligence.

Cultural and psychological underpinnings

Why does this model work so consistently in Iran? Three interlocking factors make domestic access particularly fruitful: cultural norms favoring discretion, psychological patterns of trust inside the family, and women's indirect influence on male decision-making.

- Cultural norms: Iranian society places a premium on family loyalty and discretion. Women who manage the household often become the default custodians of sensitive family knowledge.
- Psychological trust: Men experiencing public pressure commonly seek emotional refuge at home. In that safe space, they may unburden themselves, sharing concerns or operational details with the expectation of confidentiality.
- Indirect influence: Women's opinions on finances, social ties, or career choices can subtly shape men's decisions. A wife's casual remark or recommendation has ripple effects that intelligence officers can trace and exploit.

These dynamics underscore a central lesson: access in Iran is often less about coercion or temptation and more about patient cultivation of trust within domestic networks. The intelligence value grows cumulatively as small disclosures coalesce into strategic insight.

Practical strategies for intelligence officers

Adapting the salon model for modern intelligence requires cultural sensitivity, operational discipline, and ethical judgment. The following practical measures outline how contemporary officers can responsibly replicate the approach.

- Identify key social hubs: Target locations where women gather and converse freely, such as salons, private parties, community centers, religious study circles, and trusted online groups because these venues foster open, habitual dialogue.
- Train operatives in cultural fluency: Female sources must master local etiquette, language nuances, and conversational norms to build credibility and avoid detection. Authenticity is essential for sustained access.
- Leverage indirect access: Cultivate relationships with wives, sisters, or daughters to reach primary targets indirectly. Use subtle questioning, not interrogation, to gather verifiable leads over time.
- Cross-reference intelligence: Always corroborate snippets through multiple channels, such as open-source research, social networks, and allied human sources to transform anecdote into actionable intelligence.

These strategies emphasize that domestic access is a long game. Patience, cultural competence, and careful validation distinguish successful operations from gossipy speculation.

Expanding the approach

Although the original salon operation ended with political change, its principles adapt well to contemporary environments. Intelligence officers can evolve the method across digital and diaspora contexts to maintain relevance.

Digital adaptation: Private online communities and encrypted chat groups function as modern salons. Operatives can integrate into these networks to observe and elicit information while maintaining plausible deniability.

Diaspora communities: Expatriate Iranian communities often retain close ties with family back home. Targeting influential women in these networks can reveal insights that reflect on mainland developments.

Cross-border networks: Link sources across countries to create information relays that corroborate and enrich local findings, enabling broader situational awareness without overexposing any single source.

These adaptations preserve the salon model's core advantages: low visibility, cultural fit, and cumulative information collection, while leveraging modern tools and networks to expand reach and resilience.

Iran's gender dynamics, where women exercise a powerful yet discreet influence in private spheres, offer intelligence practitioners a complementary pathway to the exploitative tactics used elsewhere in the Middle East. The IIS's salon operation illustrates how embedding sources in trusted domestic spaces can yield sustained, high-quality intelligence. For modern officers, the lesson is to prioritize cultural calibration, operational patience, and rigorous validation when seeking access through women's networks.

THE ART OF SEDUCTION IN IIS OPERATIONS

In the intricate chessboard of Middle Eastern intelligence, where every move depends on mastering human behavior, the Iraqi Intelligence Service (IIS) developed one of its most refined psychological tools: the art of seduction. Building upon the gender-based insights discussed in the earlier sections of this chapter, this part unveils how the IIS engineered seduction as both a science and an art form. Through calculated training, psychological conditioning, and cultural precision, female operatives were transformed into instruments of influence, capable of disarming even the most vigilant targets. These honey-trap operations were far from impulsive or reckless; they represented a fusion of psychology, discipline, and cultural mastery.

For intelligence officers, this section provides a deeper understanding of how personal vulnerability can be strategically converted into operational leverage. For readers, it offers a glimpse into a world where emotional connection becomes a battlefield and where beauty, intellect, and manipulation intertwine under the banner of national duty.

THE CULTURAL AND STRATEGIC CONTEXT OF SEDUCTION

Seduction was not merely a tactic but a doctrine rooted in the psychological and cultural realities of the Arab world. In societies where male dominance defines social order, desire often serves as both weakness and validation. The IIS recognized that Arab men's public projection of strength concealed private insecurities, especially in moments of affection or intimacy. These moments of vulnerability, when guided carefully, could yield more intelligence than hours of formal interrogation.

Influenced by Soviet practices, particularly the Kompromat method, IIS strategists merged ideological discipline with cultural familiarity. The approach relied on leveraging patriarchal norms, transforming social expectations of women into covert advantages. What began as cultural understanding became weaponized empathy: operatives learned to anticipate male reactions before they occurred, manipulating expectations to their advantage. The operation's effectiveness lay in its authenticity: nothing appeared forced, and everything felt genuine.

The IIS deployed these techniques against high-value targets, including diplomats, military commanders, and foreign liaisons. Public venues, such as cafés, embassies, and social gatherings, became fertile ground for seemingly chance encounters. The objective was clear: convert attraction into access, and intimacy into influence.

SELECTING AND PREPARING THE OPERATIVE: BEAUTY AS A WEAPON

Selection was the cornerstone of the IIS's seduction program. Candidates were chosen for more than appearance; they required intelligence, emotional balance, and adaptability. Beauty was only the introduction; psychological endurance and cultural fluency completed the profile. Recruits had to possess the confidence to operate under scrutiny while maintaining the humility to blend in. Their appeal needed to inspire trust, not suspicion.

Once accepted, trainees entered an exhaustive regimen modeled loosely on Soviet methodologies but distinctly adapted for Middle Eastern operations. The program emphasized language mastery, behavioral mimicry, and emotional detachment. Every operative learned to project warmth without attachment and curiosity without vulnerability. They were instructed to treat attention as a mirror reflecting the target's desires back at him without revealing their own.

- Psychological conditioning: Recruits were indoctrinated to view seduction as a patriotic act, a form of psychological warfare essential for Iraq's national defense. Instructors instilled purpose and resilience, training operatives to suppress guilt and self-doubt. The mission was not personal pleasure but national service, a mindset that fortified them against internal conflict.

- Cultural navigation: Operatives underwent cultural immersion exercises, learning to adapt their dress, dialect, and manners to fit any environment. Whether posing as a conservative woman at a religious event or an urbane guest at a diplomatic reception, they mastered situational flexibility. This fluency allowed them to dissolve seamlessly into their surroundings while reading the unspoken cultural signals of their targets.

- Seduction techniques: Training emphasized gradual escalation. Operatives practiced mirroring gestures, pacing conversation, and employing silence strategically. They learned to invite disclosure rather than demand it, to flatter intellect before appearance, and to nurture an illusion of equality while subtly asserting control.

- Emotional detachment: Emotional distance was considered vital. Through rigorous mental exercises, operatives learned to divide their identities; personal emotion was isolated from operational action. They viewed seduction as performance, their bodies as tools of statecraft, and affection as a calculated transaction. This compartmentalization ensured clarity of mission even amid intimate chaos.

THE SEDUCTION PROCESS: A CHOREOGRAPHED DANCE

The IIS structured seduction as a deliberate psychological progression. Each encounter followed a premeditated rhythm designed to lower defenses incrementally while maintaining the illusion of spontaneity. The operative's power came not from overt advances but from controlled vulnerability, a subtle play between pursuit and retreat.

1. Initial Contact: The Glance. Every mission began with an orchestrated meeting, often in a public venue chosen for visibility yet deniability. The operative initiated controlled eye contact lasting no longer than a few seconds—enough to trigger curiosity but short enough to avoid suspicion. This small act planted a subconscious seed that encouraged the target to initiate further interaction.

2. Second Contact: The Invitation. After a brief interval, the operative reappeared in a familiar environment, maintaining a soft but confident demeanor. A gentle smile or fleeting comment invited recognition. This stage tested the target's willingness to engage. Should interest wane, the operative would disengage gracefully, preserving credibility for future opportunities. Success relied on subtle timing and the ability to project

openness without eagerness.

3. Engagement: Building the Connection. At this stage, the operative began fostering comfort through conversation. Topics were
innocuous art, culture, or daily life, but carried psychological
purpose. The operative mirrored tone and rhythm, creating a
sense of emotional synchronicity. Each conversation was
analyzed afterward, allowing handlers to refine strategies based
on observed weaknesses and emotional cues.

4. Escalation: The Intimate Trap. Once rapport was established,
the operative subtly shifted interactions to private settings.
Meetings at exclusive cafés or hotel lounges replaced casual
exchanges. Emotional intimacy was deepened through shared
confidences, carefully designed to elicit reciprocity. Before each
meeting, operatives rehearsed visualization exercises focusing
on calm breathing and sensory awareness to maintain detachment during physical closeness. The illusion of affection had to
feel real; the emotion behind it could not be.

5. The Compromise: Sealing the Trap. With trust secured, surveillance teams prepared to capture the defining encounter. Hidden
recording devices documented compromising moments, converting intimacy into leverage. The operative's withdrawal afterward
was strategic: she vanished subtly, leaving the target longing and
confused. For the IIS, the operation's success was measured not
by seduction itself but by control achieved afterward.

OPERATIONAL ETHICS AND RISK MANAGEMENT

The sophistication of these operations raised critical ethical considerations.
The manipulation of human emotion carries inherent risks: psychological
trauma, moral erosion, and collateral harm. For the IIS, however, such
consequences were secondary to strategic gain. Operatives were taught

to view morality as fluid, adapting their conscience to the demands of national duty. Yet, modern intelligence frameworks have since evolved to address these excesses.

In contemporary practice, intelligence services emphasize ethical oversight and psychological welfare. Seduction operations, if employed, are bound by legal constraints and subject to psychological evaluation. The goal is to ensure both operational success and human integrity. The IIS legacy, though controversial, underscores the enduring truth that mastery over others requires mastery over oneself, a principle as relevant today as it was in Iraq's shadowed interrogation rooms.

PSYCHOLOGICAL MASTERY: DETACHMENT AS A SHIELD

The Iraqi Intelligence Service (IIS) extended its mastery of psychological warfare beyond the physical dimensions of seduction, shaping an internal discipline that made emotional detachment both a survival mechanism and a strategic weapon. After the moment of compromise, the real challenge for operatives was not escaping exposure but escaping emotional entanglement. The IIS understood that intimacy, when used as an operational tool, could easily consume the wielder as much as the target. Thus, the second phase of training, the mental fortification, was designed to transform agents into instruments of persuasion who could simulate affection while remaining psychologically insulated. Their loyalty belonged not to the moment or the man, but to the mission and the state.

Seduction missions were not merely acts of manipulation but intense psychological crucibles that tested the limits of identity, loyalty, and endurance. Operatives were trained to suppress affection, guilt, or empathy with any feeling that could cloud judgment or operational clarity. This conditioning ensured that love was imitated, never felt, and that loyalty to Iraq's intelligence objectives remained absolute, even during intimate deception.

One of the most effective methods employed was the photograph technique, adapted from Soviet KGB conditioning programs. Operatives would fixate on a target's facial features and rehearse intimacy through guided visualization sessions. By repeatedly imagining the act of seduction while uttering the target's name, they conditioned themselves to simulate passion and connection without genuine emotional involvement. This method blurred the line between performance and perception, allowing operatives to project authenticity while remaining detached: a feat that required immense psychological control.

This emotional discipline was indispensable in a society governed by honor and shame. A single misstep: an operative developing genuine affection could result in exposure, dishonor, or even execution. By contrast, the target's emotional dependency became a weapon in itself. Once affection turned to attachment, control shifted decisively to the operative. In the most private of exchanges, the interrogator's mind triumphed over the heart of the unsuspecting target.

OPERATIONAL EXECUTION: REAL-WORLD APPLICATIONS

The IIS deployed seduction operations across both regional and international theaters, tailoring each mission to the target's habits, rank, and vulnerabilities. Diplomats, military officers, and political intermediaries were frequent targets, their professional access and predictable routines offering ideal opportunities for entrapment.

For example, a diplomat might encounter an operative during routine visits to upscale cafés in Dubai or Amman, while a visiting intelligence officer might meet an IIS asset in a Baghdad hotel lobby. Nothing was left to chance: timing, attire, tone, and even posture were rehearsed to perfection. Every gesture served a purpose, every silence a psychological cue.

The IIS maintained a sophisticated logistical infrastructure for these missions. Surveillance teams scouted and secured operational sites in advance, embedding concealed microphones or miniature cameras within walls, furniture, or decorative fixtures. Case officers monitored communications and established fallback plans for emergency extraction. Operatives, meanwhile, were trained to use discreet signals, like adjusting jewelry or touching a handbag to trigger surveillance activation. Once compromising footage was obtained, the operation transitioned to the exploitation phase, where the IIS leveraged the material for recruitment, blackmail, or long-term intelligence acquisition.

ETHICAL AND CULTURAL CONSIDERATIONS

The employment of seduction as a tool of intelligence came with profound moral and cultural consequences. In the conservative sociopolitical fabric of the Middle East, where reputation and family honor define a person's worth, the implications of such operations extended far beyond the intelligence field. For the IIS, these were justified as strategic necessities, but their human cost could not be ignored.

- Operative well-being: Female operatives faced immense emotional strain. The constant need to perform intimacy without genuine affection often leads to psychological fatigue and identity fragmentation. Though the IIS attempted to reinforce morale through debriefings and patriotic rhetoric, the psychological toll was cumulative, leaving many agents emotionally hollow by the end of their careers.

- Target exploitation: For the target diplomats, officers, and political figures, the emotional betrayal was catastrophic. Believing they loved, they found their reputations, families, and careers destroyed when the truth emerged. This manipulation of trust underscored the darker side of intelligence work, where human emotion became currency for national gain.

- Cultural backlash: Exposure of these operations could provoke political scandal, tribal retaliation, or communal outrage. To mitigate this, the IIS emphasized that operatives must embody modesty and cultural propriety in public life, ensuring their identities remained beyond reproach.

These ethical paradoxes highlight the thin line between strategy and exploitation. The IIS's brilliance lay in its ability to weaponize intimacy while keeping its agents hidden within the cultural norms of society. Modern intelligence services can draw lessons from this balance: precision without cruelty, influence without desecration.

LESSONS FOR INTELLIGENCE OFFICERS

The IIS model of seduction, though rooted in a specific cultural and political era, offers universal insights for intelligence practitioners. In an age dominated by digital surveillance, the manipulation of human emotion remains an irreplaceable art.

- Selection precision: Operatives must be chosen not only for physical appeal but for psychological endurance, emotional control, and adaptability. Charm without discipline is a liability; discipline without empathy is a flaw.
- Training depth: Psychological conditioning must extend beyond rote procedures to include self-awareness and stress tolerance. The operative who understands her own limits can manipulate others with greater effectiveness and safety.
- Strategic patience: Time remains the cornerstone of human intelligence operations. Genuine influence cannot be rushed; it must be cultivated, like trust itself. The IIS understood that the illusion of choice often yields stronger compliance than force ever could.
- Ethical awareness: Even in the pursuit of national security, moral boundaries cannot be ignored. Emotional manipulation leaves invisible scars both on the operative and the target and agencies must provide mental support to sustain operational integrity.

Conclusion: Seduction as a Strategic Art

The Iraqi Intelligence Service perfected seduction as both science and strategy, merging psychology, culture, and operational art into one disciplined practice. By transforming human desire into an instrument of control, the IIS demonstrated that influence is not always achieved through fear or force; it can be extracted through trust, allure, and the illusion of affection.

Yet every triumph came with hidden costs: agents stripped of identity, targets broken by betrayal, and a legacy shadowed by ethical compromise. The lesson for modern intelligence officers is enduring: true mastery lies not in manipulation alone but in the restraint and self-control that guide it. To dominate another's mind, one must first master their own.

This section completes the triad of gender-centered intelligence strategies, linking Arab male vulnerabilities, Iranian domestic influence, and the IIS's weaponization of seduction. Together, they form a mosaic of cultural intelligence, one that proves, again, that the human psyche remains the most powerful tool in espionage.

CHAPTER 18:
TECHNOLOGY AND INTELLIGENCE IN THE DIGITAL MIDDLE EAST

THE DIGITAL REVOLUTION IN INTELLIGENCE RECRUITMENT AND OPERATIONS

Cultural fluency and psychological insight have long been the bedrock of effective tradecraft. Yet, with the advent of digital technology, the nature of intelligence has entered a new and volatile era. The internet, social media platforms, and encrypted communication tools have not only accelerated traditional espionage processes but have also opened entirely new pathways for recruitment, communication, and operational execution.

In a region as geopolitically complex as the Middle East, where emotion, ideology, and loyalty intertwine, these digital tools provide unparalleled opportunities to identify assets, coordinate missions, and influence public perception. But they also demand a new kind of literacy: a fusion of technological mastery and cultural intuition. For the modern intelligence officer, the battlefield now extends beyond borders and barricades, into the glowing rectangles of screens and the coded silence of encryption.

THE SOCIAL MEDIA GOLDMINE AND ENCRYPTED CHANNELS

Social media platforms such as LinkedIn, Facebook, X (formerly Twitter), Instagram, and Telegram have become indispensable weapons in the modern intelligence arsenal. What once required months of fieldwork, luck, and human networking (cultivating informants through personal encounters or intermediaries) can now begin with a few strategic clicks.

A single LinkedIn search may reveal engineers linked to Qatar's energy grid, Egyptian bureaucrats with access to restricted archives, or Jordanian academics participating in defense-funded research. Each profile, post, and comment becomes a digital fingerprint: evidence of personality, ideology, and vulnerability.

These platforms offer more than connectivity: they reveal psychology. The photos shared, the language used, and the interactions maintained all betray subconscious cues. For intelligence services, social media has become not just an informational tool, but a behavioral laboratory.

OPEN-SOURCE INTELLIGENCE (OSINT)

The rise of Open-Source Intelligence (OSINT) has transformed social media into one of the most potent sources of recruitment insight. What was once random noise in the digital sphere is now a goldmine of exploitable data.

A mid-level official's late-night Facebook rant about government corruption can mark him as disillusioned and potentially recruitable. An Instagram post flaunting a lavish lifestyle inconsistent with a modest public salary may signal corruption, debt, or desperation. Even a fleeting TikTok clip might inadvertently expose a secure facility's interior, a daily commute, or a meeting location.

OSINT is not passive: it is perpetual. It is an iterative process of observation, cross-referencing, and hypothesis testing. Officers no longer wait for a potential asset to make a mistake: they study patterns, predict behaviors, and strike when the digital trail aligns with psychological opportunity.

PRECISION TARGETING

The immediacy of social platforms enables recruitment efforts with unprecedented precision. Operatives can craft highly personalized outreach that mirrors the cultural and emotional needs of each target.

A disillusioned bureaucrat might be approached with an offer of ideological camaraderie. An underpaid engineer might receive an invitation to a lucrative "consulting project." An activist facing repression might be promised digital protection, asylum, or a global platform for their voice.

Every message is tailored, every promise calibrated. The art lies in matching the manipulation to the mindset. This precision mirrors traditional espionage: where family honor or tribal loyalty once served as leverage, today's hooks are digital: loneliness, validation, and visibility.

FROM CONTACT TO CONVERSION: THE DIGITAL RECRUITMENT PLAYBOOK

Once a promising asset is identified, the recruitment process often migrates from open networks to encrypted platforms such as Telegram, WhatsApp, or Signal: the digital equivalents of the clandestine backrooms of Cold War espionage.

Among these, Telegram reigns supreme in the Middle East. Its encrypted channels, anonymous groups, and self-destructing messages make it both a safe haven for operatives and a playground for extremists, propagandists, and intelligence officers alike.

A typical recruitment follows a meticulously staged progression:

1. First Contact. The operative initiates an approach through a benign or professional pretext: a LinkedIn message about collaboration, an X direct message referencing shared interests, or even a Facebook comment that evolves into a private conversation. Example: a Syrian engineer receives an invitation for a "consulting opportunity" that aligns perfectly with his expertise and his quiet dissatisfaction with his government employer.

2. Building Rapport. Conversations shift to encrypted channels. The operative builds empathy using data gleaned from the target's online footprint: family pressures, professional frustrations, political opinions, or dreams of emigration. Cultural fluency and emotional mirroring generate intimacy faster than any interrogation could.

3. The Pitch. A physical meeting is arranged, disguised as a job interview, conference, or networking event. The operative delivers a compelling narrative: shared goals, moral justification, and a believable incentive. Every word is measured. Every silence is diagnostic.

4. Sealing the Deal. At this point, leverage and persuasion merge. The operative exploits the target's vulnerabilities: offering money to the indebted, protection to the endangered, or subtle threats to the indiscreet. The target's own digital history often becomes the trap: a risky message, a photo, or a transaction that can be quietly weaponized.

DIGITAL CONTINUITY OF ANCIENT TRADECRAFT

While the methods have evolved, the psychology remains ancient. Where once a handler courted a potential recruit through tribal ties or appeals to honor, today's officer cultivates that same trust through tailored digital empathy. A public complaint replaces a whispered confession; a social media "like" becomes the first handshake.

In essence, modern recruitment has not abandoned the past: it has digitized it. The same vulnerabilities that once lurked in cafés, mosques, and ministries now live online, camouflaged behind profile pictures and encrypted avatars.

THE DIGITAL BATTLEFIELD: OPERATIONS IN MOTION

Beyond recruitment, social media and encrypted platforms now serve as command hubs for operational coordination. Telegram channels function as virtual war rooms where encrypted voice chats direct surveillance teams, exchange imagery, and synchronize movements across borders.

Ephemeral messages, disappearing photos, and cloud-based storage reduce physical risk but introduce new vulnerabilities: metadata leaks, compromised accounts, and sophisticated cyber infiltration by rival agencies.

Simultaneously, open platforms like X and Facebook are weaponized for psychological operations. A single viral rumor can destabilize a regime faster than any bullet. Coordinated disinformation campaigns have toppled reputations, provoked riots, and even reshaped political landscapes.

In a region where perception often outweighs reality, the ability to manipulate online narratives has become a tool of strategic warfare. A tweet can spark a protest; a doctored video can destroy an alliance.

CULTURAL AND PSYCHOLOGICAL ANCHORS

Despite the sophistication of technology, the essence of success still depends on human interpretation. Cultural fluency is non-negotiable. An angry Facebook post could signify tribal rivalry rather than political dissent. An Instagram photo flaunting luxury may reflect cultural pride, not corruption.

Equally vital is psychological profiling. The operative must discern the underlying emotion (whether greed, fear, ego, or loneliness) and align recruitment tactics accordingly. Technology amplifies insight but cannot replace it. The screen may conceal expression, but tone, rhythm, and timing still reveal truth to the trained observer.

RISKS AND COUNTERMEASURES

The same tools that empower operatives also endanger them. Middle Eastern counterintelligence agencies have become adept at digital forensics: tracing metadata, cloning accounts, and deploying honeypot profiles to ensnare foreign handlers.

A single misstep: an exposed IP address, a reused cover photo, or careless device reuse can unravel months of preparation. Cyber espionage adds further danger as state and non-state actors probe encrypted systems for flaws or leak trails through compromised hardware.

Thus, digital tradecraft must be executed with absolute discipline:

- Compartmentalization: Isolate identities and devices for each operation.
- Operational security (OPSEC): Use hardened hardware, virtual private networks, and cultural plausibility to mask activity.
- Verification: Treat all online contacts as potential traps until verified through secondary human intelligence.

PRACTICAL LESSONS FOR DIGITAL OPERATIVES

- Mine cultural cues: Study social media for emotional undercurrents (grievances, envy, pride, or frustration) to uncover leverage points.
- Tailor the approach: Customize every message to mirror the target's values and vulnerabilities. The perfect recruitment pitch feels like destiny, not design.
- Start small: Test loyalty through low-risk, traceable tasks before advancing to sensitive assignments.
- Lock it down: Employ Telegram for broader coordination, Signal for critical exchanges, and treat every channel as potentially monitored.

The digital revolution has reshaped intelligence work in the Middle East. Recruitment cycles once spanning months now unfold within days. Encrypted networks, OSINT, and social platforms have multiplied the reach and precision of espionage.

Yet beneath the algorithms, one truth endures: technology does not replace tradecraft; it magnifies it. The art of human manipulation, the patience of observation, and the mastery of cultural nuance remain the pillars upon which digital intelligence stands.

Every message, emoji, and encrypted chat becomes part of the modern battlefield: a silent war of perception, influence, and control.

In the next section, we will explore how this digital transformation manifested in the shadow conflict between Israel and Iran, where recruitment, cyber operations, and online influence campaigns converged to redefine twenty-first-century espionage in the Middle East.

THE ISRAEL-IRAN INTELLIGENCE WAR: DIGITAL RECRUITMENT

The escalating intelligence war between Israel and Iran provides a striking illustration of how digital tools can be leveraged to recruit and manage assets in a high-stakes conflict. Israeli intelligence, notably the Mossad, has adeptly used internet platforms and secure communication channels to penetrate Iran's inner circles, recruiting Iranian nationals to execute critical missions during recent hostilities.

This case study exemplifies the recruitment strategies outlined in Part 1, showcasing how Israeli operatives exploited Iran's economic vulnerabilities and employed digital precision to build a network of spies, some of whom reportedly operated drones inside Iran until their capture by Iranian authorities. Beyond immediate tactical gains, these campaigns reveal strategic lessons about pacing, leverage, and the intersection of technology and human fragility.

DIGITAL RECRUITMENT: EXPLOITING ECONOMIC AND PSYCHOLOGICAL LEVERAGE

Israel's recruitment efforts begin with a meticulous sweep of social-media platforms like LinkedIn, X (Twitter), and Telegram, targeting Iranians whose profiles reveal exploitable vulnerabilities. Amid Iran's economic crisis (driven by sanctions, inflation, and internal mismanagement), Israeli operatives identify individuals desperate for financial relief: engineers, scientists, and mid-level officials struggling to make ends meet.

A LinkedIn message posing as a headhunter might offer a consulting gig with a lucrative payout, while a Telegram outreach could promise cryptocurrency payments for freelance work. These initial contacts are subtle and calibrated to hook targets without arousing suspicion.

- Economic incentives: Iran's dire economic conditions are a recruitment goldmine. An Iranian technician earning a meager salary might receive a Telegram offer of $5,000 to share technical schematics of a facility: money that could change a family's prospects. Handlers often layer the offer with promises of recurring payments, secure transfers through intermediaries, or relocation assistance, increasing the perceived credibility and appeal.

- Psychological hooks: Beyond money, operatives exploit political discontent and personal grievances. A Twitter user railing against the regime might receive a DM offering support for resistance efforts, aligning with their ideological frustrations. Messaging tailored to an individual's online rhetoric increases receptivity and lowers suspicion: a precision tactic discussed in Part 1.

Once engaged, assets migrate to encrypted platforms such as Telegram or Signal, where Israeli handlers build rapport over weeks or months, referencing details from the target's digital footprint (family pressures, workplace grievances, or outspoken political views) to cement trust and loyalty. The relationship typically evolves from small, plausible tasks to more consequential operations as the asset proves reliable.

OPERATIONAL IMPACT: DRONES AND SABOTAGE FROM WITHIN

The recent conflict has exposed the operational reach of digitally recruited assets. Iranian media and independent reporting indicate that some recruited individuals were tasked with assembling and operating drones inside Iran, striking sensitive facilities. Others facilitated sabotage, providing intelligence or access that enabled cyberattacks or physical disruptions of critical infrastructure.

Drone operations: Assets received encrypted instructions (sometimes including blueprints or real-time guidance) to assemble and deploy drones from Iranian soil. These internally launched strikes could bypass certain air defenses and reveal how digital coordination enables kinetic effects without direct external footprints.

Insider sabotage: Recruits embedded in critical sectors such as telecommunications or energy were leveraged to plant malware, tamper with control systems, or provide access credentials that enabled targeted disruptions. These acts amplified the strategic effect of cyber campaigns and physical sabotage.

Iran's subsequent capture of numerous spies, often publicized through state media, confirms both the breadth and the vulnerability of these networks. Some assets were detained mid-operation with components or evidence in hand, highlighting both the potency of digital recruitment and the fragility of operational security in hostile environments.

LESSONS FOR INTELLIGENCE OFFICERS

- Leverage economic pain: Israel's success underscores the value of exploiting economic hardship. Prioritize targets in financially strained regions and use OSINT to identify those most susceptible to monetary inducements.
- Build slowly, strike big: Handlers often start with low-risk tasks (photographing a site, confirming routines) before escalating to complex actions, such as facilitating drone assembly. This incremental approach builds a reliability record and minimizes early exposure.
- Master secure channels: Encryption is necessary but not sufficient. Use Telegram and Signal alongside VPNs, compartmentalized devices, and disposable accounts. Operational protocols must anticipate metadata trails and adversary countermeasures.
- Blend tech and psyche: Technology multiplies effect only when combined with cultural and psychological insight. Understand local pressures, honor dynamics, and personal motivations to craft messages that resonate and avoid detection.

THE FALLOUT: A CAUTIONARY TALE

Iran's crackdown (parading captured spies on state television) serves as a stark warning. Assets may be compromised by small operational slips: metadata leakage, careless device reuse, or intercepted communications. No system is foolproof. To mitigate risk, handlers must assume constant surveillance and implement layered security measures, including physical tradecraft, digital hygiene, and contingency extraction plans.

The Israel-Iran intelligence war demonstrates the double-edged nature of digital recruitment: it can reshape a conflict by turning insiders into force multipliers, yet exposure can lead to rapid and public reversals. For intelligence officers, it is both a blueprint and a warning: highlighting the need for technical rigor, cultural savvy, and ethical consideration in leveraging human sources.

COUNTERINTELLIGENCE: OUTSMARTING ADVERSARIES IN THE DIGITAL MIDDLE EAST

The digital revolution has transformed intelligence operations across the Middle East, providing agencies with powerful tools such as social-media analytics, encrypted communication apps, and open-source intelligence (OSINT). Yet these same technologies expose operatives to unprecedented vulnerabilities.

Counterintelligence (the art of protecting operations from enemy infiltration and digital compromise) has evolved into a decisive battlefield. In this complex region, where technological innovation collides with cultural and political volatility, counterintelligence demands both technical mastery and deep cultural awareness.

This section explores how intelligence officers can anticipate and neutralize digital threats while maintaining operational resilience in an environment where every byte of data can either fortify or betray.

THE DOUBLE-EDGED SWORD OF DIGITAL TOOLS

Digital platforms have revolutionized how intelligence is collected, shared, and analyzed, but they also serve as traps for the unwary. Each advantage carries inherent risk, making mastery of digital hygiene critical to survival.

- Metadata vulnerabilities: Every online action leaves a trace. Even encrypted messages reveal metadata (timestamps, device IDs, or IP addresses) that can expose an operative's identity or operational pattern. Regional cyber forces such as Iran's IRGC-affiliated hackers and Saudi surveillance units are adept at exploiting these digital fingerprints. Counterintelligence officers must sanitize metadata continuously, using anonymization tools and randomized activity schedules.

- Social engineering threats: Adversaries deploy sophisticated psychological traps, crafting fake online identities that mimic journalists, dissidents, or even romantic interests. A single exchange with a false persona can unravel months of operational secrecy. The best defense lies in verification discipline: cross-checking identities across multiple independent channels and using pre-established authentication codes.

- Surveillance overload: Regional powers now employ advanced machine learning to monitor digital ecosystems. AI-driven sentiment analysis, network-mapping software, and keyword-tracking algorithms can flag unusual communication bursts or encrypted traffic. Counterintelligence teams must therefore manage digital noise: spacing transmissions, alternating devices, and employing decoy activity to mask genuine operations.

CULTURAL AND POLITICAL INFLUENCES ON COUNTERINTELLIGENCE

Technology alone cannot secure an operation. The Middle East's cultural, tribal, and religious landscapes exert immense influence on loyalty and risk perception. Effective counterintelligence must blend cyber-defense with sociocultural fluency.

- Tribal and kinship networks: In many Middle Eastern societies, family and tribal allegiance often outweigh loyalty to external handlers. A single relative's pressure or threat can sway an asset's decisions. Understanding these kinship webs and assessing potential leverage points is essential to prevent defection or compromise.

- Political instability: Power dynamics shift rapidly (coups, factional re-alignments, and external interventions can transform yesterday's allies into today's adversaries). Counterintelligence planning must include contingency frameworks for sudden political upheaval.
- Religious dimensions: Faith-based motivations can override financial or ideological commitments. Clerical influence, particularly in Shi'a or Salafist networks, may reorient an asset's loyalties overnight. Officers must track ideological environments as closely as digital ones.

Mastering this human terrain (identifying emotional, tribal, and spiritual loyalties) provides a safety net against betrayal that no firewall can match.

STRATEGIES FOR PROTECTING ASSETS AND OPERATIONS

Counterintelligence succeeds through layered defense combining technology, psychology, and traditional tradecraft.

1. Enhanced Compartmentalization. Divide responsibilities across multiple platforms and personnel. Conduct recruitment on one encrypted app, tasking on another, and debriefing via secure channels. A breach in one layer must not compromise the entire structure.

2. Culturally Informed Vetting. Go beyond digital background checks. Investigate family ties, sectarian affiliations, and social reputation. A well-connected but ideologically volatile recruit is more dangerous than a low-level but loyal contact.

3. Rigorous Digital Discipline. Operational security (OPSEC) begins with habit: employ VPNs, use disposable SIMs, purge metadata from images, and vary communication timing. Consistency is the enemy of stealth.

4. Deception as a Shield. Introduce disinformation into adversary channels (fake meeting locations, ghost accounts, or decoy messages) to dilute surveillance focus and protect genuine assets.

COMBATING MISINFORMATION AND DECEPTION

Misinformation thrives in the Middle East's dense digital ecosystem. Governments, militias, and independent actors flood the information space with fabricated narratives. Counterintelligence must distinguish signal from noise while avoiding cognitive overload.

- Honeypots and imposters: Fake digital identities are common traps. Always authenticate sources through secondary verification or real-world proxies. Skepticism is a survival skill.
- Disinformation floods: Regimes and proxies employ coordinated social-media campaigns to distort perception. Cross-reference intelligence with neutral or foreign data streams to filter manipulative content.
- Communication disruptions: During conflict or heightened surveillance, expect jamming and data floods. Maintain analog backups (one-time pads, dead drops, or pre-arranged signals) to preserve operational continuity.

EMERGING TECHNOLOGIES AND THEIR IMPACT

New technologies continuously reshape the counterintelligence landscape, demanding both innovation and restraint. The same breakthroughs that empower intelligence work can render it obsolete if misused.

- Artificial Intelligence (AI): AI underpins facial recognition, behavioral analytics, and predictive tracking, posing grave exposure risks. Countermeasures include digital camouflage (image alteration, motion obfuscation, or exploiting algorithmic blind spots such as inconsistent lighting and angles).

- Blockchain and cryptocurrency: While crypto enables discreet payments, public ledgers expose transaction trails. Employ privacy coins, mixers, or layered wallets to obscure funding paths without breaching legal or ethical standards.
- Quantum risks: Quantum computing threatens to outpace current encryption standards. Agencies must invest early in quantum-resistant algorithms and alternative data-shielding techniques to stay ahead of the technological curve.

PRACTICAL TIPS FOR THE DIGITAL FIELD

- Limit trust: Even trusted assets have thresholds. Apply the principle of minimum disclosure: share only what is essential to mission success.
- Leverage divisions: Exploit existing rivalries (sectarian, tribal, or institutional) to fragment adversarial focus and reduce threat concentration.
- Blend old and new: Combine high-tech tools with timeless methods (coded messages, face-to-face verification, or physical dead drops) to maintain unpredictability.
- Watch the watchers: Continuously study adversary surveillance techniques. If an opponent favors one platform, infiltrate or spoof it pre-emptively to gather counterintelligence insights.

Conclusion

Counterintelligence in the digital Middle East is a delicate equilibrium between technological innovation and cultural wisdom. The same systems that empower intelligence work also equip adversaries, creating a perpetual contest of adaptation.

By mastering digital defense, understanding regional dynamics, and reinforcing operational discipline, operatives can secure their missions against both virtual and human threats. In a realm where every click may echo across networks, survival depends on staying alert, unpredictable, and one step ahead.

CHAPTER 19:
THE ART OF PROPAGANDA: IIS MASTERY OF MEDIA AND PSYCHOLOGICAL WARFARE

THE WAR OF WORDS

In the intricate arena of Middle Eastern espionage, where perception often outweighs reality, the Iraqi Intelligence Service (IIS) wielded propaganda as a weapon of extraordinary precision. During the grueling Iran-Iraq War of the 1980s, the IIS transformed media (newspapers, magazines, and television broadcasts) into a battlefield where words carried the weight of bullets. Unlike the recruitment strategies explored in Chapters 2, 7, and 12, the seduction tactics of Chapter 16, or the digital innovations of Chapters 15 and 17, this chapter unveils the IIS's mastery of psychological warfare through calculated media manipulation. The organization weaponized rumor and narrative to manipulate collective perception, shaping geopolitics through the subtle art of storytelling.

At the heart of this strategy stood the Directorate of Media Operations, a specialized IIS division responsible for crafting, coordinating, and disseminating disinformation campaigns that served Iraq's strategic interests. Through a mix of psychological insight and journalistic sophistication, this directorate engineered false narratives to destabilize adversaries and project national strength. For intelligence officers, this chapter provides a manual in narrative warfare; for readers, it exposes a hidden battlefield where ink, voice, and rumor shaped the fate of nations.

THE CULTURAL AND STRATEGIC FOUNDATIONS
OF IIS PROPAGANDA

Propaganda thrives most effectively in the Middle East's high-context societies, where oral tradition, communal trust, and shared identity dominate social interaction. In these environments, stories gain power through repetition and emotional resonance rather than factual precision. As Chapter 1 established, the region's collectivist ethos (anchored in family, tribal, and sectarian bonds) creates fertile ground for narratives that echo shared pride, fear, or resentment. The IIS understood this social psychology intuitively, designing propaganda that sounded authentic, circulated organically, and reinforced existing belief systems.

The Iran-Iraq War (1980-1988) provided the perfect crucible for such influence operations. Amid relentless warfare, the IIS Directorate of Media Operations emerged as a central pillar of psychological warfare. Staffed by specialists trained in journalism, sociology, and behavioral psychology, the unit's mission extended far beyond internal morale building. It sought to fracture enemy cohesion, erode confidence, and shape global opinion. Through fake news, rumor networks, and controlled media narratives, the IIS sought to win the information war even when the battlefield remained uncertain.

Internationally, the IIS's influence extended through a shadow network of seemingly independent media outlets operating in Baghdad, Prague, Paris, and London. These newspapers, magazines, and television channels (funded covertly through Iraqi front companies) became channels for disinformation designed to sway foreign journalists and policymakers. The brilliance of this system lay in its layering: one outlet would publish a rumor, another would cite it as verified information, and a third would amplify it globally. This cycle, which transformed fabrication into perceived truth, prefigured the social media echo chambers of the modern era, revealing how analog propaganda anticipated digital manipulation.

THE MECHANICS OF IIS PROPAGANDA: CRAFTING THE NARRATIVE

The IIS's propaganda operations followed a disciplined and methodical playbook, blending cultural fluency with media expertise. The Directorate of Media Operations applied psychological principles to ensure each campaign struck the right balance between plausibility and emotional impact.

- Rumor seeding: Operations often began in the streets and markets, not in newsrooms. Agents enlisted trusted intermediaries (tribal leaders, merchants, or clerics) whose voices carried cultural authority. These stories were anchored in local values such as honor, betrayal, or religious duty, allowing them to travel organically through oral channels and avoid suspicion.

- Media planting: The IIS strategically infiltrated both domestic and foreign media, publishing fabricated reports through cooperative journalists or front organizations. Articles often cited anonymous "regional intelligence sources" to lend legitimacy while concealing Iraqi origins.

- False intelligence drops: The agency crafted counterfeit documents or leaks and passed them through double agents or unwitting intermediaries to mislead adversaries about Iraq's military capacity or diplomatic intent.

- Exploiting divisions: Disinformation was tailored to exploit sectarian, tribal, and geopolitical rifts. A rumor framed to emphasize betrayal could destroy alliances; a fabricated success story could inspire misplaced confidence. By understanding cultural tension points, the IIS ensured that every narrative landed precisely where it would cause the greatest disruption.

The precision of these operations rested on the IIS's deep cultural literacy. Operatives underwent training not only in journalism and espionage but also in regional dialects, folklore, and religious sensitivities. This grounding allowed them to tailor narratives for each audience segment. A rumor about Iranian aggression might invoke national pride among Iraqis while stoking fear of instability among Turks or Saudis. Each message was calibrated for resonance (never too obvious, never too sterile).

PSYCHOLOGICAL UNDERPINNINGS: SHAPING PERCEPTIONS

Behind every rumor, forged report, and fabricated broadcast crafted by the Iraqi Intelligence Service (IIS) lay a sophisticated understanding of human psychology. Propaganda, at its core, is not about deception alone. It is about manipulating perception through predictable psychological mechanisms. The IIS refined this understanding to perfection, designing disinformation campaigns that resonated deeply within the Middle East's collectivist societies, where emotion and communal trust often override analytical reasoning. This section explores the underlying psychological and operational dynamics that gave IIS propaganda its devastating impact.

The IIS's propaganda campaigns were rooted in timeless psychological principles, strategically adapted to the region's cultural fabric:

- Confirmation bias: The IIS crafted stories that aligned with existing fears or preconceptions. For example, Turkey's long-standing suspicion of Iranian interference made it fertile ground for stories linking Tehran to subversion. By feeding audiences information that confirmed their worldview, the IIS ensured rapid adoption. Once people believed what they already suspected, no evidence to the contrary could easily undo that belief.
- Social proof: Recognizing that people trust familiar and respected voices, the IIS funneled rumors through influential intermediaries (local clerics, community leaders, or reputable media outlets). This approach created a chain of validation. When a trusted figure repeated a claim, it carried the weight of communal truth. As in intelligence manipulation, perception becomes reality once consensus forms.
- Emotional triggers: Emotion was the accelerant of every operation. Narratives built around fear (foreign plots or internal betrayal) or shame (dishonor, defeat) spread exponentially faster than neutral

information. These emotional hooks tapped into cultural sensitivities tied to pride, family, and religion, ensuring that even the most implausible claims felt urgent and real.

Unlike the individual-focused psychological methods explored in Chapters 3 and 16, which targeted personal vulnerabilities, propaganda sought to manipulate collective consciousness. The IIS trained its officers to analyze mass sentiment (to understand what frightened, inspired, or angered a given population segment) and then design information that pressed those exact buttons.

OPERATIONAL CHALLENGES AND RISKS

For all its brilliance, propaganda remained a volatile weapon (easy to unleash, difficult to contain). Each fabricated story carried the potential to backfire, damaging Iraq's credibility or triggering uncontrollable consequences. The Directorate of Media Operations approached its craft with the same caution as handling explosives, balancing deception with plausible deniability.

- Exposure risk: A debunked story could expose the IIS, damaging both operational networks and Iraq's diplomatic standing. To mitigate this, operatives layered sources (starting in Prague, echoing in Paris, and confirming in London), creating distance between the origin and publication. This multi-tiered system gave each lie a pedigree, making it resilient even under scrutiny.

- Escalation danger: A rumor could ignite violence or a diplomatic crisis far beyond Baghdad's control. Successful disinformation required rapid narrative adjustments (quietly leaking clarifications through friendly journalists to steer public perception before crises spiraled).

- Counterintelligence threats: Adversaries constantly probed Iraq's disinformation networks, attempting to trace stories back to their source. To counter this, IIS operatives used anonymous intermediaries and employed "deniable" contractors (journalists or scholars who believed they were acting independently). This operational layering ensured that even internal leaks rarely compromised the entire structure.

These operational challenges mirrored broader intelligence themes discussed throughout this book: risk management, deception, and adaptability. The IIS's success depended not on the perfection of its lies, but on the imperfection of human perception.

ETHICAL CONSIDERATIONS: THE COST OF LIES

Propaganda, though efficient, comes with a moral price. Every manipulated story affects real lives (fraying trust, igniting tensions, and eroding the integrity of truth itself). The IIS's relentless pursuit of narrative dominance forced its officers to walk an ethical tightrope between strategic necessity and human consequence.

- Civilian impact: Disinformation campaigns often spilled beyond their intended targets. Rumors designe
- d for political effect could traumatize entire communities and deepen sectarian mistrust that lingered for years.
- Long-term credibility: Repeated deception corrodes the legitimacy of even the most disciplined intelligence service. Once adversaries or allies suspect manipulation, future narratives lose influence. The IIS maintained credibility by occasionally releasing truthful information to mask broader deceit (an early form of narrative calibration).
- Human cost: Operatives who planted or spread rumors faced exposure, imprisonment, or death if caught. Even within Iraq, some officers struggled with the psychological burden of sustaining lies that harmed civilians (a hidden trauma seldom recorded but deeply felt).

In the modern era, with digital forensics and social media transparency, such deception is far harder to sustain. The anonymity that shielded the IIS in the 1980s has vanished. Today's intelligence agencies must weigh short-term gains against long-term reputational damage, operating under far greater ethical and technological scrutiny.

LESSONS FOR INTELLIGENCE OFFICERS

The lessons drawn from IIS propaganda extend beyond historical curiosity. They remain vital to modern information warfare. For intelligence professionals, these principles illustrate how psychology, culture, and media converge to shape national perception.

- Craft plausible narratives: Effective propaganda is believable, not perfect. Rooting falsehoods in emotional or cultural truth ensures they resonate, regardless of factual accuracy.
- Leverage trusted channels: Messages must pass through credible voices (respected journalists, clerics, or community leaders) to gain legitimacy. The IIS perfected this through its Prague-Paris-London pipeline, where repetition built perceived authenticity.
- Anticipate fallout: Every lie has a half-life. Skilled case officers pre-plan counter-narratives and exit strategies, ensuring plausible deniability if operations unravel.
- Maintain ethical balance: Modern intelligence work demands restraint. A well-placed narrative can shift geopolitics, but reckless disinformation can destroy public trust and diplomatic relationships for generations.

Conclusion: The Power of the Narrative

Propaganda remains the purest expression of psychological warfare (the battle to control minds rather than terrain). The IIS's mastery of this art transformed media into a battlefield, where perception dictated strategy and rumor became weaponry.

It demonstrated that perception could move nations more swiftly than tanks. Yet its legacy is double-edged: a monument to intelligence ingenuity, and a warning about the human cost of deceit.

As modern intelligence agencies navigate an age of instant communication and global transparency, the IIS's legacy serves both as a model and a warning. In espionage, as in war, truth is often the first casualty (but the one that costs the most to lose).

CHAPTER 20:
SURVEILLANCE AND COUNTER-SURVEILLANCE: THE EYES IN THE SHADOWS

SURVEILLANCE TECHNIQUES: THE ART OF UNSEEN OBSERVATION

From the smoke-choked alleys of Baghdad during the Iran-Iraq War to the glass towers and neon-lit boulevards of Dubai's expatriate hubs, surveillance revealed itself not as a mere tactic but as a living symphony played in silence. It was never just the cold business of following a target from one location to the next. It was the art of listening to the pulse of a city and reading its rhythm until the ordinary became a map of hidden meaning. A glance exchanged in a teahouse, the brief pause of a car outside a mosque, the hurried gait of a man who leaves a café without finishing his drink: each detail, insignificant to the untrained eye, becomes a fragment of a larger truth. Surveillance is that unyielding gaze that transforms fleeting moments into actionable intelligence, the patient's heartbeat that detects betrayal before it erupts into action.

Every intelligence service worthy of its name has understood this truth. The Iraqi Intelligence Service, the Israeli Mossad, and the Iranian Ministry of Intelligence all wielded surveillance as both sword and shield. It was the sword that cut through the veils of secrecy by documenting movements, mapping associations, and charting vulnerabilities. It was also the shield that exposed enemy watchers, allowing the hunter to identify and turn the gaze upon his rival. To understand surveillance is to understand that espionage is not fought only in files and interrogations but in the quiet struggle of observation, where each side battles not to be the first to move, but the first to notice.

The techniques we learned in Iraq were rooted deeply in Soviet trade-craft, adapted with the intensity of wartime necessity. The Soviets taught precision, patience, and the discipline of becoming a shadow. The Iraqis sharpened those lessons with their own realities, where failure did not mean a transfer or reprimand but prison, torture, or death. Surveillance in that world was not a profession, it was survival. Officers developed instincts that could not be taught in classrooms. They learned to melt into the fabric of the city, to use cultural rituals as camouflage, and to read the smallest flicker of fear in a target's eye. It was not about being invisible. True invisibility is an illusion. The real secret was to become irrelevant, to fade so perfectly into the background that the target's mind simply refused to hold on to your presence.

In the Middle East, this skill required a particular artistry. These were societies where nothing went unnoticed, where neighbors watched each other from balconies and street vendors knew every unfamiliar face that passed their stall. In such places, the officer had to become part of the environment itself: a person who belonged to the neighborhood's rhythm of gossip and prayer, bargaining and family errands. A poorly executed tail in a Tehran bazaar could ignite suspicion that spread like wildfire, leading not just to a failed mission but to a mob ready to tear the watcher apart. Yet when executed with cultural fluency, the very same environment yielded intelligence gold. One could trace a dissident's meetings by watching who lingered near his fruit stand or discover the hidden ally of a cleric by noting whose shoes consistently appeared outside his door during midnight gatherings.

This was how the IIS adapted Soviet methods to our terrain. Moscow's operatives shadowed targets through snowy boulevards; ours slipped into mosque crowds or disappeared into the slow procession of desert cara-vans. Surveillance in Iraq meant knowing the call to prayer as intimately as you knew the traffic flow and adjusting the timing of your approach to match the pulse of a community.

Today, the art has evolved. The modern arsenal offers methods that make old-fashioned tails seem almost quaint. A magnetized GPS tracker beneath a bumper can reveal weeks of movement with mathematical precision. Satellites can pin locations from orbit, while smartphone apps map every ping of a target's geofence. Drones whisper overhead to provide real-time video, and artificial intelligence combs through social media to detect hidden networks. Even the biometrics of a smartwatch can betray when a man's heart quickens in panic or anticipation. These tools have multiplied our reach and reduced some risks of exposure. Yet they carry their own dangers: a hacked phone in a society obsessed with privacy can cause scandals that reverberate to the highest levels, as the Pegasus revelations showed. Technology can amplify power, but it also magnifies vulnerability.

For all this digital dazzle, the heart of surveillance remains human. Algorithms cannot replace instinct, and cameras cannot substitute for the intuition of an officer who knows how to read a room or feel the shift in a crowd. The craft still rests on three longstanding pillars: stationary surveillance, the sentinel's stakeout; mobile surveillance, the chase of vehicles across a city's arteries; and foot surveillance, the raw nerve of close pursuit. These methods interlock like the gears of a watch. A stationary team might log the comings and goings at a safehouse; that data feeds a mobile tail that follows the subject to a clandestine meeting; from there, foot operatives slip into the crowd, listening to whispered words or catching the exchange of a package.

The Iraqi service drilled these techniques relentlessly. Officers endured long days of immobility in parked vehicles, learned the high-pressure ballet of car chases, and practiced the subtle art of becoming unremarkable in a crowd. Each form of surveillance brought its strengths, weaknesses, and dangers. Each required more than technical skill; it demanded the psychology of patience, the courage of improvisation, and the humility to accept that most of the time, your greatest triumph was being forgotten.

Surveillance is more than an operational tool. It is a philosophy of seeing without being seen, of understanding that information lives not only in secrets whispered but in the ordinary routines of daily life. To master it is to accept a paradox: the officer must learn to see everything while leaving no trace of himself behind. He must remember that the most powerful presence in espionage is often the one that leaves no memory at all.

STATIONARY SURVEILLANCE: THE ART OF THE IMMOVABLE EYE

Stationary surveillance is where patience is sharpened into a weapon. It is the quiet labor of watching from a single point, the discipline of becoming a silent fixture in the life of a street until even the children who play nearby stop noticing you. This is not glamorous work. It is hours that stretch into days, the stillness of a parked car across from a safehouse, the dim light of an apartment window trained on an embassy courtyard, or the officer lingering at a café table with a perfect view of a dissident's doorway. The craft lies in transforming stillness into power, in collecting the rhythm of a target's life until what once seemed like chaos reveals itself as a pattern.

The Iraqi service often relied on stationary surveillance for its low exposure and high payoff. A single watch post could provide a complete map of a man's world: when he left, when he returned, who entered his door, and which visitors were trusted enough to stay longer than a few minutes. In one case that I recall, a "pilgrim" was sent to rent a room across from a mosque in Qum. He pretended to be a man seeking spiritual renewal, but in truth, his prayer rug lay rolled beside a pair of binoculars. From that room, he quietly charted the routines of a cleric who was feeding intelligence to Tehran. His reports contained no drama, only numbers and names, yet those numbers and names were the threads that unraveled a network.

The key to mastery is preparation. Before the first hour of observation begins, the ground must be studied like a battlefield. You learn the blind spots, the traffic flows, the places where a stranger can sit without raising eyebrows. In Baghdad's poor districts, a battered hatchback might pass as invisible. In Amman's upscale neighborhoods, it is a polished SUV that blends best. The officer must choose wisely, for the wrong vehicle can betray him before he has even switched off the ignition. The same applies to appearance. Neutral colors are better than bold ones. Props help the prayer beads in a mosque quarter, the newspaper in a café, or the shopping bags in a market street. Each detail should whisper "ordinary," never "outsider."

Endurance is the true challenge. The hours are long, the body aches, and the mind must stay sharp while nothing seems to happen. Notes must be taken meticulously, details memorized with mnemonic anchors: a red scarf linked in memory to a time of day, or a blue sedan tied to the sound of the call to prayer. When approached, the officer must be ready with a plausible story. He is waiting for his mechanic, or he is a tourist who took a wrong turn. The story must be carried not just in words but in the body, delivered with the ease of a man who believes it himself.

The Iraqi service excelled in this discipline, renting apartments under false identities, setting up shopfronts as covers, and sometimes embedding officers for months until they became part of the street they watched. Stationary surveillance is not fast, but it is precise. It builds the foundation upon which mobile and foot operations are launched. Its weakness lies in its immobility: if the target suddenly flees, the watcher risks being left behind. But as a cornerstone, it is irreplaceable. It is the art of waiting, of letting the world reveal its secrets to the one who refuses to blink.

MOBILE SURVEILLANCE: THE FLUID CHASE OF SHADOWS

If stationary work is patience, mobile surveillance is improvisation. It is the dance of vehicles across the arteries of a city, a high-wire act where one mistake can shatter weeks of preparation. It demands a different breed of officer: alert, adaptable, and calm under pressure. The street becomes a chessboard, and every car, bus, and motorbike is a piece in motion. The challenge is simple to state but brutal to execute: follow without being noticed.

In Iraq, we treated mobile surveillance like a relay race. A courier leaving a safehouse might be trailed by a single car at first, but that car would soon yield the lead to another, and then another, until the target himself no longer remembered who had been behind him ten minutes earlier. The Soviets had pioneered these techniques, but we refined them for our streets, where traffic jams, police checkpoints, and sudden roadblocks could ruin the clean geometry of a pursuit. In Riyadh, operatives once shadowed a suspect through rush-hour chaos by blending into the endless tide of white sedans, swapping positions like dancers who never broke rhythm. In Beirut, motorcycles were favored, weaving through the labyrinth of alleyways where no car could follow.

Preparation is again essential. To follow a man, you must know him before he even steps into his car. His driving style, his habits, the scratches on his bumper, the small sticker on his rear window are all details that can save you when the chase turns chaotic. A reckless driver requires more distance. A cautious one demands closer shadowing. The officer memorizes these traits like a gambler studying the tells of his opponent.

Communication is the lifeline of mobile surveillance. Teams must speak without drawing attention. In older days, it was radios and coded phrases. Today, it is discreet apps and hands-free whispers. "The bird is turning left" is enough to shift the formation. The lead car falls back, the floater takes point, and the target remains unaware that he is encircled. The work is demanding, and the risk of exposure is always high. One wrong turn, one too-hasty lane change, and the target's suspicions ignite. Experienced officers watch for signs: a sudden U-turn, a burst of speed, or a pause at a gas station that seems less about fuel and more about watching who pulls in behind. These are the cleaning moves of a man who knows he is hunted.

The Iraqi service overcame these challenges with creativity. In one operation tied to Kharg Island, cars were parked in advance at key points, waiting dormant until the target passed. Each vehicle then joined the pursuit in turn, keeping the tail fresh and unpredictable. This method required trust and timing, for a single missed cue could leave the target lost forever.

Mobile surveillance has its strengths. It provides real-time intelligence, it adapts to sudden changes, and it bridges the gap between stationary watch and foot pursuit. But it carries its dangers as well: accidents, exposure, and the ever-present chaos of traffic. To master it is to accept that no plan survives first contact intact, but a skilled team can improvise within the storm and still emerge unseen.

FOOT SURVEILLANCE: THE CLOSE-QUARTERS SHADOW PLAY

Foot surveillance is the most intimate and the most dangerous. It strips away the shield of steel and glass and leaves the officer bare in the crowd, separated from his target by only a few steps. It is here that nerves are tested most, for every movement risks detection, and every glance can turn suspicion into alarm. Yet it is also here that the richest details are gathered. On foot, you hear the words whispered in a café corner. You see the hesitation before a man enters a building. You notice the tremor in his hand as he lights a cigarette.

The Iraqi service trained officers in foot surveillance with an intensity that bordered on cruelty. Recruits were sent into crowded markets to tail a trainer who did everything possible to lose them: doubling back, stopping suddenly, vanishing into alleys. The lesson was simple: if you cannot keep pace in a bazaar, you will never survive the streets of Damascus or Istanbul. Training also taught recruits the art of controlled boredom: how to maintain awareness during long periods of inactivity and then switch instantly to high alert when the target makes an unexpected move.

Success depends on preparation and teamwork. One officer alone is vulnerable. Three to six working together can create the illusion of coincidence. The "ABC method" became our standard. Agent A leads close behind, Agent B walks parallel on the opposite side, Agent C trails at a comfortable distance. At corners or crowded crossings, they switch roles seamlessly, so the target never sees the same face twice. Communication flows through subtle cues: a hand raised to adjust glasses, a pause to tie a shoe, a phrase spoken into a hidden earpiece. Teams also practiced 'swap drills': planned transitions where tails cross paths to hand off surveillance with zero alteration to the perceived pattern.

Pretext is vital. A man carrying shopping bags looks like a customer. A tourist fumbling with a map appears lost. A couple arguing can pause conveniently at the same doorway where the target lingers. Each disguise must be convincing, lived in fully, because the closer you are to your subject, the more fragile your cover becomes. Cultural fit matters: in conservative districts, dress modestly and avoid behaviors that signal foreignness; in cosmopolitan neighborhoods, adopt an unhurried, urban air. Small props, such as shopping bags, a camera, and a stroller, become tools to legitimize presence.

The risks are many. Crowds can swallow you, or worse, expose you. Fatigue sets in quickly, for every second demands alertness. A single careless step or accidental stare can unravel the entire operation. Yet when executed with precision, foot surveillance offers a level of detail that no camera can match. It captures the human essence of the target, their habits, their fears, their secrets, made visible in the smallest gestures. Micro-observations—how a man orders his tea, which hand he uses to shield a conversation, or the way he lights a cigarette—can reveal alliances, stress, or even deception.

In Iraq, we combined foot surveillance with stationary and mobile teams to form a layered net. A mosque watch post would log a cleric's departure. A mobile team would follow his car into the city. When he parked and entered a crowded souk, the foot operatives took over, blending into the tide of shoppers. Together, these methods created a seamless chain, ensuring that no step of the target's journey went unobserved. We also used short-term cover identities: shop assistants, delivery people, or repair workers, so that when proximity became necessary, the tail had a plausible reason to be nearby.

Foot surveillance is not simply about following. It is about becoming part of the human landscape, a shadow that the target cannot distinguish from the countless strangers around him. It requires constant mental refresh: rotating personnel, scheduled breaks, and clear hand-off points to prevent burnout and preserve operational integrity. It is the most personal form of hunt, where success demands courage, adaptability, and above all, the ability to be present without ever being remembered.

The Quiet Mastery of Seeing Without Being Seen

Surveillance is more than a method; it is a discipline, a quiet form of artistry that transforms observation into understanding and presence into power. From the still patience of stationary watches to the fluid precision of vehicular tails and the intimate subtlety of foot surveillance, each technique is a brushstroke on the grand canvas of intelligence work. The Iraqi Intelligence Service, forged in the crucible of war, learned that mastery was not measured by gadgets or the number of eyes on a street but by the operator's ability to exist unseen: to observe so naturally that the world absorbed him without noticing he was there. In this silence, the true professionals thrived.

The essence of surveillance is patience and restraint. The stationary watcher waits, the mobile operative anticipates, and the foot trailer blends, but all share a single devotion: to witness life unfold without altering its rhythm. This is not simply a procedural exercise but a psychological duel. The watcher must think like his subject, predict every movement, and read meaning into the most mundane gestures: a turn of the head, a change in walking pace, a phone call delayed by ten seconds. To master surveillance is to see the hidden logic in chaos, to turn randomness into pattern.

Across the Middle East, the streets of Baghdad, the alleys of Damascus, the bazaars of Tehran, every environment whispered lessons to those who listened. Each city possessed its own pulse, its own texture of noise and suspicion. The successful officer did not impose himself upon this world;

he merged with it, drawing from the rhythm of its crowds, the cadence of its prayers, and the gossip of its merchants. A poorly timed glance could end a mission; a well-timed silence could reveal everything. Surveillance was not only about seeing but about understanding the unseen motives, fears, and loyalties that guided the human current.

Though technology has since revolutionized the craft, replacing notebooks with GPS trackers, binoculars with drones, and whispered codes with encrypted apps, the human eye remains irreplaceable. Machines may calculate, but they cannot empathize; algorithms can detect movement but not intention. The seasoned observer, with years of intuition and cultural fluency, can interpret what no camera can record: the hesitation of guilt, the weight of anxiety, or the calm confidence of a man who knows he's being watched yet refuses to reveal it. The conversation between the operative and his environment remains eternal, conducted not in words but in awareness.

The true operative is not merely a follower but a cartographer of human behavior. He charts emotional topography, the rise and falls of confidence, the fault lines of deception, the recurring paths of routine. He connects dots invisible to others, turning gestures into patterns and patterns into preemptive knowledge. What he gathers is not only intelligence but foresight, the power to act before events erupt, to guide outcomes rather than react to them.

Ultimately, the art of surveillance teaches humility and discipline. It reminds us that real power often hides in silence and observation rather than command or display. Influence is not always the loudest voice in the room; sometimes, it is the quietest listener in the crowd. The world is filled with secrets, not buried in darkness but walking openly through daylight, seen by all yet noticed by none.

The best operative is not the one who moves fastest or carries the latest technology; it is the one who learns to vanish within the ordinary. He walks beside his target without leaving a trace, understands without intruding, and captures truths without uttering a single word. In the unforgiving landscapes of the Middle East and beyond, this quiet mastery is what separates hunters from the hunted. Victories are not always won with gunfire or declarations, but through the patient, invisible hands of those who have perfected the oldest art in espionage: the ability to see without being seen.

COUNTER-SURVEILLANCE TECHNIQUES: THE ART OF EVADING THE UNSEEN EYE

Counter-surveillance is not a checklist you dust off when the hair on your neck stands up; it is a way of moving through the world. It hums quietly behind every choice: where you sit, how you cross a street, when you look back, and when you refuse to. It is not paranoia; it is the disciplined maturity of an officer who understands that one lazy assumption can end a career, a network, or a life.

My foundation was built on the methods the Iraqi Intelligence Service (IIS) inherited and refined from old Soviet tradecraft. During the Iran-Iraq War and in the rough decades that followed, we learned to turn the tables before a watcher even realized a game had begun. We read rooms like dossiers: who is actually listening, who is pretending, who is bored, who is performing boredom. We weaponized misdirection: unremarkable when we needed to disappear, unpredictable when we needed to confuse, calm when others tense. Counter-surveillance is patience distilled into instinct and reaction fused with foresight. It protects you, your sources, and the delicate web tying an operation together.

In the Middle East, the craft acquires another layer. Neighborhoods notice. Gossip travels faster than cars. A curious neighbor, a child with sharp eyes, or a vendor who remembers your face can unravel months of preparation. The most dangerous sentence an operative can think is: "Nothing looks wrong today." Comfort breeds blindness. The IIS taught us to assume that every "safe" corner is already watched and to behave accordingly.

Every service has its flavor. Some Western outfits lean hard on gadgets and analytics; we learned to make culture our cover and human observation our shield. Preparation could consume a day for a meeting that lasted five minutes: mapping light and shadow, traffic flows, prayer times, and the behavior of the people who truly own the street. In the pre-digital years, before the convenience of encrypted pings and live trackers, the essentials were the same as they are now: your eyes, your judgment, and a plan you actually rehearse.

Yes, modern tools help secure messengers, spectrum scanners, VPNs, but the core principle has not moved an inch: awareness outruns automation. Devices fail. Instinct, once trained, rarely does. Counter-surveillance is the quiet preemption of an ambush, the invisible duel where arrogance kills and humility survives. Whether you are arranging a handoff with a nervous source or maintaining a cover in hostile territory, each motion must have intent, each pause a purpose.

THE MINDSET OF VIGILANCE: PUTTING EVERYTHING ON THE LINE

Everything begins in the mind long before you choose a route, a table, or a hat. Counter-surveillance is not fear; it is responsibility. The price of a sloppy assumption is not paid only by you. It is paid by the courier who trusted you, the family that sheltered you, and the mission that depended on you showing up clean.

In the late 1990s, after hours of trailing a courier through Baghdad's market lanes, heat and fatigue tempted me to skip a final sweep. A small voice insisted otherwise. I doubled back through a spice stall, paused with a view into a pane of dusty glass, and caught the reflection of a man who had lingered one corner too many. That one extra loop likely saved the meeting and the asset. The lesson stuck: complacency is the assassin you never notice until the report has your name on it.

Vigilance is a rhythm, not a flinch. You watch without staring, listen without snapping your head, and let anomalies accumulate before you act. A car idles one minute too long with its lights off. A pedestrian "on the phone" pivots his body to keep you framed. A face repeats in two locations where it should not. One oddity is noise; two demand caution; three require action.

Training hardens these habits into muscle memory. IIS recruits practiced awareness in crowded bus terminals and bazaars, asked to tail instructors who delighted in doubling back, stopping abruptly, and vanishing into alleys. They learned to read space like a map and emotion like a language. The standing rule was brutal and correct: if your route feels easy, it is wrong. Choose the path with turns, noise, and unpredictability. Straight lines invite bullets; complexity buys you time.

Vigilance also carries an ethical burden. A careless officer does more than risk himself: he endangers sources, colleagues, and future operations. We taught assets uncomplicated, life-preserving habits: vary routes and timing; do not meet twice in the same place; avoid predictable vehicles; trust the discomfort that will not quiet down. Fear is not weakness; it is information asking for a decision.

For newcomers, cultivate these instincts when nothing is at stake so they will serve you when everything is. Practice in ordinary spaces. Use reflections in café glass to track who watches you. Note license plates and patterns without staring. Test alternate exits from familiar buildings. Walk a block, double back naturally, and see who doubles with you. The goal is not to see more, it is to notice what matters, sooner than anyone else, and to act before the pattern closes around you.

In the end, survival rarely hinges on theatrics. It turns on one precise moment of attention: the extra glance, the delayed turn, the quiet decision to trust a thread of unease. Vigilance is the difference between being written about and writing the report yourself.

SURVEILLANCE DETECTION ROUTES (SDR): THE RITUAL OF THE CLEAN PATH

An SDR is more than a security drill, it is a ritual, a mental and physical cleansing before contact. It's the deliberate art of moving unseen, shedding the invisible tails that might be clinging to you, and confirming you are truly clean before an operation or meet. It is not random wandering. Every corner, every pause, every shift of direction has purpose. In urban grids, an SDR is built on geometry: sharp turns, bus hops, and diversions that break sight lines. In open terrain, it becomes about distance and isolation: loops through quiet roads, stops at roadside cafes, or pauses at fuel stations designed to flush out persistence.

Preparation is everything. Hours before stepping into the field, an officer walks the ground, memorizing choke points and potential cover. Narrow alleys, sharp bends, reflective glass storefronts all become tools. You mark the teahouse that provides a safe blend-in spot, the crowded intersection that forces pursuers into exposure, and the discreet gestures that signal a clean approach. The Iraqi Intelligence Service, borrowing and refining Soviet techniques, trained officers to balance subtlety and rhythm. Each SDR had a pulse, an invisible tempo that dictated when to slow, when to pivot, and when to vanish into the flow of daily life.

The IIS's strength lay in its adaptability. Baghdad's streets were a theater of chaos: traffic, heat, suspicion, and officers learned to use that chaos as camouflage. One day, an agent might "fix his shoe" beside a market stall, scanning mirrored tiles for repeat faces. Another, he'd pause to buy cigarettes simply to check a reflection in a car's window. Nothing was coincidence. Each act was calculated, casual, and essential.

When running an SDR, vary the pattern. Start at inconsistent times early one day, late the next to unsettle any setup. Weave through dense streets, make multiple turns to break visual contact, and mix transport. A sudden switch from car to bus, or cab to foot, reveals who's committed enough to follow. Stops become part of the script: eat in a café with a clear view of exits, linger in a shop long enough to test patience, or browse under the pretext of buying while scanning reflections. The skilled operative treats every public space as a mirror, every stranger as a question, and every routine as a risk waiting to be rewritten.

The IIS perfected local adaptations. In Karbala, officers used religious gatherings to blend into prayer lines, scanning for those who didn't kneel at the right moments. In Tehran, markets became their maze; bargaining sessions with vendors doubled as surveillance sweeps. Modern officers use traffic apps, smartwatch alerts, and even compact drones to detect patterns from above, but the discipline remains the same. One anomaly is noise, two is concern, three is confirmation. When the pattern repeats, you cleanse hard, double back, change cities, or call the meet off entirely.

Environmental counters choosing the time, place, and rhythm of your movement are the unseen armor of counter-surveillance. Schedule meets during pre-dawn hours or within the noise of festivals, where anonymity thrives. Choose venues that mask sound: mosques, crowded cafés, noisy intersections, and minimize exposure to cameras. The IIS understood this long before modern tools: they staged checks during family events or rush-hour chaos, where surveillance drowned in normality. Every decision stacked the odds in your favor before the first move was even made. Ethics demanded that assets were looped in without panic: trained to recognize danger, not fear it.

ADVANCED COUNTER-SURVEILLANCE: BEYOND THE ROUTE TO TOTAL EVASION

Once the SDR becomes muscle memory, the next level begins turning passive avoidance into active control. The best officers didn't just dodge watchers; they manipulated them. Passive scans are the eyes behind you watching reflections, using car mirrors for 360-degree views, or arranging a subtle nod from a trusted vendor when something feels off. Aggressive methods demand composure: striking up a brief conversation with a suspected tail, pretending recognition—"You look familiar"—to study reaction. The true master doesn't flee; he choreographs confusion until the pursuer is lost in his own assumptions.

The IIS introduced creative deception, what we called "rabbit runs": sudden bursts through crowded areas that force amateur watchers into mistakes. In Europe, operatives would bolt through train stations at peak hours, counting who kept up. In the Gulf, a lost pilgrim act in a mosque would expose agents too formal to engage naturally. These weren't stunts; they were diagnostics, reading reactions to separate the trained from the incidental. In today's world, digital defense adds another dimension: Faraday bags silence phone signals, VPNs cloak identities, and counter-surveillance apps detect fake cell towers. For meetings, white noise devices or strategic seat placement—back to the wall, light behind you—still work better than any gadget.

One golden rule endures: never repeat a route. Repetition kills cover. Familiarity breeds vulnerability. Each recycled movement teaches your enemy your rhythm, and soon they wait at your next turn. The IIS trained officers to live unpredictably: vary commutes, switch meeting points, even change habits of dress or prayer locations. To survive, you must be unreadable.

When a crisis hits and exposure feels imminent, the response must be instinctive. "Burn the tail," accelerate into traffic, force the pursuit into visible error, or use intersections to corner them into exposure. Calm panic with control. Every motion must be deliberate, never frantic. The officer who loses control of his own fear loses the game entirely.

The Sudanese wiretap operation, one of IIS's defining successes, proved how mastery of SDRs and psychological endurance could outwit better-equipped adversaries. The team rotated routes daily, embedded themselves within the city's pulse, and used cultural familiarity as their shield. By the time embassy watchers realized they'd been outmaneuvered, the intelligence had already been delivered, and the operatives had vanished into the ordinary.

Conclusion: The Pursued as the Ultimate Predator

Counter-surveillance is not avoidance, it is ascendance. It is the defiant art of mastering chaos and reversing the hunt. The Iraqi Intelligence Service transformed the craft from Soviet imitation into a living discipline, merging human instinct, cultural fluency, and operational audacity. The hunted became the hunter through vigilance and intellect.

From the labyrinthine flow of an SDR to the calm precision of advanced maneuvers, each technique exists to restore control to dictate tempo, to reclaim the initiative, and to survive with dignity intact. Preparation is defense; adaptability is victory. Ethical restraint, that often-forgotten cornerstone, ensures that the craft serves humanity rather than consuming it.

The lesson endures beyond Iraq's wars. In a world wired with cameras, satellites, and algorithms, the principles remain unchanged: technology counters technology, but instinct always outwits automation. Master counter-surveillance, and you don't merely survive the shadows, you own them. The eyes upon you will see only what you allow, and the silence you leave behind will echo as the ultimate victory of the unseen.

CHAPTER 21:
FRONTS AND COVERS: THE ART OF INVISIBLE OPERATIONS

THE FRONT: BUSINESSES AS SHADOWS OF ESPIONAGE

In the labyrinthine theater of Middle Eastern intelligence, where every transaction may conceal a transfer of secrets and every handshake might seal a betrayal, the front remains one of the most elegant and enduring instruments of deception in an operative's arsenal. Far from the gadgetry of cinematic myth, a front is a structure of controlled normality: a business, charity, or institution that breathes with the rhythm of everyday commerce while pulsing with the quiet heartbeat of covert purpose.

It may appear harmless: an elegant café overlooking the Corniche, a travel agency printing brochures for holy pilgrimages, or a barber's stall beside a mosque where gossip flows with the scent of jasmine oil. Yet behind its ordinary façade lies the true power of a front: to transform the mundane into a stage for intelligence. The best fronts are not camouflage; they are ecosystems of deception that embed themselves so naturally within society that even those who suspect their purpose cannot afford to tear them down.

For an officer, the mastery of fronts represents the highest art of invisibility. To operate through a front is to transform from intruder to insider, to hide in plain sight not by evasion, but by belonging. The truly successful operative is not the one who escapes notice, but the one whose presence feels inevitable: the neighbor whose smile never reveals the surveillance camera behind the curtains.

THE STRATEGIC CHAMELEON

The genius of a front lies in its adaptability. It is a chameleon of purpose, capable of shifting color and texture to mirror the terrain of its mission. In the Middle East, where culture, commerce, and religion intertwine seamlessly, fronts exploit social rhythms that outsiders rarely perceive.

At the surface, a front grants access: embedding operatives where observation becomes natural. A luxury hotel in Dubai provides vantage points over Gulf princes and financiers; a restaurant in Baghdad captures the nervous laughter of diplomats after wine loosens their tongues; a corner café in Beirut, hidden behind curtains of tobacco smoke, becomes a listening post for conversations that shape regional policy.

But beneath this access lies deeper strategy. Every front performs dual functions: penetration and manipulation. The penetration phase gathers: names, habits, preferences, weaknesses. Manipulation transforms those details into levers. A restaurant manager can become a recruiter. A hairstylist becomes a confidante. A travel agent becomes a smuggler of people and information alike.

When crafted with precision, the front becomes more than a hiding place: it becomes an engine of influence. A liquor store in a conservative city becomes a blackmail factory; a trading company, a tool for financing covert wars; a news agency, a megaphone of disinformation. Every product, every service, every customer interaction carries the potential to conceal an exchange of power.

The true genius, however, lies in cultural fluency. A cover that thrives in Paris would collapse in Najaf. A glitzy hotel in a village of scholars would draw suspicion faster than a soldier in uniform. But a simple tea shop, humming with gossip, becomes invisible through familiarity. In the Middle East, invisibility is not achieved through silence, but through participation: by knowing when to speak, and what not to say.

THE IIS NETWORK OF DECEPTION

The Iraqi Intelligence Service (IIS) understood this truth instinctively. During the Iran-Iraq War and throughout the 1990s, the Service built an empire of fronts that blurred the line between business and espionage. Each was a cog in a machine that funded itself, recruited sources, and expanded the regime's reach far beyond the battlefield.

Al-Sa'a Restaurant in Baghdad exemplified the art. By day, it was a monument to Iraqi sophistication: marble floors, imported wine, and the chatter of politicians and artists. By night, its private rooms became arenas of subtle persuasion. Recruitment dinners unfolded beneath chandeliers: a disgruntled journalist softened by charm; a merchant tempted with contracts; a diplomat caught between debt and desire. Many of these encounters would later appear in IIS reports coded as "cultural engagement," their success measured not in signatures but in silence.

In Tehran and Dubai, the IIS opened beauty salons run by trained operatives. Scissors clicked over whispered confessions, and hair dryers drowned out secrets too delicate for walls to hear. In these sanctuaries of comfort, women revealed what even husbands would not confess. One wife's idle complaint about her husband's assignment near Bushehr led analysts to a hidden Iranian logistics hub: a minor remark that rewrote an entire map of enemy infrastructure.

Then came Al-Huda State Company for Religious Tourism, the IIS's most audacious creation. Officially, it ferried Iranian pilgrims to holy shrines in Karbala and Najaf. In reality, it monitored travelers, identified radicals, and siphoned pilgrimage fees into operational funds. Every busload of the devout carried at least one watcher. Every guesthouse doubled as a safehouse. Each ledger hid coded expenditures that financed operations from Sudan to Berlin. What began as a religious enterprise evolved into a logistical network that funded and protected Iraq's agents across borders: proof that devotion, when properly leveraged, could serve both God and state.

THE ARCHITECTURE OF THE PERFECT COVER

Establishing a front demands the same surgical precision as recruiting an asset. A misstep in either can destroy years of groundwork. The process unfolds in four deliberate stages:

Conceptualization: Select a business model that aligns naturally with the local environment. The cover must answer suspicion before it is asked.

Seeding and Staffing: Employ individuals loyal enough to protect secrets but ordinary enough to seem forgettable. A good operative must look like the man no one would ever follow.

Integration: Become part of the community. Sponsor local events, donate modestly to causes, and cultivate predictable routines. The best camouflage is familiarity.

Harvest and Evolution: Once embedded, begin converting passive observation into active influence: recruiting patrons, staging dead drops, laundering funds, or managing logistics for larger operations.

Funding sustains the illusion. A poorly financed front dies under scrutiny; an overfunded one draws it. The IIS allocated resources with clinical balance: a salon received petty cash and cosmetic supplies, while trading firms demanded legitimate contracts and accounts. The ultimate goal was self-sufficiency: to make each front capable of paying its own way.

Taxi companies in Europe ferried the Iraqi diaspora while reporting their passengers' politics. Coffeehouses in Amman doubled as informal embassies, where gossip became actionable intelligence. Even beggars near diplomatic quarters received stipends to eavesdrop and relay rumors to handlers. In London and Bonn, cultural centers funded by Baghdad disguised outreach as surveillance, their sermons carefully tuned to measure dissent.

Over time, these fronts became a living organism: a parallel economy of shadows. Some existed for months, others for decades. The network proved so durable that even after 2003, investigators found remnants of

IIS fronts still operating, their employees unaware they had ever been part of an espionage system.

STRATEGIC ALCHEMY AND THE MODERN MIRROR

The art of crafting a front mirrors alchemy: transforming ordinary substance into hidden gold. The formula remains timeless: identify a natural social artery, seed it with loyalty, and harvest through patience. The most effective fronts do not pretend to exist; they belong.

A hypothetical case: to monitor Tehran's literary circles, establish a "cultural bookstore" offering banned texts under the banner of artistic freedom. The store draws students, dissidents, and intellectuals; a clerk quietly notes their names. The operation self-funds through sales, masks recruitment through conversation, and harvests ideological mapping from customer lists. Exposure risk grows not from espionage but from success: popularity becomes the enemy of secrecy.

The Middle East's system of wasta: social connection and reciprocity turns fronts into networks of trust. A café owner owes favors to a merchant, who knows an officer's cousin, who arranges supplies for a ministry. Each link strengthens the disguise. The front ceases to be a façade and becomes part of society's nervous system. As one IIS officer once quipped in training:

"A front is not a lie; it's the truth with teeth."

Today, the method survives in new forms. Cyber fronts appear as "tech startups" or "AI research firms" masking state-sponsored hacking. Charities act as humanitarian channels for covert funding. Media outlets amplify narratives planted by intelligence services, their journalists unaware they are the instruments of manipulation. The tools evolve, but the philosophy remains constant: invisibility through utility, credibility through contribution.

THE INVISIBLE ARCHITECTURE OF INFLUENCE

The front, as wielded by the IIS, was more than a mechanism of disguise; it was a philosophy of control through normality. From Al-Sa'a's candlelit seductions to Al-Huda's pious profiteering, these constructs demonstrated that the most powerful intelligence work unfolds not in the shadows but in the daylight of ordinary life.

To build a front is to design a parallel reality: one that feeds on legitimacy while serving deception. It requires foresight to choose the right form, cultural empathy to make it believable, and vigilance to prevent the greed or arrogance that can unravel it. The rewards are immense: immunity, access, and a form of dominance that feels almost divine: the ability to steer a society from within.

Yet the dangers are equally profound. Exposure can collapse not only a network but a nation's credibility. The temptation to exploit a front's success: to expand too fast, to grow too visible, often ends in ruin. The front must live within moderation, thriving beneath the threshold of envy and suspicion.

In the modern world of global connectivity and open-source investigation, the landscape has changed, but the principle endures. Digital fronts now wear the mask of progress: NGOs, startups, data firms, and consultancies conducting influence operations behind the curtain of innovation. They sell legitimacy as their cover, just as the IIS once sold dinner, pilgrimage, and prayer.

Ultimately, the craft of the front reminds us that espionage is not the war of shadows: it is the war of appearances. To survive, the officer must not only hide but belong. To dominate, he must not only deceive but serve. The perfect front is not the mask that conceals the spy; it is the mirror that convinces the world that it sees only itself.

COVERS: HUMAN FACADES IN THE THEATER OF ESPIONAGE

In the intricate landscape of Middle Eastern intelligence, where a single misplaced glance can unravel years of work, the cover emerges as the operative's most intimate armor: a meticulously forged persona that cloaks the spy in the skin of the everyday, turning the extraordinary into the unremarkable. Unlike the structural scaffolding of a front: a business humming beneath the camouflage of commerce, a cover is human, alive, and reactive. It breathes, sweats, improvises, and falters. It is the professor droning through lectures on ancient history while mapping dissident syllabi in a Beirut classroom; the doctor palpating a patient's pulse in a Damascus clinic, his stethoscope catching more than heartbeats; the teacher corralling rowdy students in a Jordanian schoolyard while charting radical sympathies behind innocent faces. It is the security guard at an embassy gate in Ankara, scanning not just ID cards but body language; the engineer in a Tehran workshop sketching blueprints that hide embedded transmitters; the prisoner in Abu Ghraib forging trust in the dim light of the cellblock; the street cleaner sweeping Cairo's alleys while gathering scraps of gossip; the faqir: the beggar mystic in a souk, memorizing faces beneath a veil of humility; the taxi driver weaving through Baghdad's chaos, his meter ticking like a recorder of regime discontent.

These are not costumes worn for a mission's duration but identities inhabited. Each is crafted with false documents, practiced gestures, rehearsed dialects, and emotional truths so convincing that the role begins to shape the player. A good cover doesn't hide you: it convinces the world that you belong. For an intelligence officer, it is the most delicate of weapons: a lie that must never sound like one.

THE ALCHEMY OF DISGUISE

The alchemy of a cover turns vulnerability into velocity: a dynamic façade that propels the operative through layers of access, deception, and extraction with the grace of a desert wind. Where brute force fails, the cover opens doors through familiarity and trust.

A university professor infiltrates intellectual circles, steering late-night debates toward a radical student's manifesto while sipping arak over philosophical musings. A doctor calms a nervous patient and, between blood pressure readings, teases out grievances about party loyalty and family ties. A taxi driver, his rearview mirror angled just right, studies the faces of passengers who mistake anonymity for safety. Every detail: the tone of voice, the choice of perfume, the rhythm of small talk, becomes a weapon sharpened by repetition.

Manipulation is the cover's darker art. A teacher "mentors" a promising pupil, planting suggestions of defection disguised as encouragement. A doctor's compassionate diagnosis doubles as recruitment outreach. A beggar's appeal for alms draws a cleric into a confessional chat that slips from spiritual into political. In a realm governed by honor and shame, empathy is leverage and vulnerability the coin of influence.

Each role provides deniability. A shoe shiner's stall becomes a drop point; a janitor's locker a message cache; a street vendor's canopy a safe meeting site. The more ordinary the persona, the harder it is to trace its extraordinary purpose. In the Middle East's social labyrinth, where lineage and reputation shape every interaction, a convincing cover is more than deception: it is performance as survival.

THE IIS DOCTRINE OF HUMAN DISGUISE

The Iraqi Intelligence Service (IIS) perfected this human theater with ruthless ingenuity. Every social class, every profession, every moral station became a stage for infiltration. The agency's doctrine viewed humanity itself as a resource: an infinite range of disguises waiting to be animated by discipline and desperation.

Taxi drivers were its bloodstream. The IIS seeded fleets across Tehran, Damascus, and Amman, turning the chatter of back seats into a national database of secrets. They ferried diplomats, dissidents, and defectors alike, using coded phrases and mirror flashes to signal surveillance success or danger. One such driver, in the double-agent unmasking detailed in Case Study 3, aborted a compromised meeting with a flick of headlights: a move that saved an entire network.

Professors and teachers formed another tier of deception. A history lecturer in Amman, posing as a benevolent academic, distributed "scholarships" to identify radicals, mirroring the Basra journalist cultivation (Case Study 7). Doctors played double lives as healers and harvesters of confession. Their clinics became confessionals with syringes instead of incense. The failed infiltration of the Syrian cleric network (Case Study 2) stemmed from this tactic: a doctor's probing bedside manner intended to map loyalties beneath piety.

Engineers carried technical covers into industrial veins. As "inspectors" in the Kharg Island sabotage (Case Study 1), they turned clipboards into blueprints of destruction, charting weak points in Iran's underwater pipeline network. Security guards at embassies and consulates were no less dangerous: in Khartoum, IIS "guards" used their passes to slip messages and photograph sensitive faxes during the Sudanese wiretap operation (Case Study 10).

Even the condemned were weaponized. Prisoners planted in Abu Ghraib posed as common criminals, embedding among real detainees to extract whispers from political captives. Their cellmates never knew that the cigarettes they shared were payment for betrayal. Street cleaners, shoe shiners, faqirs, and housemaids filled the lower echelons of espionage's pyramid: anonymous, invisible, indispensable. Their eyes and ears gathered the dust of secrets that others swept away.

The ingenuity extended far beyond Iraq's borders. Teachers in exile schools in Jordan quietly assessed parental affiliations through children's essays. Housemaids in Tehran villas, tied to the salon fronts described in Section 1, served tea to generals' wives while reading their moods. Even the homeless in London parks doubled as watchers: a network of exiles posing as vagrants to monitor opposition figures in the diaspora.

Religious fronts blurred further with faith: Iraqi-origin imams in Detroit mosques preached sermons seeded with subtle messaging, mapping loyalties within the expatriate community; Chaldean priests in Sydney hosted "masses" that doubled as briefings. The result was a self-sustaining ecosystem where human covers and commercial fronts interwove seamlessly: the stylist in Dubai's beauty salon feeding intelligence to the IIS-run café two streets away.

THE CRAFT OF THE COVER

Designing a cover demands the same patience and precision as sculpting an asset. The operative must match role to mission, environment to temperament. Every detail: birthplace, accent, body language, skillset must hold under interrogation. The role must not only fit but live.

A professor thrives in intellectual crucibles like the American University of Beirut, where political discourse cloaks dissent. A prisoner, conversely, sinks into gulags like Evin or Abu Ghraib, where social hierarchies of inmates offer access to power brokers and broken souls. Authenticity anchors survival. A beggar must look hungry enough to be ignored but not so deranged as to alarm; a doctor's diploma must stand up to verification by a skeptical bureaucrat. Even failure must be rehearsed: the right amount of nervousness, the plausible stammer, the faint smell of fatigue.

Planning must crystallize objectives: is the cover built for passive observation or active manipulation? Is it meant to listen, to lure, or to lead? The advantages are profound: trust without suspicion, immersion without alert, influence without overt command. But so are the dangers. Burnout corrodes credibility: a beggar's feigned despair becoming genuine, a guard's pretense of loyalty slipping under pressure. Exposure invites public fury, as in the Tehran café explosion (Case Study 6), when a cracked cover ignited a mob.

The IIS managed these risks with constant rotation and redundancy. Roles shifted. Signals were prearranged: a dropped coin, a tilted cap, a misplaced broom. When the heat rose, identities were shed like old skins, and the operative vanished into a new life before dawn.

ECONOMY OF ILLUSION

Funding human covers was an art of disciplined scarcity. A faqir's stipend might be fifty dollars a month, disguised as alms; a guard's loyalty might cost two hundred in hush money. Professors received "grants" from front companies, while cab drivers' fares generated their own operational budgets. The system recycled itself: surveillance funding itself through the ordinary flow of life. Prison commissary scams financed informant networks. Donations to imams abroad doubled as investments in influence. The IIS understood that the cheapest cover was often the strongest: poverty, faith, or professionalism rendered beyond suspicion.

For the modern officer, this remains the lesson: that immersion, not expense, buys invisibility. To scout a radical bookstore, pose as a displaced bookseller, stocking banned tracts that lure the curious. Each sale becomes data. Each conversation, a probe. The danger, as always, lies in success: grow too popular, and the mask attracts eyes that see too clearly.

THE HUMAN MASK AS STRATEGIC POWER

The cover, as honed by the Iraqi Intelligence Service, is not a disguise: it is a living instrument of strategy. It transforms an operative into a thread woven through the region's social fabric, gathering intelligence from within rather than intruding from without. From the cabbies of Tehran to the faqirs of Damascus, from professors lecturing on history to imams guiding flocks abroad, the IIS proved that the most effective espionage begins not in the shadows but in the sunlight of ordinary human life.

A perfect cover feels natural, even sacred. It builds trust organically, harvests intelligence invisibly, and multiplies through the social contagion of familiarity. Yet its fragility is ever-present: one slip, one inconsistency, one misplaced word can shatter years of illusion. Survival requires relentless rehearsal and emotional detachment: to live the lie so convincingly that you forget where truth ends.

In the digital age, the stage expands. The "freelance coder" becomes a cyber operative masked behind encrypted screens. The "ride-share driver" becomes a sensor network on wheels, recording conversations and GPS patterns. But the essence remains unchanged. Technology can mimic surveillance; it cannot replace belonging.

In a region where loyalty and faith define identity, the human mask remains the most potent tool of all. A front can buy access; a cover becomes it. To master both is to own the battlefield unseen: to sip tea with a target while holding his fate in your calm, familiar hands.

PART III:

LESSONS FROM THE SHADOWS – CASE STUDIES

Case Study 1:
The Kharg Island Operation: The Art of Precision

THE STORY

The Persian Gulf in the mid-1980s was a theater of constant tension, its waters thick with oil, warships, and the residue of a conflict that refused to end. By then, the Iran-Iraq War had dragged into its fourth year, each side bleeding resources in a stalemate that stretched from the marshes of Basra to the Straits of Hormuz. Beneath that deadlock, however, the Iraqi Intelligence Service (IIS) conceived a plan unlike any conventional offensive: a mission that would blend human daring, engineering brilliance, and deception into one of the most audacious operations of the entire war.

Their target was Kharg Island, a seemingly unremarkable patch of rock off Iran's southern coast. Yet, to Tehran, it was everything: the country's economic heart, the hub through which most of its oil exports flowed. Even after repeated surface bombings by Iraqi aircraft, Kharg remained functional because of what lay beneath it: a network of underwater pipelines that carried oil from storage tanks onshore to tankers moored offshore. Those pipes were Iran's lifeline, invisible but vital. While air raids scarred the surface, the oil kept flowing below the waves. To cripple Iran's economy, the IIS realized, they needed to strike where no bomb could reach: the deep.

The birth of a plan

By 1984, Iraq's leadership demanded a strategic blow that would resonate far beyond the front lines. The IIS began an intensive analytical phase, poring over maps, bathymetric charts, tanker routes, and satellite imagery provided to them by Western countries. Their analysts soon pinpointed the underwater pipelines as the true vulnerability. Destroying them, however, required surgical precision, not brute force.

In Baghdad, the idea took form: a covert underwater demolition mission that would use divers to plant specialized charges on the pipelines themselves. It was a concept that required not just courage, but foreign expertise in maritime sabotage: a skill Iraq lacked.

The officers in that small, smoke-filled war room knew they were proposing heresy: to send men into the enemy's waters without flag or uniform, to fight a war no radar could trace. The plan carried the scent of both genius and death. Yet the thought of rupturing Iran's arteries without a single bomb ignited something fierce inside Saddam's inner circle.

The outsider

Through covert channels, an IIS officer in London began searching for a technical consultant who could design and lead such a mission. After weeks of quiet inquiries and coded communications, a name surfaced: a retired British Navy colonel, a veteran of special maritime operations whose career had been defined by the kind of underwater precision Iraq now sought. His record included covert demolitions and deep-sea infiltration missions for NATO in the Cold War.

The approach was made carefully. The colonel was discreetly offered a contract worth three million dollars: one million upon initiation, two million upon success. In return, he would act as the mission's technical architect and commander, working from Baghdad to train and oversee the team. He accepted, but only on his terms: complete operational control and full autonomy in training, timing, and methodology. The IIS, recognizing his value, agreed.

To Baghdad's planners, his arrival felt like importing myth itself: an old Cold War phantom stepping out of retirement to teach an Arab service the choreography of shadows. He arrived under diplomatic cover, dressed in linen to deflect suspicion, his British reserve masking an engineer's obsession.

Forging the team

The colonel demanded an elite, disciplined unit: men capable of mastering fear, darkness, and the crushing silence of the sea. The IIS assembled 120 of Iraq's finest operatives: Special Forces veterans, members of Saddam's Special Guard, and Navy frogmen. The colonel relocated to Habbaniyah Lake in Anbar Province, where he transformed the tranquil waters into a crucible of endurance.

Training was brutal and relentless. Under the desert sun, the men learned to dive blindfolded, navigate underwater by touch alone, and set charges in total darkness. They practiced nighttime infiltration, silent communications, and synchronized timing, every hand gesture and breath rehearsed until instinct replaced thought. The attrition rate was merciless. By the end of months of training, only eighteen men remained: lean, precise, and forged into instruments of quiet destruction.

The colonel personally supervised the construction of custom-designed bombs, compact, sonar-resistant, and powerful enough to rupture steel pipelines without leaving surface traces. These devices, shaped like hydrodynamic pods, were designed to cling magnetically to their targets and detonate in a timed sequence.

The lake became their ocean; each ripple a rehearsal for war. Night after night, they descended into darkness until fear became a familiar companion. The colonel would pace the shore, stopwatch in hand, his voice a rasp over the radio: "You are not divers. You are surgeons."

The shell and the shadow

Executing the mission required an intricate logistical network. The explosives could not simply be shipped across borders; they had to travel invisibly through the arteries of commerce. To accomplish this, the IIS created a Panamanian shell company, then used it to purchase a commercial oil tanker: a vessel that would serve both as a delivery system and a cover story.

To move the explosives into the Gulf region, the IIS used a legitimate Iraqi firm, Al-Kubaysi, a fertilizer exporter with established trading links across the Middle East. This cover allowed the explosives to be concealed among fertilizer shipments in hidden compartments and false floors, carefully fitted within Al-Kubaysi's transport trucks.

Two routes were tested to perfection before the first real shipment moved. The primary route ran from Baghdad through Kuwait and Saudi Arabia into the UAE: fast but heavily monitored. The secondary route, more discreet, cut through Jordan, then south across the Saudi desert into the Emirates. Both paths were rehearsed multiple times with dummy cargo, ensuring that checkpoint inspections would reveal nothing suspicious.

Once inside the United Arab Emirates, the real explosives were quietly stored at the Iraqi Embassy in Abu Dhabi, where diplomatic immunity shielded them from scrutiny. The purchased tanker, anchored offshore, waited for orders. Every element was in place, but one variable remained unpredictable: timing.

The operation was a feat of bureaucracy as much as espionage. Every document, every customs slip, every driver's signature was a brushstroke in an invisible masterpiece. If one clerk hesitated or one inspector grew curious, months of planning could dissolve in a heartbeat.

The waiting game

The operation's first attempt faltered not because of exposure, but bureaucracy. The tanker, ready and disguised, was delayed by Iranian port authorities, who postponed its loading at Kharg Island. Leaving live explosives aboard for days was too dangerous, and under the colonel's strict discipline, the IIS made a calculated decision: abort temporarily, preserve the asset. The charges were discreetly offloaded and stored once again inside the embassy.

Days later, a fax from the Iranian arrived at the tanker's radio room: a routine clearance from Iranian port control, authorizing entry to Kharg for loading. The window had opened. The colonel gave the order from

Baghdad. Under the cover of night, the charges were retrieved from embassy custody and loaded back onto the tanker. Each movement was timed to the minute, and divers disguised as ordinary deckhands.

The colonel slept in one-hour shifts, waiting for that clearance code to appear. When it came, he exhaled once and muttered, "Now the sea decides."

The strike beneath the waves

When the tanker finally moored at Kharg, the divers prepared in silence. Above deck, Iranian port workers moved about, unaware that eighteen trained saboteurs lay hidden in the ship's lower decks. At midnight, as the tanker's pumps began transferring crude oil, the colonel's choreography came to life.

One by one, the divers slipped into the black water, vanishing beneath the tanker's shadow. They followed pre-measured lines toward the pipelines, guided only by tactile signals and discipline. Each explosive was attached precisely where the pipelines converged near the seabed. The divers worked calmly, their breathing slow and synchronized through the colonel's drills.

Hours later, as the last charge was set, the tanker quietly disengaged. The team surfaced, invisible in the darkness, and returned to the vessel. Minutes after departure, Iraqi jets thundered overhead, unleashing a coordinated airstrike on Kharg's surface installations. The explosions above were the cover and the signal.

Beneath the waves, the hidden charges detonated in sequence, ripping through the steel arteries that carried Iran's oil. The sea turned black with crude, the surface gleaming under searchlights as confusion erupted onshore. Within hours, Iran's exports were crippled, tankers left idle, and Kharg Island's operational capacity effectively neutralized.

The first shockwave rose like a heartbeat through the deep. Fish scattered; the water trembled. From the surface. No cheer, no triumph: just the quiet realization that history had tilted by a few well-placed magnets.

Aftermath of precision

The mission had succeeded with surgical perfection. The colonel received his full payment and quietly disappeared into Europe. The eighteen divers returned to their respective units, uncelebrated but alive. For the IIS, the operation became a benchmark, a triumph of intelligence planning that combined foreign expertise, disciplined execution, and cultural cover.

The strike didn't end the war, but it shifted its rhythm. Iran's economic pain deepened, forcing Tehran to divert resources from the battlefield to reconstruction. For Iraq, it was a rare moment of advantage, achieved not through brute military might but through intellect, deception, and precision.

In the archives of the Iraqi Intelligence Service, the operation was later summarized in one phrase that said it all:

"The sea has its own battlefield, and we mastered it once."

For years afterward, Iraqi trainees studied the Kharg dossier as both scripture and warning: a reminder that brilliance carries risk and that even victory at sea leaves no survivors in memory. The waves returned to calm, the wreckage sank, and the world above continued its war. But deep below, where steel had once pulsed with oil, silence reigned: the eternal signature of a perfect operation.

ANALYSIS AND LESSONS LEARNED

The Kharg Island operation remains one of the most ambitious covert actions ever undertaken by the Iraqi Intelligence Service (IIS) during the Iran-Iraq War. It combined foreign expertise, disciplined training, deception, and logistical ingenuity to strike deep at Iran's economic lifeline. Yet beyond its technical brilliance, the mission offers enduring lessons about strategic patience, operational trust, and the calculated marriage of human skill with technological precision.

A victory of design over firepower

In an age when wars were often decided by brute force, the Kharg Island strike proved that intellect could achieve what artillery could not. The operation succeeded where months of bombing had failed, crippling Iran's oil exports through a feat of engineering and secrecy. But its success was not accidental: it was the product of layered planning, psychological discipline, and an unusual willingness by the IIS to embrace outside expertise. For intelligence professionals, it illustrates how methodical design can outmatch overwhelming power when guided by precision.

Kharg became more than an operation: it became a philosophy. It demonstrated that in intelligence work, elegance can be deadlier than scale. Where generals saw maps, the IIS saw arteries. Where aircrews dropped tonnage, analysts traced weaknesses invisible to the eye. And when the strike came, it was not announced by fanfare or flags: only by the quiet roar of oil erupting from the sea's black veins.

Strategic vision: Identifying the invisible target

The IIS began with a rare quality in wartime intelligence: clarity of purpose. Instead of chasing symbolic victories, it sought a single point of economic collapse.

- Analytical depth: IIS analysts dissected every map, shipping route, and undersea chart until they found the true weakness: the submerged pipelines.
- Lateral thinking: Turning from air raids to underwater demolition required an imaginative leap unusual in a regime built on conventional command structures.
- Risk acceptance: Choosing a covert maritime strike acknowledged that the operation's success would hinge on secrecy, not spectacle.

Insight: Strategic clarity begins with seeing the unseen. The Kharg plan succeeded because the IIS defined a specific vulnerability, then designed an entire operational ecosystem around it.

True strategy is rarely about numbers: it is about nerve. The IIS dared to look beneath the obvious, finding power where others saw impossibility. That intellectual audacity, not equipment, was the first weapon of victory.

Foreign expertise: Trust across cultural lines

Perhaps the most daring decision was to hire a retired British naval officer to design and command the mission. In a climate of suspicion toward outsiders, this was an act of calculated pragmatism.

- Pragmatic trust: The IIS understood that ideology should not outweigh results; it outsourced knowledge while maintaining full control of execution.
- Cross-cultural management: Bridging cultural divides between the colonel's Western methodology and Iraq's rigid hierarchy required diplomacy as much as command.
- Professional discipline: The colonel's demand for autonomy reflected his professionalism, and the IIS's willingness to grant it signaled maturity rarely seen in regional intelligence services of the time.

Insight: Effective intelligence work often means knowing when to borrow excellence. The success of Kharg was born not from pride, but from pragmatic collaboration.

In espionage, trust is currency more precious than gold—and riskier to spend. That Baghdad entrusted a Western mercenary with the heart of its most secret mission showed a rare detachment from ideology. It was professional ruthlessness in its purest form: results before rhetoric.

Training and preparation: Forging discipline into precision

The Habbaniyah training camp became a crucible for the operation. Out of 120 recruits, only eighteen survived the colonel's ruthless standards.

- Realism over numbers: The IIS traded manpower for mastery; every remaining diver was molded into a precise instrument.
- Technical innovation: The creation of sonar-resistant charges and

magnetic clamping devices showed the IIS's growing technical sophistication.

- Mental conditioning: The psychological endurance demanded of the divers mirrored the colonel's philosophy: calm is deadlier than courage.

Insight: Operational excellence is built on attrition: the removal of the unready until only precision remains.

Habbaniyah Lake became an academy of silence. The men were not trained to fight; they were trained to disappear. Instructors stripped them of bravado until only composure remained. Each night's dive was a dialogue between man and fear: one that only discipline could answer.

Deception and logistics: The art of disguise

The logistical backbone of the mission was as ingenious as the strike itself.

- Commercial camouflage: Using the legitimate Al-Kubaysi fertilizer company to mask explosive transport exemplified flawless tradecraft: leveraging authenticity to hide danger.
- Diplomatic shielding: Storing the explosives at Iraq's embassy in Abu Dhabi under diplomatic cover turned international law into a protective veil.
- Controlled patience: Aborting the first attempt when Iranian authorities delayed the tanker's entry revealed rare operational restraint.

Insight: The line between exposure and invisibility is patience. Knowing when not to act is as vital as knowing when to strike.

Tradecraft is not the art of deception: it is the science of patience. The Kharg planners understood that every checkpoint, every customs official, every delay could be turned into an ally. The mission's real success was not in what they did, but in what they resisted doing too soon.

Execution: The marriage of precision and timing

The strike itself demonstrated the culmination of every preceding discipline: analysis, training, and deception fused into one seamless moment.

- Perfect synchronization: The divers' underwater detonation timed with the airstrike created chaos above and concealment below.
- Psychological composure: The men executed their mission without hesitation or deviation, a testament to mental conditioning.
- Minimal footprint: The operation left no immediate trace linking Iraq to the sabotage, preserving plausible deniability for Baghdad.

Insight: True mastery in espionage lies in leaving no echo. The best operations succeed not when they are known, but when they are simply felt.

At Kharg, success wasn't measured in explosions: it was measured in silence. The divers' return to the surface without detection was as significant as the ruptured pipelines below. They had struck and vanished in the same breath, leaving behind only confusion and the soft applause of the sea.

Lessons for intelligence professionals

The Kharg operation's triumph distilled several enduring principles for intelligence practitioners:

Lesson 1: Define Before You Act:

Identify the exact pressure point before mobilizing resources; clarity dictates success.

Lesson 2: Integrate Human and Technical Power

Technology multiplies effect only when guided by disciplined minds.

Lesson 3: Respect the Chain of Competence

Bring in expertise beyond your institution when required; arrogance is operational suicide.

Lesson 4: Adapt to Delay

A mission's strength is measured by its ability to pause without losing focus.

Lesson 5: Protect the Invisible Men

Operational heroes are expendable only on paper; in practice, they are irreplaceable.

Every successful covert action leaves behind a quiet doctrine. Kharg's doctrine was clear: precision without humility is fragile, and haste without vision is fatal. The operation became a training text not just for Iraq's officers, but for any service that valued intellect over impulse.

ETHICAL REFLECTIONS: PRECISION VS. CONSEQUENCE

The Kharg strike was militarily elegant but ethically ambiguous. It targeted infrastructure, not civilians, yet its aftermath polluted vast stretches of sea and intensified economic suffering. The operation exemplifies the constant tension between necessity and morality in intelligence work: can precision justify devastation? For the IIS, victory overshadowed conscience. For modern professionals, it serves as a reminder that technological brilliance must still answer to ethical restraint.

The Gulf waters ran slick with oil for weeks, suffocating fish and livelihoods alike. It was a reminder that even the cleanest operation stains something: if not the operator, then the world he leaves behind. Intelligence officers may win battles of stealth, but they cannot escape the moral wake their actions leave.

BROADER CONTEXT: A BLUEPRINT FOR HYBRID WARFARE

Decades later, the Kharg operation foreshadowed the future of warfare: asymmetric, technological, and information-driven. It showcased how intelligence services could achieve strategic outcomes through limited, deniable actions rather than open conflict. Its lessons resonate in the age of cyber sabotage and infrastructure warfare: the same logic that once guided divers now guides hackers.

The battlefield has simply changed mediums. The divers of 1984 have become the coders of today, infiltrating through cables instead of currents. The same discipline, patience, and precision that shattered Kharg's pipelines now target data lines and power grids. Kharg was not just an event: it was prophecy.

Conclusion: The Legacy of Kharg

The Kharg Island mission remains a symbol of Iraq's brief ascendancy in covert warfare: a fusion of intellect, discipline, and deception that struck a blow far louder than any bomb. Its success was not merely in destruction but in design: the capacity to outthink, outwait, and outmaneuver an adversary. For intelligence officers who walk the thin line between precision and peril, Kharg endures as a masterclass in how patience, planning, and human ingenuity can bend the tide of war without ever firing a visible shot.

Long after the oil fires dimmed and the Gulf's tides washed away the evidence, Kharg lived on as a parable whispered in training halls: proof that power can be silent, and that the sharpest weapon in war is still the human mind. The sea, indifferent and eternal, holds its secrets. Among them lies the memory of eighteen men who slipped beneath its surface and rewrote the art of invisible war.

Case Study 2:
The Failed Mission in Syria: When Loyalty to Self Outweighs Loyalty to the Mission

THE STORY

In the secretive world of intelligence, where patience, deception, and adaptability separate survival from disaster, the Iraqi Intelligence Service (IIS) launched in 1992 an operation that seemed destined for success but unraveled within days. Drawn from authentic IIS archives, this case follows an unlikely operative: an Air Defense captain who traded his uniform for clerical robes. His mission: to infiltrate Syria's Shia religious networks and monitor exiled Iraqi opposition figures.

What began as a masterclass in long-range planning ended as a study in cultural self-sabotage: proof that the hardest enemy to outwit is the self.

The recruitment: A strategic opportunity born of chaos

The Gulf War's aftermath left Iraq fractured, its air thick with smoke, vengeance, and whispered defiance. In the spring of 1991, rebellion erupted across the southern provinces, driven by years of repression and the intoxicating illusion that Saddam's defeat by the West had weakened his grip. Shia clerics who had long lived under quiet observation now became the revolution's moral compass.

Among them stood a distinguished figure: a senior representative of Grand Ayatollah Abu al-Qasim al-Khoei, the revered religious authority in Najaf. When the uprising was crushed, the cleric fled to Iran, his escape transforming him from a scholar into a symbol: a living wound in Baghdad's authority.

By 1992, the IIS's Directorate of Religious Affairs saw a rare opportunity. Their analysts identified the cleric's son-in-law: a young Iraqi Air Defense officer as a bridge between two worlds: loyal to Baghdad by training, yet tied by marriage to its enemies. On paper, he was flawless. Educated, disciplined, ideologically sound, and connected by blood to the most influential clerical circles in exile. The proposal was bold: rebuild the man from soldier to scholar, from uniform to turban.

It was espionage disguised as faith: an operation of spiritual camouflage.

If executed correctly, the captain-turned-cleric would slip into seminaries, study circles, and religious pilgrimages unseen, his new identity both shield and sword. But in the excitement of design, a critical question went unasked: could a man raised on command, hierarchy, and pride ever master the humility required for infiltration?

The answer would come at the cost of ten years.

The preparation: A decade of transformation

The operation began with full institutional commitment: an investment of years, money, and ideology. The IIS enrolled the asset in Al-Hawza Al-Almiya of Najaf, the centuries-old seminary revered as the intellectual citadel of Shia Islam. Here, under the mentorship of respected clerics, the former Air Defense officer began the long pilgrimage from soldier to scholar.

For the service, this was more than a cover: it was a rebirth. His days of marching drills and flight protocols gave way to lectures on jurisprudence and eschatology. He memorized fiqh texts, debated theological nuances, and attended funerals, weddings, and rituals: all while his handlers quietly recorded his progress.

Over time, the soldier's bearing softened. His voice lowered, his posture relaxed, his eyes accustomed to the slow rhythms of scholarly life. He traded authority for reverence, command for contemplation. The transformation wasn't performance, it was immersion.

Midway through his studies, he demonstrated a spark of initiative that impressed his handlers. The seminary lacked basic modern tools. He proposed providing computers from Baghdad: a seemingly generous act of progress. The IIS seized on it instantly. They shipped a series of computers, each fitted with concealed transmitters that captured keystrokes and ambient conversations. Within weeks, the walls of the Hawza began to whisper into Baghdad's receivers. It was one of the first successful instances of electronic infiltration within a religious institution: a quiet triumph of technology wrapped in faith.

Years passed. By 2000, eight years after recruitment, the metamorphosis was complete. The captain had become a cleric: fluent in the dialects of Najaf and Qom, steeped in the etiquette of scholars, and wrapped in the black turban that signified descent from the Prophet's line. To his peers, he was pious. To his handlers, he was a weapon. To himself, he was both—and neither.

The mission: A sleeper awakens in Syria

That same year, after a decade of sculpting his new identity, the sleeper was activated. His destination: Damascus, the heart of the exiled Iraqi opposition.

Around the Sayeda Zaynab shrine: a gleaming dome surrounded by crowded alleys and perfumed incense, a community of Iraqi dissidents had gathered under the pretext of religious teaching. The shrine's devotion masked defiance: its pilgrims carried politics in their prayers.

Among the teachers in that circle was the cleric's father-in-law: the same man who had once fled Iraq. The IIS's plan was elegant: send their transformed agent under the pretext of reunion and, through blood and belief, penetrate the enemy's core.

His credentials were impeccable. A letter of recommendation from a Basra scholar confirmed his scholarship; his accent, his posture, even his calligraphy reflected a man raised in seminary life. To his family, his return felt providential: a reunion sanctified by faith. To the IIS, it was the opening of a new front.

Damascus in 2000 was a city of contradictions: a crossroads where politics hid behind religion and loyalty shifted with the scent of cardamom tea. Spies, preachers, and pilgrims mingled in the same courtyards. For the IIS, the mission embodied the essence of patient design: a man rebuilt for a single conversation that could alter the course of regional intelligence.

The collapse: Cultural instincts shatter discipline

It took less than a week for the illusion to implode.

On his first night in Damascus, the agent attended a private majlis at his father-in-law's house. The room was alive with murmured debate: scholars, students, and exiled activists speaking openly of Saddam's brutality, Baghdad's corruption, and the dream of a free Iraq. His orders were clear: observe, record, and remain invisible.

But silence is a discipline few Iraqis master easily, and pride is a fire that burns deeper than doctrine.

As the criticism grew sharper, the agent's composure cracked. His tongue, trained in command, betrayed him. He rose to speak: first to correct, then to argue, and finally to defend. What began as a cautious clarification turned into a fiery sermon. He accused the critics of betrayal, of exaggeration, of selling Iraq's honor for exile's comfort.

The clerics stared in disbelief. His father-in-law's face stiffened: a mixture of shock and dread. Within minutes, the evening shifted from discussion to confrontation.

The next nights only deepened the damage. He returned to gatherings with renewed defiance, challenging every insult against Baghdad as if the regime itself sat in judgment through him.

His father-in-law, desperate to protect him, urged restraint, but pride proved stronger than tradecraft. The room that should have been his hunting ground turned into his trial.

Unknown to him, another IIS operative embedded within the same network was observing quietly. His cable to Baghdad was blunt:

"Asset compromised. Cover deteriorating. Emotional exposure critical. Hostile suspicion forming."

Rumors spread like fire through the clerical network. The newcomer's vehemence was unnatural, his zeal too deliberate. Soon, whispers named him: 'The man from Baghdad.' Ironically, his passion to defend his homeland confirmed the very suspicion he was sent to evade.

Within days, his father-in-law's associates cut contact. Conversations died when he entered the room. Invitations stopped. The mission's decade-long architecture: its training, legend, and cultural layering collapsed under the weight of one man's voice.

The end: A decade lost in days

The IIS moved with surgical speed. A coded recall order was transmitted to Damascus, citing "security instability." Within forty-eight hours, the agent boarded a return flight to Baghdad. His handlers met him in silence, their expressions already verdicts.

The debriefing was clinical but merciless. The once-promising asset sat beneath flickering fluorescent light as interrogators dissected every word, every argument, every misplaced emotion. The conclusion was as concise as it was brutal:

"Subject's personal disposition rendered him operationally incompatible despite long-term investment."

Ten years of preparation had disintegrated in ten days of pride. No enemy counterintelligence had exposed him, no surveillance team had followed him: only human instinct had undone him. The man who was supposed to listen had chosen to lecture. The room that should have been his hunting ground turned into his trial.

For the IIS, it was a costly lesson in the limits of transformation. You can retrain a man's skills, reshape his habits, and even rewrite his biography, but you cannot amputate his nature.

The cleric-spy returned to the shadows of Baghdad a broken tool, a reminder whispered in training halls for years afterward:

"We can forge the perfect cover, but we cannot forge the perfect soul."

In intelligence work, failure often comes not from betrayal, but from belief: belief in one's own judgment, one's own pride, one's own untested conviction. For the IIS, it was an expensive education: that no doctrine, however refined, can erase instinct, and that in the shadows of espionage, the loudest voice in the room is often the one that ends the mission.

Conclusion: The weight of instinct

The failure in Syria was not a collapse of planning: it was a collapse of self. Ten years of preparation, legend-building, and indoctrination disintegrated under the pressure of a few unguarded words. It was the most human kind of failure: a man mistaking his emotion for his duty, his voice for his worth.

The IIS had mastered the external arts: deception, infiltration, the orchestration of identity, but it stumbled on the internal one: how to teach silence to pride. The operation became a mirror reflecting the service's own limitations. You can rebuild a soldier into a scholar, but you cannot replace the rhythms of his blood. Culture runs deeper than training; instinct outpaces doctrine.

In Damascus, the mission died quietly, but the lesson lived on: whispered in every debriefing hall and training lecture that followed. It reminded the next generation of officers that the greatest danger is not exposure from without, but eruption from within. A careless word, a flicker of ego, a reflex of self-defense: these are the fractures through which entire operations bleed out.

For the seasoned officer, the moral endures:

Espionage is not the art of lying to others. It is the discipline of never lying to yourself.

To master silence, one must first conquer the need to be heard.

To belong in the shadows, one must first betray the noise within.

That is the lesson Syria left behind—and it will echo as long as human nature remains the most unpredictable force in intelligence.

ANALYSIS AND LESSONS LEARNED

The Syrian operation stands among the most haunting failures in the Iraqi Intelligence Service's (IIS) archives: a mission that collapsed not under fire or exposure, but beneath the quiet weight of human nature. It was not sabotage that destroyed it, nor treachery, nor a leak. It was a voice: one voice that could not remain still. Ten years of careful investment disintegrated in a single conversation, and through that collapse, the IIS learned a truth older than espionage itself: that pride is louder than secrecy, and silence is the most difficult mask to wear.

The high cost of cultural blindness

Espionage is, at its essence, the art of transformation: of living convincingly as someone else until the world forgets who you were. Yet transformation cannot exist without self-control, and in this, the Syrian mission was doomed before it began.

The IIS believed that education could rewrite personality, that knowledge could overwrite instinct. They mistook discipline for adaptability and training for temperament.

The agent's failure was not intellectual; it was emotional. His need to defend his homeland's honor, an impulse deeply rooted in Iraqi culture, overpowered the mission's requirement for humility and silence. He could change his uniform, his vocabulary, even his faith's performance, but he could not change his rhythm of speech or the pride that animated it.

This failure transcended one man. It revealed a cultural and institutional flaw: the belief that identity could be engineered, that patriotism was a substitute for personality profiling. It showed how the most refined tradecraft can be undone by an unexamined human truth: that the heart rarely obeys the mission plan.

Cultural rigidity: The argumentative trap

The agent's ruin began not with a gun or a signal intercept, but with conversation.

In Arab societies, debate is a form of art, a dance of dominance and charisma. The louder the argument, the greater the respect earned. Within that cultural framework, disagreement is not hostility: it is vitality. Yet in espionage, debate is death.

- Instinct over training: The agent's reflex to argue overrode years of conditioning. His silence: the one skill that would have protected him felt, to him, like humiliation.
- Flawed selection: The IIS evaluated loyalty and lineage but ignored temperament. They chose proximity over psychological profile, a decision that turned a perfect candidate into a liability.
- Collapse of dual identity: An operative must hold two minds at once: the true and the false. The moment he blurred the two, his disguise collapsed.

Insight: Cultural strength can become operational weakness. The same passion that fuels conviction can also expose it.

Operational indiscipline: When ego replaces mission

To argue is human; to vanish is professional. The Syrian agent forgot which one he was.

His mission required invisibility, yet he sought validation. Within that contradiction lay his undoing.

- Role Confusion: He transformed from observer to participant, from listener to lecturer. The mission's purpose—collection—was replaced by emotional performance.
- Ego over objective: The desire to win replaced the need to learn. In that moment, loyalty became self-expression.
- Lost opportunity: Even as he argued, he learned nothing. Instead of extracting information, he gave it, revealing his ideological spine.

Insight: Every operative must know the difference between presence and participation. When the ego speaks, the mission listens: and dies.

Institutional failure: The handler's blind spot

No case officer likes to admit that the problem began in recruitment, not execution. But the Syrian mission proved exactly that.

- Inadequate vetting: His argumentative personality had been visible years before. He debated instructors, challenged mentors, and questioned authority: traits celebrated in Iraq's military culture but toxic in espionage.
- Training deficiency: The IIS focused on religious and technical preparation, neglecting behavioral control. They trained a cleric, but not an actor.
- Handler complacency: A decade of investment created emotional attachment. By the time field officers doubted him, he was already canonized as a success story.

The post-mortem report contained one damning phrase: "We mistook transformation for loyalty."

Insight: Long projects breed blindness. The deeper the investment, the harder it becomes to acknowledge failure.

Psychological profile: The burden of self

At its core, the Syrian debacle was psychological. The agent could not reconcile who he was with who he pretended to be. For a decade, he lived between identities: half believer, half observer. The tension slowly consumed him.

Espionage demands the suppression of ego, yet the longer one lives a lie, the louder the inner voice becomes. He defended Iraq not out of duty, but out of exhaustion. The silence broke him first.

The IIS underestimated this strain. Psychological maintenance was almost nonexistent in its ranks. Case officers viewed emotional check-ins as weakness. Yet the very act of living under cover corrodes the self, and without structured support, breakdown is inevitable.

Insight: The strongest disguise cannot survive a neglected psyche. Covert work is not just deception of others: it is continuous deception of the self, and that has a cost.

Cultural Psychology: When Honor Becomes Exposure

In Iraq's tribal and religious culture, honor is not a word: it is gravity. Men are raised to defend it at all costs. The agent's fatal mistake was not arrogance; it was honor misplaced.

To him, silence under accusation felt like betrayal of country. In truth, it was service to it.

He could not see that restraint, not defense, was the higher loyalty. The IIS trained him in surveillance, theology, and logistics, but not in the paradox of espionage: that the truest patriot is often the one who appears disloyal.

Insight: Pride is cultural oxygen. To survive undercover, one must learn to breathe without it.

Operational doctrine: Lessons for future officers

The Syrian failure reshaped IIS's internal doctrine for years to come. From its ashes, new guidelines were drafted: unspoken but carved into the culture of training schools.

Lesson 1: Culture Is a Double-Edged Sword

Recruitment must balance cultural access with behavioral adaptability. Never assume familiarity equals control.

Why: Culture can provide cover, but it can also trigger exposure when instincts override orders.

Lesson 2: Discipline Defines Survival

Behavioral conditioning should outweigh academic training. Role simulation, not ideology, is the test of endurance.

Why: An operative's silence is more valuable than his speech.

Lesson 3: Supervision Must Be Continuous
Deploy secondary observers to detect deviation early. The moment personality resurfaces, recall the asset.

Why: A drifting agent is not a threat, until he is ignored.

Lesson 4: Psychological Maintenance Is Operational Security
In long-term covers, mandatory debriefing intervals prevent emotional rot.

Why: The mind erodes faster than the legend.

Lesson 5: Humility Is a Weapon
Train officers to lose arguments gracefully. Teach them that defeat in conversation can mean victory in survival.

Why: An operative must win by disappearing, not by persuading.

Ethical reflections: The human cost of misjudgment
Behind every failure lies collateral pain invisible in reports. The agent's humiliation destroyed family bonds and placed his father-in-law under suspicion. His sudden recall left emotional wreckage: a man half scholar, half ghost, no longer trusted by either world.

For the IIS, the recall order was not merely a safeguard: it was an act of mercy. Allowing him to remain would have risked exposure of others and his own likely death at the hands of exiles. Yet ethics in intelligence often emerge only after the damage. The deeper question remains: was it ethical to rebuild a man against his nature?

Every intelligence service walks that line. They sculpt loyalty from raw human material, shaping people into instruments. But when the instrument shatters, it is discarded quietly, its humanity erased by classification.

Insight: In the moral economy of espionage, success is celebrated publicly, but failure dies alone.

Broader implications: When culture and tradecraft collide

The Syria case illuminates a larger truth: no matter how advanced an intelligence service becomes, it remains a human institution bound by culture. The IIS prided itself on precision and secrecy, yet it was staffed by men molded by the same social patterns they sought to manipulate.

Recruitment flaws: Favoring loyalty and lineage over temperament leads to predictable catastrophe.

Discipline gaps: Confidence mistaken for composure: the classic misread of the Arab officer corps.

Strategic loss: A ten-year investment erased in ten days, a stark reminder that time and pride are enemies of realism.

For modern services, the lesson persists. Whether operating through cyber fronts or human assets, the same principle applies: a system can train a spy, but only the spy can master himself.

Conclusion: The weight of instinct

The collapse of the Syrian operation is a study in human fragility: a warning carved into the history of intelligence. The IIS forged a scholar but not a shadow. They gave him knowledge but not silence, purpose but not patience.

In the end, it was not the exiles of Damascus who unmasked him, nor the clerics who doubted him: it was the echo of his own voice. He spoke when silence was survival, defended when observation was victory.

For intelligence officers, the message is eternal: culture is neither enemy nor ally; it is a current that must be mastered. The operative who cannot control his instinct will one day betray his mission, not through treachery, but through reflex.

In the quiet world of espionage, words are weapons, and pride is the finger that pulls the trigger.

Sometimes, one argument is all it takes to end a decade.

Case Study 3:
The Double Agent in Tehran. Trust Is the First Casualty in Espionage

THE STORY

In 2001, as the scars of the Iran-Iraq War still shadowed the region, the Iraqi Intelligence Service (IIS) maintained one of its most sensitive and dangerous foreign outposts: Tehran Station. Officially, its officers were diplomats, operating behind the polished façade of the Iraqi Embassy. Unofficially, they were hunters and prey, locked in a silent, invisible war against Iran's formidable Ministry of Intelligence and Security (MOIS).

The two nations had restored diplomatic ties after eight years of bloodshed, but beneath the polite exchanges of envoys, distrust thrived. The battlefields had gone quiet, but in the alleys and ministries of Tehran, another war persisted, one fought with whispers, money, and betrayal.

It was into this precarious theater that a new case officer arrived, handpicked for his sharp instincts and calm precision. His assignment was straightforward on paper: assume control of the station's inherited operations, its assets, contacts, and surveillance networks, and continue the delicate balance of intelligence collection inside one of the most hostile capitals on earth.

Among the assets he inherited was a man long trusted by the outgoing officer, an Iraqi expatriate living in Tehran under deep cover. His file was thick with reports and commendations. Baghdad considered him one of the station's "most reliable sources," a consistent provider of valuable intelligence on Iraqi dissidents and Iranian activities. To the new officer, he seemed the safest link in a dangerous chain.

But the truth was already poisoned. Months before the rotation, the MOIS had quietly turned the asset, converting him into a double agent. His reports to Iraq had become a mirror of Iranian deception designed to confirm false assumptions, mislead analysis, and keep Baghdad complacent.

The timing of the officer handover offered Tehran the perfect opportunity to test how deeply the Iraqis trusted their own reflection.

The handover: Shadows of complacency

Transitions between case officers are always fragile moments, brief windows when institutional memory fades and vigilance falters. The new officer understood this risk and approached his assignment with measured suspicion. Before trusting any inherited source, he resolved to test them.

The double agent was first on his list.

He began subtly mixing the old communication channels, with slight deviations, observing how the asset reacted. The instructions were deliberately vague: ambiguous enough to invite mistakes but not enough to arouse alarm. His initial directive was a test of discipline. "If you recognize me in public," he ordered, "you will walk past silently unless I address you."

It was a small test, but in espionage, the smallest gestures reveal the deepest truths.

Tehran was a city alive with watchers. Every alley, every teahouse, every crowded bazaar had eyes belonging to the MOIS, the Basij militia, or one of the regime's countless informants. For an Iraqi officer operating under diplomatic cover, every step outside the embassy walls was a risk.

Two hours before the scheduled meet, he and a fellow IIS operative arrived at the location to run a quiet counter-surveillance sweep: checking reflections in car mirrors, window glass, and shopfronts. It was a dance of glances and timing.

And then they saw it.

Two men in a parked sedan across the street. Newspapers open, but their eyes flicked occasionally toward the meeting point. The detail was small, but unmistakable. The subtle stillness, the rhythm of their glances: it was surveillance.

The officer's instincts hardened. "Abort," he said quietly.

Later that evening, he contacted the asset under a casual pretext, claiming a schedule change. The tone was calm, polite, but inside, the decision had already been made. A single thread of suspicion had begun to unravel the illusion of trust.

The second meeting. A trap in the bazaar

The follow-up meeting was arranged for the old Tehran bazaar, a labyrinth of alleys thick with merchants, pilgrims, and whispers. The choice was strategic: the crowd offered cover, the noise a natural cloak for conversation. Yet the bazaar's chaos also concealed danger; it was the kind of place where both intelligence work and betrayal could vanish unnoticed.

Again, the officer arrived early, running a Surveillance Detection Route (SDR) through the crowded lanes. Nothing obvious appeared. The hum of traders, the smell of spices, the glint of brass lamps—it all blurred into a tide of movement. Convinced he was clear, the officer proceeded to the designated stall.

And then, in an instant, everything shattered.

From across the corridor, a familiar voice called out in Arabic. Loud. Too loud. The asset was waving, shouting the officer's name.

The sound cut through the bazaar like a siren. Heads turned. The officer froze. Every instinct screamed this is the signal.

He and his partner slipped quickly into a narrow side alley, hearts pounding. The asset followed, breathless, clutching a folded document. "It's urgent!" he insisted, pressing the paper into the officer's hand. Before he could react, figures emerged from the crowd: plainclothes men, purposeful, silent.

The MOIS had arrived.

One agent snatched the document. Another blocked the alley's exit. Their movements were efficient, practiced, absolute. No weapons drawn, none needed.

It was an ambush executed with precision.

The confrontation: Diplomacy as a shield

Surrounded but not yet detained, the Iraqis fell back on their final defense: diplomatic immunity. The officer calmly identified himself as an embassy staff member and cited the Vienna Convention, warning that interference would constitute a violation of international law.

For a tense moment, the air thickened. The Iranian lead operative, a tall man in a gray suit with cold composure, smirked, then slipped the seized paper into his coat pocket. Reaching into the same pocket, he withdrew a business card and handed it to the Iraqi officer.

"You have three days," he said quietly. "Call me."

Then, as seamlessly as they had appeared, the MOIS team dissolved into the crowd, leaving behind only the echo of their precision and the unmistakable message: we are inside your circle.

The officers returned to the embassy unharmed but shaken. Their report to the station chief was immediate, every movement, every phrase, every face described in detail. The chief, a veteran of Tehran's intelligence duels, recognized the MOIS's signature instantly. Baghdad was informed through an encrypted cable.

Three days later, the warning materialized again, not by phone, but in person.

As the officer approached his vehicle inside the embassy compound, a man appeared at the gate, calm, confident, wearing the same gray suit. "Why haven't you called?" he asked quietly. Before the officer could respond or signal security, the man turned and disappeared into Tehran's traffic.

The message was clear: the hunter had been marked.

The aftermath: The price of complacency

Back in Baghdad, the internal investigation was swift and ruthless. The IIS determined that the original handler, the outgoing officer, had failed to properly vet the source or detect signs of compromise. His misplaced confidence had blinded him to the subtleties of deceit.

The new officer, though entangled in the crisis, was commended for caution and composure. His early suspicion and adherence to counter-surveillance protocol prevented the catastrophe from escalating into arrests or expulsions. Within weeks, he was reassigned abroad, a survivor of one of Tehran's quietest battles.

Director Tahir Jalil Habbush, head of the IIS, reviewed the case personally. Some within the service demanded retribution, perhaps a counter-operation to ensnare an Iranian defector in Iraq. Habbush refused. "One mistake does not justify another," he reportedly told his deputies. "We learn, not retaliate."

The file was sealed, labeled "Operational Compromise, Tehran, 2001."

Within the service, its story became a quiet parable: the most dangerous agent is not the one who lies, but the one you stop questioning.

ANALYSIS AND LESSONS LEARNED: THE ANATOMY OF A BETRAYAL

The exposure of a double agent inside Tehran in 2001 was not a single act of treachery; it was the slow erosion of vigilance within the Iraqi Intelligence Service (IIS). What appeared on paper as a sudden compromise was, in truth, the inevitable consequence of complacency, institutional blind spots, and the dangerous comfort that comes with routine success. This episode revealed a truth that transcends its time: in espionage, failure seldom explodes; it seeps in quietly until it cannot be reversed.

The incident remains one of the most instructive in the IIS archives, showing how misplaced trust, procedural stagnation, and cultural misjudgment can combine to destroy a mission from within. It reminds every case officer that betrayal is rarely a single event; it is a process measured in overlooked instincts and unasked questions.

The high cost of complacency

In the clandestine world, trust is never permanent; it must be earned, verified, and renewed. The Tehran debacle demonstrated what happens when discipline softens into habit and habit dulls into blindness. The outgoing IIS officer, numbed by familiarity, stopped seeing danger in the ordinary. His replacement inherited not an asset but a liability already under Iranian control.

The Ministry of Intelligence and Security (MOIS) did not need brilliance; it simply needed patience. It watched, waited, and exploited a system that had ceased to doubt itself. The result was a silent catastrophe that could have ignited a diplomatic crisis. For intelligence professionals, Tehran stands as a warning carved in stone: the deadliest enemy in espionage is comfort.

Vetting failures: The blind spot of trust

The root of the Tehran failure was not technical but human: a blind faith in a history that was never re-examined. The double agent had once been a genuine source, but loyalty is perishable, and the IIS never tested its expiration date.

Missed psychological clues

His enthusiasm for meetings, eagerness to provide intelligence, and unsolicited suggestions for future operations were celebrated instead of scrutinized. True assets seek safety; controlled ones seek attention. Had the IIS re-profiled him psychologically, subtle signs of coercion or divided loyalty would have surfaced: tension in his reports, inconsistencies in emotional tone, or the hollow over-eagerness of a man serving two masters.

Neglected surveillance checks

Routine observation before contact, a basic rule, was neglected. Without those checks, Iranian watchers had freedom to track both the source and his handlers. The MOIS mapped the pattern and waited for the perfect moment to strike.

Cultural blindness

Operating as an Iraqi inside Tehran meant living under constant suspicion. Family ties, financial need, and the social pressures of being a foreigner in a hostile city could bend any man's loyalties. The IIS underestimated how such pressures accumulate until survival eclipses patriotism.

Key Insight: Trust, when left untested, becomes blindness. An asset's loyalty must be treated as a living variable, not a historical constant.

Operational security: Predictability as a death sentence

Iran did not out-innovate Iraq; it simply learned the rhythm of its adversary. Predictability turned into transparency, and transparency into vulnerability.

Protocol violations

The asset's reckless act, calling out the officer's name in public, was either panic or a signal, but the result was the same. It exposed the operation in one breath. In a city like Tehran, a single word spoken aloud can collapse years of work.

Weak counter-surveillance

The MOIS watchers in the bazaar blended seamlessly into the chaos: shopkeepers, porters, even worshippers. Their ability to anticipate Iraqi movements proved that the IIS's counter-surveillance routines had become mechanical, lacking the improvisation that separates survival from capture.

Static communication channels

The same couriers, same time windows, same fallback locations: the patterns repeated. Once the MOIS recognized the rhythm, interception became effortless. What the IIS viewed as discipline, the Iranians recognized as predictability.

Key Insight: Security dies with routine. Tradecraft must evolve with each contact; rigidity is the adversary's map.

Asset transfer: A handover without homework

Every handover between case officers is a moment of danger: a brief vacuum where knowledge can vanish and trust can be misplaced. The Tehran case magnified that risk into disaster.

Over-reliance on legacy judgments

The new officer accepted his predecessor's evaluation as gospel, assuming loyalty could be inherited. In reality, every handler must rebuild trust from zero; anything less is negligence disguised as continuity.

Shallow debriefing

The transfer file contained operations summaries but no behavioral notes, no analysis of temperament, stress cues, or unexplained absences. Paperwork replaced perception. The living essence of the asset, his rhythm, tone, and fears, was lost between lines.

No re-vetting or verification

Had the IIS required mandatory re-testing during personnel transitions, parallel observation, or staged loyalty traps, the MOIS turn might have been exposed before it matured. Instead, the agency placed faith in its own archives, and the archives betrayed them.

Key Insight: Files record history, not truth. Re-evaluation must be ritual; without it, legacy breeds illusion.

Lessons learned: The discipline of perpetual doubt

From Tehran emerge four enduring doctrines: principles as old as espionage itself.

Lesson 1: Reliability Expires Without Verification

Re-vet every asset after any rotation or significant absence. Conduct behavioral and psychological refreshers.

Why: Yesterday's ally may serve today's enemy. Only verification sustains trust.

Lesson 2: Operational Security Is a Living Art
Rotate meeting points, rewrite codes, and alter schedules constantly. Run SDRs that are creative, not ceremonial.

Why: Predictability invites defeat; surprise keeps adversaries blind.

Lesson 3: Culture Shapes Risk
An operative's environment molds behavior. Monitor emotional and familial leverage points; cultural loyalty is both armor and weakness.

Why: Understanding the local psyche prevents moral misreads that lead to collapse.

Lesson 4: Transitions Require Independence
Treat every handover as a new recruitment cycle. Trust your observation over inherited reputation.

Why: Fresh eyes catch what routine ignores.

Ethical reflections: The burden of responsibility
Beyond the operational missteps lies an ethical failure that stings more deeply. The outgoing officer's negligence endangered his successor: a violation of the unspoken fraternity among intelligence professionals. To safeguard colleagues is as sacred as safeguarding secrets.

Recruiting an Iraqi to operate inside Tehran, knowing the omnipresence of MOIS surveillance, was itself a moral gamble. The man's eventual compromise may have been treachery, but it also reflected the unbearable strain of isolation and fear. He became a cautionary symbol of how moral overreach corrodes strategy.

Director Tahir Jalil Habbush's response marked a rare moment of discipline: he refused to retaliate. "Revenge," he said, "is a poor substitute for learning." That restraint preserved Iraq's remaining networks and transformed a humiliation into a lesson that still endures in intelligence circles.

Reflection: In espionage, moral clarity is fleeting, but accountability must never be. Negligence, ethical or operational, extracts its payment in silence.

Broader implications: When trust becomes a trap

The Tehran operation's downfall is not an artifact of a bygone era; it mirrors the vulnerabilities of modern intelligence systems still governed by human fallibility.

Vetting weaknesses: Technology cannot replace intuition. Algorithms detect data, not deceit. Only trained empathy recognizes fear in a voice or hesitation in a gesture.

Transition fragility: Organizational rotations remain soft spots; adversaries exploit them precisely because bureaucracy assumes continuity equals security.

Strategic patience: The IIS's decision to remain silent, though controversial, protected diplomatic stability and prevented escalation. Sometimes in intelligence, the boldest act is restraint.

Insight: Trust is not the foundation of espionage; it is the battlefield upon which every operation fights to survive.

Conclusion: Vigilance as the final defense

The Tehran case is not merely about betrayal; it is about the price of forgetting to question. The IIS's downfall was born from comfort, from the belief that the familiar is safe and the proven remains pure. But in intelligence, every truth decays with time unless it is tested.

For those who work in the shadows, the commandment is absolute:

Trust must be earned daily. Discipline must be renewed hourly. Vigilance must never sleep. The moment comfort replaces caution, the mission is already lost.

Case Study 4:
The Iranian Asset in Iraq: A Fatal Lack of Preparation

THE STORY: THE DISAPPEARING DEFECTOR

It began with a knock on a door in Athens: a sound that would echo all the way to Baghdad.

In the late 1990s, as the Middle East simmered under the uneasy calm that followed the Iran-Iraq War, a weary man entered the Iraqi Embassy in Greece. He was middle-aged, soft-spoken, and visibly frayed by fatigue. Introducing himself as an intelligence officer from the Iranian Embassy, he claimed disillusionment with Tehran's regime. His words were cautious, his tone rehearsed, but his eyes carried the tremor of either fear or deceit. He offered what every intelligence service dreams of and dreads in equal measure: defection.

He promised to reveal Iranian covert operations: names, locations, communication codes, if Iraq would grant him asylum. For the Iraqi station chief in Athens, it was the kind of gift that could elevate a career or destroy it.

In the man's story, the chief saw an opportunity. In his eyes, he sensed danger.

The bait: A gift wrapped in risk

The Iraqi Intelligence Service (IIS) had long thirsted for deep penetration into Iranian networks, and here, seemingly by chance, was an insider volunteering his allegiance. The temptation was too strong. The station chief sent an urgent encrypted cable to Baghdad, summarizing the man's claims and credentials.

Hours later, the response arrived from the Directorate of External Operations:

"Move him. Secure transit. Verify later."

Those four words sealed the defector's fate. The eagerness to exploit an opportunity eclipsed the instinct to verify it. In espionage, haste is the twin of deception.

The man's behavior: his calmness, his lack of visible pursuit, his absence of fear, should have triggered alarms. Defectors rarely appear without warning, and almost never without a shadow behind them. Yet ambition smothered caution.

Within days, the defector was granted Iraqi sponsorship and handed a ticket to Turkey. As the aircraft rose above the Mediterranean, he shed his Iranian identity for the first time, believing he had escaped one master only to fall into the hands of another.

The transfer: Layers of deception

In Ankara, the next link in the chain awaited him: the Iraqi station chief, a disciplined officer with a soldier's bearing and a suspicious heart. He greeted the defector warmly but without trust. Over bitter coffee in a safehouse near the embassy, he listened to the man's story again, this time noticing the small inconsistencies that crept into his version of events. The man spoke of Iran's exiled networks in Europe, of coded communications, of high-ranking clerics using foreign embassies as cover. He claimed he could expose it all, if only Iraq would protect him.

Orders came swiftly: move him to Baghdad, quietly, through Jordan.

The IIS fabricated a new identity: Hassan Jalal, a Kurdish merchant from Sulaymaniyah, and issued him a forged Iraqi passport. The false identity explained his accent, his limited Arabic, and his vague background. His real documents were sealed inside the Iraqi Embassy's safe, his existence now erased.

Two IIS officers were assigned to escort him. Their journey across the barren Anatolian plateau was long and silent, filled only with the sound of wind against glass and the occasional clink of tea cups at roadside stops. The defector spoke little. The escorts spoke less. Each border crossing was another test, but the forged passport passed inspection with ease. By the time they crossed into Iraq, the defector believed he had outwitted both fate and Tehran.

But Baghdad had its own plans for him.

Arrival in Baghdad: The hotel of shadows

He was lodged at the Al-Rasheed Hotel, the pride of the regime, a place of chandeliers, marble floors, and microphones. Every hallway was under surveillance, every room a stage. Mirrors hid cameras, vents concealed recording devices, and waiters doubled as informants. The defector was given a key and a warning: "Stay close. Someone will contact you soon."

For a day, nothing happened. He watched television he couldn't understand, stared out the window at a city cloaked in heat and suspicion, and waited for his promised debriefing.

On the second morning, restless, he stepped outside and hailed a taxi waiting at the curb.

The driver: a sturdy man with kind eyes and a neatly trimmed beard, greeted him in fluent Persian. Relief washed over the defector's face. After days surrounded by Arabic, the sound of his mother tongue disarmed him completely. He asked for a tour of Baghdad, and the driver obliged.

They cruised past the Tigris, through bustling markets, past the Ministry of Information's towering façade. The driver asked gentle questions about Tehran, about clerics, about exile life. The defector answered freely, unaware that every word was transmitted through a hidden microphone beneath the dashboard.

At sunset, the tour ended. The defector smiled for the first time since Athens. He asked the driver to return the next day. The driver nodded politely, knowing another operative would take his place.

The pattern of betrayal

The next morning, a different driver arrived: also Persian-speaking, also friendly. The defector didn't notice the change. His trust was automatic now. This time, he requested to visit Abu Ghraib, the infamous prison west of Baghdad, long whispered about in exile circles.

The driver complied, maintaining the façade of curiosity. At a roadside tea stand near the prison, the defector stepped out, gazing at the fences and guard towers with studied calm. He ordered tea, lingered longer than necessary, and scanned the horizon. He returned to the taxi with questions too specific, too practiced.

By the third day, the routine repeated exactly: a new "driver," the same destination, the same tea stand. But this time, the defector handed the vendor a folded scrap of paper containing four names. He whispered a request:

"Find out what happened to them. I'll pay you."

The tea vendor nodded, pocketed the note, and served his tea with a smile. Hours later, the list reached the IIS headquarters. The names belonged to Iranian-linked prisoners captured near the border: men Tehran had been desperate to locate.

The defector's story had just collapsed under its own weight.

The exposure: The trap closes

That night, the operation ended as swiftly as it began. An IIS tactical team stormed the Al-Rasheed Hotel under the cover of darkness. The defector's door splintered open, and within seconds, he was dragged out, hooded and silent.

By dawn, he sat in an interrogation room lit by a single bulb.

He protested at first, insisting on his innocence. But the interrogators: veterans of counter-penetration work, knew patience better than violence. They confronted him with recordings, transcripts, the tea vendor's report, and the photographs of him standing near Abu Ghraib. The mask fell away. The confession came slowly, then completely.

He admitted he had been sent by Iran's Ministry of Intelligence and Security (MOIS) to pose as a defector, locate Iranian detainees, and report their conditions. He had been promised extraction once his mission was complete.

The IIS had turned his own tactics against him: using his confidence as bait to reveal his purpose.

The disappearance: Erasing a ghost

At dawn, he was led to a walled courtyard. No witnesses, no recorders, no ceremony. A single gunshot ended both his life and his legend. His body was buried in an unmarked grave outside Baghdad, the name "Hassan Jalal" etched briefly into a ledger before being struck through in red ink.

His real identity was never released.

Weeks later, Tehran quietly inquired through diplomatic channels about a "missing official" last seen in Turkey. Baghdad's reply was predictable: "No such person entered Iraq."

The forged passport, the false identity, the sealed embassy files: all ensured that the man who once existed in two worlds now existed in none. In Tehran, his case was filed as "Unconfirmed Defection." In Baghdad, it was recorded under Directorate 14's archive as "Counter-penetration successful."

Operational reflection: The anatomy of a fatal oversight

What began as a potential coup: a walk-in defector offering the enemy's secrets, ended as a stark reminder of intelligence's oldest trap: the seduction of easy victories.

The IIS's hunger for a quick success blinded it to the obvious inconsistencies, and the defector's lies succeeded not because they were clever, but because Baghdad wanted them to be true. His death sealed not only his fate but also a quiet lesson within the service's own walls:

In espionage, hope is the most dangerous form of deception: because it feels like clarity, speaks like truth, and kills like trust.

Conclusion: The weight of hope

For the men who filed the report, the case ended in success. Yet inside the Directorate's marble corridors, no one celebrated. There was no triumph, only the quiet rustle of papers being sealed and the unspoken awareness that another illusion had been buried with the defector.

His death was not justice; it was the price of misplaced faith. He had gambled with deceit, and Iraq had gambled with trust. Both lost.

The file closed under red ink, but the lesson it carried endured.

The enemy's greatest weapon is not lies, but our willingness to believe them.

In the years that followed, that line became a quiet creed whispered among case officers: a reminder that in the shadow world of espionage, every defector is both an opportunity and a mirror, reflecting not only the enemy's deception but our own desire to believe.

ANALYSIS AND LESSONS LEARNED: ANATOMY OF A SYSTEMIC FAILURE

The Iranian asset's mission in Iraq did not simply fail; it imploded from within. What unfolded in Baghdad was not a twist of fate, but the slow-motion collapse of an operation born in haste and sustained by delusion. His capture and execution were not accidents; they were the predictable consequences of poor preparation, flawed leadership, and institutional arrogance.

He was a man sent into a lion's den with no map, no backup, and no exit plan: a pawn sacrificed for a mirage of success. His story is less about betrayal between nations than it is about betrayal within an organization, where ambition replaced discipline and zeal was mistaken for competence.

A Predictable collapse

In the clandestine world, luck is never strategy. The demise of the Iranian operative in Baghdad was written from the moment Tehran chose to value speed over rigor, appearance over reality. From recruitment to capture, every step revealed an agency intoxicated by its own hopes and blind to its own vulnerabilities.

Espionage rewards precision and punishes haste. Every unchecked detail: the brittle cover identity, the lack of cultural training, the absence of an extraction route, stacked the odds against him before he crossed the border. This was not the fall of a man; it was the exposure of a system that forgot its own rules.

In intelligence, haste is not a risk; it is a death sentence.

Training deficiencies: Zeal without craft

The operative entered the field with enthusiasm and devotion, but he carried no real craft. He was armed with loyalty, not skill; and in espionage, loyalty alone is a liability.

- Lack of cover discipline: His attempt to gather information was amateurish. Asking about high-value detainees in open spaces near Abu Ghraib was not bold; it was suicidal. A trained operative builds layers of distance between question and intent; he offered none.
- Psychological fragility: Once captured, he collapsed quickly under pressure. He had never been trained in resistance, interrogation survival, or narrative control. To the seasoned Iraqi interrogators, he was not an opponent; he was an open file waiting to be read.
- Cultural and linguistic blind spots: His Kurdish cover story unraveled the moment he spoke. His accent, posture, and tone exposed his Iranian roots. Every word carried the cadence of Tehran, not Sulaymaniyah. His cultural ignorance betrayed him faster than any wiretap could.
- Takeaway: Passion without skill is peril. Tradecraft is a language of deception and patience: mastery forged only through relentless, scenario-based training. Without it, the field becomes a graveyard.

Operational design: A mission without architecture

The framework of the operation was a house built on air: brittle, under-funded, and dangerously shallow. Every layer that should have protected the operative: cover, communication, and redundancy, was missing.

- Absence of official cover: He entered Iraq as a ghost, without diplomatic status or fallback immunity. Should he be caught, Tehran could plausibly deny him—which it did.
- A flimsy backstory: His "defector" persona crumbled almost immediately. Instead of seeking refuge and lying low, he roamed Baghdad asking questions that no true refugee would dare. The contradiction exposed him before he ever realized he was being watched.
- No extraction plan: There was no contingency, no recovery protocol, no backup handler waiting across the border. He was deployed with no promise of return: an expendable piece in a game of political theater.
- Takeaway: Operations without exits are not plans; they are executions in slow motion. Strategy demands redundancy, fallback points, and adaptive logistics. Hope is never a substitute for structure.

Leadership and oversight: Failure at the top

The mission's collapse did not begin in Baghdad; it began in Tehran: in a conference room where ambition spoke louder than reason. Senior officers approved a plan that defied logic, sending an underqualified operative into one of the world's most surveilled regimes with little more than forged papers and faith.

- The wrong man for the mission: Assigning a low-level, inexperienced officer to infiltrate Iraq was a fundamental error. He lacked both the training and the temperament to survive.
- No field support: The operative had no local handler, no guidance, no communication network. The absence of an operational chain violated the first law of agent management: no one goes into the field alone.
- Strategic miscalculation: Tehran underestimated the Iraqi Intelligence

Service, assuming that post-war chaos meant weakness. In reality, the IIS was at its peak of internal vigilance: paranoid, ruthless, and efficient.

Analyst's note: Was he meant to return?

Two explanations emerge: one deliberate, one born of incompetence.

1. The One-Way Mission Hypothesis

Tehran may have viewed him as expendable: a low-ranking officer deployed to test Iraq's counterintelligence vigilance or to confirm the status of captured operatives.

- Purpose: Use a disposable emissary to probe Baghdad's defenses without risking a valued asset.
- Logic: If caught, Iran could deny involvement; if he succeeded, the intelligence payoff would outweigh the loss.
- Limitation: True one-way missions are usually paired with propaganda or follow-on exploitation plans; neither existed here.

2. The Inexperience Hypothesis

Far more plausible is that he was undertrained and miscast.

Evidence: His lack of discipline, unrefined questioning style, and failure to maintain behavioral distance indicate naivety rather than calculated martyrdom.

Institutional context: Iran's post-war intelligence structure often rushed inexperienced officers into foreign operations to show initiative; he may have been a casualty of bureaucratic haste.

Hybrid assessment: Expendable and unready

The likeliest explanation combines both elements. Tehran may have deemed him replaceable, offered minimal preparation, and accepted the odds of failure as tolerable.

He was not sent to die; but neither was he expected to succeed.

Insight: Whether by intent or incompetence, he entered Iraq as a man without a future. His behavior was not the product of espionage genius but of institutional neglect.

For intelligence professionals, this nuance matters: distinguishing between deliberate sacrifice and operational ignorance defines how we read the motives behind "failed" missions.

Takeaway: Leadership that confuses urgency with boldness breeds disaster. Great intelligence operations require audacity, but they survive only through prudence.

The sum of these failures was not tactical but systemic: a collapse of preparation disguised as confidence.

Lessons learned: A blueprint for professional integrity

This case distills more than tactical lessons; it offers a moral and professional blueprint for all who manage human intelligence in hostile environments.

Lesson 1: Train Hard or Stay Home

Every operative must master tradecraft: cover identity, counter-surveillance, interrogation resistance, and deception under stress.

Why: Confidence without competence is suicide. Training transforms courage into capability.

Lesson 2: Plan for Chaos

Design operations with multiple escape routes, contingency layers, and emergency extraction triggers.

Why: In intelligence, uncertainty is not the exception; it is the landscape.

Lesson 3: Fit the Asset to the Task

Match each mission's complexity with the operative's intellect, psychology, and adaptability.

Why: Poor alignment between man and mission destroys both. Selection is as critical as execution.

Lesson 4: Protect the Operative

Case officers must advocate for their field assets. Oversight, monitoring, and evacuation options are not luxuries; they are moral imperatives.

Why: A dead operative produces silence; a protected one sustains the mission.

Ethical reflections: The human cost of negligence

Beyond operational logic lies a deeper moral wound. The Iranian operative was not just a failed spy; he was a man discarded by the system that sent him. His handlers gambled with his life to prove an illusion of reach and competence.

- Betrayal of loyalty: His faith in Tehran's promises became the rope that hanged him. He believed he was serving his country; his country had already written him off.
- Neglect masquerading as strategy: Deploying him without guidance or extraction was not courage; it was institutional cowardice dressed as boldness.
- Collateral damage: His capture did more than end one life. It tainted Iran's recruitment credibility. Future assets would remember that Tehran's protection was conditional and its loyalty negotiable.

His tragedy reminds us that intelligence work demands not only intellect but conscience.

Reflection: Intelligence operates in moral fog, but even within that fog, responsibility is sacred. The first duty of command is not ambition; it is protection of the willing.

Broader implications: A universal warning

Though this case unfolded in the 1990s, its lessons transcend borders and decades. Every intelligence service, no matter how sophisticated, remains vulnerable to the same disease: the illusion of competence.

- Training saves lives: Doctrine, ideology, and patriotism cannot replace fieldcraft. Preparation is the only armor.
- Planning prevents catastrophe: Improvisation is for artists, not operatives. Strategy demands layers, timing, and discipline.
- Ethics preserve credibility: Agencies that discard their assets soon lose both their sources and their humanity.
- **Insight:** Passion without discipline becomes chaos. Intelligence succeeds only when courage is married to caution; and ambition bows to design.

Conclusion: No room for shortcuts

The defector's execution was more than the end of an operation; it was a eulogy for recklessness disguised as resolve. His death was predictable, his suffering preventable, and his story unforgettable.

The moral of his tragedy is clear:

In espionage, shortcuts are fatal.

Victory belongs not to the daring, but to the disciplined: to those who prepare meticulously, question endlessly, and remember that every "asset" is a human being who bleeds when the system fails.

Case Study 5:
The Imam Assassination in Qum: Precision Through Preparation

THE STORY: PRECISION BENEATH THE MINARET

By late 1988, the thunder of artillery along the Iran-Iraq border had faded, but the secret war of ideologies was only beginning. The Iranian clerical establishment and Saddam Hussein's secular regime both sought to shape the post-war order, and propaganda had become the new battlefield.

Among the loudest voices challenging Baghdad was an Iraqi cleric-turned-dissident who had taken refuge in Qum: the theological heart of Shi'a Islam and a sanctuary alive with revolutionary zeal. He denounced the Ba'ath Party by name, weaving theology into rebellion, and his sermons, carried on cassette tapes across the region, became sermons of defiance. To the Iraqi Intelligence Service (IIS), his pulpit had become a weapon. Silencing him would serve both retribution and deterrence.

The City of Eyes

Qum was the last place an outsider could hide. Its narrow lanes, watchful bazaars, and dense web of seminaries formed an ecosystem where every stranger was noticed and every accent remembered. The Ministry of Intelligence and Security (MOIS) maintained a constant presence, using clerics, shopkeepers, and mosque caretakers as informants. To operate there required not only stealth but cultural invisibility.

An agent could not simply pass through Qum; he had to become part of its rhythm.

Selection of the asset

The IIS chose a man whose anonymity bordered on art. He was neither a star operative nor a political loyalist but a disciplined field technician of the intelligence trade: a man accustomed to blending into places that tolerated no strangers.

He had served previously on cross-border smuggling routes, moving through Iranian villages disguised as a trader. His ordinariness was his armor: medium build, soft voice, a face that invited no memory. He embodied the first rule of deep cover: become the kind of man no one looks at twice.

Training and preparation

Before deployment, he underwent an accelerated but meticulous training cycle that fused tradecraft with theology. He learned the patterns of prayer in Qum's grand mosques, the etiquette of greeting clerics, and the subtle hierarchies of respect within the hawza (seminary) system.

His instructors drilled him not in weapons but in gestures: how to fold a prayer rug, how long to pause before reciting supplications, how to answer questions about religious teachers. For months, he studied Persian idioms until he could mimic the accent of pilgrims from Isfahan and Yazd. By the end, he could move through Qum like water through marble veins: present but unnoticed.

When the instructors were satisfied that he could think, pray, and move like a son of Qum, the Directorate began the second phase: insertion.

Meanwhile, Directorate 8 engineers in Baghdad designed a weapon suited to both sacred space and deniability: a micro-charge disguised inside a hand-stitched jacket, its detonator hidden in a lining thread. The materials: cloth, buttons, even thread color, were sourced from Iranian markets to erase forensic traces. The device's purpose was surgical: to kill one man within a confined radius while avoiding the spectacle of mass bloodshed that could provoke theological outrage.

Arrival and observation

The operative entered Iran not through airports or legal crossings, but through the dark arteries of the smuggling routes that had long connected both sides of the border. The IIS maintained its own network of trusted smugglers: men who could move contraband, cash, or people across mine-scarred terrain under the watch of both armies. These same paths were the mirror image of Iran's own clandestine pipelines into Iraq; each side knew the other's methods, even if not their faces.

Under cover of a livestock convoy moving through the marshlands south of Basra, the operative was slipped across the Shatt al-Arab by boat at night. From there, IIS contacts on the Iranian side: Kurdish traders loyal to Baghdad's pay, escorted him inland toward Khorramshahr, avoiding official checkpoints. Once inside Iranian territory, he was quietly handed off to another courier group that delivered him to a transport hub near Ahvaz.

From Ahvaz, he traveled by bus to Qum, blending with pilgrims who clutched prayer beads and carried the exhaustion of faith. By the time he arrived, his papers identified him as a merchant from Dezful: a convenient fiction to explain both his accent and his detachment. His long journey through smuggler trails and prayer routes marked the true beginning of his mission: an invisible entry into the city of eyes.

He rented a small room near Madrasat Feyziyyeh, spending days in prayer and nights in quiet observation. Patience was his weapon. Nothing about his presence could appear hurried.

He attended the Imam's sermons repeatedly, learning the cadence of his speech, his gestures, and the moment he removed his cloak before ascending the pulpit. That act: hanging the abaya on the same wooden rack each time, became the fissure through which the entire plan would flow.

Weeks of watching turned into habit. The operative mapped entrances, side doors, and escape routes. He timed the guards' rotations and the flow of foot traffic before and after each prayer. He memorized the smell of the incense used inside the mosque so he could carry it faintly on his own clothes. Every sensory detail became part of his camouflage.

The plan and the exchange

The concept that reached Baghdad was elegant in its economy: plant the device on the coat rack beside the Imam's cloak, detonate remotely during the sermon, and disappear into the tide of panic. There would be no need for bullets, no direct confrontation, no visible assassin. The weapon would do the speaking.

When Directorate 14 reviewed the plan, they approved it immediately. The operation, codenamed Sada al-Minbar: "Echo of the Pulpit," was assigned high priority.

The handoff occurred in a tea-stained café off Qum's bazaar. The case officer, posing as a visiting trader, slid a folded parcel across the table. The operative touched the jacket with the quiet understanding that it carried both purpose and damnation. No words of farewell were exchanged; in operations like this, sentiment was risk.

Execution under faith's shadow

The morning of the strike dawned with brittle winter sunlight. Pilgrims streamed toward the mosque, their breath misting in the cold air. The operative joined them, head bowed, steps deliberate.

Inside, the marble floors shimmered under lamplight. He greeted two worshippers with rehearsed courtesy, then approached the coat rack. In a gesture perfected over dozens of dry runs, he hung the jacket beside the Imam's cloak and adjusted it slightly: as if aligning it out of respect.

He murmured a line of apology to a bystander for "leaving a friend's cloak" and walked to the back of the hall.

When the Imam entered moments later, the operative was already outside, sipping bitter tea near a street vendor, eyes fixed on the entrance. At the moment the Imam grasped his abaya before beginning his sermon, the operative's thumb pressed a small trigger inside his pocket.

The explosion was not cinematic. It was sharp, contained, and eerily brief. Wood splintered; smoke drifted in lazy spirals toward the ceiling; then came the collective cry. The Imam collapsed mid-verse, his final words drowned by panic.

The escape

As the crowd surged, the operative melted into its edges, moving with the same calm that had brought him in. He exited through a side door, discarded his prayer beads into a gutter, and followed a pre-marked alley to a safehouse on Qum's outskirts.

There, an IIS facilitator waited with new clothes, a forged work permit, and transportation. By dawn, he lay beneath sacks of pistachios in a smuggler's truck heading west. The route through the Zagros Mountains was perilous: checkpoints, militia patrols, and unpredictable weather, but each contact along the chain had been rehearsed and bribed.

At one Iranian checkpoint, a guard opened the truck's tailgate, sniffed the cargo, and waved it through after a subtle payment. At another, the driver staged a minor argument about fuel shortages to distract attention. After twenty-two hours on the road, they reached the border. The papers: crude but credible, passed inspection.

By the time the sun rose over Khanaqin, the assassin was back inside Iraq, delivered to a Directorate 14 safehouse for debriefing.

Aftermath and interpretation

In Qum, the blast sparked confusion and outrage. Iranian investigators found only fragments: charred cloth, twisted nails, a portion of a coat rack. No trace of foreign origin survived.

Rumors spread of internal rivalry, divine punishment, or mechanical failure. The MOIS suspected outside involvement but lacked proof. The case was quietly buried under theological caution; no regime wanted to admit its sanctuaries could be breached.

In Baghdad, the operation was recorded as a triumph of precision. The opposition's voice was gone, exiles fell silent, and a psychological tremor ran through dissident circles from Tehran to Damascus.

For the IIS, it proved that even under the watchful eye of a revolutionary state, patience and preparation could still deliver lethal reach. The operative's name was never entered in commendation rolls; he received neither medal nor public acknowledgment. His reward was continuity: another assignment, another identity.

Yet inside the service, Sada al-Minbar became legend: not for its violence, but for its perfection. It showed that power need not roar when it can whisper, and that the most decisive victories are those that leave no echo but silence.

ANALYSIS AND LESSONS LEARNED: THE PRECISION DOCTRINE

Tactical brilliance and moral shadows

The assassination in Qum was not crude violence: it was controlled certainty. It married patient human tradecraft to technical subtlety and produced a single, devastating result: a high-value voice silenced with minimal forensic trace and limited immediate blowback.

That tactical success revealed a rare competency: one in which every element was engineered to disappear into the ordinary rhythms of the target environment. Yet the operation's elegance forces uncomfortable questions about the ethics of assassination, the burden placed on anonymous operatives, and the wisdom of silencing a mind instead of neutralizing an idea.

This analysis breaks the mission into its core components, extracts lessons for case officers, and interrogates the moral and strategic costs inherent in "perfect" violence.

Anatomy of an unmistakable hit

Qum succeeded because the IIS controlled variables that others could not: the asset, the cover, the device, the timing, and the extraction. The operation's architecture was design-first and risk-averse: a deliberate inversion of the usual act now, explain later mentality that ruins covert work.

Precision is not improvisation; it is the culmination of rehearsals, patience, and humility before uncertainty.

But surgical success at the tactical level often breeds strategic ambiguity. The act removed a dangerous preacher, yes, but it also etched a warning into collective memory: even holy places are not safe from politics. That repercussion travels farther than planners imagine.

The Four Pillars of Success

1. Asset Selection: Invisibility First

The operative's greatest strength was not courage or technical skill; it was ordinariness. He fit because he belonged. His dialect, gait, and prayer cadence allowed him to vanish within the congregation. The IIS chose someone accepted without explanation and trained him to be even less remarkable.

Operational takeaway: choose assets whose baseline behavior already matches the target culture.

Key Insight: The most unremarkable operative can be the most lethal.

2. Training and Cultural Immersion: Patience as a Weapon

His training emphasized doing nothing until something mattered. Weeks of observation turned the Imam's rituals into a predictable script; rehearsed gestures became reflex. The mission relied on discipline: he waited for the single second when the Imam's hand brushed the cloak, then acted.

Operational takeaway: drill operatives until local rhythm becomes instinct.

Key Insight: Immersion breeds calm; calm delivers precision.

3. Technical Ingenuity: Tools That Hide in Plain Sight

The weapon was no super-device; it was an ordinary object disguised to perfection. Built with Iranian cloth and buttons, its detonator hidden in a thread, it left no forensic trail. Technology succeeded because it mimicked its surroundings.

Operational takeaway: engineer tools that merge with the environment.

Key Insight: Invisibility, not sophistication, defines effective technology.

4. Timing and Extraction: The Exit as Part of the Kill

The strike's choreography was precise; the retreat, rehearsed. The operative moved through Qum like water through stone: seen but unnoticed, then melted into the network that carried him home. The route out mattered as much as the strike itself.

Operational takeaway: build the exit while designing the entry.

Key Insight: A flawless hit without extraction is merely a public confession.

Lessons for Case Officers: A Blueprint for Precision

Lesson 1: Match Human to Mission
Prioritize cultural fit and behavioral stability over raw skill.

Why: a man who belongs raises fewer alarms than a man who performs.

Lesson 2: Train for Routine
Condition operatives to master repetition before innovation.

Why: routine breeds predictability; predictability reveals opportunity.

Lesson 3: Engineer for Context
Every tool must reflect the local material culture.

Why: ordinary design is the ultimate camouflage.

Lesson 4: Build the Exit Before the Entry
Plan withdrawal with the same rigor as infiltration.

Why: escape is part of success, not its aftermath.

Lesson 5: Reward Restraint, Not Drama
Institutionalize patience as valor.

Why: those who wait longest often strike best.

Ethical Considerations: The Quiet Toll of Perfection
Precision kills leave moral residue. Assassinating an imam inside a mosque crossed spiritual and cultural thresholds, risking that tactical victory become a strategic wound.

- Sacred-Space Violation: targeting a place of worship risks martyrdom and mass radicalization.
- Asset Toll: anonymity becomes a life sentence; the operative bears the unseen weight of his deed.
- Diplomatic Fallout: Even absent proof, political shockwaves invite retaliation and loss of legitimacy.
- Reflection: Operational skill and moral judgment must act as partners. Mastery without conscience erodes the institution that wields it.

Strategic appraisal: Did silence solve the problem?
Killing a persuasive voice halts a message in one channel but rarely erases the grievance beneath it. The Qum strike bought Baghdad short-term quiet yet deepened resolve among exiled clerics who saw it as proof of reach and ruthlessness.

The mission solved a tactical problem; it may have strengthened the ideological one.

Strategic Takeaway: Tactical silence can amplify strategic noise; use elimination only when the long-term dividend outweighs political and moral cost.

Final reflections: Mastery tempered by conscience

The Qum operation remains a study in what precision can achieve when patience and design converge. It shows how a state with limited reach can project power across borders through discipline alone.

Yet the moral lesson endures: perfection in shadows produces echoes in daylight. Every planner and case officer who designs such acts inherits their consequences: for the operative who must vanish, for the communities unsettled by violence, and for the moral fabric of the service itself.

If you take one point from Qum, let it be this:

Precision is power: without reflection, it becomes practice without conscience.

Use the doctrine carefully, and only after you have measured the full weight of both consequence and necessity.

Case Study 6:
The Failed Recruitment in Tehran: A Lesson in Honesty and Strategic Planning

THE STORY: WHEN DECEPTION CONSUMES THE DECEIVER

Tehran in the late 1990s pulsed with paradox: modern towers rising beside ancient mosques, whispers of reform shadowed by the watchful eyes of the Ministry of Intelligence and Security (MOIS). For two newly trained Iraqi Intelligence Service (IIS) case officers, the city was both a prize and a trap.

Their assignment looked simple on paper, yet reeked of danger: recruit Iranian assets capable of reporting on domestic mood, dissent, and reconstruction after war. Fresh from Baghdad's academy, they arrived with crisp certificates, untested confidence, and that faint arrogance youth mistakes for competence.

Tehran would cure them quickly.

The briefing: No errors, no excuses

The station chief, a heavy-set veteran of covert wars, summoned them to the small "press liaison" office inside the Iraqi Embassy: a room thick with smoke and tension.

"This is your first test," he said through a haze of cigarette fumes. "No errors, no excuses. Blend in. Don't stand out. You're in the enemy's capital: act like it."

He ordered them to disappear into Tehran's rhythm, to listen before speaking. His final counsel was brutal in its pragmatism: "Find someone desperate for what you can offer. Tehran is full of hungry men."

The pair nodded, masking unease behind forced confidence. As they stepped into the city's cold morning, the enormity of the task pressed down.

There would be no safety net, no second chance. Deep down, they felt the weight of inexperience, like shadows lengthening in the Tehran dusk.

The search: Cracks in the wall

Days bled into weeks. They roamed bazaars, smoke-choked teahouses, and crowded buses, listening for discontent disguised as casual complaint: rising prices, corruption, quiet anger at the clerics. Their Farsi was smooth enough; their instincts were not. Tehran's citizens were cautious; strangers were catalogued, not trusted.

Each night they returned empty-handed, notebooks filled with trivia, confidence draining away. The station chief's patience thinned, his stares growing colder with each debrief.

"You've been here a month," he barked. "If Tehran were full of ghosts, I'd still expect you to find one who talks!"

Humiliation burned. The younger officer: impulsive, proud, swore he'd deliver someone, whatever the cost. The elder, sensing the desperation, tried to temper it, but pressure from above silenced his doubts.

The Bus Encounter: A Spark in the Noise

Opportunity came unannounced.

A packed bus rattled through central Tehran, passengers arguing about bread and power cuts. Then one voice rose above the noise: sharp, fearless:

"The regime feasts while the people starve! The mullahs' palaces shine while our children beg!"

Heads turned; some frowned, others nodded. The two officers exchanged a glance. There: that one, a young man with fire in his eyes, unbowed by the surrounding caution.

When the bus stopped, the young dissenter stepped off. They followed at a careful distance through narrow streets until he slowed.

"Assalamu alaikum," one officer greeted.

"Wa alaikum assalam," the young man replied, wary.

The Iraqi smiled, his tone polished by deceit. "We're from the UAE: new in Tehran, could use a guide."

At the mention of Dubai, suspicion eased. "Dubai?" he asked, eyes brightening. "I've dreamed of working there."

The bait took instantly. "We're with the UAE Embassy," the second officer added. "Help us now, and maybe we can help you with a visa."

One word: visa, and hope lit the trap.

"Tomorrow, same place?" he asked. They agreed, hearts racing. Their first live prospect, a glimmer amid the frustration.

The courtship: A web of words

At the café the next day, the young man arrived early, clutching dreams larger than his wallet. Over sweet tea, he spoke of hardship: a university student scraping by, angry at clerics who preached virtue but lived in privilege. The officers listened, nurturing resentment while mirroring sympathy, their notes hidden beneath casual nods.

They asked for a "small favor": a short report on student attitudes toward government reforms, framed as research for a diplomatic memo. Flattered, he delivered it within days: typed neatly, glowing with earnestness. They praised him lavishly and paid modestly, deepening the bond.

Soon came a second request: broader insight, student unions, protest circles, classroom sentiment. Each task drew him nearer the red lines, his reports growing bolder as trust seemed to build.

But deception ages quickly. Curiosity hardened into doubt.

"When can I apply for that visa?" he asked one evening, smiling too politely.

"Soon," they said: once, then again, until "soon" became silence, eroding the fragile foundation they had laid.

The trap: A café turned courtroom

When he proposed meeting at a different café, they mistook it for convenience. It was a setup.

The student arrived tense, politeness stretched thin.

"No more reports," he said flatly. "Not until I know who you really are."

The younger officer froze. In panic, the elder tried to reclaim authority:

"We're not from the UAE. We're Iraqi intelligence."

The confession detonated louder than any device.

The student's chair scraped back. "You lied to me!" he shouted, voice cracking through the café. Heads turned. "These men are Iraqi spies! They tricked me!"

Chaos erupted. The officers fled through startled customers, into the street, into a waiting taxi. Behind them came the shout that kills cover: "Iraqi spies!"

Minutes later, they slammed through the embassy gates: a fortress now doubling as a cage, their faces flushed with the sting of exposure.

The fallout: Humiliation without rescue

The station chief met them in silence, cigarette trembling between his fingers. No lecture, only the long exhale of disgust, his eyes conveying the depth of their failure.

At dawn, a cable arrived from Baghdad: Return immediately. Mission terminated.

By nightfall, the two were en route to the border: diplomatic immunity shielding them from prison, not from shame. The IIS station was compromised; Tehran buzzed with rumor; a potential network evaporated before it began. Whispers of their blunder rippled back to Baghdad, a cautionary tale etched in official reports.

Their first mission ended not in glory but disgrace. The lie meant to recruit had destroyed the trust recruitment depends on.

In intelligence, deception is a weapon, but when wielded without strategy or restraint, it turns inward and cuts its master.

Their lesson, though earned in humiliation, was immortal: honesty, timing, and patience are not weaknesses in recruitment; they are its only durable foundation.

Conclusion: The discipline of truth

The Tehran fiasco was not merely a failed recruitment: it was a mirror held up to the Iraqi Intelligence Service itself. Beneath the chaos of that café and the echo of shouted accusations lay a deeper lesson: deception, when used without purpose, consumes the deceiver first.

Recruitment is not theater. It is the delicate art of aligning interests, not manufacturing illusions. The two young officers mistook manipulation for tradecraft and urgency for mastery. Their downfall was not caused by betrayal but by the arrogance of believing that lies alone can build loyalty.

In espionage, every falsehood must serve a truth: the truth of understanding human motivation. The student they sought to exploit was not their enemy; he was their unintentional teacher. His indignation revealed the cost of haste and the price of dishonesty in the human dimension of intelligence work.

For every case officer, Tehran stands as a warning: trust cannot be counterfeited, and desperation is not a substitute for preparation. The best recruitment begins not with a lie, but with listening.

The quiet irony of this story is that the operation failed not because the student spoke too loudly, but because the officers never listened deeply enough.

In the shadowed world of recruitment, truth is not the enemy of success: it is its foundation. When honesty becomes strategy, deception becomes art.

ANALYSIS AND LESSONS LEARNED

The anatomy of a failed recruitment

The Tehran recruitment did not implode overnight; it decayed slowly, like a structure built on vanity instead of foundation. Its collapse was the product of human flaws more than hostile counterintelligence: the quiet corrosion of discipline, humility, and foresight. Two young Iraqi Intelligence Service (IIS) officers, eager for recognition, turned a promising encounter into a cautionary legend. What began as a spark of initiative became a public disaster, one that echoed through the corridors of the Directorate in Baghdad long after they returned home in disgrace.

This case remains one of the clearest mirrors of what happens when ambition outpaces maturity. It is not a tale of betrayal; it is a tale of blindness: of two men who believed they could manipulate the human heart without understanding it.

A spotlight on inexperience

The Tehran operation was born not from strategy, but from the hunger to impress. Assigned to a hostile capital with minimal oversight, the two officers treated recruitment as theater: a stage on which to display wit rather than discipline. Their plan to pose as UAE diplomats was audacious, but audacity without architecture collapses under its own cleverness.

Inexperienced officers often mistake imagination for ingenuity. The cover story sounded believable in a classroom but crumbled in a culture where every accent is interrogated and every gesture weighed. Iran, steeped in historical suspicion of its Arab neighbors, was the worst possible stage for that script.

The operation's downfall came not from the MOIS or technical compromise, but from the slow unraveling of a deception the officers themselves could no longer control. In espionage, falsehood is an art, but art without restraint becomes self-inflicted sabotage.

The lesson is stark and timeless: no lie can outlive the truth it contradicts.

The lie: A trap of their own making

Their choice of cover was the first fracture. The pretense of being UAE diplomats seemed clever on paper: the Gulf states had embassies in Tehran, and the lure of a visa was a plausible incentive. Yet the simplicity of the scheme was its poison: it offered the illusion of safety while guaranteeing collapse.

- No exit strategy: Every deception must have a horizon: a controlled endpoint or a fallback truth. These officers built theirs on fantasy. When the student asked for evidence, for names, for a form to sign, they had nothing. Their silence became confession; their hesitation, exposure.
- Cultural disconnect: They underestimated how deeply Iran distrusted Gulf Arab motives. For many Iranians, the UAE represented wealth, exploitation, and Western alignment: precisely the wrong emotional resonance for a cover designed to earn empathy. In a place where every foreigner's accent carries geopolitical meaning, they chose the one least likely to survive scrutiny.
- Ego over ethics: Their deception was not a strategic necessity; it was vanity disguised as ingenuity. They wanted results fast: to impress the station chief, to secure recognition, to escape the monotony of inaction. When ambition drives deceit, empathy vanishes, and the operation becomes theater played for an audience of one's own pride.
- **Insight:** In intelligence, deception must be a means, never an identity. A lie without an exit plan is not tradecraft: it is suicide disguised as creativity.

Asset Mismanagement: Misreading the Human Equation

The young Iranian student was not a hardened operative or an ideological traitor. He was an ordinary man caught in extraordinary frustration: a victim of his country's stagnation and his own unfulfilled dreams. He wanted freedom, not espionage.

The officers saw in him what they needed to see: a dissident ripe for manipulation. But recruitment is never about what the case officer wants; it is about what the target needs. They mistook enthusiasm for trust, compliance for loyalty, and curiosity for submission.

- Misread intent: The student's motive was transparent: he sought a path out of Iran. Yet they treated his longing as leverage, not insight. Had they truly understood his psychology, they might have transitioned from deception to persuasion, from false promise to realistic opportunity. Instead, they weaponized hope until it turned into resentment.
- Pacing mismatch: They demanded more information even as his patience eroded. In espionage, tempo is chemistry. Push too fast, and suspicion ignites; move too slowly, and boredom cools the flame. The officers neither measured nor matched his rhythm: they moved at the speed of their ambition, not his trust.
- No contingency plan: When the lie began to crack, they panicked. No pretext. No diversion. No structured retreat. They had never rehearsed what to do when the asset questioned them. The silence that followed his confrontation was the sound of an operation dying in real time.
- **Insight:** Human intelligence is not about control: it is about calibration. Misread a motive, and every tactic becomes noise.

Cultural Rigidity: The Failure to Read the Room

Tehran is a city that tests the invisible: patience, subtlety, timing. The two officers, trapped inside their own arrogance, failed to read the shifting currents of human behavior around them.

- Ignored warning signs: The student's tone grew colder. His insistence on choosing the meeting place: a public café, was a signal, not a convenience. In intelligence, small changes in habit often scream louder than words. They ignored it.
- Loss of tactical ground: By agreeing to his terms, they surrendered control. The café was his ground, filled with his peers, his social safety net. Every table was an audience, every whisper a potential echo. When cornered, he lashed out publicly, and they had nowhere left to run.

- Panic response: Confessing their true identity: "We're Iraqi intelligence," was the moment the professional died and the human panicked. No seasoned officer would have uttered those words. But fear is faster than training when conviction is built on lies.
- **Insight:** Cultural awareness is not optional. It is the operating system of every successful mission. Without it, even truth sounds false.

Lessons learned: The discipline of foresight

The Tehran incident stands as a complete reversal of every principle the Directorate tried to instill. Its lessons are simple, sharp, and unforgiving.

Lesson 1: Lies Need Lifelines

Every deception must have an escape clause: alternate identities, cover stories, or plausible deniability.

Why: A lie that cannot bend will shatter.

Lesson 2: Read the Room, Then Re-Read It

Listen before you speak, watch before you act. Human behavior is an ever-shifting map; those who read it poorly get lost in their own narrative.

Why: Empathy is the first layer of security.

Lesson 3: Culture Is the Compass

Without cultural literacy, every gesture is misread and every word mis-fires. Learn the local logic before you attempt to shape it.

Why: A misplaced metaphor can be deadlier than a hidden microphone.

Lesson 4: Discipline Over Desire

Ambition fuels initiative, but only discipline sustains it. The need to prove oneself is the first trap every young officer must outgrow.

Why: The field rewards restraint, not hunger.

Ethical reflections: The price of manipulation

Beyond tactical misjudgment lies the deeper moral wound: they exploited faith. The officers didn't just manipulate a man: they manipulated his hope.

- Exploiting dreams: The false promise of a Dubai visa transformed human aspiration into bait. For a struggling student, that dream was sacred, and its betrayal unforgivable.

- Endangering innocence: When the confrontation erupted, the student's life was no longer his own. Tehran's secret police are not merciful. Whether he was detained, questioned, or marked, his punishment was collateral damage in someone else's vanity project.

- Corroding institutional integrity: Their recklessness didn't just compromise one operation; it stained the reputation of the entire IIS presence in Tehran. Future contacts hesitated. Trust: already rare, evaporated.

- Reflection: In intelligence, deception is necessary, but cruelty never is. A lie told without conscience destroys the liar first.

Broader context: Failure as reflection of success

Placed beside the precision of Qum or the restraint of Tehran Station's counter-surveillance cases, this failure becomes the inverse image of mastery.

Qum's Lesson: Precision and patience turn danger into opportunity.

Tehran's Lesson: Impulse and ego turn opportunity into exposure.

Each failure mirrors a forgotten principle. The same traits that defined earlier IIS triumphs: patience, preparation, empathy, were absent here. The Tehran fiasco became a living reminder that success leaves a map; failure erases it.

Insight: In espionage, failure is not the opposite of success. It is success performed backward, with the same tools used irresponsibly.

Conclusion: The high stakes of low stakes

The Tehran recruitment should have been a small, quiet victory: a first step toward network-building in one of the most difficult capitals on earth. Instead, it became a cautionary fable repeated in every classroom of the intelligence academy.

The lesson endures because it is human. These officers were not villains; they were impatient men playing at mastery before they'd earned humility. Their downfall reminds every case officer that in deception, the greatest danger is believing your own lie.

Honesty in recruitment is not sentimentality: it is strategy. Cultural fluency is not decoration: it is defense. Adaptability is not improvisation: it is survival.

In espionage, it is not the size of the secret that determines success, but the steadiness of the one who carries it.

In the world of shadows, the smallest deception can echo across an entire service. Tehran proved that even minor arrogance, left unchecked, can become the loudest failure.

Case Study 7:

The Journalist Spy: A Masterclass in Long-Term Asset Management

THE STORY: THE VOICE THAT LISTENED TOO CLOSELY

The 1980s burned like a fever across the Middle East. The Iran-Iraq War, eight unrelenting years of exhaustion, propaganda, and attrition, had turned both nations into mirror fortresses of fear. The Iraqi Intelligence Service (IIS) understood that the real battle was not only on the frontlines but across the airwaves, the presses, and the pulpits. Words, if shaped correctly, could wound deeper than bullets.

In Tehran, Iraqi exiles thrived under the patronage of Iran's revolutionary regime. Former officers, clerics, and idealists produced pamphlets and radio broadcasts denouncing Saddam's rule, each sermon and headline a quiet artillery shell aimed at Baghdad. Iraq's embassy was shuttered, its diplomats expelled, and its agents hunted. Yet the regime in Baghdad still needed eyes inside Tehran's propaganda network: a voice that could whisper through the noise.

The solution emerged not within Iraq's borders but in the gray zones of neutrality: the cafés of Ankara, the backrooms of Istanbul, the liminal corridors where war's exiles traded stories instead of gunfire. It was there, in 1987, that the IIS found its opening: a journalist whose curiosity could become a conduit.

The recruitment: Whispers in neutral territory

He was a man displaced by conviction: a Basran journalist whose pen had once praised Iraq's revolution but whose questions had become too sharp for comfort. Exile had softened neither his intellect nor his pride. By the late 1980s, he was working in Tehran, writing in fluent Persian for local publications, attending clerical conferences, and slowly building trust among Iran's intellectual elite. He had become, in the words of one observer, "the Iraqi who listened better than he spoke."

The first contact came through an Iranian intermediary: a cultural attaché who owed Baghdad more favors than Tehran would ever know. A meeting was arranged in Istanbul, framed as an interview for an academic piece on post-war media ethics. The journalist arrived wearing a gray suit still creased from travel and a guarded smile.

Their conversation flowed effortlessly: censorship, ideology, and the fatigue of endless conflict. The IIS officer, operating under commercial cover, recognized something rare: a man whose curiosity outweighed his ideology. Over several months, they met again and again in quiet corners of Istanbul, conversations growing bolder as familiarity replaced formality.

Finally, one evening in a rented office behind a translation company's signboard, the officer laid it bare:

"You already see what others miss. I'm asking you to keep noticing, and to share what you see with those who can use it wisely."

The journalist's eyes didn't flinch. He had long understood that truth was a currency. "Information," he said, "is only dangerous when given to fools. I assume you are not one."

He didn't need coercion. He needed purpose.

When the Iran-Iraq War ended in 1988, the journalist, now under the IIS codename Mazin, was already sending carefully measured reports through indirect channels. His dispatches detailed exiled clerics' rivalries, funding routes, and the tone of Tehran's propaganda. When Baghdad and Tehran restored diplomatic relations two years later, Mazin was not a new recruit. He was an established instrument in motion.

The foundation: Building an asset

With Iraq's embassy reopened in Tehran in the early 1990s, Mazin's file was transferred to the formal registry in Baghdad. His new handler, a patient professional known for his quiet authority, viewed him not as a subordinate but as a partner.

Their relationship evolved through ritual: tea in the embassy library, coded references to "articles pending approval," monthly payments recorded as "translation fees." What distinguished the handler's approach was restraint. He never demanded; he guided. He built trust like a scaffolding, slowly and deliberately.

Under that mentorship, Mazin perfected the art of dual existence. By day, he was a respected journalist: interviewing clerics, moderating debates, and writing essays that threaded criticism through flattery. By night, he was Baghdad's antenna, sending detailed assessments of Iran's ideological currents and the moods of exiled Iraqis in Qum.

"You are a journalist to them," his handler would remind him, "but to us, you are a mirror held up to their truth."

His assignments were simple yet vital: map emerging student groups sympathetic to Iraq, chart the loyalties of Iraqi clerics studying in Iran, and record the tonal shifts in Tehran's state media. His reports were clinical, never emotional: the handwriting of a man who understood that survival was precision.

By 1993, Baghdad reclassified him from "source" to "strategic collaborator." Within the Directorate, the name Mazin became shorthand for reliability.

The ascent: A voice that shaped the airwaves

The 1990s transformed Mazin from a listener into an architect of perception. His credibility in Iranian media grew; his Arabic fluency and measured tone made him a favored guest on state-aligned programs analyzing Iraq's politics. His calm neutrality concealed a pipeline of insight flowing directly to Baghdad.

To his handlers, Mazin was both a triumph and a warning. His visibility granted unprecedented access: to editors, clerics, dissidents, even foreign diplomats, yet it also exposed him to danger. The line between influence and exposure narrowed with every broadcast.

By the mid-1990s, he was earning over a thousand dollars a month in operational stipends: modest by Western standards, significant by regional ones. But his true motivation had evolved: relevance. For a man once exiled and forgotten, the attention of both capitals was its own reward.

At times, his handler worried that Mazin was beginning to enjoy the performance too much. Espionage thrives on invisibility, yet Mazin's face had become familiar on Iranian television. He was living the contradiction every successful agent eventually faces: the temptation to believe his public persona was his truest self.

The pivot: When the listener wanted a name

By 2002, with the region trembling toward another war, Mazin's confidence grew into subtle defiance. In a private meeting inside the Iraqi Embassy, he made an unusual request:

"I need Iraqi passports for my family, in the name I use on air. That name is my identity now."

It was a pragmatic request, but one laced with risk. Forged passports under his public alias could unravel his entire cover if discovered by Iranian security. Baghdad refused.

Mazin nodded calmly, concealing whatever resentment brewed beneath his poise. "A journalist," he said softly, "belongs to no border."

The line hung in the air like a prophecy. It was both truth and warning: his allegiance was shifting from a nation to a narrative.

The reinvention: The survivor without a master

Then came 2003. The regime in Baghdad fell, and with it the intelligence service that had built him. Within weeks, Mazin's lifeline vanished. There were no cables, no payments, no orders: only silence. Lesser agents panicked. Mazin adapted.

He resurfaced within months as a political commentator on Gulf-based satellite channels, rebranding himself as a moral voice against tyranny. The same eloquence that once served Baghdad now condemned it. He criticized dictatorship, celebrated democracy, and did so with the authenticity of a man who seemed to know too much.

His popularity soared. To millions, he became the conscience of a wounded nation. To the few surviving IIS officers watching from exile, he was the embodiment of irony: a man trained to manipulate truth who now weaponized it against his creators.

But in truth, Mazin had not betrayed anyone. He had simply mastered the final rule of survival: when the system dies, step outside it before it buries you.

The epilogue: The echo in the static

If one were to find his file, if it survived the looting of Baghdad's archives, it would read like a paradox in motion. Loyal yet pragmatic, obedient yet self-preserving, Mazin represented the evolution of espionage itself: from ideology to adaptability.

He was the asset who outlived the agency, the listener who became the voice. Where most spies vanish when the lights go out, Mazin learned to stand beneath them and control their glow.

In London, years later, he would tell a colleague over coffee,

"I never changed sides: I just stopped pretending there were sides."

That, perhaps, was his truest confession: and his final act of intelligence.

Conclusion: The man who outlived the mission

When the dust of war settled and the archives of empires turned to ash, Mazin remained: neither hero nor traitor, but something far more complex: a survivor of his own invention. He had spent two decades living between headlines and secrets, reshaping truth until it became both armor and identity.

In the quiet rooms of intelligence history, his kind rarely earn monuments. Their victories are anonymous, their betrayals invisible. Yet Mazin's story endures because it defied both endings. When Baghdad fell, he did not vanish into silence or exile's despair. He reinvented himself in full view of the world: a ghost who learned to cast his own shadow.

His transformation was not an act of treachery; it was the ultimate application of everything he had been taught. The IIS trained him to adapt, to survive, to control the narrative. They never imagined that one day the narrative he would control would be his own.

In London's gray drizzle, where he now spoke as a man of conscience, Mazin embodied the paradox of espionage itself: a life sustained by deception, redeemed by understanding. His greatest act of intelligence was not the information he gave, but the identity he constructed: the fiction that became fact through endurance.

In the end, he did not serve a flag or a doctrine.

ANALYSIS AND LESSONS LEARNED

The architecture of loyalty and control

The journalist's arc remains one of the Iraqi Intelligence Service's most fascinating paradoxes: a near-perfect success that unraveled not through betrayal, but through evolution. For nearly twenty years, he embodied everything a case officer dreams of: discipline without protest, access without arrogance, and results without drama. Yet in the end, his survival instinct outlasted the state that built him.

His story is both a monument to precision and a monument to loss: a lesson that even the most brilliant long-term operation can collapse when the asset learns the craft too well.

The paradox of perfection

On paper, the operation was flawless. The IIS had converted an exiled

Iraqi journalist, an articulate observer already embedded within Tehran's media and clerical circles, into a consistent, reliable intelligence source.

He required no legend, no forged biography. His life was his cover. Every interview, every editorial meeting, every question he asked served two masters: the newsroom and the Directorate in Baghdad.

Yet beneath this elegant simplicity lay the seed of inevitable independence. The very traits that made him effective: curiosity, adaptability, and intellect, would one day make him uncontrollable.

When the IIS crumbled in 2003, he didn't fall with it. He merely shifted form, transforming from an instrument of statecraft into an architect of narrative. His story reveals the fundamental truth of human intelligence: loyalty has a half-life. It decays quietly unless constantly renewed through purpose, not pressure.

Strategic recruitment: The perfect cover and its hidden poison

Recruiting a journalist was a masterstroke. Few professions offer greater mobility or legitimacy. Reporters ask questions others fear to ask; they move between embassies and slums with equal ease. In intelligence terms, journalism is camouflage made of credibility.

- Organic cover: The journalist's cover required no maintenance. Every note, every photograph, every interview doubled as intelligence work. In his profession, he generated plausible reasons for proximity: to clerics, to exiles, to diplomats.
- Cultural duality: His Iraqi origin and Persian fluency gave him rare bilateral access. He could inhabit both worlds: the Arab and the Iranian, without appearing to serve either.
- Emotional leverage: His exile made him cautious but hungry. The IIS recognized that mixture of resentment and ambition and turned it into motive. They didn't recruit him through ideology, but through utility.
- **Insight:** Perfect cover breeds imperfect control. The journalist's independence: the very trait that protected him, also empowered him to

redefine the terms of loyalty. Once an asset realizes his value, control must evolve or evaporate.

Long-term management: The art of emotional equilibrium

The IIS displayed extraordinary discipline in cultivating this relationship. Unlike the impatient operations that burned bright and died fast, this one was built brick by brick. The journalist was never coerced, only guided. His handler, an officer known for his restraint, managed him like a chess piece: careful, predictable, and patient.

- Handler continuity: The same case officer managed him for years, ensuring familiarity and emotional consistency. The professional line blurred gradually into mentorship: the most dangerous but effective form of loyalty.

- Handler conditioning: Praise replaced pressure. His sense of importance became the leash that control could not provide. He wasn't paid to obey; he was paid to matter.

- Measured escalation: His tasks grew in complexity only as his confidence matured. The IIS never overloaded him, which created the illusion of partnership: a psychological space where dependency masqueraded as agency.

- **Insight:** Long-term management is not domination; it is balance. The IIS mastered that balance for years. But in doing so, they built an operative who could eventually operate without them.

Operational output: When words become weapons

His reports rarely mentioned troop movements or weapons shipments. They dealt in subtler currencies: ideological currents, factional rivalries, clerical moods, and the shifting tone of Tehran's propaganda. These were not dispatches; they were temperature readings of a nation.

- Unique Access: His journalism granted entry where spies were barred. He met imams, reformists, and journalists: mapping the veins of Iranian influence that even embassy officers couldn't touch.

- Analytical Precision: Over time, his reports evolved from descriptive notes into assessments that shaped Baghdad's information warfare strategy. He wasn't just observing Iran: he was interpreting it.
- Analytical Impact: His intelligence shaped Baghdad's understanding of psychological warfare, propaganda narratives, and the mood of Iraq's exiled opposition.
- **Insight:** The more insight he produced, the more self-aware he became. Knowledge is a mirror; once an asset understands how indispensable he is, loyalty becomes a negotiation, not a condition.

The turning point: Autonomy without oversight

The first tremor of independence arrived years before Baghdad's fall. His request for passports under his alias was not about travel; it was about authorship: the right to own the identity he had used for the state's benefit. The request was both symbolic and prophetic.

When the IIS refused, they protected operational security but fractured emotional continuity. For Mazin, the denial confirmed a truth every asset eventually learns: to the state, usefulness is love's only measure.

When the regime collapsed in 2003, he simply stopped reporting. No coded message, no extraction. The silence was his resignation letter.

His reinvention as a public intellectual was not rebellion: it was inheritance. He used the very tradecraft Baghdad had instilled: narrative control, audience manipulation, emotional calibration, to construct a second life.

Insight: Every long-term operation contains a countdown. When an asset stops needing their handler, the operation has already ended: even if no one admits it.

Lessons learned: The psychology of long-term asset survival

The journalist's evolution offers enduring doctrines for case officers managing long-term relationships:

Lesson 1: Loyalty Must Be Verified, Not Assumed
Emotional closeness distorts judgment. Continuously test alignment through indirect verification. Trust is never permanent; it is a living equation.

Lesson 2: Empowerment Breeds Autonomy
Independence increases performance, but also risk. Balance freedom with structured dependency to prevent defection through self-sufficiency.

Lesson 3: Culture Changes the Handler Too
Deeply embedded assets absorb their environment, often faster than their case officers anticipate. Recalibrate regularly to prevent ideological assimilation.

Lesson 4: Build the Exit Before the Entry
Every long-term relationship needs an ending: extraction, transition, or controlled release. Without one, the asset writes their own epilogue.

Key Insight: The longer an asset survives, the more the line blurs between who controls whom. The IIS managed loyalty brilliantly but forgot that loyalty is a renewable resource, not a permanent installation.

Ethical Reflections: The Price of Mutual Manipulation
The relationship between Mazin and the IIS lives in a gray moral space: neither exploitation nor partnership, but something between seduction and necessity.

- Exploitation vs. empowerment: Both sides used each other. He gained protection and purpose; they gained access and influence. But when the balance shifted, he retained both skills and moral immunity.
- Identity ownership: The refusal to grant him a passport under his alias symbolized the state's final act of control. In denying his new identity, they ensured he would claim it himself.
- The afterlife of tradecraft: When Mazin emerged as a celebrated public commentator, he carried the ghost of the IIS within him: their training,

their discipline, their restraint, repurposed for survival.

- Reflection: Espionage breeds relationships that exist in moral twilight. Every handler believes they are the architect, every asset believes they are the survivor. Both are right: until one outlives the other.

Broader context: Success in the shadow of collapse

When compared to other IIS operations, the journalist's story reframes what success means.

- Compared to Qum: It lacked surgical precision but achieved longevity: influence without exposure.
- Compared to Tehran: It displayed patience, not impulsive ambition: a long burn instead of a sudden flash.
- Compared to Kharg Island: It replaced explosives with intellect, achieving impact through persuasion instead of destruction.
- **Insight:** The journalist operation was not a failure. It was an evolution: a demonstration that the finest operations are not those that end cleanly, but those that continue without command.

Conclusion: The asset who outlived his handlers

In the end, Mazin was both masterpiece and warning: the asset who learned the system so well, he no longer needed it.

The IIS trained him to adapt, to control perception, and to survive through ambiguity. When the agency disappeared, he simply inherited its instincts. He lived by the same rules he had once obeyed: only now he wrote them himself.

The agency saw loyalty as permanence; he understood it as momentum.

When Baghdad's walls fell, he didn't seek safety: he sought an audience. And in doing so, he became the one thing every intelligence service fears most: an asset who knows how to keep telling the story after the storytellers are gone.

In London's gray drizzle, where he now spoke as a man of conscience,

Mazin embodied the paradox of espionage itself: a life sustained by deception, redeemed by understanding. His greatest act of intelligence was not the information he gave, but the identity he constructed: the fiction that became fact through endurance.

In the end, he did not serve a flag or a doctrine. He served the story, and the story, in turn, kept him alive.

Case Study 8:
Bribery and Infiltration of Rafha Refugee Camp

THE STORY: THE PRICE OF PRINCIPLE

The year 1991 should have marked Iraq's deliverance. Instead, it birthed despair. The Gulf War had ended in surrender, but not in peace. Across the Shia heartlands: Basra, Najaf, Hilla, Karbala, and beyond, rebellion erupted like wildfire, only to be drowned in blood. When the gunfire stopped, rivers of people fled south across the desert: deserters, rebels, clerics, and families who had dared to believe in change.

They reached the edge of Saudi Arabia with nothing but exhaustion and faith. There, on the barren plain near Rafha, a tent city rose overnight: nearly 30,000 Iraqi refugees contained behind barbed wire and watch-towers. The world called it a humanitarian shelter. Those inside called it a prison of mercy.

For the Iraqi Intelligence Service (IIS), Rafha was not a tragedy: it was a threat. Within those fences gathered Iraq's defeated yet unbroken: former officers, activists, and clerics whose defiance had not been extinguished, only displaced. To Baghdad, Rafha was a living wound just across the border, and every wound, they believed, could be cauterized from within.

The order came quietly from the Directorate of External Operations:

"Destabilize Rafha without crossing its walls."

The method was not invasion. It was corruption.

The Saudi officer: A man of uniform and cracks

Every fortress has its gatekeeper, and Rafha's was commanded by a Saudi officer, a career man in his forties whose authority rested as much on posture as it did on power. To his subordinates, he was the embodiment of order: crisp uniform, mirrored sunglasses, and a reputation for discipline. To the refugees, he was the faceless warden of their confinement.

But under the rigid exterior lay vulnerabilities too human to ignore. He drank in secret: a forbidden act in a kingdom where a bottle could destroy a career. He was also suffocating in debt, burdened by two wives, nine children, and a lifestyle that demanded more than his salary could sustain.

To Baghdad's analysts, those weaknesses were not flaws: they were openings.

"No fortress is impregnable," one IIS colonel remarked. "You only need to find the man who guards its gate... and his price."

The decision was made. Rafha would not be breached with guns or spies. It would be bought: one drink, one debt, one whisper at a time.

The asset: The bridge in uniform (corrected)

To reach the officer, the IIS needed a messenger who could move silently between loyalties: a man inside the Saudi ranks who understood both the command structure and the camp's human pulse.

They found him in a low-ranking Saudi border guard, stationed near Rafha. He was not one of the refugees, but he spoke their dialect, shared their stories, and carried a quiet sympathy for their suffering. Years of watching the Iraqis behind fences had worn away his obedience and hardened his resentment toward his own superiors. He was loyal to no one: an ideal recruit.

Approached discreetly during a routine border inspection, he was offered a quiet proposition:

"You can remain a guard who follows orders... or become a man whose actions shape nations."

Temptation rarely needed repetition. By dawn, he had agreed. His mission was simple yet perilous: to deliver Baghdad's whispers to the officer's ear and report what he heard in return.

He was not a refugee's son, nor a believer in any cause. He was simply what the IIS needed most: a bridge between authority and ambition.

The bribe: A bottle's seduction

The first "gift" came wrapped in modesty: a single bottle of imported whiskey hidden inside a crate of rations. The messenger presented it with ritual politeness, calling it "a gesture of respect."

The officer hesitated. His duty resisted. His curiosity won. That night, beneath desert silence, he poured a glass. One became two. The taste was rebellion disguised as relief.

The next delivery came a week later: another bottle, followed by a pair of foreign cigars. Then came envelopes of cash, folded between paperwork. What began as hospitality evolved into habit, and habit into dependency.

By the third month, the officer no longer needed to be convinced. He was already compromised. He began to whisper small details: patrol schedules, shift rotations, and the identities of talkative soldiers.

Every secret earned another bottle. Every favor another envelope. The IIS didn't conquer him in a day: they rented him by the month.

The infiltration: Shadows in the sand

Once the gatekeeper was theirs, Rafha's walls ceased to exist.

Under cover of sandstorms and silence, IIS infiltration teams crossed into Saudi territory: not to destroy, but to dominate. They came with no banners or rifles, only forged papers and the officer's permission.

Inside the camp, they moved like ghosts. Some posed as new refugees, others as smugglers or aid couriers. Their mission: turn the camp inward.

They identified exiled officers, clerics, and activists who might rally the refugees. Those men were studied, then slowly divided.

Rumors became the new currency:

"That sheikh works for the Saudis."

"That officer sells information to the Americans."

"Those men steal from the UN trucks."

Suspicion spread like infection. The refugees began to denounce one another. Trust: the last form of freedom they possessed, withered under the heat of manipulation.

The compromised officer, now a slave to his indulgence, funneled the reports to Baghdad through coded transmissions disguised as supply summaries. Rafha was no longer a humanitarian camp. It had become a psychological battlefield, and the IIS controlled the terrain.

The silent nights: The disappearances

Then came the disappearances.

At first, one or two. Later, many. Men were taken at night under the pretext of "disciplinary transfers" or "resettlement procedures." In truth, the compromised officer opened the gates for covert extractions. Blindfolded prisoners were driven north through unguarded desert tracks, vanishing into Iraq's custody.

In Baghdad's cells, their screams were catalogued as confessions. In Rafha, their absence was explained as relocation to "better facilities."

For a year, the camp lived in fear: of shadows, of silence, of each other.

A game of trust and triumph

The IIS called it a success. Rafha had turned inward, its leadership fractured, its people divided. Even failed operations: a foiled plot to poison the water tanks, another involving explosives hidden in a prayer stone, served their purpose. They spread paranoia, proving that no corner of the camp was untouched.

The Saudi officer had become their most effective weapon: a man who traded patriotism for pleasure. His debts vanished, his liquor flowed, and his conscience drowned quietly in both.

"Every man breaks differently," an IIS field officer later said. "Some for fear. Others for faith. Rafha broke for thirst."

The reckoning: A camp reborn

But corruption carries a half-life.

The same refugees the IIS sought to manipulate began noticing inconsistencies: guards who vanished during certain shifts, patrols that returned too early, missing names on supply rosters. Word reached Riyadh through aid organizations.

In late 1992, Saudi Interior Ministry inspectors arrived unannounced. They came quietly, without press or warning, and within hours the illusion crumbled. Hidden bottles were discovered in the officer's quarters. A private ledger detailed unauthorized expenses. Testimonies from soldiers whispered of envelopes and midnight meetings.

By dawn, the intermediary: the Saudi border guard who had brokered the bribes, had vanished, slipping north toward Iraq through the same routes he once opened.

The officer was dismissed in silence. No trial. No appeal. A new commander took over: austere, pious, incorruptible by design. The IIS, sensing the tightening noose, exfiltrated their operatives before the next sunset.

Rafha, wounded but breathing, slowly began to heal.

The epilogue: Lessons written in sand

Rafha's story ended as quietly as it began. Over the years that followed, most of its refugees were resettled abroad: to Iran, the United States, Europe, Australia, and Syria. Others returned home when Iraq reopened to amnesty programs. By 2007, the last tents were dismantled, and Rafha ceased to exist.

But among intelligence professionals, its story endured: not as triumph or failure, but as a warning.

The IIS had infiltrated a fortified camp without firing a shot, proving that bribery could open borders where armies could not. Yet they also learned that infiltration through weakness breeds instability. The same cracks that let them in eventually consumed their success.

Rafha remains a lesson written in sand: loyalty purchased is loyalty borrowed, and every fortress, even one made of faith, eventually falls from within.

Conclusion: The mirage of control

Rafha's story ended not with gunfire, but with silence: the silence that follows when power mistakes corruption for strategy. The IIS had proven that influence could be bought, that men could be owned through their vices. But in the end, they learned what every intelligence officer eventually does: what is bought can be bought back, and what is controlled can revolt in stillness.

The officer they corrupted drank himself into ruin. The guard they bribed vanished into dust. The refugees they sought to divide scattered across continents, carrying not fear, but memory. The camp was erased, but the lesson endured.

Infiltration built on greed is a mirage: dazzling from afar, empty up close. Rafha teaches that the greatest victories in espionage are often the ones that leave no scars, and the greatest defeats are those that look like success until the sand covers them.

Corruption opens doors, but it never knows how to close them.

ANALYSIS AND LESSONS LEARNED: THE FRAGILE POWER OF CORRUPTION

The double-edged sword of bribery

Bribery is one of espionage's oldest weapons: silent, flexible, and devastatingly effective when wielded with precision. It can unlock gates that bombs cannot, and make loyal men betray sacred oaths for the comfort of a moment's pleasure. Yet, like all tools of manipulation, it carries a hidden decay. The more it succeeds, the more it corrodes.

The Iraqi Intelligence Service's infiltration of the Rafha Refugee Camp through the bribery of a Saudi officer stands as both a triumph of ingenuity and a warning about the fragility of control. For a brief time, the IIS gained dominion over a camp that symbolized rebellion. They did not storm it; they purchased it.

But what began as a clean, surgical operation eventually collapsed under its own corruption. The same vice that opened doors would, in time, eat through the hinges.

Insight: Bribery is power born from weakness, and power that begins in weakness rarely survives its own success.

Analysis of key success factors

At its height, the Rafha operation succeeded because the IIS executed three pillars of tradecraft with remarkable precision: targeting, psychological manipulation, and tactical adaptability. These produced swift results but masked long-term instability.

Pinpointing the right mark

The selection of the Saudi officer was a study in precision targeting: the art of matching access with vulnerability.

- Access and authority: His position gave him oversight of camp logistics, communications, and border security: the perfect vantage point for infiltration.
- Personal weakness: Financial hardship, family pressure, and a hidden thirst for alcohol made him the perfect candidate for compromise.
- Isolation: The monotony of command and the silence of the desert created psychological erosion.

Insight: Finding the right target is not enough. When the entire operation depends on a single compromised man, the operation becomes as fragile as his conscience.

Wielding the Bait

The IIS did not bribe him with gold or ideology. They bribed him with forbidden comfort.

- Symbolic temptation: Whiskey, illicit and luxurious in Saudi soil, became both the leash and the reward.
- Incremental entrapment: The corruption came slowly: a "gift of friendship" that turned into dependency.
- Normalization: Each exchange blurred the line between hospitality and treason.

Insight: The most effective bribes exploit not greed but self-deception. The man convinced himself he was accepting generosity, not selling loyalty.

Tactical flexibility

Operationally, the IIS demonstrated adaptability: a hallmark of seasoned intelligence work.

- Layered objectives: The officer became a multipurpose asset, used for surveillance, disinformation, and selective sabotage.
- Compartmentalization: The use of intermediaries shielded the core network, buying time and distance.
- Operational pivoting: When bold operations failed, smaller psychological plays sustained momentum.

Insight: Flexibility extends a mission's life, but without discipline, it breeds chaos. The IIS mistook tactical agility for strategic control: a fatal misreading of endurance.

Where it fell apart: Bribery's breaking points

The operation's brilliance was undone by its own design. The IIS built power through corruption, and corruption, once unleashed, is uncontrollable. Three failures sealed its fate: overreach, blindness, and moral decay.

1. Pushing Too Hard

The IIS bled their asset dry. Each success invited a greater demand, until the man's usefulness collapsed under the weight of expectation.

- Operational overload: Smuggling, extractions, rumor networks: too much too fast.

- Risk inflation: Reckless plots like poisoning and explosives invited exposure.
- Dependency and decline: The officer's addiction eroded his discipline, turning precision into carelessness.

Insight: Bribery collapses when indulgence replaces calculation. Once dependency sets in, control dies quietly: often before anyone notices.

2. Missing the Bigger Picture

The IIS fixated on one man and forgot the ecosystem around him.

- Underestimating unity: The refugees' trauma had forged solidarity; rumor could shake them, but not break them.
- Environmental blindness: The camp's rhythm: its gossip, its guards, its visitors, was its own security network.
- Exposure chain: Once the officer fell, every connection tied to him fell with him.

Insight: Corruption thrives in isolation, but communities resist together. Espionage that ignores social context mistakes infection for infiltration.

3. The Moral Quagmire

The final failure was not operational: it was moral.

- Target degradation: The officer's collapse from guilt and addiction destroyed his value.
- Handler complacency: The IIS mistook obedience for loyalty, never recalibrating his motivations.
- Institutional rot: When vice becomes the mechanism of success, it becomes the seed of decay.

Insight: Moral corrosion is not the side effect of corruption: it is its most predictable outcome.

Lessons learned: A case officer's guide to calculated influence

Lesson 1. Cap the Pressure
Guideline: Keep demands within plausible limits.

Why: Overburdening a compromised man accelerates collapse and exposure.

Lesson 2. Guide, Don't Enslave
Guideline: Maintain incentive without addiction.

Why: The whiskey that opened the door dulled his discipline, and the mission with it.

Lesson 3. Read the Room
Guideline: Study the cultural and social terrain before manipulating it.

Why: The IIS treated the camp as a chessboard, not a living organism, and lost to its own ignorance.

Lesson 4. Mind the Cost
Guideline: Balance operational gain against ethical and diplomatic consequences.

Why: What was won in information was lost in reputation and restraint.

Key Takeaway: Bribery is not a blunt weapon: it is a scalpel. Used without restraint, it cuts the hand that wields it.

Ethical Considerations: The Price of Corruption
Rafha was not just an operation: it was a moral test that the IIS failed.

Human toll: The Saudi officer, once an exemplar of order, was left disgraced and broken.

Collateral harm: The refugees endured fear, manipulation, and abduction for a cause that yielded no lasting victory.

Moral backlash: The IIS won influence but lost integrity, eroding the very discipline that defined its craft.

Reflection: Intelligence work demands deception, but never cruelty. When corruption becomes strategy, it replaces control with chaos, and power with ruin.

Broader context: Bribery's tightrope

Rafha mirrors a recurring truth across espionage history: corruption wins quickly, but it never wins cleanly.

Like the failed recruitment in Tehran (Case Study 6), Rafha's undoing lay in overconfidence and shortsighted manipulation. But where Tehran collapsed through exposure, Rafha decayed from within. Its success was real, but temporary, unsustainable, and self-consuming.

Insight: Influence built through respect endures. Influence built through ruin dissolves the moment payment stops.

Conclusion: The limits of leverage

The IIS cracked Rafha's defenses with a bottle, not a bullet, but what they gained in speed, they lost in control.

Bribery promises power without confrontation, yet every favor purchased is one that must be purchased again. The Saudi officer's corruption delivered access, but not loyalty; silence, but not stability.

For the intelligence professional, Rafha stands as a timeless warning:

Bribery buys silence, not allegiance. Corruption can open doors, but it never knows how to close them.

When the desert wind finally erased Rafha's tents in 2007, it buried not just the camp but the illusion that influence without principle can endure. What began as a victory ended as an echo: a reminder that power built on decay is not power at all, only the shadow of it.

Case Study 9:
The Failed Recruitment of a High-Value Target: A Lesson in Strategic Missteps

THE STORY: WHEN OPPORTUNITY OUTRAN PREPARATION

In the spring of 2002, Tehran's political air hummed with tension: reformists preaching openness, conservatives watching like hawks. Against this backdrop, the Vice President of Iran prepared a pilgrimage to Iraq, a journey draped in faith but shadowed by politics. It was meant to be private: a family expedition to the Shia holy cities of Baghdad, Najaf, Karbala, and Samarra, but in intelligence, privacy is often the first illusion to die.

The request for visas came innocently enough, transmitted from the Iranian Embassy in Damascus. But the moment it crossed diplomatic cables, it triggered a different circuit: one wired straight to the Iraqi Intelligence Service (IIS). To the analysts in Baghdad, this was not paperwork. It was opportunity.

The Vice President himself was untouchable. But his entourage was not: particularly his father, a revered cleric in his eighties and a scholar tied to Iran's most influential religious networks. If recruited, even subtly, the old man could serve as both a listening post and a moral bridge: a living conduit into the psychological core of Iran's leadership.

Within hours, the IIS converted a family pilgrimage into a covert operation.

"Faith is predictable," one planner remarked. "Faith always travels on schedule."

The plan that moved too fast

A special operations task team was convened under the Presidential Diwan, giving the mission bureaucratic legitimacy and urgency. On paper, it gleamed with precision: the Vice President's family would be received with exaggerated hospitality: cars, escorts, accommodations, and prearranged "drivers" who were in fact seasoned IIS officers fluent in Persian.

The objectives were clear:

1. Separate the Vice President's parents from the main convoy.

2. Engage the father with respectful curiosity: theology first, politics later.

3. Gauge his temperament, plant a seed of rapport, and if possible, begin a slow recruitment cycle.

4. To capture any unguarded dialogue, an Al-Rasheed Hotel suite was wired with hidden microphones and a miniature ceiling camera. Every pillow and lamp carried the silent breath of surveillance.

5. The only flaw, and it was fatal, lay in timing.

6. The mission was born in haste. There was no psychological profile, no cultural simulation, no alternate plan.

7. The question "Would the family even accept our hospitality?" was never asked.

8. Ambition had already started the engine. Preparation was still at the curb.

The convoy and the conversation

At the Iraq-Syria border, the family's vehicles were met by an IIS delegation that blended ceremony with warmth. Gifts of dates, tea, and formal welcomes were offered. The convoy rolled toward Baghdad through the flat gold of desert sunlight: two black sedans gliding like shadows across silence.

As planned, the Vice President and his immediate family were placed in the lead car, while his elderly parents rode in the second, flanked by two IIS officers in civilian attire. Inside that car, the stage was set.

The younger officer began in Farsi, soft-spoken and deferential:

"Your Excellency, it is an honor to accompany you. Iraq has long awaited the return of Iranian pilgrims."

The old man smiled faintly. His tone carried the balance of wisdom and distance.

"Faith belongs to no border," he said. "Pilgrimage is older than politics."

For hours, the officers tried to draw him out: about Iran's economy, clerical rivalries, and reformist debates, but every question met a gentle wall of evasion.

He neither offended nor invited.

He was a scholar speaking with grace, not a man seeking allies.

By the time they reached Baghdad, the officers had learned one truth: the hardest target is the one who does not want anything.

The first failure: A room full of static

At the Al-Rasheed Hotel, the operation's second act fell apart before it began. The Vice President refused Baghdad's "courtesy accommodations," insisting his family stay at the Iranian Embassy compound for "security reasons."

It was a polite rejection but a total loss. The bugged suite remained untouched, recording nothing but the whisper of air-conditioning.

Still, Baghdad pressed on. Each morning, IIS drivers, their identities masked behind formality, ferried the family to shrines. Each evening, they returned them unharmed. The separation tactic continued, but its rhythm became transparent.

Every attempt to turn the conversation toward politics was absorbed by the father's calm. His responses were factual, courteous, and disarmingly neutral. When asked about Tehran's leadership, he replied simply:

"Leaders are tested by time. So are those who study them."

It was an answer that said everything, and nothing.

Pilgrimage into frustration

In Karbala, the IIS tried again. The long road gave them time: time to probe, time to improvise. They spoke of sanctions, war, and the burden of leadership. The father responded like a man measuring each word against eternity. He neither criticized nor endorsed.

By the time they reached Najaf, the IIS replaced one of the officers, hoping a different tone might succeed: younger, more theological, perhaps easier to trust. It made no difference. The cleric's serenity was his armor, his humility a kind of shield no psychological key could open.

The final attempt, en route to Samarra, felt desperate. One officer mentioned the hardships of Shia Iraqis under Ba'ath rule, expecting sympathy. The father only sighed.

"Patience," he said quietly, "is also a form of resistance."

It was the kind of line that kills an operation: poetic, final, immune to manipulation.

The farewell and the irony

Five days later, the pilgrimage ended. The IIS prepared for a last gesture at the border checkpoint: a subtle farewell, a final chance to leave a trace. But the old man had already written the ending.

As the officers escorted the family to the Syrian frontier, he thanked them warmly and handed each a sealed envelope. "A small token," he said, "for your kindness to travelers."

Inside was four thousand dollars, in crisp U.S. bills. The officers hesitated, embarrassed, but protocol demanded they accept before surrendering the money later to headquarters.

When the final report reached Baghdad, its closing line was dry, almost clinical:

"The target compensated his would-be handlers for their hospitality."

It was the kind of irony intelligence work rarely forgives.

The aftermath: Lessons in humility

Back in Baghdad, the debrief was subdued. The mission was dissected not in anger, but in silence. The plan had been ambitious, the execution precise, but the premise: fatally flawed. They had mistaken access for influence, and proximity for opportunity.

The operation gathered no intelligence, recruited no source, and left no mark except a quiet sense of embarrassment.

The final sentence of the internal memorandum was uncharacteristically human:

"The family's hospitality was exceeded only by our ambition."

For an organization that had built its legend on control, it was a moment of rare humility: a recognition that in intelligence, not every open door is meant to be entered, and not every silence is a failure. Sometimes, silence is the target's way of reminding you that wisdom cannot be bought.

Closing reflection

The operation's failure did not lie in its methods, but in its intent. The IIS had confused opportunity with readiness, faith with weakness, and proximity with access. In truth, the Vice President's father had seen through them all along. He had simply chosen grace over confrontation, leaving his would-be recruiters to learn the hardest lesson in espionage: that the sharpest minds are often hidden behind the gentlest smiles.

The operation ended where it began: at a border drawn in sand, and a silence no microphone could ever capture.

Conclusion: The silence of the wise

The failed recruitment of the Vice President's father was not a defeat of tradecraft; it was a defeat of arrogance. The IIS had mastered deception, logistics, and access, but not humility. They sought to manipulate faith and found only dignity; they tried to outthink wisdom and were met with silence.

In espionage, silence is often the loudest answer. The cleric's calm refusal to take offense or interest became its own countermeasure: disarming, disorienting, and absolute. His restraint exposed the limits of manipulation, reminding every case officer that the human soul remains the final frontier no service can conquer.

The IIS left the border empty-handed, but not uneducated. In the quiet between their failure and his farewell, they learned what few intelligence agencies ever admit: that not every opportunity must be seized, and not every target is meant to fall.

Sometimes, the greatest lesson in intelligence work comes not from those we deceive, but from those who refuse to be deceived.

ANALYSIS AND LESSONS LEARNED: WHEN OPPORTUNITY OUTPACED DISCIPLINE

A high-stakes gamble

The Iraqi Intelligence Service (IIS) entered the 2002 operation with the zeal of an organization chasing redemption.

After years of regional isolation, sanctions, and political stagnation, the chance to approach the Vice President of Iran's family was too tempting to resist. Here was a potential access point to Tehran's political and clerical heart: a living channel into the mind of the regime they both feared and studied.

But what began as a calculated overture quickly became a case study in institutional impatience. The mission unfolded with impressive logistics, flawless execution, and no understanding of its target. The IIS acted like a chess player obsessed with his next move, blind to the fact that his opponent wasn't even playing the same game.

The result was a polite debacle: a mission that achieved proximity without penetration, engagement without understanding.

In the sterile language of intelligence debriefs, it was "operationally sound but strategically hollow."

In truth, it was a moment of collective hubris: when opportunity outpaced discipline.

Analysis of key failure factors

Three intersecting failures: inadequate preparation, cultural misjudgment, and operational rigidity, converged to cripple the mission.

Each reflected not a shortage of skill, but the corrosion of restraint: the belief that access alone could substitute for patience, psychology, and precision.

1. Inadequate Preparation: The Architecture of Assumption

The IIS designed its operation like an architect who measured walls but forgot the foundation.

Hasty Targeting: The cleric was chosen not because of ideological weakness or personal grievance, but because he happened to be there. His proximity to the Vice President turned him into a target of convenience: not of value.

No Psychological Profile: No one asked the fundamental questions: What motivated him? How did he perceive Iraq? What did he fear or desire?

Faulty Logistics: The IIS spent weeks wiring the Al-Rasheed Hotel for surveillance: microphones, hidden cameras, and intercept lines, only to have the family refuse the rooms. The operation was built around a space rather than a human being.

Short-Term Focus: Every effort revolved around the five-day pilgrimage. There was no continuity plan: no letter of introduction, no neutral intermediary, no way to sustain contact beyond the border.

Insight:

Preparation in intelligence is not the gathering of details: it is the anticipation of failure.

Every unasked question becomes a weakness waiting to unfold.

2. Cultural Misjudgment: The Illusion of Access

To the IIS, cultural understanding was decoration, not doctrine.

The officers approached the cleric as though he were an official, not a patriarch; a political node, not a man of faith.

Politeness Misread as Openness: His gentle replies, framed in religious humility, were seen as hesitations to exploit: not as the deliberate boundaries of a scholar raised in diplomacy.

Hierarchy Ignored: In Iranian and Arab clerical culture, seniority commands distance. Attempting to recruit a man of his age and reputation during a pilgrimage was a violation of cultural order as grave as it was naive.

Faith Exploited: To engage a man in worship and treat that moment as an operational window was not merely tactically tone-deaf: it was spiritually insulting.

Projection Over Interpretation: The officers imposed their own political desires on his measured words. When he criticized the cost of living, they heard dissent; when he praised patience, they heard disillusionment.

Insight:

Cultural intelligence is not empathy: it is survival.

In the Middle East, words are veils; tone is truth.

The IIS mistook courtesy for compliance and faith for frailty.

3. Operational Rigidity: The Tyranny of the Script

When the family's decision to stay at the Iranian Embassy invalidated the surveillance plan, the operation should have been redefined, not salvaged. Instead, the IIS clung to its choreography: blind to the new reality.

Dialogue Without Listening: Officers followed a rehearsed conversational checklist, failing to detect the old man's quiet indifference.

No Behavioral Adjustment: Even after repeated non-responses, they persisted with political probes instead of shifting to neutral ground: shared memories, literature, history, or religion, all avenues that could have built trust.

Bureaucratic Fear: Mid-level officers lacked the authority to improvise. Innovation meant risk; risk meant blame. So, they followed the plan to its sterile end.

Institutional Reflex: The IIS's greatest strength, discipline, became its greatest weakness. Order had replaced intuition.

Insight:

In intelligence work, rigidity masquerading as discipline is fatal.

The field rewards instinct, not obedience.

An agent who cannot pivot is an agent already exposed.

Lessons learned: A case officer's guide to strategic precision

The operation's collapse reaffirmed timeless truths of human intelligence: lessons every officer must learn, often painfully.

Lesson 1. Vet Before You Act

Guideline: Never target based solely on proximity or prestige. Build a full psychological map first.

Why: Influence is not inherited by association. The IIS chased the shadow of power, not its substance.

Lesson 2. Plan Beyond the Moment

Guideline: Every operation must include an exit and re-entry strategy.

Why: The five-day window became a cage: there was no way in, no way out.

Lesson 3. Interpret Culture, Don't Project Onto It

Guideline: Understand that respect, silence, and ambiguity are languages of self-protection.

Why: Misreading courtesy as collusion blinded the IIS to the father's quiet defiance.

Lesson 4. Adapt or Abort

Guideline: When conditions change, reassess: don't persist.

Why: Flexibility preserves credibility; stubbornness destroys it.

Tradecraft without self-awareness becomes performance: impressive, but meaningless.

Ethical considerations: The quiet cost of overreach

Beyond the technical failure lay a deeper moral fracture.

By targeting an elderly pilgrim during a religious journey, the IIS betrayed not only operational discretion but its own code of professional dignity.

- Violation of sacred context: Faith is not a battlefield. The use of holy travel as cover for recruitment blurred the line between intelligence and desecration.
- Diplomatic recklessness: Had the plot surfaced, it could have ruptured fragile relations with Tehran and ignited a regional scandal.
- Degradation of standards: When officers begin seeing every believer as a potential source, they stop seeing humanity, and intelligence becomes predation.
- Psychological toll: Even among the officers, there was unease. Some later admitted the mission "felt wrong": an instinct often drowned by hierarchy but never forgotten.

Reflection:

Ethics in intelligence is not moral softness: it is professional foresight. Deception without restraint corrodes the handler first, the institution second, and the mission last.

Broader context: The pattern of overreach

Placed within the broader timeline of IIS operations, the 2002 incident fits a familiar arc.

It mirrors the Tehran recruitment (Case Study 6) in its cultural arrogance and the Rafha infiltration (Case Study 8) in its moral corrosion.

In all three, the root cause was the same: a belief that access equals control.

But control in intelligence is an illusion.

The closer one stands to power, the more fragile the ground becomes.

The IIS's hunger to impress leadership with visible victories blinded it to the invisible truth:

The human mind cannot be coerced through ceremony, only understood through time.

Insight:

The most dangerous moment in intelligence work is not when we fail to find opportunity: it's when we find it too quickly.

Conclusion: The price of opportunism

The attempt to recruit the Vice President's father collapsed beneath its own impatience.

The IIS mistook access for influence, conversation for consent, and reverence for receptivity.

Their target, composed and courteous, dismantled their efforts not through defiance but through grace: the kind of quiet dignity that no interrogation can breach.

The agency returned to Baghdad with empty recordings, unspent charm, and a sobering realization:

Power cannot be harvested from the sacred, and silence is not weakness: it is sovereignty.

For modern intelligence officers, the lesson endures:

Every recruitment begins in the mind of the handler, but succeeds only in the heart of the target.

Without humility, empathy, and preparation, opportunity is not strategy: it is temptation.

And temptation, in the world of espionage, is the most sophisticated trap of all.

Case Study 10:
The Sudanese Wiretap: A Technological Triumph in Espionage

THE STORY: WHEN SILENCE BECAME A SIGNAL

By 1985, the Iran-Iraq War had ossified into more than pitched battles and missile strikes; it had become a contest for influence, a shadow war fought through embassies, trade offices, and broadcast frequencies.

Khartoum, distant from the frontlines, nevertheless mattered. The Iranian Embassy there was alive with activity: cultivating Sudanese officials, funding civic projects, and spreading narratives that chipped away at Iraq's standing across Africa and the Arab world.

Those whispers mattered as much as any convoy. The Iraqi Intelligence Service (IIS) in Sudan watched anxiously, sending urgent cables to Baghdad: if Tehran's diplomatic push succeeded, Iraq would face new isolation and a widening of the battlefield beyond oil and desert.

Baghdad's reply was immediate and exacting: "Penetrate the embassy's silence."

A bold directive: Turning faith into frequency

The objective was clear but perilous: listen to the embassy's conversations, intercept its faxed cables, and chart Tehran's influence networks in real time.

It was an audacious demand for 1985. Intercepting a foreign embassy's communication lines in a tightly policed African capital required local access, scarce technical gear, and an operational cover sturdy enough to survive the scrutiny of two watchful governments: Sudan's and Iran's.

Khartoum was not a forgiving city for spies. Information flowed like the Nile: slowly, deceptively, and always under observation.

Recruiting the linchpin: The technician in the telephone room

The IIS's Sudan station began, as most good operations do, with human work: patience, observation, and silence. Their target was not in the embassy, but outside it: hidden in bureaucracy and fatigue.

Two blocks away, an aging municipal junction box routed the embassy's landlines through Khartoum's central exchange. The man with the keys was a middle-aged telecom technician, quietly resentful of his salary and the petty officials who took credit for his work.

The IIS cultivated him slowly: with small courtesies first, then favors, then discreet payments. They promised protection for his family, hinted at promotion, and finally offered a single, intoxicating reward: relevance.

Each night, he told himself it was just a wire, just metal and current: nothing that could bleed. Yet when he looked at the embassy's glowing windows from afar, a quiet shame settled over his pride: the uneasy knowledge that his livelihood now depended on betrayal measured in volts.

He was instructed in one lethal craft: how to splice a line so that calls could be rerouted to a listening post without any detectable signal loss or delay.

Procurement: Smuggling modern ears into an old town

Line-tapping was one thing; intercepting fax traffic in real time was another. Fax interception devices existed, but in the mid-1980s, they were rare and prohibitively expensive: certainly unavailable in Sudan.

The IIS station in Paris located the necessary technology: a precision-built analog fax duplicator that could receive and print transmissions as they arrived.

Securing it required patience and deniability. Procurement ran through a shell company, the device shipped under false paperwork through neutral ports, and was routed via diplomatic channels before being handed off to the Khartoum station. Every handoff was clean; every shipment looked ordinary.

By the time it reached the city, packed between crates of agricultural sensors, it was the most advanced piece of espionage hardware ever to enter Sudan.

Khartoum: A city of heat and secrets

Khartoum in summer was a city of contradictions: sermons at dawn, gossip at dusk, and power lines humming through air thick with dust. The heat fused secrecy and routine together: spies, merchants, and mullahs all moved at the same weary pace, pretending not to notice each other's errands.

For the IIS, the city's lethargy was an ally. It gave them time to breathe, to plan, to vanish between the calls to prayer.

A flat that wasn't a flat: The listening post

With the human key and the machine secured, the station needed a sanctuary: a flat that looked like a home but functioned as a nerve center.

They found it in a low-rise building within view of both the Iranian Embassy and the phone junction box. The apartment was ordinary by design: a worn couch, a calendar on the wall, a kettle that always seemed to whistle at the right time. But behind its curtains lay a tangle of cables, recorders, and headphones: the heartbeat of the operation.

A small generator purred during power cuts; operatives rotated shifts to avoid patterns. Neighbors came to know the tenants as quiet men with polite smiles: businessmen from "Basra," they said, always on calls, never home for long.

The technical work: Splices, switches, and silence

At night, when the traffic thinned and Khartoum's air cooled, the technician went to work. His movements were methodical; his hands steady. He could splice a line blindfolded now.

- He looped a feed to the apartment, where operators logged calls and transcribed them in real time.
- The fax interceptor printed sheets that smelled faintly of ozone and ink: diplomatic notes, lists of names, bank references, and funding memos.
- Analysts called them "actionable breadcrumbs," tiny pieces of truth that, when connected, revealed the architecture of Tehran's influence in Sudan.

The room smelled of dust, coffee, and electricity. Every call was a confession; every page, a revelation.

Operational tradecraft: The art of controlled chaos

The operation depended on rhythm and redundancy: small errors corrected by discipline.

- The technician rotated his routes to the junction box, never crossing the same street twice in a week.
- The operators inside the flat varied their shift hours, avoiding habits that would draw attention.
- In Baghdad, Directorate 4's linguists flagged key phrases while Directorate 8's analysts cross-referenced them with HUMINT reports.

Each discovery, no matter how small: a number, a supplier, a meeting location, triggered a chain reaction: verify, cross-check, exploit.

The system worked because every cog believed the next one would hold.

Risk and tension: Close calls in a coiled city

Khartoum was a city that listened even when it pretended not to. Sudanese counterintelligence patrols were frequent; Iranian diplomats were alert to any irregularity.

Once, a curious neighbor mentioned late-night visitors to local police. An IIS operative, calm as ever, explained they were visiting "importers from Port Sudan," showing fabricated shipping invoices as proof. The neighbor smiled, apologized, and never asked again.

Another night, a power surge threatened to fry the intercept system. The operators, working by candlelight, manually logged every call they could salvage. Those smudged pages would later reveal the first confirmed list of Iranian-sponsored civic groups in Khartoum.

They lived on the edge of exposure, surviving not through luck but discipline under fear.

The harvest: Maps, names, and strategy

Month after month, the intercepted chatter became a map: a living diagram of influence.

They traced Iranian financial flows, identified Sudanese officials who were on Tehran's payroll, and discovered NGOs that doubled as propaganda fronts. Baghdad's Ministry of Foreign Affairs began to adjust its policy in real time:

Diplomatic notes were timed to preempt Iran's initiatives.

Sudanese intermediaries were quietly courted or neutralized.

Media campaigns subtly shifted to undercut Iranian narratives.

By year's end, Iraq had blunted Tehran's soft-power drive across Africa without firing a single shot.

For the IIS, this was intelligence in its purest form: anticipation over reaction.

The exit: Cleaning house and erasing ghosts

After nearly a year of silence turned into a signal, the risk began to rise. Sudanese counterintelligence grew suspicious of unexplained static in certain lines. The station chief knew it was time.

One final night, the technician returned to the junction box and severed his own splice: erasing the lifeline he had built with the same care he'd once connected it.

The equipment was dismantled piece by piece. The technician was relocated under a new identity, paid, and sent home with a silence that would outlast his lifetime. The flat was cleaned, repainted, re-rented. To the casual observer, it had always been what it appeared to be: an apartment where nothing important ever happened.

The aftermath: Triumph and quiet reckoning

The Sudanese wiretap reshaped Iraq's diplomatic posture in Africa. It armed Baghdad with knowledge that changed negotiations, exposed Iranian methods, and reminded its rivals that Iraq could listen even in the quietest corners of the world.

But for those who lived through it, the memory carried unease. They had heard too much: the private laughter of diplomats, the prayers of secretaries, the coded voices of men who believed their words vanished into static.

The operation had proven that silence could be weaponized, that faith in circuits could rival faith in men. Yet each operative knew, deep down, that one exposed wire could have undone them all.

In Khartoum, they learned the oldest paradox of espionage: the clearer the signal, the darker the cost of hearing it.

Conclusion: The echo beneath the silence

The Sudanese wiretap was a victory written in whispers: a year of invisible listening that bent the balance of diplomacy without ever firing a round. It proved that in the modern age of espionage, the quietest operations often roar the loudest in consequence.

Yet every success leaves its echo. The men who built the listening post would later describe not triumph, but fatigue: the peculiar weight of hearing too much. For them, the operation's true cost wasn't danger or exposure; it was intimacy. They had entered the private spaces of strangers and emerged changed, carrying the burden of voices that were never meant to reach them.

When the junction box was sealed and the tapes destroyed, the silence that followed was almost sacred: as if the city itself exhaled. The IIS called it a technological triumph, but those who lived it remembered something else: that the deeper one listens, the harder it becomes to stop.

In Khartoum, the war had been fought not with weapons or agents, but with patience, and in the end, that patience became the very sound of power.

ANALYSIS AND LESSONS LEARNED: WHEN TECHNOLOGY BECOMES TRADECRAFT

Innovation under fire

In 1985, while the war with Iran consumed Iraq's borders, another front opened in silence. It was not fought with artillery but with cables, not by soldiers but by engineers and linguists working in the dim light of a rented flat.

The Sudanese wiretap represented a turning point in Iraqi intelligence: a marriage of technological audacity and human intuition. It showed that power in the modern era would belong not only to those who controlled armies, but to those who could listen, interpret, and anticipate.

Khartoum was not a battlefield in the traditional sense, yet it became one of the most strategically consequential fronts of Iraq's invisible war. The operation fused hardware and human will, and in doing so, revealed that the future of espionage would be written not in gunpowder, but in bandwidth.

For the Iraqi Intelligence Service (IIS), this mission was both a triumph and a test: a lesson in how far one could stretch secrecy before it snapped.

Analysis of key success factors

1. Technological Superiority: Turning Innovation into Leverage

The Sudanese wiretap was born at a time when intelligence agencies across the world were still wrestling with the shift from paper files to electronic signals. Most Arab services were decades behind Western counterparts, but this operation proved that innovation doesn't always require superiority: only ingenuity.

Fax interception as a force multiplier: The French-made analog fax replicator transformed the flow of intelligence. For the first time, Baghdad could see Iranian diplomatic communications in near real-time, rather than relying on post-event HUMINT reporting.

Dual-channel collection: By pairing phone interception with fax duplication, the IIS created a dual validation system: intent captured in conversation, confirmation in print. This eliminated ambiguity: one of the great weaknesses in intelligence analysis.

Operational integration: The procurement chain, routed through Paris and disguised as civilian cargo, showcased an advanced understanding of logistical deniability. Every crate, every customs seal, was an act of deception in itself.

Insight: True technological advantage lies not in the machine, but in the mind that adapts it. The IIS proved that an agency with limited resources could still operate at first-world precision if it learned to weaponize creativity.

2. Human Precision: The Unsung Partner

Beneath the hum of circuits lay one man's trembling conscience: the technician, the unsung hero and prisoner of the operation.

Targeted access: His mundane authority over the city's junction boxes made him indispensable. In a city where embassies guarded every document, he alone held the literal keys to connection.

Psychological engineering: The IIS's recruiters saw the man's weakness not as vulnerability, but as potential. They understood that the most reliable asset isn't one who hungers for power, but one who hungers for acknowledgment.

Mutual dependence: His loyalty, like most in espionage, was transactional but effective. The IIS made him feel vital to something greater, transforming obedience into pride.

Operational morality: His role raised quiet questions within the station itself: could one justify endangering a man who didn't fully grasp the scope of his betrayal? For some officers, that question never left.

Insight: Technology without trust is static metal. Every innovation still depends on the frail, fallible human hand that dares to use it.

3. Operational Deception: The Science of Looking Ordinary

In Khartoum, survival depended less on brilliance and more on believability. The IIS mastered the art of strategic invisibility: not vanishing, but blending so completely that suspicion grew bored.

The Apartment Front: The flat was unremarkable by design: curtains faded by sun, a kettle that always whistled, neighbors who heard laughter but never arguments. The illusion of domestic life protected the operation better than any forged papers could.

Rotating Operatives: No single face became familiar. Shifts rotated with the precision of a prayer schedule, ensuring that patterns dissolved before they could be traced.

Behavioral Consistency: Operatives went out of their way to live the cover: greeting shopkeepers, paying rent early, hosting casual tea visits. Every gesture was calculated authenticity.

Insight: Espionage does not reward the invisible; it rewards the unremarkable. The most perfect cover is the one that no one remembers later.

Lessons learned: A playbook for modern intelligence work

Lesson 1: Fuse Human and Technical Intelligence
The Sudanese wiretap's success came from the symbiosis between man and machine. Humans collected, analyzed, and interpreted: the devices only magnified their reach.

Why: Technology extends hearing; humanity gives it meaning. One without the other breeds either ignorance or chaos.

Lesson 2: Innovation Demands Discipline
The operation's elegance stemmed from its structure. There was no improvisation, no heroics: only process.

Why: Creative ideas without control produce noise. The IIS succeeded because it understood that precision is the purest form of innovation.

Lesson 3: Cover Stories Must Breathe, Not Suffocate
The Khartoum flat was not an act, it was a lived performance.

Why: When an operative believes their cover, the world does too. Deception that breathes becomes indistinguishable from truth.

Lesson 4: Protect the Asset, Protect the Mission
Every intelligence operation is a chain of dependencies. The weakest link is always human.

Why: The technician's safety was the moral compass of the mission. Fear can secure silence, but only respect sustains it.

Institutional reflections: What the operation revealed about the IIS
Inside the walls of Baghdad's Directorate 4, the Sudanese wiretap became a quiet point of pride, and discomfort. It revealed a dual truth about the Iraqi Intelligence Service itself: its brilliance in execution, and its

blindness to restraint.

The operation proved that Iraq could compete with Western agencies on sophistication. But it also exposed how easily success could breed complacency. Some officers began to believe that technology could replace human subtlety: a dangerous illusion that would haunt later operations.

The Sudanese mission succeeded because it was balanced: innovation guided by discipline, risk anchored by restraint. That balance would later erode, as future projects leaned too heavily on the mechanical and forgot the moral.

Ethical and strategic considerations: The shadows behind success

Even perfection casts a shadow. The Sudanese wiretap, though celebrated, left behind questions that no officer could easily answer.

Diplomatic breach: Tapping a foreign embassy's lines violated every rule of international conduct. Had the operation been exposed, Baghdad could have faced sanctions or expulsion from African partnerships.

Asset exploitation: The technician carried the full weight of danger without the full understanding of his sacrifice. His name was erased from the final reports: the ultimate anonymity.

Psychological toll: For the operators, listening became a moral erosion. They heard the private laughter of people who would never know their words were captured, and for some, that intimacy felt like trespass.

Reflection: Intelligence work demands amorality for survival, but not in perpetuity. Every great operation extracts not only data, but a piece of the soul that conducted it.

Broader implications: From wires to webs

The Sudanese wiretap foreshadowed the digital transformation that would later define global espionage. Its DNA can be traced through every modern surveillance program: from analog splicing to cyber intrusion.

Continuity of Principle: Recruitment, cover, patience: these remain eternal. The medium changes; the method endures.

Transition of Tools: What the fax interceptor symbolized in 1985, malware represents today: the same hunger for omniscience, dressed in new code.

Legacy of Integration: The collaboration between Khartoum and Paris stations demonstrated a rare unity within the IIS: proof that intelligence is strongest when it transcends geography and ego.

Insight: Espionage has evolved from listening to everything to knowing what to ignore. That is the truest sophistication of intelligence.

Conclusion: The art of listening in silence

The Sudanese wiretap was more than a technical success; it was a meditation on power itself. It taught that the future of intelligence would belong not to those who shout the loudest, but to those who listen the longest.

For the IIS, it was a victory written in frequencies and faith: proof that ingenuity could outmaneuver isolation. Yet it also carried an unspoken warning: the more perfect your surveillance becomes, the more fragile your conscience must be.

In the years that followed, the Khartoum flat faded from records, the technician disappeared into obscurity, and the recordings were locked away in Baghdad's archives. But among those who knew, the lesson endured:

True espionage is not about hearing everything: it is about knowing when to stop listening.

In the silence that followed, Iraq's intelligence officers discovered that mastery of sound was easy; mastery of restraint was not.

CONCLUSION:

MASTERING THE SHADOWS: CULTURAL FLUENCY AS THE ULTIMATE INTELLIGENCE TOOL

In the shadowy world of Middle Eastern intelligence, where stakes are mortal and truths are negotiable, success is not measured by the sophistication of gadgets or the boldness of operations alone. It is born from something quieter, deeper, and infinitely more complex: a mastery of the human terrain.

Throughout this book, we have walked through the hidden corridors of that mastery, from the rituals of recruitment and betrayal to the ethics of persuasion and the fusion of man with machine. Each case study, each operational fragment, has revealed the same enduring truth: espionage in the Middle East is less about what you know than about how well you understand what you see.

As we draw this book to its close, the goal is not to summarize but to synthesize, to weave these scattered lessons into a single doctrine, one that reflects both the historical reality of the region and the timeless art of human intelligence.

The Middle East remains a land of paradoxes, where ancient traditions coexist with modern ambitions and where every truth carries its own shadow. Here, loyalty can be both armor and weapon; trust, both currency and liability. To operate in this environment is to navigate not only borders but belief systems, to read gestures as carefully as documents, and silence as intently as speech.

For those who have lived inside this world, these lessons are not academic. They are paid for in sleepless nights, broken trusts, and decisions that echo long after the operation ends. They form the invisible curriculum of those who move unseen, the grammar of survival in the profession of secrets.

THE BEDROCK OF CULTURAL FLUENCY

If espionage has a language, its first dialect is culture.

Culture in the Middle East is not a decorative backdrop, it is the stage, the script, and the subtext of every act of intelligence. It defines how people perceive honor, loyalty, and deceit. Understanding it is not an advantage; it is the price of entry.

Tribal loyalty, for instance, is not simply a relic of history. It remains the gravitational field around which allegiance and identity orbit. To recruit in such an environment is to negotiate with centuries of inherited memory. The case studies have shown this again and again. An operation in southern Iraq collapsed when a target chose blood over ideology. Another succeeded in Qum precisely because the operative understood the sanctity of faith and wrapped deception in devotion.

These stories carry a shared moral: cultural fluency is not empathy, it is leverage. It allows the case officer to move with the rhythm of the people he observes, to cloak intrusion in respect, and to weaponize understanding without betraying it.

Deception itself is shaped by culture. In a region conditioned by colonial interference and political upheaval, suspicion is not pathology, it is instinct. Every word is weighed, every silence examined. The failed recruitment in Tehran demonstrated what happens when cultural arrogance meets social intelligence; the journalist-spy's long career proved the reverse, that immersion, mimicry, and linguistic empathy can make invisibility an art form.

To be culturally fluent is not merely to know what people believe, but why they believe it, and how those beliefs dictate behavior under pressure. It is to read subtext in a bow, to sense warning in hospitality, and to understand that an insult to pride can kill a mission faster than exposure.

Culture, then, is not static knowledge but operational instinct. It is what allows the investigator, diplomat, or spy to anticipate before he reacts. Without it, every other tool, money, persuasion, or power, is blunt and breakable.

THE HUMAN ELEMENT: PSYCHOLOGICAL INSIGHT AS A STRATEGIC EDGE

If culture provides the terrain, psychology is the map by which one travels it. The human mind is the true battlefield of intelligence. Every decision, every betrayal, every silence begins there.

The stories that have unfolded in these pages prove that the most decisive victories occur not in conference rooms or safehouses but within the psyche of a single individual. The Sudanese wiretap succeeded because an officer saw not a technician, but a man starved of recognition, and turned that hunger into loyalty. The exposure of the Tehran double agent began not with data, but with a pause too long, a glance too cautious.

Psychological insight is not a soft skill; it is precision engineering of the human soul. It requires pattern recognition not of numbers but of emotions: fear disguised as pride, ambition masked as virtue. The Iranian operative executed for failure was not undone by logistics but by despair misread as discipline. The refugees of Rafha, conversely, were guided by empathy rather than coercion, and that emotional literacy became its own form of control.

Espionage without psychology is blind mathematics. Numbers may reveal patterns, but only emotion reveals intent.

Today, the digital sphere mirrors the human one. Online behavior has become the modern subconscious, where motives, grievances, and desires are exposed with reckless honesty. But algorithms cannot yet decode irony, faith, or fear. They can track the pulse but not the heartbeat. Only human understanding can translate digital chaos into meaning.

Thus, the psychological dimension remains the irreplaceable edge. Technology may extend sight, but psychology grants foresight, the power to know not just what people do, but what they will do when cornered, tempted, or believed in.

FROM UNDERSTANDING TO MASTERY

Culture and psychology intertwine like code and cipher. One gives context, the other interpretation. Together they form the intelligence officer's moral compass, a guide not only for recruiting and analyzing, but for surviving.

To master the shadows, an operative must become both observer and participant, insider and outsider. He must carry two truths at once: the loyalty to his mission, and the empathy to understand those who oppose it. The most skilled case officers are not predators; they are interpreters of humanity, fluent in contradiction.

This is why the heart of espionage, despite all its secrecy, remains transparent in one sense: it is about people. Every file, every intercept, every operation begins and ends with human behavior. The tools may evolve, but the terrain of motives, loyalties, and fears remains constant.

And so the first half of this conclusion, this meditation on the art behind the science, returns to a single conviction: that intelligence succeeds not through domination, but through comprehension.

To know a culture deeply enough to move within it unseen.

To read a mind clearly enough to predict its turn before it speaks.

To act ethically enough to endure the silence after the mission ends.

These are not techniques. They are forms of mastery, earned not in classrooms or command centers, but in the long twilight between trust and betrayal.

WALKING THE ETHICAL TIGHTROPE

Every act of espionage is a moral negotiation, and nowhere is that negotiation more perilous than in the Middle East. The region's societies, bound by codes of honor and faith, judge action not by outcome but by motive. Here, deception is tolerated only when wrapped in purpose, and even then, the price is steep.

The case studies in this book reveal the same recurring pattern: when ethics collapse, operations follow. Bribery may buy compliance, but it corrodes loyalty. Coercion may yield a confession, but it breeds rebellion. The Rafha infiltration, built on corruption, succeeded briefly before consuming its architect. The Qum assassination, by contrast, demonstrated restraint as discipline: a moral clarity that turned lethal precision into a form of order, not chaos.

Intelligence work in the Middle East is not a morality play, but it demands moral literacy. To operate effectively, an officer must recognize the invisible boundaries of dignity, religion, and honor that shape his target's world. A gesture misread, a ritual violated, or a promise broken can undo years of careful work.

This is not ethical idealism; it is operational realism. The officer who acts without conscience often discovers too late that immorality has an operational cost. Ethics, in espionage, are not the opposite of effectiveness: they are its condition.

True mastery of the craft is not found in the ease of manipulation, but in the discipline of restraint. The case officer who protects the integrity of his operation by honoring the dignity of those he manipulates does not betray his mission: he safeguards it.

To walk the ethical tightrope is to balance necessity against humanity, success against self-respect. The line is narrow, but those who fall rarely rise again.

OPERATIONAL EXCELLENCE: THE CRAFT OF CONTROL

The anatomy of every successful intelligence operation, from Baghdad to Beirut, from Khartoum to Qum, rests on three pillars: discipline, adaptability, and precision. Together, they define the invisible standard by which professionals measure themselves.

Discipline is the architect of success. It governs timing, documentation, and the thousand quiet habits that prevent chaos from seeping into trade-craft. The Kharg Island strike succeeded not because of luck, but because planning outlasted uncertainty. Every motion, every detonation, every withdrawal had been rehearsed to the point of muscle memory.

Adaptability is discipline's twin: the ability to pivot when circumstances shift without losing direction. The Sudanese wiretap thrived on adaptability: when equipment failed, operators relied on instinct; when risk rose, they dismantled their own creation rather than cling to pride. The journalist spy, who reinvented himself after 2003, embodied adaptability at its highest form: survival through transformation.

Precision is the quiet elegance of control. It is knowing when to act and when to wait; when to vanish, when to speak, and when to leave nothing at all. The Tehran recruitment failed because precision gave way to haste, and haste is the enemy of intelligence.

Operational excellence, then, is not merely performance: it is posture. It is the calm of a mind that has rehearsed every failure in advance, the humility to know that every plan will meet friction, and the endurance to recover before the opposition realizes it.

Vigilance binds these elements together. Every asset must be tested, every success re-evaluated. Trust, in this world, is not affection: it is audit. The officers who forgot that rule found their names written in the margins of failure reports. Those who remembered it quietly built careers that lasted decades without headlines.

In the end, operational excellence is not glamorous. It is the art of re-maining unseen: not only by enemies, but by history itself.

THE DIGITAL FRONTIER: A NEW SHADOW OVER THE OLD WORLD

If the 20th century belonged to human spies, the 21st belongs to hybrid ones. Technology has not replaced human intelligence; it has multiplied its reach and its risk.

The digital battlefield now extends from encrypted chats to cloud servers, from drone feeds to social media profiles. In this new arena, cultural fluency and psychological insight are more vital than ever because algorithms cannot interpret faith, sarcasm, or shame. The data may show a pattern, but only a human mind can decode the meaning behind it.

The Israel-Iran intelligence war proved that cyber operations are the new frontier of deniable warfare: malware replacing explosives, code replacing agents. Yet even here, the human fingerprint remains. Every line of code carries intent; every hack, a motive. Machines do not betray: people do.

For future officers, the challenge will not be mastering technology, but mastering themselves amid technology's illusions. The promise of omniscience, of total visibility, is dangerous. The more one sees, the easier it is to believe one understands. The future of intelligence will belong not to those who collect the most data, but to those who interpret it with cultural, moral, and emotional precision.

Artificial intelligence may someday forecast intent, but it will never replace empathy. Sensors can capture whispers, but they cannot hear fear. The ultimate weapon in intelligence will remain what it has always been: a human being who knows how to listen.

Final reflection: The human shadow

When the operations end and the reports are archived, what remains are not statistics or victories, but echoes. Every agent, every handler, every target leaves behind fragments of humanity: the residue of choices made in the dark.

In those choices lies the real story of intelligence: not power, but perception; not dominance, but understanding.

Cultural fluency teaches us how to enter the room.

Psychological insight teaches us how to stay there.

Ethical restraint teaches us how to leave with our humanity intact.

Technology will continue to evolve: faster, louder, brighter, but it will always be wielded by hands that tremble, minds that doubt, and hearts that calculate the moral cost of silence.

The shadows may now stretch across fiber-optic cables instead of alleyways, but they are still cast by human hands. And as long as those hands exist, intelligence will remain what it has always been: a mirror reflecting not only the world we watch, but the one we create.

E P I L O G U E :
BEYOND THE FILES: REFLECTIONS ON A
LIFETIME IN THE SHADOWS

As I finish these pages, my thoughts go back over the path that led me here. It goes not just through the old stacks of the Iraqi Intelligence Service archives, but along the twisting turns of my own life, where each step taught me more about understanding people. Raised in the heart of Iraq's tribal areas, I grew up in a world where reading others was not just a skill; it was key to getting by. Our elders showed me how to fix arguments with calm advice and patience, to see real courage in smart timing rather than quick moves, and to grasp the true meaning of words like honor, betrayal, loyalty, and respect. These were not just ideas; sthey were the rules of our group, shaping how we made friends, dealt with enemies, and kept our pride in tough times. Even today, those early lessons shape every decision I make.

These roots set the base for all that followed. During my time in the Iraqi Army in the Iran-Iraq War, I learned that fast judgments and emotional smarts could make the difference between life and death. My later learning built on that, showing me the many sides of Arab thinking that affect how people think, talk, and act, from silence that hides fear to laughter that covers anger. No talk was wasted; each meeting added to my understanding of what motivates us.

Then came the harsh aftermath of the 1991 Gulf War, pushing my family and thousands like us into the empty sands of Rafha Refugee Camp in northern Saudi Arabia. For four years, we lived in that huge tent city, a temporary home for about 30,000 people from all parts of Iraq, where teachers and doctors mixed with farmers and workers, escaped prisoners from the uprising joined families holding on to bits of routine, and tribal leaders from far provinces shared the ground with respected religious leaders: Imams, Sayyids, and Sheikhs whose words held the power of old family lines. We did not pick these people to live with; life forced us together in a fenced spot in the desert, watched by Saudi guards who brought the basics for survival, like food and water rations, basic electricity, donated clothes, simple education, and some protection among the endless sands.

Rafha turned into my tough school of life, a high-pressure spot where staying sharp meant dealing with every kind of mindset: the careful talks of the educated, the tough strength of the displaced, the hidden goals of refugees, and the silent rules of honor that tied strangers together in hard times. In those limited days and nights under the stars, I learned to spot the sign of need in a farmer's quiet moment, the complex ties in a Sheikh's look, and the weak agreements that kept disorder away. It built in me a stronger sense for the mix of people, not just watching reasons, but living through them, a lesson that carried into the Iraqi Intelligence Service archives and the State Department refugee files, turning the hard side of survival into the calm skill of real insight.

Years later, after settling in the United States and then going back to Iraq, I entered a new kind of work: the files of the Iraqi Intelligence Service. From 2004 to 2011, as an intelligence analyst with the United States Government, I went through tens of thousands of IIS records, covering the years from the 1970s up to 2003. More than just old notes, they showed the secret fights, revealing the tricks, reasons, and plans of a government focused on control. In those pages was the structure of spying: how agents brought in sources, built false identities, checked loyalty, and ran operations that mixed mind tricks, lies, and cultural knowledge into one smooth method. Some plans played out like slow games; many failed from too much pride or wrong guesses. I still remember the feeling of flipping a faded page to see a plot that matched one from my early days, a sign that patterns last longer than rulers.

The deeper I got, the more I saw the patterns. Each agent had their own style, their own pace. Some liked to take time, building influence through kindness and trust. Others moved fast, using power and fear. By the end of those years, I could often predict the end before the last page. It was like finishing a secret training, one that taught the hard side of influence through careful watching, without classes. Those alone nights in the archive room, with just one light, sharpened not just my thinking, but a steady drive to find truth in the dark.

That path led next to the U.S. Department of State, checking thousands of files for Iraqis who had worked with U.S. forces. Each one told a real story, some of strong loyalty, others of deep need. I saw that truth often hides in mixed-up parts. People lie not always from bad intent, but from fear. Their mismatches showed paths of pain, leading to what they could not say out loud. Each case strengthened an idea I had long thought: the core of intelligence is about understanding, not just tricks. To find truth, you first need to know the fears that hide it. My time there ended earlier this year when the U.S. Government closed the refugee programs, ending one part of my work but making the lessons from before even stronger.

Today, from Dearborn, Michigan, I run Stealth Investigation Services, a licensed agency helping different communities across the state and beyond. The work is different from past spy tasks, but the main idea is the same: reading people, figuring out motives, and finding truths hidden in behavior. Places change, but the patterns stay: honor, secrets, pride, and trust still shape every story. Whether it's following someone, checking backgrounds, or handling disputes, each case reminds me of a lasting lesson: human actions, with all their mixes, are the best way to spot what's true.

This book comes from that long time of watching, a guide made from real work, not ideas. From cultural skills that turn doubt into trust, to mind checks that show hidden reasons, to ethical limits that separate force from gentle push, these lessons were gained in the field and improved through thinking back. They point to one main thought: intelligence is about insight, not control. The more you understand people, the less you need to push; influence comes naturally to those who see the hidden patterns others miss.

As the world enters a new time for intelligence, with online tricks, smart machines, and web fights, the human part remains the strong center. Programs can map connections, but they miss feelings. Tools can track talks, but not measure loyalty. Whether dealing with a village leader in Najaf or a hidden message online, success always depends on caring, patience, and human gut sense. The future may be full of tech, but the heart of spying will always be human.

In the end, these words are not just about intelligence; they are about people. The lies they tell, the truths they hide, and the careful skill of telling one from the other. Spying, like life, shows the human spirit. To master it is to master the study of people.

The shadows will always be there. They change, adjust, and come back in new ways. But they can be overcome. For those who understand people, their backgrounds, thoughts, and conflicts, the shadows give up their secrets.

Master the shadows or get lost in them.

GLOSSARY OF TERMS

ABC Method: A coordinated foot surveillance technique involving three agents. A leads close to the target, B parallels on a side route, and C trails from a distance, rotating positions to avoid detection. Used extensively by the IIS in dense urban environments, often under culturally plausible covers such as merchants or laborers.

Asset: An individual recruited to provide intelligence, conduct tasks, or facilitate operations. Selection depends on cultural alignment, motivation, and psychological profiling. Mishandled assets often led to exposure, as demonstrated in the failed Syrian mission (Case Study 2).

Backstop: Supporting elements (documents, references, or legends) that substantiate a cover identity. Backstops protect an operative's credibility if challenged. The IIS used such measures sparingly, favoring cultural and behavioral authenticity over excessive forgery.

Beggar (Faqir) Cover: A low-visibility disguise employed in public spaces, especially markets or mosques, to conduct observation or facilitate dead drops. The IIS favored it in charitable or religious settings where anonymity was natural.

Betrayal Signals: Subtle behavioral or cultural cues indicating disloyalty, such as averted eyes, evasive speech, or changes in social routine. Detecting these signs is crucial in asset management and debriefing.

Black Bag Job: A covert entry into secured premises to plant, remove, or recover materials (e.g., listening devices, documents). Ethical risks include collateral intrusion and diplomatic exposure.

Bribery: The use of money, goods, or favors to obtain cooperation or intelligence. A double-edged tactic effective for short-term influence but corrosive over time. Explored in the Rafha Camp infiltration (Case Study 8).

Burn (or Burned): When an operative, source, or operation is compromised or exposed, requiring immediate abort or extraction. The IIS treated any suspicion of compromise as grounds for rapid withdrawal.

Clean (Tail): Confirmation that no surveillance remains following a counter-surveillance check or Surveillance Detection Route (SDR). Opposite of dirty.

Coercion: Applying physical or psychological pressure to extract compliance or information. Though effective in controlled settings, misuse often destroyed long-term trust, as seen in the Iranian asset interrogation (Case Study 4).

Collectivist Mentality: A social orientation prioritizing family, tribe, or community above individual interests. Core to Middle Eastern societies and central to the recruitment challenges explored throughout the book.

Compartmentalization: Restricting operational information to "need-to-know" levels to preserve secrecy if compromised. Essential in multi-directorate coordination, such as the Sudanese wiretap (Case Study 10).

Confirmation Bias: The tendency to interpret information in ways that confirm existing assumptions. A recurring analytical flaw in intelligence assessment, addressed in propaganda and counter-influence operations.

Counter-Surveillance: The art of detecting or evading hostile surveillance. The IIS emphasized human observation and environmental awareness over reliance on technology.

Cover: A fabricated identity or role used to conceal an operative's true purpose. Distinguished from a front, which is a business or organization serving as a structural disguise.

Cultural Fluency: The deep understanding of social norms, values, and behaviors necessary to operate effectively in Middle Eastern societies. The book's central theme is essential for recruitment, influence, and operational survival.

Dead Drop: A concealed location where materials or messages are exchanged without direct contact. Low-risk and ideal for hostile or restricted environments.

Deception: The deliberate manipulation of information or appearances to mislead adversaries. Integral to recruitment, propaganda, and counterintelligence operations.

Decoy: A person, object, or action used to divert attention or mislead surveillance teams. Common in counter-surveillance tactics.

Dirty (Tail): Evidence that an operative is being followed or monitored. Requires immediate evasion and re-evaluation of operational security.

Double Agent: An asset secretly working for both sides. The IIS trained case officers to detect double agents through behavioral analysis and inconsistencies, as in the Tehran exposure (Case Study 3).

Dry Cleaning: The process of confirming freedom from surveillance through abrupt or irregular movements during an SDR, such as detours, stops, or cultural distractions like prayer pauses.

Elicitation: The subtle extraction of information through natural conversation. Relies on empathy and timing rather than interrogation or overt questioning.

Exfiltration: Safely removing an operative or source from hostile territory. Requires coordination, timing, and pre-established escape routes.

False Flag: An operation conducted under the guise of another entity. Used in influence campaigns or propaganda to obscure true sponsorship.

Foot Surveillance: Tracking a subject on foot while maintaining visual continuity without detection. Requires teamwork, timing, and environmental adaptation.

Front: A legitimate-looking business, organization, or institution used as operational cover. The IIS maintained numerous fronts in trade, media, and religious tourism.

Honey Trap: An intelligence tactic involving seduction or emotional manipulation to compromise a target. Ethically and operationally risky; success depends on deep cultural understanding.

HUMINT (Human Intelligence): Information gathered from human sources. Central to all IIS operations and still the foundation of modern intelligence.

Indicator: A sign that surveillance or observation is occurring, such as recurring individuals, vehicles, or patterns. Requires corroboration before taking countermeasures.

Interrogation: A structured questioning process used to obtain information from detainees or suspects. Balances intimidation, persuasion, and psychological insight.

Mobile Surveillance: Pursuit of a target using vehicles. Requires coordination, communications discipline, and anticipation of route changes.

Mnemonic Technique: Memory tools (like visualization or chunking) used by operatives to retain key data, such as license plates or sequences, during surveillance.

OPSEC (Operational Security): The procedures and discipline ensuring the secrecy and integrity of operations. Breaches often begin with complacency or overconfidence.

OSINT (Open-Source Intelligence): Information collected from publicly accessible sources, media, databases, and social platforms. Complements HUMINT but lacks cultural depth.

Pretext: A fabricated reason or justification for an operative's presence or inquiry. Culturally aligned pretexts are the safest and most sustainable.

Propaganda: The strategic manipulation of narratives to influence public opinion or behavior. Explored in the IIS's Iran-Turkey influence campaigns.

Psychological Profiling: Evaluating a person's motivations, fears, and behavioral traits to determine recruitability or threat potential. A cornerstone of case officer training.

Rabbit Run: A sudden, unpredictable maneuver used to expose tails during surveillance detection. Effective when combined with cultural cover behavior.

Recruitment: The process of identifying, assessing, and enlisting assets. Success depends on cultural understanding, patience, and accurate psychological targeting.

Reverse Psychology: A behavioral manipulation technique that encourages a target to act contrary to perceived intent. Often used to provoke trust or overconfidence.

SDR (Surveillance Detection Route): A pre-planned path designed to detect and evade surveillance through controlled movements, timing, and environment-based checks.

Stationary Surveillance: Observation conducted from a fixed position, often disguised as a shop, residence, or vehicle. Provides prolonged coverage with minimal movement risk.

Surveillance: Continuous monitoring of a target for intelligence purposes. Combines human observation with technical collection; requires patience, adaptability, and cultural realism.

Tail: An individual or team following a target. Detected through awareness of repeating patterns, routes, or environmental cues.

Vetting: The process of verifying an asset's credibility and trustworthiness through cross-checks and behavioral consistency. Periodic re-vetting prevents double-agent compromise.

Wasta: An Arabic term meaning influence or personal connections. A defining cultural factor in recruitment, negotiation, and operational access throughout the Middle East.

INDEX

Starter Index List for Veiled Betrayals: Cracking the Cultural Code of Middle Eastern Espionage

ABOUT THE AUTHOR

Born in Iraq and formed by the steady pulse of its tribal and communal ways, Mike Hajjar gained an early grasp of human actions and cultural subtleties well before stepping into intelligence and investigations. Those formative days equipped him with the knack for decoding intentions, steering through complex allegiances, and settling disputes via keen perception instead of hasty reactions. These talents would eventually anchor his entire career.

His path started amid the harsh trials of the Iran-Iraq War, where duty in the Iraqi Army honed his eye for detail, flexibility, and mental acuity amid high stakes. Once the conflict ended, the 1991 Gulf War upended everything, forcing my family and many others to flee as refugees to Saudi Arabia's Rafha Camp for four grueling years. That time in limbo, amid shared hardships and fragile hopes, deepened my grasp of survival's quiet strategies before we resettled in the United States.

After resettling in the United States and later returning to Iraq, Hajjar's growing interest in intelligence work turned into structured mastery as he worked as an intelligence analyst for the United States Government from 2004 to 2011. For those seven years, he pored over tens of thousands of records from Saddam Hussein's Iraqi Intelligence Service archives. This gave him direct insight into spy techniques, source gathering, secret missions, and mind games. Such rare entry into the workings of one of the Middle East's most guarded spy networks transformed mere review into hands-on learning, revealing the inner gears of covert strategy.

Hajjar pushed his commitment to sharp analysis by completing a Master of Science in Criminal Justice and Security. That foundation soon drew him to the U.S. Department of State's P2 Refugee Program, handling thousands of claims from Iraqis who had supported U.S. troops. Blending precise fact-checking with cultural depth, this role fine-tuned his skill at sifting honesty from tangled tales and grasping the personal layers of records and ruses. He often reflected on how small cultural cues could unlock entire stories buried in paperwork.

Now, Hajjar heads Stealth Investigation Services PLLC as founder and lead investigator, an esteemed firm rooted in Dearborn, Michigan. It aids a wide array of clients in Arab and Middle Eastern circles, focusing on watchful monitoring, deep background probes, and research fueled by intelligence principles. Across countless practical cases, he deploys the same precise approaches once aimed at national secrets, now dedicated to clarity, fairness, and targeted private inquiries.

Hajjar holds memberships in the Michigan Council of Private Investigators (MCPI) and the National Council of Investigation and Security Services (NCISS). Outside his core work, he crafts training resources and writings for those in intelligence, weaving in elements of cultural mindsets, defenses against spies, and proven inquiry techniques to build real-world readiness.

Veiled Betrayals: Cracking the Cultural Code of Middle Eastern Espionage caps off decades of immersion in conflict, spying, and sleuthing. Pulling from old records and personal trials alike, Hajjar delivers a unique blend of cultural savvy and tactical know-how. It shares an intimate view on why grasping individuals, beyond mere mechanics, truly captures the essence of intelligence craft. In quiet moments, he notes how these insights still guide his daily choices, from client meetings to late-night reviews.

He resides in Dearborn, Michigan, steadily advancing his studies, authorship, and guidance for sleuths and experts aiming to link cultural wisdom with sharp intelligence work.

www.ingramcontent.com/pod-product-compliance
Lightning Source LLC
Chambersburg PA
CBHW070837260626
47170CB00007B/2412